INTERNATIONAL ACCLAIM FOR

Away

"A dazzling novel . . . written by a major novelist at the height of her considerable powers." — *Globe and Mail*

"*Away* is a novel of extraordinary depth. . . . The people and the periods come vividly to life, at times creating a near cinematic effect." — Saskatoon *StarPhoenix*

"Her writing shimmers with lyric sensuality." — *Vancouver Sun*

"*Away* celebrates the talismanic power of memory and the possibilities inherent in the lyricism and magic that exist just beyond the edges of reality." — *Kirkus Reviews*

"[*Away*] is a treasure . . . a passionate and powerful story." — *Winnipeg Free Press*

"An elegiac, lushly lyrical, enchanting family saga. . . ." — *Publishers Weekly*

"An extraordinary achievement; highly recommended." — *Library Journal*

"Few contemporary writers chart the intimate relationship between inner and outer landscapes with the passion, elegance and evocative power of Urquhart." — Kitchener-Waterloo *Record*

"*Away* is a ravishing evocation of the lives of those whose souls are irrevocably touched by nature." — *The Independent*

"Urquhart's blending of the spiritual and political sides of the Irish makes an amazing story told in a language that is melodious and laden with complex imagery." — *Booklist*

JANE
URQUHART

AWAY

EMBLEM
McClelland & Stewart

First published in trade paperback with flaps 1993
Trade paperback edition first published in 1997
This Emblem edition published 2010

Emblem is an imprint of McClelland & Stewart Ltd.
Emblem and colophon are registered trademarks of McClelland & Stewart Ltd.

LIBRARY AND ARCHIVES CANADA CATALOGUING IN PUBLICATION

Urquhart, Jane, 1949–
Away / Jane Urquhart.

First published: Toronto: McClelland & Stewart, 1993.
ISBN 978-0-7710-8642-7

I. Title.

PS8591.R68A9 2010   c813'.54   C2010-901586-X

We acknowledge the financial support of the Government of Canada
through the Book Publishing Industry Development Program and that of
the Government of Ontario through the Ontario Media Development
Corporation's Ontario Book Initiative. We further acknowledge the support
of the Canada Council for the Arts and the Ontario Arts Council for our
publishing program.

Printed and bound in the United States of America
This book is printed on paper that is 20% recycled.

McClelland & Stewart Ltd.
75 Sherbourne Street
Toronto, Ontario
M5A 2P9
www.mcclelland.com

1 2 3 4 5   14 13 12 11 10

For my mother, Marian Quinn Carter,
and my father, Walter Carter,
and for the Quinn family

In memory of my Godfather Danny Henry,
my grandmother Fleda Quinn,
and Thomas J. Doherty

The three most short-lived traces: the trace of a bird on a branch, the trace of a fish on a pool, and the trace of a man on a woman.

– an Irish triad

I

A Fish on a Pool

THE women of this family leaned towards extremes.

All winter they yearned for long, long nights and short precise days; in the summer the sun in the sky for eighteen hours, then a multitude of stars.

They kept their youth – if they survived – well past their childbearing years until, overnight at sixty, they became stiff old ladies. Or conversely, they became stiff old ladies at twenty and lived relentlessly on, unchanged, for six or seven decades.

They inhabited northern latitudes near icy waters. They were plagued by revenants. Men, landscapes, states of mind went away and came back again. Over the years, over the decades. There was always water involved, exaggerated youth or exaggerated age. Afterwards there was absence. That is the way it was for the women of this family. It was part of their destiny.

Esther O'Malley Robertson is the last and the most subdued of the extreme women. She was told a story at twelve that calmed her down and put her in her place. Now, as an old woman, she wants to tell this story to herself and the Great Lake, there being no one to listen. Even had there been an audience of listeners, the wrong questions might have been asked. "How could you possibly know that?" Or, "Do you have proof?" Esther is too mature, has always been too mature, for considerations such as these. The story will take her wherever it wants to go in the next twelve hours, and that is all that matters; this and the knowledge that for one last night she will remain beside the icy, receptive waters of the Great Lake.

She paints a landscape in her mind, a landscape she has never seen. Everything began in 1842, she remembers her grandmother Eileen telling her, on the island of Rathlin which lies off the most northern coast of Ireland. Esther allows rocks, sea, to form in her imagination. There would be a view of a coastline with cliffs. It was the morning that an unusual number of things came in with the tide, causing celebration and consternation among the islanders and permanently fixing the day itself in legends that are recounted around fires at night. "Your great-grandmother's name was Mary," Old Eileen had said to Esther. "She lived with her widowed mother in a cabin three fields from the sea. And it was Mary who was the first to approach the beach that morning."

The night before, a furious storm had reduced the circumference of the island by at least ten feet. It had snatched overturned curraghs from the shore and dispatched seven of Mary's favourite boulders to God knows where. The sandy beach nearest the girl's cabin had been made off with as well and had been replaced with a collection of stones resembling poor potatoes. No one – not even those who had spent some time on mainland beaches – had seen their like before and they were rumoured to have come from a land where no grass grew and nothing breathed. Parts of the neighbouring cliffs had tumbled into the ocean's embrace, taking with them several sheep. It would come to be said that these animals had been replaced by less domestic and less stupid beasts who scuttled into the earth at first light and whose cries could be heard coming from the hills at twilight the third Sunday of every month from then on.

Esther has seen elemental upheavals of this nature from her own, Canadian parlour windows. Great Lake tantrums, she

4

calls them, Loughbreeze Beach uproars. Her house is solid but it has always responded to stimuli. Made of slender pine boards, lined with cedar, insulated with sawdust, it is alive with a forest life never experienced by walls of stone or brick or cement. When the vehement storms that mark the end of summer come tumbling in over the lake, each gust of wind, each eruption of thunder, is felt in the house's timbers, until, late at night, in the confusion of sleep, the women of this family have been known to believe that the house has *become* the storm; that some ancient quarrel is going on between that which is built and that which is untouched, and that the house might fling itself in a moment of anguish into the arms of its monstrous liquid neighbour.

The old house on Loughbreeze Beach is like a compass situated on the southern boundary of the province called Ontario, on the extreme edge of the country called Canada. Each of its many windows gazes stolidly towards one of four principal directions. When Esther looks to the east she sees a germinating jetty from where, over the course of time, things, in her life, had moved away. When she gazes to the south she sees the ever-present lake and its horizon. To the north lies the cedar wood, beyond which a threatening piece of machinery can occasionally be glimpsed. And past the orchard – in the west – the pier, the conveyor belts, the freighters of the cement company clutter up the shore of the lake.

Over the years the women of the family who have ventured out into the world have carried pictures of Loughbreeze Beach with them in their minds; its coloured stones shining through water, the places where fine pebbles give way to sand, certain paths the moon makes across the lake's surface on autumn midnights. And some of the girls in the family were unable to leave the lake at all. It was in them to seek forever the beaches they

5

were born near and to walk in landscapes where something liquid glistened through the trees.

~

A hundred and forty years before and thousands of miles away, the girl Mary had been the first to witness the beginning of the miracle. Stumbling across the new stones whose texture made walking difficult, she had turned to face the ocean which had robbed her of her favourite boulders. She had been, in those early days, cursed with the gift of eloquence – a gift that would be taken from her forever one hour later. The sea responded to her rant by turning an odd shade of whitish green and swelling up as if it were about to reveal a hidden volcano, and Mary watched, stunned, as thousands of cabbages nudged one another towards the shore. Soon the vegetables completely covered the new stones while behind them the ocean was divided into bands of colour; darks and lights separated by ribbons of glitter. The glitter, it turned out, consisted of a large quantity of silver teapots, so perfectly designed against spillage that they proved very seaworthy as they bounced cheerfully towards the beach. The darker bands revealed themselves to be barrels of whiskey – enough barrels of whiskey to keep any who might want to be, drunk every Saturday night for decades. Flung across two of these barrels was, as Mary gradually perceived, a human form; its head thrown back, one half of its face hidden by a profusion of dark, wet curls. As the barrels that carried it approached the shore, Mary waded through fifty clanking teapots to meet it, and found an exhausted young man who, when she grabbed his shirt in her fists, opened two sea-green eyes and spoke the name Moira before falling once again into semi-consciousness.

Esther knows that at that moment her red-haired great-grandmother would not have wanted to go on living, or at least to go on living in the way she normally had. Time would have frozen, her childhood would have disappeared, and the present would have descended upon her like the claws of a carnivorous bird. "Landscape," Old Eileen had said to Esther, "shrank to a circle that could be measured by Mary's arms, and in that circle the only familiarity was her own brown skirt swaying in a sea that had transformed itself into an undulating carpet of precious metal and wrinkled leaves."

Mary heard the barrels creak as they touched and separated in the current. She heard the surf pant. But mostly she looked at the young man whose sodden shirt she held firmly in her hands – the dark curls pasted to his left cheek, the eyebrows like ferns, the lashes resting on the bones beneath his eyes. She absorbed, in these few moments, more knowledge of a man's body than she ever would again. One of his arms rested, palm upwards, in the water, the sleeve torn open at the spot where his elbow bent. She saw the fortune lines on his hand, the blue rivers of veins under the marble skin, the creases on the vulnerable places of wrist and inner elbow. She saw the Adam's apple and tendons of his exposed throat and the hollow between his collarbones just above his chest. By grasping his shirt she had revealed one of his nipples; the sun had dried the dark hairs around it so that they moved like grass in the breeze, as did the similar hairs that grew down from his belly towards the mystery that his trousers held. Fabric was glued by sea water to his legs and Mary could see the shape of the hard muscles of the thigh and the sharp slice of shinbone, and then the marble skin and blue veins of his bare feet. In the time that it took the sun to travel from one cloud to the next, Mary had learned so much of him that she would have been able to scratch the details of his features on a rock or mould an exact replica of him from clay. She recognized, immediately, that he came from an otherworld island, assumed that he had emerged from the water to look for her, and knew that her name had changed, in an instant, from Mary to Moira.

~

"Never allow anything to change your name," Esther's grandmother had warned her when she began to tell this story. "My poor mother – your great-grandmother – was destined to live out the actuality of Ovid's intention. *Of bodies changed to other forms I tell.* Never allow anyone, anything to change your name," she repeated. "My name is Eileen, yours is Esther. Let's keep it that way."

The twelve-year-old child, Esther, had been, even in her short life, pushed towards beaches by lightning and sand. She carried with her the same red curtain of hair and the same disturbing necessity for water, for passion and pain, as had the girl in the north of Ireland. Esther, however, was learning her lessons early from an old woman who had herself been silenced by passion before the age of twenty, and who had only now chosen to speak of the past.

"You are changing your name," Esther had said to her. "Right now you are changing your name from Eileen – from Great-Aunt Eileen to Grandmother. Everyone's name is changing – Grandpa Liam, Grandma Molly – and all because *you* are changing your name." Esther's face had clouded. She pulled a blue hair ribbon from her head – an expression of anger. "You are the name changer," she said.

"That is not quite the same." The old woman stared hard at Esther, who was squirming uncomfortably on the sofa her father called Wicklow Beach. "I always knew I was your Grandmother even if you didn't. I am speaking of the kind of name change that turns you into someone else altogether, someone other than who you are, the change that takes you off to somewhere else. By the time I finish this story you will have decided to hug the land – the real earth – the trees in the orchard, the timbers of this house. You will have decided never to go away."

"Oh," said the child that Esther had been, trying to adjust her ears to the sound of the old woman's new voice.

Now Esther stands on one of the house's creaking verandahs and looks towards the jetty where everything had, at one time or another, moved away from her. A man, a few beloved horses, the possibility of children. It seems odd to her that a jetty this important could have disintegrated, could have transformed itself into a rough collection of rocks rearranged by storms and trees that have grown to maturity in soil that has collected among boulders. But she knows that were she to step into a boat and glide near the spot on a clear, calm day, she would be able to look over the gunwales and see the old pilings, water-logged and green, wavering beneath the surface like an unconscious memory. Then she would be able to look along the shore and see an aluminum pier and a hulking freighter taking blasted limestone to a refinery.

Except at the front where the Great Lake pounds and the beach stones form ever-changing terraces – solid waves of their own in response – Loughbreeze Beach Farm spreads in ruin around Esther. The parts of it that are not being claimed by that which is unclaimable are being excavated by industry: the growing quarry, the impossible earth-wound made by the cement company. Meadows she played in as a child, woodlots, cornfields, and pastures have disappeared into this gaping absence. Past midnight, when the lake is calm, Esther has, for the last ten years, been able to hear huge machines grinding closer and closer to the finish of her world. One morning a week she spends with the old wringer-washer laundering the cloths she uses to remove the limestone dust from her furniture. One evening a week she walks past the twisted unpruned trees in the orchard, past rotting snake-rail fences, past the obsolete nineteenth-century farm equipment that lies like the scattered skeleton of an extinct animal in the long grass. This evidence of decay the property of a cement company, and soon the evidence itself will be eliminated.

~

The girl in Ireland had let go of the young man's shirt, placed her hands beneath his arms, and gently removed him from the two whiskey barrels that had served as his raft. Clearing a path through cabbages and teapots, she had dragged her treasure up onto the beach to let it dry in the sun. She had put her two warm hands on either side of his cool face and ran her thumbs along the bones above his eyes, the delicate skin of his eyelids. She traced his collarbones with her fingers and tentatively touched the soft hair on his belly. Disturbed by the chill of the sea that had enveloped his body, she lay down beside him on the beach, loosened her long red hair across his shirt, and placed her head on his chest. He stirred as she did this and spoke the word "Moira" once again. When she dropped her arm lightly across his narrow hips a cold hand came up to meet hers. The sun rose higher in the sky, drying her skirt, his trousers, causing the silver vessels to wax radiant. Mary relaxed, watching the steam rise from her skirts, measuring the size of the hand she held against her own until the warmth of the stones around her and the sun above made her drowsy.

That is how her mother, the priest, and a handful of other islanders had found her early in the afternoon, surrounded by cabbages and teapots, asleep in the arms of a dead young sailor.

~

Esther's mind is skilled at building inner landscapes, those she has never seen, those that lie beyond the views her windows frame. There was, for instance, a grand house built by her father on a hill three miles to the north. It was struck, because of its high elevation, by lightning and it had burned to the ground. There was a resort hotel built by her father on a peninsula ten miles to the east. It was buried, because of careless farming practices and because of its low elevation, by sand. And fifty miles to the northeast the original O'Malley homestead – a territory of rock and scant pasture – is now composed of rotting log buildings and rock torn open by prospectors. The traces of wounds left behind by industry are permanent. Fragile architecture abandoned by settlers is not.

All of this propelling Esther towards her place; her large bedroom with its view of the lake, her barns and fields and orchards. Her father, defeated by houses and hotels, had collapsed himself into his wife's family at Loughbreeze Beach, had kept accounts and had run for public office. He had opened a shoestore in the village of Colborne, two miles up from the lake. He had spent leisurely hours inventing names for the cumbersome pieces of furniture in the house. He had given his daughter access to water.

It was what her grandmother, daughter of an Irish girl named Mary, had wanted for the twelve-year-old Esther, and she had wanted it despite her certain knowledge of the impending curse of the mines. "For God's sake," she had yelled, "stay where you are, be where you are." She had thumped the floor with her cane, "Try to understand, but try not to interpret."

"Any interpretation is a misinterpretation," Eileen had told Esther. "Remember that."

~

Delight and fear had broken over Rathlin Island like a pair of consecutive tidal waves.

It had been a hard winter and a long one, so the appearance of the cabbages had been met with general rejoicing – Mary's widowed mother being one of the chief rejoicers. From the four principal points of the island, the sparse population set out for Mary's beach where it collected cartloads of the vegetable, each family throwing in a few teapots for good measure. Never before had there been so bountiful a harvest. No potato patch, no garden plot, had yielded such abundance, and the smell of boiled cabbage would pervade the island for weeks to come.

As for the arrival of the whiskey, it was considered a miracle beyond all telling. Tempered over the centuries by scarcity and the slavish daily labour necessary for survival, the island's population was neither wasteful nor foolhardy. A life of debauchery was, in fact, simply beyond the powers of its collective imagination. The liquor was put in the custody of the priest, stored behind the church, and distributed whenever wakes or weddings demanded it, thereby alleviating, for many years, the financial anxiety that normally accompanied such occasions.

But as the priest, Mary's mother, and all the other islanders knew, no unplanned harvest was reaped without cost. Sudden wealth such as this was a gift from "the Formoire, the ones from the sea, the others." All the green and brown and silver objects

on the beach could only have been deposited by them in payment for something stolen. There was fear in this. From the
moment the first few islanders stood that day on the hilltop,
surveying with astonishment the totally transformed beach –
the prone couple, the new dark stones, the vegetable matter,
the wooden casks, the fine silverware – they knew what it was
that had been taken.

Mary, they believed, was lying in the arms of her faery-
daemon lover; or, what was more likely, what was left of Mary
was lying in the arms of what was left of her faery-daemon
lover, he having returned – with her – to the sea from which he
had undeniably emerged.

Those who looked down at the beach that morning crossed
themselves and turned to Mary's mother with compassion in
their eyes. They knew, and she knew, that Mary was away.

After the great excitement connected to the collecting and
squirreling away of cabbage, cask, and silver had died down,
the islanders turned their attention to the body of the young
man. Some ventured the opinion that it should be left where it
was in the hope that the tide would reclaim it. Others suggested it be burned, right there, on the beach. No one wanted
to touch it for fear that they themselves would be "touched"
and then "taken" as Mary had been. As islanders, they prided
themselves on the fact that few of their people had been
snatched. One old woman once, and a couple of babies
removed in their cradles. Mostly, it was believed, the faeries
confined their abductions to the mainland. Still, the islanders
knew of the ones who lived under the waters and this abandoned body clearly belonged to one of them. After much delib-
eration and examination from a safe distance, Father Quinn
made the final decision. The young man's body was human, he
announced, borrowed most likely by "them" for the purpose

of seducing Mary, and then abandoned when the job was done. In fairness, it ought to be given a decent burial, though not, of course, in consecrated ground. Prudence demanded, however, that only she who had been touched touch the body, and so Mary herself should prepare it for its final rest.

Mary had awakened to the sound of her mother's voice calling her name and a view of the fluttering silken hairs on the young man's chest. "I'm Moira," she whispered, her mouth near his unbeating heart.

"Mary!" her mother shouted, and the daughter heard the sound of her old name but did not respond to it.

"Mary," her mother called, venturing closer, "he's gone back and it's you who must tell me if he's taken you with him."

"My name is Moira," said Mary, sitting up and staring out to sea, one hand grasping the young man's curls possessively.

"And how," asked her mother, her voice ringing through the air, "how would you be getting a name such as that?"

"He gave it to me," she said, simply.

The islanders stood in a group, wide-eyed and silent. Mary's mother began to weep. There was no doubt in any mind now that this girl on the beach, sitting on the strange black stones, was merely a flimsy replica left by "them" or by him in Mary's place.

Father Quinn began to shout instructions. "Moira!" he yelled (for there was no doubt in his mind either). "Moira, this body beside you must be prepared for burial and you shall have Mary's mother's cabin in which to do this. It's only you who can wash the body and lay it out for it's only you that has been touched. I'll send some of the men to carry it and dig the ground to bury it. Mary's mother can stay with a neighbour. It's only you who can touch it, Moira, do you understand?"

And when she did not answer he shouted again more clearly, "Do you understand?", for although he had heard her speak her name he was not quite certain that she used words in the manner of the island people.

Mary nodded, her hair ablaze in the early afternoon sun. She looked at her own live arms, her long legs, and then at the still limbs of the young man. Her heart was full to bursting. Everything about him was hers now, all hers forever.

~

"You are only three generations away from all this," Esther remembers her grandmother saying. "You are only two generations away from me. Don't think it couldn't happen to you, too. Pay attention." And Esther allowed the pale, slim body of a drowned sailor to reveal itself, limb by limb, muscle by muscle in her inner theatre. She was being shocked and moved and shamed by skin and ribs and collarbones, just as, later in the story, she would be tossed and shaken by the gestures of a young dancer.

~

Mary had returned a stranger to the rooms in which she had lived her short life. She had been touched, had become significant, and because of this all around her had become insignificant, distant beside the still reality of the young man's body, now lying on the litter that the men had made and later carried to her table.

The day had grown darker as a memory or aftershock of the night storm drifted across the atmosphere. Outside the small window a single hawthorn twitched and then shivered in a sudden breeze. Mary added more turf to the fire and gathered water from the rainbarrel to warm for the washing. She removed the young man's clothes, now stiff with dried sea water, recognizing the parts of his body she knew from the beach, and learning, instantly, the parts that she didn't know. The skin at the back of his knee brought tears to her eyes because of its perfection; his groin was a dark flower. As she held up first one hand then the other to wash them, she saw the light of the candle shine through the translucent skin that connected his fingers as if they were partly webbed.

She dressed him in a clean pair of her dead father's trousers and one of his shirts, and then undressed him again because he looked so fragile and helpless in clothing several sizes too large for him. Then she boiled and ironed his own sea-wrecked clothing. While she worked her eyes travelled back and forth from his calm face to the window where she could see the priest scuttle over the stones like a large insect, cleansing the beach with his holy water. Before she dressed the young man again she tore a ribbon of fabric off each of his ruined garments and tied the strips into a knot that she would keep.

She dampened his hair and combed out his curls with her fingers. She removed one black curl with a knife and tucked it in her underbodice, and then removed a skein of her own hair and placed it in the breast pocket of his shirt. Repeating the process she cut another of his locks and one of her own and solemnly braided them together. Then, drawing a stool up to the table where the young man lay, she sat down to watch out the length of the night.

Rathlin Island being in the far north of the country, and this being early summer, light drained imperceptibly from the sky until, some time before midnight, the light of the setting sun was replaced by that of the rising moon. Inside the cabin Mary spoke softly to the one she knew was a friend to her, comforting him as she might have comforted a child. She thought only occasionally of Father Quinn and his holy water, believing him to be powerless now in the radiance of this new holiness. She had never been awake in the cabin at this hour and was pleased to discover the night-life; spiders dropping, silent on silken threads, a blur of moths' wings near the candle, and abrupt mice on delicate feet. She felt contented, knowing her life's destiny to be fulfilled, her heart to be given or taken away. In the manner of her old eloquence, which she vowed she would never make use of again except to address him, she began to make words for him and to sing these words to him in a clear, quiet voice:

Dark houses will never swallow you,
Nor graves, nor any other thing that's closed.
It is you who will always have bright skies above you,
The ceiling of water through which you moved.

My heart is made of the soft wings of moths,
Or the silver threads that spiders make in the night.
You who swam easily into my hands,
Carrying with you the Otherworld's light.

That night, while Mary sang to the young man, hearth fires burned bright all over the island and fireside gatherings blossomed in each small dwelling. In the tiny villages of Cleggan and Kinramer, Church Bay, Ballygill and Ballycarry, tales of the Sidhe were told and the properties of Fetch, Pookah, Banshee, and Love-Talker were discussed. One old man remembered his mother telling him of a fisherman she knew from the mainland who was abducted by a mermaid. Another said that his own dog had been stolen and had come back with a troublesome predilection for hens' eggs. The children of the old god Lir were brought to mind, how they had spent hundreds of years as swans, confined to the turbulent waters of the Moyle, which churned through the strait separating the island from the mainland. Even Robert the Bruce was reported to have been fetched by the famous spider of the seven webs he had watched while hiding out in one of the island's caves. It was the consensus of opinion that it was always the brightest and the best that "they" were after. Mary, they agreed, had been a child given to spending far too many hours on the seaside . . . almost as if she were hoping to be fetched, standing as she did on the sand, her skirts hitched up to reveal long white legs, her red hair blowing towards the sky.

The next morning the men who came to collect the corpse, in order to put it into the grave they had dug five fields back from the sea, found Mary still singing. They handed her the canvas sack and watched as she fitted the young man's body into it, lifting first his legs, then his hips, then his shoulders. She touched his lips with her fingers before pulling the canvas over his face. Then, without looking at the men, she pushed his curls under the fabric and sewed a seam over the curve of his skull.

Esther walks on this last evening – a June evening pregnant with light – through the twisted orchard. Petals from scant blossoms are falling from unpruned boughs as she creeps by, and her eyes are filled with the low sunlight that she remembers from after-dinner baseball games. Using a stick that has been greyed and smoothed by a journey on the Great Lake, she pokes angrily at rusted remains – a galvanized pail, a trough with its bottom missing – relics from the time when the painted barns stood tall and milk from gentle-eyed cows was still brought to the table. Relics from the time when she was twelve and her grandmother Eileen had decided to spin out a story.

Though she is eighty-two, and age has weakened her heart, arthritis crippled her hands, Esther takes pride in the fact that her eyesight is "acute." She likes the sound – and the meaning – of the word "acute." It suggests a state of alertness; an animal assessing the danger or pleasure of being where it is.

She pauses now and then to look out over the lake and up into the sky above it where gulls swerve, catching the low sun on their white bellies and exploding into shine. She remembers her father calling them "star gulls" on evenings like this one. She remembers old Eileen sitting with the family on the open front porch, saying, "Once I used to look for a white sail," and then saying nothing at all.

She comes to the end of the orchard and slowly pivots, turning her back to the posted signs that announce DANGER EXPLOSIVES to the aluminum pier, the conveyor belt, and she begins the creeping walk back. The sun is no longer in her eyes and the old house hovers – a white ship moored in a sea of long grass, the cedar bush crouching on one side of it, the lake an apron unfurled on the other. There are hay rakes and iron ploughs scattered and rusting all around her. Underneath grass, earth, rocks, and charred timbers on the hill three miles away there are thick chunks of solid glass and a few fragile pieces of doll's china that no one knows about. Under the sand of the peninsula that reaches out into the lake there exist rooms whose wallpaper depicts bridges, willows, and streams – the scenery of a foreign land. Under the water at the end of a germinating jetty there are pilings clothed in seaweed that remember the search for a white sail and a pale hand.

She has spent the past month preparing for the eventuality

of this last evening and tomorrow's last morning. Entering the old house now she stares at the furniture, the drawers and crevices she has filled with messages – messages to no one in particular. Small bits of paper are taped to the legs of tables and to the seats of chairs; they are pinned to sofas and hooked rugs. They clutter up boxes of costume jewellery and hang from the ends of old tools in the woodshed. Even the odd pane of new clear glass has a story attached to it. Depending on her mood, she had written either something simple – "John broke this one . . . he was not punished" – or something more precise and factual, listing dates, events, and places. Occasionally her own emotional history was recorded. On an old copper boiler she had written the words "I wept for joy. The lake was calm and light engorged the kitchen"; words that will mean nothing to the others who find them. Attached to the metal case of a gold pocket-watch that rests alone on the dining-room table is a luggage tag, and on this is written, "There was often one of us who was away."

If the case were to be opened, no timepiece would be revealed, only thin glass under which rests a lock of black hair, braided together with a red-golden tress and fashioned into a circle. Near this lies a bone hairpin around which is twined a single long thread of the same red-golden hair, a shard of turquoise china, and one black feather, old, torn, and seemingly neglected.

The smooth wooden stairs creak under Esther's feet as she advances down the hall to the large room with the view of the lake. Outside, the poplars at the front of the house are catching the fire of the final sunset. Because the wind has picked up and the lake has grown restless, it is difficult to separate the clamour of approaching machinery from the crash of waves on beachstones. Esther thinks of the million-year-old fossils that decorate these stones and how the limestone record of their extermination has brought about the demise of her own land-scape, the enormous hole in the earth, the blanket of concrete dwellings that is obliterating the villages she knew as a child. As she climbs into the sleigh-bed that has always been in this room, she knows that what she wants is to give shape to one hundred and forty years. She wants to reconstruct the pastures and meadows that have fallen into absence – the disassembled architecture, the great dark belly of an immigrant ship, a pioneer standing inland stunned by the forest, a farmer moving through the beams of light that fill his barn.

Esther pulls the quilt up closer to her neck as the cool lake air reaches her from the window. She will not sleep on this final night, instead she will tell herself the long story until dawn, the way old Eileen had told it to her during after-school twilights.

In her mind's eye, the young girl her great-grandmother was flickers like a distant torch on the opposite side of an ocean. Esther sees the dance old Eileen's arms performed as she told the story, her hands moving like moths towards the flame.

At the quarry the men will work all night, shifting the gears of their machines under artificial light.

Esther, too, will work all night whispering in the dark.

At first it was believed that Mary would die; that she would waste away, abandoning a body that had already been "left behind." As time went by, however, and she seemed stronger and more beautiful than ever, it began to appear that other steps would have to be taken. She did nothing but sing quietly – there was no other form of speech – the songs she had invented during her night vigil with the corpse. She performed her chores methodically and easily – too easily, her mother thought – as milk turned to butter with a few light touches of the churn and eggs were produced by hens the moment the girl stepped outside to collect them. Her bread rose to ridiculous heights in the oven and the sweet berries for which the islanders spent hours searching began to appear in profusion all around her mother's cabin.

As streams of golden tea poured from silver teapots all over the island in the following months, the women, young and old, considered the predicament. They feared Mary, but did not wish to offend her, fearing the retribution of "the others" more. They wondered if she would bring a changeling into the world and, if so, what dark powers it would have. Some of them secretly hoped that the girl had been given the ability to do cures, particularly for the complaints of women and the diseases of children.

The men, when they gathered round their turf fires at night, never mentioned Mary's name at all, but a mental picture of her stirred their thoughts and sometimes their groins, leading them to believe that they must avoid her altogether lest they begin to be astray themselves. One by one they crept into the damp church on the bay, slipped behind the dark curtain of the confessional, and whispered their secret longings into the ear of Father Quinn. It was when this venerable person, himself, started having unsettling dreams concerning red hair and snow-white breasts that he decided something must be done before the whole island became possessed.

Father Quinn was not a young man, but not so old as to be beyond desire. When he awoke some mornings, his normally severe countenance in the silvered glass seemed altered, inflamed by something just beneath the skin that wanted to burst out. Mary might have been in his dreams all night disguised as a tree or even as a single leaf moving in the breeze just beyond his grasp, and he straining to touch it. All day, then, he would be remembering the veins of that leaf and its delicate structure.

It was with a great deal of reluctance that he climbed the road that led from Church Bay to the girl's cabin. He would swing incense over her, thoroughly drench her with holy water. He brought along his censer, a glass vessel filled with liquid, and a chip of the tooth of Saint Patrick. He carried dried stems of heather with which to thrash the "other" from her if need be. He had begun to pray before he left his cold rooms at the back of the church, and he had continued to pray as he fortified himself with a drop of the miraculous whiskey stored conveniently nearby. He prayed that her cheeks would fade, her bosom sag, her teeth rot, and her eye lose its lustre. He prayed that her waist would thicken and that a wart would grow on her nose. And he prayed that if the Lord could not arrange these alterations he himself would cease to be tormented by her, her infirmity would cease to be his affliction, that she would be taken completely by "the others," and that nothing disturbing would be left in her place.

Mary, however, had gone, as she did on certain days now, down to search for he who had been given as a gift to her. He had fallen into her life as Wednesday falls into the middle of the week, and it was often Wednesdays that she sought and found him. Her pale swimmer. It was Wednesday when he had washed into her arms, and he would crash over her, she knew, every Wednesday for eternity. Her wave. Her breaker.

Wednesdays she woke with the smell of the sea in her room, her mouth requesting fire and salt and her arms aching. Something like thunder shook the furniture of the cabin and beyond its walls fuchsia and whitethorn trembled. She ate handfuls of her mother's precious peppercorns and rubbed her thighs until they burned with the turf that awaited the fire, until her body, inside and out, shrieked and sang, and the little grey village outside the window stepped backwards and withdrew. Then she burst from the house to the sea, in fever.

She bathed immediately, loving the weight of drenched clothing that pulled her farther into the sea and then the lightness of her limbs as she threw her clothing back to the shore. She floated, and waited.

His song was like no other song. It rasped and whimpered and told her secrets she had known for centuries. Her arms were full of him, he entered her and passed right through her. He enveloped her like her own skin and she a stone sinking under his weight. He forced her to want other elements to breathe beyond that which was available in the ordinary air, and then, moments later, the air was no longer ordinary. If she had been asked to describe him, she would have said that he was the exact spot where the sea touches land, the precise moment of the final reach of surf. That was the place and the time of him. She would forever, then, seek shorelines and beaches.

Father Quinn dragged his equipment laboriously towards Mary's door and was met by the handsome bulk of Mary's mother leaning over her vegetable patch, examining the new green leaves of potato plants.

"I've come to bring Mary back, Norah," he said, "by whatever means God sees fit."

"Well, she's not here," said the woman. "Even she that is here is not here."

"And what does this creature do all day?" asked the priest, trying to keep pictures of her red mouth and white throat out of his mind as he spoke.

"She's mostly singing," said her mother, "and whispering to someone I can't see."

"Does she pray, then?"

"No, it's not prayers she's saying."

"Well, I'm certainly hoping that it's you who are praying, Norah Slattery. This cabin will be needing all the prayers anyone might be whispering."

"Sometimes it's rhymes she says." Mary's mother looked embarrassed. "Rhymes," she added, lowering her voice, "with words like heart and treasure and darling in them. The songs have those words as well."

The priest's own heart sprang in his chest and then quieted. His conscience slapped him hard. He wanted to hear these songs sung by Mary's own mouth, and she singing them for him alone. He looked down at his censer and holy-water bottle lying on the earth where he had dropped them. They look

25

ridiculous, he thought, glinting in the sun with potato plants and weeds bobbing all around them.

"I've brought some holy water," he said absently, "in case it might help. That and some incense."

"She won't be back till sundown, that's certain," said Mary's mother. She picked up her apron and let it fall again, looking oddly girlish as she did so, despite her age and size. Then she turned her face away and made her confession. "I can't help thinking, Father," she said, "that she's the same daughter that I gave birth to. Not a hair on her head has changed and she still calls me Mother. Is it, do you think, Father, that this is what 'they' would have me believing?"

"Consider this," the priest replied. "'They' leave an exact replica of that which they've taken, in its place. This girl is an exact replica. She is here but she is not. The word 'exact' is important. Every hair that's on her head is an exact replica of every hair that was on her head. Do you see it, Norah? There is nothing about her would have changed except that she is changed. The question is how to get her back. Sometimes it takes seven years. Sometimes they never come back. Sometimes they waste away."

"Should I be turning her out of doors then, Father, if she's not my daughter at all?"

"Ah no, Norah, for if Mary were to come back she would need to exchange herself, and she wouldn't be able to find herself to exchange."

"Oh," said Mary's mother, confused, "it's like that then, is it?"

"Yes," Father Quinn said in a tired voice, "that's what it's like . . . exactly." He glanced at the tooth chip where it rested in its silver-and-glass reliquary. It looked powerless and decayed. For a moment he wondered whether it had been broken from a human, never mind a divine tooth. He thought of Mary's

26

gleaming teeth, of her mouth. "That and her calling herself by a different name." He was silent for a moment, thinking. "Still," he said eventually, "it might be a good thing for her to be off the island, were she to leave it in a natural way."

The moment he spoke these words he experienced a feeling of loss so shattering he was forced to catch his breath. Composing himself he added, "In a natural way, as if she really were Mary, not this . . . Moira." He remembered her walking the roads of the island, her hair a-fly. Then he imagined the roads without her on them. He was not fond of the island's roads, he decided; the hills, the sea stirred his heart, but not the roads.

"And what way would that be, Father?" Mary's mother stood with her hands clasped piously in front of her.

"Death or marriage," the priest said, surprising himself with the bluntness of his answer. "Both natural, so that if Mary came back she'd know where to look for herself."

"But who would be marrying one who is away?"

"One who doesn't know," replied Father Quinn. "One who doesn't know," he repeated slowly, though he believed in his heart that there were plenty who would marry her skin and hair even if they did. "Or perhaps," he continued, a new idea striking him, "one who knows but doesn't believe."

"In God!?" asked Mary's mother, shocked.

"Doesn't believe," answered the priest, "that a person can be away at all."

Brian O'Malley's cottage was situated some two miles east of Ballyvoy in the collection of dwellings that went by the name of Coolanlough. Hills swept up on either side of it, rising to the cliffs a mile away. To approach these promontories you had to walk beside the still lakes known as Dhu, Faddon, and Crannog – the latter with its ancient man-made island floating on its surface. From the cliffs you could look at Rathlin Island and the waters of the Moyle that churned in front of it, or you could turn to the left and examine Ballycastle Bay and the town that rose behind it. With your back to the sea you could watch the swift shadows of clouds darken the surfaces of the already dark lakes. Below, on the beach, there might be one or two dulse gatherers and, to the left and right of Rathlin, fishing boats bobbing like small, floating sea birds. Moving purposefully past these curraghs might be the Rathlin-Ballycastle ferry. This small vessel knew no schedule, returned sometimes hours, sometimes days after it set out. Once when it was owned by Sean MacDonnell, who lived on the land, it wintered on the island. Once when it was owned by Fergus MacFee, an islander, it wintered on the land; its furious respective owners cursing God and the sea.

Father Quinn had been lucky and unlucky. The day was fair, the crossing easy. But unlucky because, since the day was fine, he was unlikely to find his friend Brian O'Malley at home. The priest carried a copy of Horace under his arm, guiltily, knowing that this was not the real reason for his visit. Normally the two men met once or twice a month to talk about Latin, mathematics, and philosophy, and O'Malley's cottage was the best place for that. But, Quinn reminded himself, he should be grateful that the walk from Ballycastle to Ballyvoy was not as lengthy as that to Coolanlough, and on a fine day Ballyvoy was where O'Malley was most likely to be found.

Eventually the priest rounded a bend in the road that led up from the harbour town. Now he could see the straggling cottages and cabins that made up the village. He heard wind and birds and his own determined footsteps on the gravel, then the expected sound of sustained chant coming from the hedgerows. Quinn joined in unconsciously, mouthing noun declensions, moving with facility into verbs and then shouting enthusiastically long Latin sentences concerning Roman campaigns until the other chanting voices ceased and a tall form emerged from an opening door in the shrubbery that lined the side of the road.

"Well," said the schoolmaster, "how is it that you've come on a day such as this?"

Behind him the voices that had been dutifully reciting broke into chaos. Words and laughter burst out from summer leaves. Great scuffling erupted.

"Creeping up like this you might have been one of the inspectors of the old days." Both men remembered when hedge schools such as this had been forbidden by law. "I've most of the children here though they're itching to be gone, if it's some talk you're after."

Father Quinn was passing the old leather book from hand to hand nervously. Four or five blackbirds paced at his feet. "It's about something else I've come," he said, "besides Latin."

Two small boys rolled out of the entrance and wrestled in the dust on the road. The dark birds spun away.

"Back in with you," roared O'Malley. "On with Caesar. Do the part on England. Recite in whispers."

The boys disappeared. Hisses slipped through the wattle, thatch, and lattice of the old structure. *"Britannia est magnum insulum,"* the voices announced in unison.

"Magna insula!" shouted O'Malley, tossing his head back briefly in the direction of the greenery. "We've been looking carefully at your *Lives of the Saints*, if it's that. And grateful we are for the loan of it."

"Fine, fine," said Father Quinn, "but, no, it's not that."

"Should I send them off, then?" The whispering beyond the leaves stopped. The very air seemed to listen. The priest looked furtively up and down the road as if he were about to perform an act for which there should be no witnesses. "If you have no objection," he said, "it might be best."

O'Malley turned and entered the shrubbery. "Two more sentences," he demanded, "and then be gone for the day. And say them slowly and clearly in the voice of Caesar."

"Insula natura triquetra, cuius unum latus est contra Galliam," the children droned. *"Huius lateris alter angulus, qui est ad Cantium, quo fere omnes ex Gallia naves appelluntur, ad orientem solem, inferior ad meridiem spectat."*

"Until tomorrow, then!" O'Malley boomed. "And think about Caesar."

Thirteen children exploded through the makeshift door and hurtled past the priest. Most were barefoot. Father Quinn watched them scatter across the road in the direction of freedom, their clothing like torn pennants waving from fragile poles.

Shortly afterwards, their tormentor appeared in the sun. "There's one or two of them have the makings of a scholar," he said. "But there's not a poet in the lot of them. More's the pity."

"And your own poems?" asked the priest, politely.

"Ah those . . . they come now, if they come at all . . . very slowly." The schoolmaster looked suddenly shy. "I've one on the recent shipwreck though, if you'd like to hear it."

So, thought the priest, the silver and the whiskey were not divine providence after all. "Speak it to me," he said.

O'Malley cleared his throat:

Their nautical hearts were brave
And the cliffs of Antrim steep.
Lordly was the wave
And darkling was the deep.
The ship had sailed a thousand leagues,
A thousand leagues or more,
But the sight of the cliffs of Antrim
Was the site of its final shore.

Through the several verses of the poem the priest admired his friend's strong face, noticing the lines on the forehead and the cut of the angular bones, and then the creases made by worry, thought, and kindness around the dark blue eyes. He needed a haircut, thought the older man, but the hair itself was neatly combed, though greying and thin at the temples. Altogether the man had a pleasant countenance. What would she who was over on the island think, he wondered, of a face such as this.

The schoolmaster finished his recitation and looked towards the stones at his feet. One of his laces had broken this morning. He mostly kept his poems private, guarded against the world. But Father Quinn was his closest friend – though he came from the island and they met infrequently – and his verses were received by the priest in a friendly manner. Their views on certain other subjects, however, diverged dramatically.

"Fine," said Father Quinn now. "A fine poem and filled with noble sentiments."

Brian O'Malley took the compliment, as always with mild embarrassment. "Oh, there's nothing in it," he maintained quietly, "that hasn't been said before."

Both men were silent, knowing this to be true.

"Shall we walk towards the cottage then?" O'Malley touched the priest lightly on the shoulder.

They walked some distance in silence, the priest with his hands behind his back. Normally he would have complimented his friend on his few square acres of native landscape, its cliffs and pastures, the dark lakes and the sea in the distance. He would have commented on a neighbour's lambs or a new calf. He would have continued with reference to the splendid view of Rathlin Island that could be had from this or that point, and he would have ended with a long speech on the island as being the best bit of rock that God had ever flung into the sea. But his thoughts were elsewhere, on a white neck, a green eye, a burning halo of hair.

"What is it then?" O'Malley eventually asked.

The priest looked hard at his birthplace, then into the eyes of his friend. "There's a terrible fever sweeping the island," he whispered.

"Not the cholera again?" The faces of all his pupils leapt into the teacher's mind.

The men had stopped walking.

"No, it's a fever of the mind," said Father Quinn, though he, of all the islanders, knew it was a fever of the body as well. "There's one on the island," he continued, "who is away."

"Now Father . . . this is mere superstition. How it persists is beyond –"

"No, listen: you don't believe it but it's tragically true. She's had one from the sea for a lover and now she's away. Wasn't she

32

found asleep and he lying drowned in her arms, and the beach stones all changed and she, too, changed utterly?"

They were walking again. "And how is it that she's changed?" asked the teacher.

"She's . . ." Father Quinn's voice caught on the word. "She's beautiful."

"And was she not before?"

"She's beautiful," insisted the priest, ignoring the question, "and she's only speaking now in verses and songs." Father Quinn strode angrily ahead so that O'Malley had to hurry to keep up. "And it's the men of the island, old and young, that are stricken with the fever. Tossing, they are, on their beds at night, and then stumbling into my confession box during the day to tell me their wild thoughts. And they've gone all soft, no one planting or fishing, or planting and fishing without their hearts in it and having all their dreams at night taking unholy courses. And she, herself, down by the sea on that ungodly beach, singing to no one we can see, and sometimes" – the priest reddened with shame – "sometimes swimming naked."

"I don't believe it!" asserted O'Malley.

"Ah, but it's true, I've seen her my –" Father Quinn broke off suddenly.

O'Malley swallowed a smile. The shadow of a cloud pursued the two men down the road, shaded them briefly, then went on momentarily to darken the schoolmaster's white cottage which had just come into view.

"I've never seen the likes of it," Father Quinn went on. "Everything blooming at her doorstep – and none of it planted, mind – and they say when there's rain falling, it falls everywhere but on her mother's cabin and she in it."

"And this poor, unfortunate drowned creature, who was he, then?"

"I've already told you who he was. He was one of *them*. Sure he'd stolen some poor mortal's flesh to be visiting her, but one of them it's certain. Didn't he bring an unholy flood of whiskey with him? That and a gathering of silver teapots so plentiful you couldn't walk but you'd be crushing one beneath your heel."

O'Malley referred to the recent shipwreck and his own poem about it.

"Ah yes," said the priest darkly, "and who was it I wonder who caused this poor ship to founder? She has a look on her would tempt God himself." Quinn's face went soft. "Never mind bring one of them up from the sea."

So she *was* beautiful before, thought O'Malley, but he kept his own counsel.

Entering the cottage's gloom, the priest remembered his mission with distaste. I haven't the cunning, he thought, of the true matchmaker. Already I've revealed too much. I've forgotten what I meant to say.

"She's good natured," he began now, "and not likely to be away much longer, I'd think. Perhaps –"

"Would you show her to me, Father?" the schoolmaster interjected.

"Perhaps with some prayers and some holy water . . ."

"I'd like to see her."

"Some long prayers might bring her back soon."

The schoolmaster squatted near the hearth, his broad back to Quinn, blowing on the ashes, hoping to find some fire to boil water for the tea.

"Does she say the poems loud enough to hear?"

"With some prayers she'll not be saying them at all. Her mother says she works hard. I'll do all I can to bring her back. If you come in a month . . ."

"I'll come with you," Brian said, "in the morning."

"But she's . . ."

The schoolmaster rose, having managed to coax a flame from the remaining turf. "I'm of a mind," he said, "to see her as she is. I'm of a mind to see her now." He poured some water from a pail into the kettle.

The priest walked back and forth across the flags. He hadn't the heart to speak anymore about Mary, and his spirits were too low to introduce the topic of philosophy.

O'Malley set the kettle to boil.

"What was the name of that ship?" the priest asked for want of something better to say.

"*Moira*," said O'Malley. "The *Moira* was her name. She came out of Belfast, I believe."

The priest registered the name but did not comment upon it. "And where was she bound?"

"For America, I think they said, a place called Halifax."

"She hadn't gone that far on her journey, then."

"No," agreed the schoolmaster, "she hadn't gone far at all."

SHE awoke at first light, swimming upwards from deep, green dreams.

The desire for the sea was on her. Liquid.

This was the only room she had ever known. From that small window she had watched her father's departing sail, her small hand flat against the cool glass.

Now the room was bathed in blues and greens; the furniture dim as if holding onto night.

In her dreams her father's sail collapsed into a green horizon. Gone.

His wake had tumbled around and eventually out of her memory. Coffinless. The singers and the smokers. Herself near her mother's skirts and all the women wailing.

She had waited for him to return for three years until even his absence became absent.

Now she lay in the dawn with the desire on her and armies of new words in her mind requesting that she say them.

"His forehead," she whispered, the words pushing out past her lips, "his long arm."

She lay flat on her back with her hands open on her stomach, the idea of his arm as real as if it glistened there before her.

"Just below the surface," she began, "with the tatters of your shirt around it and the fluid between us, the flower of your hand turning in the ocean's mind, your arm a bright banner, your forehead an approaching sail. My own arms pushing wind aside to plunge them into salt. Let me breathe this green with you and be with you. Our breastbones touching."

Her bed was hard and dry. Sheets rasped, papery, against her skin and blankets were heavy on her limbs. Anything solid was an impediment when there was this sea change upon her. Her body, it seemed, was composed of salt fluids: blood and tears.

She left the cabin quietly, timing each footfall to coincide with her mother's snores and settling the doorlatch back into place soundlessly. Soon her bare feet were covered with dew and the bottom of her skirt drenched in it. Her mind already awash with love, her eyes fixed on the black beach over which she had to walk in order to swim. Dark morning birds lifted away from the earth she walked on, her words spinning in the sky then flying over the fields to the shore.

She would swim until cold and exertion caused her body to ache and her mouth to gasp. Then she would swim harder and he would begin to take shape. She would see his ribs in the sand ripples and something in the surf would begin to speak to her. "Moira, Moira," until all of him, a taut muscle, glided by her side. Salt-lipped, slick-thighed. And afterwards they would stagger to the black beach where she put her head on his still chest.

There was great wealth in this, great treasure. She had him, even when far from the sea in all the new words that sang and spoke in her mind and spilled from her lips. And then the pictures he had shown her: distant harbours, far shores, rivers penetrating foreign continents, a glimpse of a strange dome or monument, a riot of flowers the colour of flame dancing on a weird strand, mountains flickering on a horizon. He would open his hands under the water and there would be steeples, towers, forests, a crowded wharf.

She could build him with stones and smooth driftwood, with salt water and sand, the architecture of his body fragile and impermanent, the sea reclaiming it when she turned again towards the world. But the next time she needed him the materials would come into her hands as she swam and she would know the pleasure, the craft of reconstruction.

This morning, as always when she awakened on the beach, he was gone. As she stood to return to her mother's cabin, the world drew fractionally closer. She saw the ferry crossing from Ballycastle in the direction of Rue Point, her own island. It would dock, she knew, at Church Bay, only a few hundred yards from the spot that she used to call home.

INSIDE the not-so-picturesque ruins of Bunnamairge Friary, one mile east of Ballycastle, side by side on camp-stools, sat Osbert and Granville Sedgewick, bachelor sons of Henry Austin Sedgewick the Third. Osbert was making a watercolour of one of the Friary's few remaining arches, and Granville was composing his forty-third lament concerning the sorrows of Ireland. Both were cold, damp, and generally uncomfortable, but unshaken in the belief that, despite the mud and water that filled their shoes and the wind that threatened to snatch their creations from their laps, they were communing happily with the spirit of their country's past.

Ever since the first Irish Sedgewick had been granted estates in Glen Taisie in the early seventeenth century, this family's members, unlike many Anglo-Irish landed gentry, had exhibited nothing but surprise, delight, and a certain charmed mystification whenever they examined the details of their surroundings. Dedicated collectors of almost everything, they had dragged an extravagant amount of information and unprecedented numbers of specimens and objects into their damp, ill-lit halls, going about the task with such zeal it soon appeared they wanted all of County Antrim under glass. They scoured the coastal cliffs for birds' eggs, flora and fauna, the moors for ancient carved stones, and the cabins of their tenants for quaint bits of folklore and songs. Their satchels bursting with the finest sketchbooks and round cakes of green watercolour paint, they committed hundreds of views to paper, and stairwell after stairwell of the ancestral home was filled with these fading efforts, the rest of the house being stuffed to capacity with cases and shelves.

By Osbert and Granville's time, the floorspace in the halls was as crowded as the rest of the house as a result of their father's discovery of, and subsequent enthusiasm for, the art of taxidermy. One of every creature, great or small, that crept or ran or flew or swam in and around County Antrim was now on display at Puffin Court (so called because of Henry Austin the First's obsession with this unusual bird which flourished on the nearby cliffs and which he was said to resemble to an uncanny degree). The puffin itself was well represented in the stuffed menagerie, appearing as guardian figures in cases filled with smaller, and more nervous, native birds. It also perched, or rather stood flat-footedly, on the backs of the horse and cow, the only two large beasts available in County Antrim since the demise of the Irish stag in prehistoric times. The puffin did not appear with the foxes but, for some inexplicable reason, a small example stood among the hounds, all of whom had been docile family pets, but who now exposed their yellowed teeth to full advantage.

Henry Austin Sedgewick the First had authored a lengthy Latin text on the puffin – *Fratercula arctica Hibernica* – much of which was written from the puffin's own point of view. "*Ego sum Fratercula arctica,*" it began. "*Habito in ora Hibernica.*" All ten copies still remained in Puffin Court's vast and dusty library. Until quite recently, no further Sedgewicks had managed to get their musings into print, though many of the library's shelves sagged under the weight of ancestral day books, scrapbooks, diaries, and handwritten, handbound odes and epics. Only the previous year, however, a London firm had published twenty of Granville's laments in a small leather-bound edition, an encouragement that had inspired him to produce, in the following few months, over two dozen more.

Granville could not compose at all, however, unless he sat, as he now did, in close proximity to some crumbling evidence of Ireland's former glory, and hence his portable lap desk, which he kept in his knapsack, was one of his most cherished possessions. It had travelled with him to all of North Antrim's most interesting locations; from the Giant's Causeway to Bruce's Cave on Rathlin Island, from Oisín's Grave to Doonfort at Fair Head, from Dunseverick Castle to Carrick-A-Reed. Now, while his brother applied another grey wash to the old stones depicted in his watercolour, Granville was writing his lament for Bunnamairge Friary and the Black Nun he knew was buried under its threshold.

The Sedgewicks were a fair-minded if eccentric family and Osbert and Granville were as well loved by the peasantry as any pair of landlords could ever hope to be. The tenants had given up trying to understand the family during the incumbency of Henry Austin the First and had lapsed into a kind of bemused acceptance of what was termed "the antics of themselves." Several of the older men in the community kept their minds busy inventing new folklore to relate at their firesides during Osbert's and Granville's note-taking visits so as not to disappoint the young masters whom much of the male peasantry had come to know, thirty years before, during the Great Walk Making Employment – a project conceived by Henry Austin the Third when Osbert and Granville were small boys.

In a particularly ambitious attempt to get yet another facet of County Antrim onto his demesne, if not into the house itself, the father of the boys hired fifty of his tenants to help him create suitably romantic and lengthy walks for his children. One of these promenades, two miles long and liberally scattered with man-made grottos of every description, was known as the Cave Walk. Its crowning glory was a structure made with thousands of bottles from the Ballycastle Glass Factory inserted into mud and wattles so that their necks and mouths were exposed to the air in hopes that the wind might blow into them and create "a symphony of sound." The Cliff Walk was never completed owing to the difficulty of getting rocks large enough and precipitous enough and in sufficient quantity onto the property. Many arbours, however, sprang up at this time, as did fountains of varying intensities. Three or four artificial lakes were created, complete with the man-made islands called crannogs. Osbert's and Granville's creative careers had begun at the ages of six and eight when their father had commanded them to sketch, and then compose a sonnet about, one of the little crannogs. Although's Osbert's drawing was far superior to Granville's, despite the former's younger age, Granville displayed a natural aptitude for poetry. From that day on they pursued their chosen gifts, happily, never once intruding into the other's territory, but almost always working together.

The old Friary was a great favourite with the brothers for several reasons. First, it could be reached easily, after a pleasant hour-and-a-half stroll, downhill, from Puffin Court towards the sea. Second, its history was undeniably tragic as well as undeniably finished – a requisite for Granville's laments if not for Osbert's watercolours – and third, it was, of course, connected to the Roman Catholic Church for which all of the Sedgewicks, who were, naturally, Protestant, had great affection. They were charmed by their tenants' passionate faith, by their beads and Hail Marys and crucifixes. At the time of the Catholic emancipation in 1829, bonfires were lit and torches were waved at Puffin Court in response to those glowing all over the neighbouring hills. As might be expected, this gave rise to great suspicion in the minds of the other Protestant gentry and Presbyterian farmers in the region, but as the years went by, and the Sedgewicks goodnaturedly went on with the business of collecting gulls' eggs and mineral specimens, and as they appeared in the appropriate church with regularity, this lack of judgement on their part came eventually to be ignored.

The Black Nun upon whom Granville now mused was buried beneath the Friary's portal because, in a moment of extreme humility, she had expressed a wish that, when dead, she be trodden upon by those entering and those leaving the religious house where she had lived. Why she inhabited a friary was never fully explained, though it may have had something to do with her role as a prophet. During her lifetime she had made a number of predictions, none of which had, as yet, come true, but all of which might, if one were merely to wait long enough. She predicted that Knocklaid Mountain would explode, caus-ing a muddy flood for seven miles in all directions. She pre-dicted that Rathlin Island would disappear into a dense fog and never be seen again. She predicted that Finn Mac Cumhail's great dog Bran would return to Ireland in the form of a leopard hungry for British blood. And she predicted that Ireland's lib-eration and independence would be announced by the appear-ance of a ship with sails of flame in Ballycastle Harbour. This last prediction fascinated Granville who had great sympathy for the cause of an independent Ireland. He intended to focus two stanzas of his lament on a description of this mythic ship – the sparks showering the sky, the fire reflected in the water, the Black Nun herself, her face glowing, joyfully haunting the pro-phesied event. Then, because this was, after all, a lament, he intended to have the whole scene evaporate before the poet's very eyes, leaving him longing for,

All days evermore,
The sails of sun, the victory won,
The joy upon the shore.

Granville had given little thought to what might become of his family holdings were this grand liberation to take place. It seemed as vague and unlikely to him as his stuffed puffins and demesne seemed eternal. It was the myth of the desire for freedom that appealed to him – all the longing that filled the very air. The ongoing sense of emotional trouble. Ever since the first poem in his series – "A Lament on the 1704 Act to Prevent the Further Growth of Popery" – he was obsessed by the sorrow that seemed to be embedded in the stones beneath his feet. Resolution, he knew instinctively, would change the tone of the landscape, the faces of the cottiers, the melancholy of the people's music, and the passion and stoicism of their survival – in short, all that he and his ancestors had come to love. And so, without being aware, he supported this delicate balance of injustice and defiance on the one hand and sorrow and poetry on the other. That, and the rich cloak of imagination and invented worlds that protected the peasants around him from the cold reality of their unchangeable lot.

"How is it going at O'Malley's school?" asked Osbert, bending down to reach the little pot of water that stood at his feet. "A damp season for it, I'd say."

Both brothers loved and supported the "little hedge academy," as they called it, it being one of the few to survive the advent of state education, once it had become legal to educate Catholics at all. Osbert occasionally gave free drawing lessons to the children, and Granville, who had written "A Lament on the Demise of the Bardic Schools of Ireland," donated books. The children were invited once a year to Puffin Court and given the run of the Cave Walk while Granville and the hedge schoolmaster compared poems.

"They've a fair bit of thatch," said Granville, "it shouldn't be too bad. Punic wars, is what they're doing now, I think." He paused and stared into the distance. "I wonder if this Black Nun had a youth?" he mused.

"They say school's been out for a couple of days. O'Malley's gone to the island with the priest."

"Ah . . . the priest-philosopher. Was he here, then? Pity I hadn't known. I could have asked him about the nun." Granville began counting syllables. "Can you think of a word that rhymes with cloister?" he eventually asked, "or perhaps another, something besides hosiery for rosary?"

"He was only to be gone overnight but he's not returned." Osbert squinted at his arch. "Usury," he said, "not exact but close enough."

Overhead a family of hawks circled once or twice before departing for the cliffs at Fair Head. The brothers worked for some time in silence until Granville completed a draft of the lament, with his characteristic dotting of i's and crossing of t's all the way down the page, and looked towards the island's cliffs off shore. "Surely the priest couldn't keep O'Malley away from the school for more than a day. They've usually argued it out in three hours or so."

"It was to look at a woman that he went over there. There's a woman on the island they say is 'away.'"

"'Away' . . . off with the faeries, is she?"

"Not this one," said Osbert, tying his portfolio. "They say this one has a daemon lover."

"Is that so?" said Granville, closing his notebook and capping his pen, "How interesting."

As the brothers climbed the path that led from the Friary the rain began in earnest. Simultaneously, two black umbrellas unfurled, and just at the moment when the fabric became taut with the accustomed and satisfying snap Osbert recalled another of the Friary's legends, one that had been omitted from his brother's lament. It was rumoured that the friars, just before their final eviction, had buried the contents of their treasury at the most distant point to which a candle's light reaches when placed in the east window of the now ruinous chapel.

The absence of light on the one hand, the absence of darkness on the other, and where the two absences meet, treasure. He thought of the woman on the island who was away. Then, as he and his brother walked through the rain into the glen towards their demesne, these two concepts became wedded, somewhere in the back of his mind.

ONLY traces of her previous self, her previous life remained when she was not by the sea. Fragments.

She remembered how to perform various chores: stirring, pouring, hoeing, encouraging flame. But her memory could have been anybody's memory; a pattern borrowed from a passing brain, the routine of an ordinary day, instructions dictated to her from outside of herself. Now bend, now lift, now fold. Dry activity. And herself a mere memory of herself.

Porridge, potato, a knife, three or four earthenware bowls, the rough wool of her mother's skirt in a house where nothing shone. The solid hand at the end of her wrist that reached and grasped, just the trace of a hand from before, covered in shadow. The real, now, was a hand shimmering under water, distorting in the liquid atmosphere. The full, liquid caress.

And so, when she saw the two men enter through her door, they were just ideas of men she remembered from before; the priest a black hulking shape, heavy in one of the room's corners, the other dressed in muted colours. And their voices coming at her from far across the air.

"We've come to pray, Mary."

Her mind riveted on the young man's torn collar and the words in her mind building it. Where grew the flax that made the woven threads in plaid, now torn beside the curve of your neck where my fingers are. A corner plastered on a collarbone. Some stitches sewn and soaked with brine. You are gentle, gentle, gentle as the sea you sail. Threads unravelling at your neck.

She saw the priest crouch and assemble his portable altar, but he was far from her. She felt the holy water fill her hair, but it was tepid and useless and ran in futile tracings to her throat. She brought the memory of her hand to the place beneath her jaw to rid herself of it and then saw the moisture glistening on her fingers. The water when she placed it in her mouth was not the moisture she desired.

The priest was saying words in Latin while the other man moved, a brown blur, from corner to corner of the room. The lukewarm water ran between her shoulder blades and across her face, like tears.

"Pater noster . . . In Deo speramus, Te Deum laudamus."

She recalled the mole on his left cheek, his eyelashes. She had words somewhere about his eyelashes and their cousins, his perfect brows. She had seen his lashes beat, back and forth, like the fronds of miniature angel's wings, and then she had seen them hold still.

A terrible sadness poured over her. Where had she gone? Where had she gone? If she were to return, how terrible the loss of this singular enchantment? Her homeland was a city underwater that she'd never seen except when he'd shown her – the spires, the steeples spilling from his open hand.

"No," she said quietly, and it was the first word she had spoken.

"No," she said again into the distance of the room.

"Cast off this shadow, Mary," the priest was saying "that stands between yourself and God."

He advanced towards her with the large crucifix. Mary saw the young naked man that hung from the cross and reached tentatively to caress the sand waves of his ribs. But it was not Christ that she touched.

"Say a prayer to him, Mary."

She floated away and turned her face towards the small window and the sea. A rectangle of sun lay on the floor beside the table. Something in Mary decided to step inside the golden light. The priest placed the crucifix carefully on the table and turned towards his friend whose gaze was fixed on the bronze radiance of sun-filled hair. Quinn reached for his breviary and nervously thumbed the pages, searching for further prayers.

Each day since his arrival on the island O'Malley had witnessed this ceremony; the priest stiff and wilful, the girl soft and absent . . . her eyes partially covered by lashes, her gaze averted, her face impassive. Once he had seen the priest, in desperation, extend his arm as if to strike or embrace her, and the schoolmaster, himself, had instinctively moved forward to prevent the anticipated invasion. Father Quinn's arm had dropped helplessly back to his side. The men exchanged a quick look of anger, but they never spoke of the incident.

In fact, since their first conversation in O'Malley's cottage, they rarely discussed the girl at all. Once or twice the priest had asked, "What am I to do?" or "How's it all to end?" And his friend had replied, "When you convince yourself and her that it's all nonsense . . . that and your congregation . . . that will end it." But Father Quinn had exclaimed, "Nonsense! And she with that look on her!"

Mostly the two men spent the quiet evenings and their walks to and from Mary's cabin comparing facts gleaned from their recent reading. Between them they shared the ownership of the *Supplement to Address the Defects of the 5th, 6th and 7th editions of the Encyclopaedia Britannica*, purchased from the Sedgewicks at reasonable cost upon the arrival of the eighth edition in their library. There had almost been a quarrel between the friends when the Supplement became available, O'Malley claiming that he should have it for the little hedge school and Quinn insisting that he needed it to instruct his parishioners – though few of them could read and many of them spoke only Gaelic.

They had finally resolved the argument through joint ownership, and now they were systematically reading the four volumes from A to Z, or, in Quinn's case, from Z to A, so that they were able to exchange volumes somewhere around the middle of the alphabet. Because they had only the Supplement, there were large gaps in their learning, but they comforted themselves with the idea that, the number of knowable things being infinite, there would always be gaps in their knowledge, and because the body of knowledge was steadily growing it was futile to lust after the eighth edition of the Encyclopaedia since there would soon be a supplement to it as well.

They had recently completed the first half of their reading, had exchanged volumes, and were able now to discuss things together that appeared near the beginning or the end of the alphabet.

A few weeks earlier they had talked about the excellent article on the term "Absentee," pleased that it had singled out the English landlords of Ireland as the most fitting example of this condition, and pleased also that O'Malley's own landlords, Osbert and Granville Sedgewick, flatly refused to leave Ireland at all. Tonight, as luck would have it, they had come to the long dissertation on "Beauty," which they were examining with great enthusiasm, the first half of the alphabet being conveniently housed in the priest's rooms.

The ideas put forward in several texts on the subject were described in the article. O'Malley, who held with the assertions of a certain Mr. Knight, was shouting now, as he always did when in the heated pursuit of knowledge.

"For God's sake, Quinn, can't you understand that there is a kind of beauty that is universal and cannot be caused by association? Singular beauty. It jumps out at you! You've never seen its like before! You gasp! You associate it with nothing. It thunders in on you. It is what it is. It's like nothing else."

"That is heresy!" exclaimed the priest. "What you are talking about is sensuality and selfish gratification! Beauty should be a reflection of all that we have *learned* is good in the world. Not an independent assault on the senses. Are you telling me . . . would you say that a harlot can be beautiful? Can that which is wicked be beautiful? Ah no, my friend, it cannot. Can a lie be beautiful? No, of course not . . . only truth."

"So, then, if the truth be beautiful and if the truth about a beautiful woman be that she's a harlot, does not her physical beauty combined with this truth create a larger beauty? This is where your theory leads, Quinn. And now answer *me*."

"Why is it that you're always twisting my words so that I'm not certain where my sentences began?" Father Quinn thumped the calfskin cover of Volume One which lay on the table between them. "I said only that which is *good* can be beautiful. It's only the Devil that makes us see a wicked woman as beautiful because the Devil clouds the truth, the Devil" – Father Quinn looked up at O'Malley from under bushy, rigid eyebrows – "the Devil clouds the truth through our selfish desire to have our senses gratified. He's a man of the flesh is the Devil."

"What about power and danger, then . . . and the sublime? There is always power and danger in sublimity. And yet you would not call power beautiful. You would not call danger beautiful. I've stood on cliffs with you and looked across to other cliffs with you. How beautiful, you've said, how sublime."

"It's only a manner of speaking." The priest suddenly looked old and tired. "And, of course," he added, "they are God's creations."

"So is the harlot God's creation," said O'Malley, softly, as if he were thinking of something else.

"That's where you're wrong, Brian." The priest rose to prepare for bed. "She is the creation of something else altogether. I'm not even certain that it's evil, but it's not of God's world and it's not of God's creatures."

As they lay awake on their respective beds, thinking, neither of the men admitted to himself that he had been discussing the woman they visited each day.

On his fourth, unanticipated morning on the island the schoolmaster woke before dawn, restless, and in no mood for further conversation. He had intended, when he planned the visit, to stay only a day, but the weather had turned rough the first night, causing the ferry to rest at the island, and again the second evening, lengthening the same vessel's stay in Ballycastle. By the time the sea and air became serene, he was caught in the web of the little drama, anxious for an outcome of one form or another, and captivated, more than he knew, by feelings of pity and tenderness for the speechless young girl.

Odd memories of his life before the ideas in books began to direct it circulated through his mind: certain small cities he had constructed in sand as a child, a starlit walk home from Ballycastle on the cliffs after the fair when he was an adolescent, the way he had learned to identify all the ships in Ballycastle harbour and all the small ships he had attempted to make in their image. Where were they now, those fragile constructions of sticks and cloth and string? He recalled the polished clarity of the beach stones under the water where he sailed his toys. He remembered fishing in Lough Crannog – the flash of a silver trout – the stories his grandfather told him in Irish, a hawthorn tree left standing, still standing in the centre of his father's field. Spring sowing came back to his mind; the morning chill, the mounds of dark earth, himself, his father, the neighbours bent in silent concentration over their meagre plots.

He moved his legs and shifted the position of his body under the blanket. Light was entering the room. The framed lithograph of the Sacred Heart of Jesus came into focus on the wall and then the sparse furniture of the priest's kitchen where O'Malley had spent the night. There was a smell of mildew from the priest's oilskin jacket which hung from a nail on the wall and which was never able to dry fully, and another odour, slightly sour, which emanated from the milk can near the sink. O'Malley realized, with distaste, that little in the priest's house was fresh; nothing shone with the health and cleanliness of the girl's hair in the sunlight. He thought of his own rooms; his cottage where a broom had rarely, since his mother's death, been pushed into its corners, and he knew that the odours here – the smell of a solitary life and celibacy – were familiar to him.

He flung his legs over the side of the bed and reached for the jumper he had tossed on the floor the previous night. He pulled on his boots, buttoned his trousers, and walked out into the morning, heading for the black beach where the miracle or tragedy had taken place. He would look for materials to build toy boats, he decided, try to regain the joy, the freshness. Perhaps a poem might be composed on the view. But, at the back of his mind, unadmitted, was the hope that he might catch a glimpse of the girl swimming or simply gazing out to sea, or maybe he would be able to hear her sing one of her songs.

The beach was empty when he arrived. He forgot the toys completely, sat down heavily, and rested his arms on his knees. It wasn't long before he began to toss the black stones into the water, one after another, sadly and at lengthening intervals. Their uniformity annoyed him and he searched for a variant, something larger or sharper with which to attack the surf. His grandfather had said that a handful of nails tossed into the advancing waves could cause the children of the sea to become powerless – temporarily. According to the old man it was the ninth wave that was the most potent, the most dangerous. It would have been the ninth wave, then, that caused the change in the girl. There had been a time – long ago – when O'Malley had believed such things.

He found a bone hairpin as he ran his hands back and forth over the stones behind him. Holding it to the sky, he saw one bright thread of hair trembling in the breeze. Before he began his walk across to the wharf to enquire about the ferry, he wrapped the hair around and around the pin and placed it in the breast pocket of his old cotton shirt. He wondered if he had just missed the girl by a sliver of time.

When he reached the jetty the bell for eleven o'clock mass had begun to ring. The sky had turned dark and the wind was rising in preparation for another storm.

When the ferry was cancelled for the fifth time, Brian O'Malley, suspicious though he was of superstition, saw it as an omen. He could not get off the island, it occurred to him, until this drama with the girl had reached some kind of conclusion. The thought of the children, running free, forgetting their noun declensions, or of his two small fields that would be wanting attention by now, evaporated when he touched the bone hairpin in his breast pocket.

He took to walking, that morning, back and forth across the edge of the bay that made up the harbour. Fishermen watched him, with curiosity, though they themselves had been, and were capable of being again, as entranced as he. The storm was gathering strength. Curraghs were pulled up on shore. Brian continued his wandering, angrily, everything about him blown by wind. He applied Platonic, and finally, in despair, Cartesian modes of reasoning. He even prayed a little, said a few Aves for deliverance. The rain began. He stood utterly still under the downpour with his head bowed and his fists clenched. There was nothing for it. He was a ruined man. He would have to find some way to marry her.

The low rainclouds blowing in from the sea were obliterating the cliffs of his own landscape. He was soaked through and filled with a sharpness of sensation that made him want to see everything far away in a clear light – not just these stones glistening with rain and shifting under his boots but his own cottage surrounded by its three lakes, the land extending away from it a mile towards the cliffs. The little hedge school and the vast estate of Puffin Court. The gentle uplift of Doonfort, the track to his door. All this he wanted on a clear map, now, knowing that if he were able to arrange her presence there his geography would be changed forever.

Suddenly and inexplicably he remembered his mother and the game she had played with him when he was a boy – a guessing game of question and response centring on the objects in their cabin. "What way are you?" they would ask each other until the accumulated answers brought the solution to the puzzle. Once, when he had been the fire and trying to confuse his mother, he had felt language grow and blossom in his mouth like flowers. "What way are you, Brian?" she had asked, and at the age of eleven he had said, "I am hot and difficult and lie under an open roof. I send my thoughts to the sky. I consume myself but am forever being rebuilt by others. Without me you would starve and freeze and your stories would remain untold."

Those words came back to him now. He had never, he knew, written or spoken better since.

By the time Brian reached her cabin with the saddened priest in tow it was late in the afternoon. The weather all around the rocks of Rathlin and the coast of Antrim was in chaos.

The girl's mother let them in with a sigh.

"He's after marrying her," the priest rasped into the woman's ear. "It's as I predicted," he added without enthusiasm.

Brian walked to where Mary sat, her face turned towards the grey, rain-streaked window.

He would make her speak.

He touched her shoulder. She looked at him, startled. "I've come," he said, "because I am certain that you must be my wife. It will be good so. We will have children and I will be kind to you."

She turned again to the window, but she had heard him. He perceived that her eyes followed an individual raindrop down the left-hand pane of glass, then rose again to begin the journey with another. Her forearms jerked slightly as if they were being pulled by invisible strings. Brian crouched beside her so that his face was level with her hair.

"I will not disturb the place you think you've gone to," he said softly. "I will not force you back."

Because of the storm he could hear the surf pounding angrily, though the cabin was nearly a quarter of a mile from the shore. For reasons he did not fully understand he told her that the same sea washed the shore near the place where he lived.

The girl brought one hand up to the cool glass, each finger connecting with a teardrop of moisture on the other side. She traced the rain absently, then regarded him with calm eyes.

56

She is not afraid of me, he thought. I will make her speak.

"Will you not give me an answer?" He was startled by the catch of emotion in his own voice. He waited. In the silence he remembered again his mother's game. It was played, he knew, by mothers and children all over the county.

"What way are you?" he asked.

A slight smile visited the girl's face. She looked directly at the man who had been, until this afternoon, a blur to her.

The mother and the priest felt a veil fall between them and the couple.

Wind rattled the door. Brian placed one hand tentatively on Mary's forearm and asked again, "What way are you?"

Waiting, he placed his forehead on his outstretched arm. His posture embarrassed the priest in its resemblance to impassioned prayer. Abruptly he knew that he had underestimated the extent of his friend's loneliness.

"Please . . ." Brian said to the floor whose flags stared blankly back at him. "Please speak to me."

The priest coughed, and the woman, remembering some distant moment of passion in her own life, turned her back on the scene. Then all three heard Mary's voice. She had placed her hand on O'Malley's hair.

"I am here but I am not here," she said. "I will be your wife but I will not be your wife."

"You are here," said Brian. "You can feel the warmth of my hand through your sleeve. I can see the same raindrops as you can, running down the glass."

She looked at the schoolmaster's hair and felt the texture of it beneath her palm, sensed the solidity – the actuality – of the body that crouched at her side.

And then she fell weeping onto the schoolmaster's shoulder. Unbuckling. Beginning to enter the world again.

DURING her pregnancy her longing for beaches diminished, her mind turned inland.

Sometimes this required an effort on her part but mostly the presence of the child in her body tied her to the earth, the cottage, the fire. She knitted small jackets and sewed small shirts, the shape of her thoughts changing with the shape of her torso. Responding to the gentle attentions of her husband, his kindnesses, she was pleased when he began to teach her to read and write. Soon she was able to mark out the English alphabet on a slate and to fashion her own name on the same black surface. The conversations of the men interested her, though she never participated, and this caused her to look forward to Father Quinn's monthly visits in a way the girl on the island never could have. Quinn, himself, relaxed and relieved, believing he had cured the girl – brought her back with his holy water – and undistracted by the bulk of her present form, was at his most eloquent and didactic. Eventually Mary came to know the Supplement to the fifth, sixth, and seventh editions of the Encyclopaedia almost as well as the men.

Brian managed his two fields and taught the hedge school when the weather and the season permitted the children to attend. He was delighted by his bride; her quiet good nature, her domestic skills, her cleverness. His life was rich; they never once discussed the time that she had been away. Unlike Father Quinn, he believed it had been the strength of his own love that had caused the change in her – that and her removal from the island. Her mother, mad with joy at her daughter's alleged return to the world, sent verbal messages with the passengers on the ferry and, sometimes, a garment for the anticipated child.

At first Mary had searched for the other one. Walking to the cliffs, she had climbed down to the shore by the steep descent known as Grey Man's Path, mornings, before her husband had awakened. But the sea had shown her nothing but drumming surf and, it being autumn, its coldness had denied her entry. She returned, pale and private, to a room full of silent questions where Brian had prepared the breakfast and the tea. She felt as though she had been betrayed by something she could no longer imagine. In her dreams, sometimes, she dived into green and her fists clutched dark, wet curls. But once she was pregnant even these dreams visited her less and less. Before leaving the island she had placed the little circle of black and red-gold hair inside the case for a pocket-watch from which the timepiece had been removed, and now this lay, undisturbed beneath her undergarments in the upper right-hand drawer of a chest. Sometimes, when she was arranging laundry, or searching for a garment, the cold surface of metal touched her hand and she remembered, but she closed the drawer again and turned her back to the wall of her house that was nearest the ocean.

In the evenings Brian continued to teach her as though she were one of the children at the school.

She knew English, it being encouraged on the island by the priest who believed it was necessary for any kind of advancement. He had even, in his leisure time, taught a handful of the boys to read and write in this language; it had never occurred to him that a girl might need this skill. During the time, however, that Mary had been known for the curse or the gift of eloquence, it had sometimes been English words that sprang to her lips – often thoroughly confusing the adults who happened to hear her. But most of the time her speeches were composed of a combination of this relatively unknown language and Irish Gaelic, leading to the supposition, on the island, that her announcements were aimed at no one in particular and need not be paid attention to at all.

Now it was the shape of the English words that caught her fancy, their silence on the slate after the deliberate noise of putting them there. She said to her husband that they were like a collection of sticks and stones tossed up on a beach. He told her then of the game one plays with an unbroken paring of an apple, tossing it over the shoulder, and the shape it makes on the floor forming the first letter of the name of the one you will marry. But they did not attempt this, knowing B's and M's to be an unlikely outcome of such a venture.

Finally Mary was able to read aloud and copy lessons from a schoolbook filled with simple rhymes intended for children. There was something in the clean music that brought to her traces of songs and poems she herself had made during her last months on the island – songs she had remembered and forgotten at the same time. They made her pause in her reading sometimes, and look towards the window and the sea.

But the repetition of the lessons, in time, robbed them of their strange significance. Soon she was able to recite:

I saw a ship a-sailing,
A-sailing on the sea.
And Oh, it was all laden
With gifts for you and me.

> There were comfits in the cabin
> And apples in the hold.
> The sails were made of silver,
> The masts were made of gold.

without recalling a foreign shore spilling from a pale hand. And finally she was able to write the word "away" on her slate without looking up and around to determine whether its awful power had caused the calm solidity of the evening to disintegrate and waves to wash over the cabin.

By the time the baby, Liam, was six months old, she had learned so many words that she carried on her studies on her own. The book she liked best was *Easy Lessons in General Geography*. On its maps she was able to see the island of Ireland shrink in comparison to the other, larger land masses, and her own island, Rathlin, disappear altogether from some representations of the world. She examined, with astonishment, engravings of deserts, jungles, and mountain ranges, exotic beasts that jumped or thundered through life in vast inland territories, birds too huge to fly, mice too huge to scamper, and strange human figures dressed as birds or beasts themselves. She learned that there were thousands of different languages in the world and wondered about the possibilities and the clamour of unfamiliar collections of sounds.

Night after night the small book in her hands overwhelmed her. The very idea of Poland left her stunned; its cities and rivers and paintings and population and indistinguishable sounds all going on while she was quiet in their cottage. And when she had recovered from Poland the page describing Holland would disorient her to such an extent that she would have to put the book down so that she could compose herself before facing Silesia.

"Is it true, then?" she would ask Brian after being shocked by the Maltese Islands or Tasmania, her eyes huge as if seeing it all there in front of her.

Laughing, he would cross the room, stand behind her with his arms encircling her neck so she felt the dry wool of his jumper next to her cheek. "Soon I'll teach you Latin," he would whisper, "and Greek."

Italy. Greece. Their temples built themselves in her imagination. She needed, she said to Brian, an example of the colour turquoise, as that was the colour of the sea there. He searched for days and then appeared with a shard of china where two and a half turquoise birds were frozen in flight. The baby clasped it in his fist and then put it in his mouth from where it was rescued shining. "It's a sky colour," she said then, "a colour of birds." "So I believe," Brian replied. Mary carried the fragment in her apron pocket from then on, so that it would not harm the baby. It nudged in her a frail image of a landscape shown to her by a pale hand, but the memory was confused with the jumble of information gathered from her recent reading.

Her legend, which had preceded her to the mainland, stayed with her, of course, and denied her the kind of easy company another young wife might have had with those of the same sex, so she was often alone when Brian was working. But she was not unhappy. The world held her full attention, the same world from which she had been parted two years before. It absorbed her in exaggerated ways. Its vastness – continents, seas, and solar systems – described in the book seemed to break through the bounds of her body while she was reading. And the rest of the time the particularities of her daily life with its attendant objects and rituals gave her calm pleasure. The child alone was universe enough for her, his perfect body in her hands: the clear eye and small ear, sweet breath and smooth skin. But blankets and buckets, water or milk in a jug, a shelf that displayed her few pieces of blue willow china, a cast-iron pot, a knife, puddles outside the door, turf ready for the fire all gave her joy.

Brian had not called her back but she had come nevertheless into the world he had offered to her. The other had drifted away on a concealed current, floated elsewhere, visiting her only occasionally at night in dreams that disappeared in the new light of these mornings at the sound of the child's awakening cry.

On a sunny autumn day in 1845 the Sedgewick brothers were working on their shell collection – a full morning dedicated to conchology.

Osbert had his watercolours arranged in front of him – rose, a touch of ochre, soft grey, eggshell white, burnt umber – and his thoughts moved cheerfully back and forth, as he worked, from these colours to gold, which he had been reading about in the eighth edition of the Encyclopaedia the night before; that pure substance, stabilizer, he believed, of the universe. He imagined veins of it as the earth's ligaments, a binding force without which the planet would simply fly to pieces. He disapproved of mining it, he had explained to Granville, for precisely this reason. All this removal of purity from the ground could lead only to disastrous consequences. Some of the sorrows of Ireland, he maintained, were undoubtedly based on the fact that gold was not prevalent in the makeup of the country's rocks. Instead of trying to get the precious metal out of the earth, he told his brother, scientists in the unhappy countries should be trying to invent ways to get more of it *in*.

Granville was busily writing down facts, and being so occupied was not nearly as happy as his brother. "*Solenisis*," he wrote doggedly, "or shell of a razor fish. Sometimes seen burrowing in sand but known to possess the ability occasionally to move rapidly through water by opening and shutting its valves. Water enters through the inhalant orifice and exits through the efferent orifice."

"*Tellina solidula*," he wrote next.

The brothers sat in leather chairs with their backs to a cabinet filled with similar and very dirty hundred-year-old puffins' eggs. As this strange bird (sometimes called the sea parrot) laid its eggs at the bottom of a muddy burrow bored into a cliff, it had been impossible for Henry Austin Sedgewick the First to lay his hands on a pristine specimen. Subsequent attempts to remove the grime had been to no avail, and now they stood, row upon row of them, covered with a thin veneer of hundred-year-old mud, the least dusted collection on the property. On the bottom shelf, to the left, was a small gathering of black, leather-like cases, known to protect the eggs of a certain variety of shark and called "mermaid's purses" by the peasantry. Near them, mounted on a silver stand, was a shark's tooth which was said to have facilitated the teething of Osbert and Granville themselves and whose presence in the house was a result of a bit of folklore collected by their father.

"Stories are getting grim at firesides these days," said Granville abruptly, turning his attention away from the task at hand.

The sunlight that moved through the dusty bubbled glass of the large arched window on the other side of the room chose this moment to expose the extent of wear on the northern side of the Persian carpet. Two and a half hundred years of Sedgewicks had trod there, carrying their prized specimens to the cases that lined the walls.

"Political talk?" enquired Osbert. "Uprisings?"

"Not exactly," said Granville. "Tinkers, travelling people are bringing tales of incredible hardships in the West."

"Terrible hardships in the West," agreed Osbert. "Always have been. Some of them are without windows and, as a result, without views. Sublime scenery though. Do you remember our puffin hunts with Father in Donegal? We must go back . . . perhaps next year. This shell needs just a suggestion of red ochre."

"Yes, but now they say that there's not enough to eat."

"Never have had enough to eat," said Osbert. "Subsist on potatoes, for God's sake." He scrubbed, almost with annoyance, at the ochre. "Remarkable root, however," he added, "in that one *can* subsist upon it. *Solanum tuberosum.* Who brought it from Peru – Raleigh or Drake? Thought they were truffles, didn't he . . . or they?"

"Raleigh never visited Peru."

"Are you certain?"

"Quite."

"Well then . . . must have been Drake."

"They're saying," Granville persisted, "that there is something wrong with the potatoes."

"Insects, I expect. Filia beetles undoubtedly. Tiny things but rather wonderful when examined microscopically. The adult is about one-sixteenth to one-eighth of an inch long. I drew them once, I think . . . can't remember."

"They say the leaves turn black and there's a sweet, rotten smell," said Granville, "and the potatoes decompose before you can get them out of the ground. James Flanaghan told me that last year's harvest, in the West, was partly ruined but that this year's is non-existent."

"Is Flanaghan the one who told you that remarkable story about that robber . . . what was he called?"

"Black Dan O'Reilly."

"Oh yes . . . and wasn't there something about gold . . . something about a hand?"

"Black Dan O'Reilly's quest for the golden hand. He was the one that began by stealing chickens . . . but he wanted more.

66

So he moved on to piglets, but he still wanted more. He stole cattle, and wanted more, so then he stole fine silver from the gentry . . . but he wanted more. In the meantime he fell in love with a virtuous girl who wanted him to be virtuous too. But she knew him well – that he always wanted more – so she told him of a golden hand that she'd heard of that was buried in a bog and that it was the most of everything and that he should try to find it. Encrusted with jewels and all that."

"Did he find it?"

"No, but he was kept honest trying."

"Was it there?"

"Osbert, this is folklore."

"Yes, but a golden hand is undoubtedly a Celtic artifact. Probably the story contains *some* historical accuracy. They often do, you know. Did Flanaghan happen to mention which bog the girl was referring to?"

"He did . . . but I've forgotten."

"I'll ask him then."

"Yes . . . I've it written down somewhere but rather than have me hunt it up it would be faster if you ask Flanaghan. He and Boyle think it will happen here as well."

"What . . . golden hands in the ground . . . robbers?"

"No, this potato disease."

There was shouting out in the garden where some of the men were working, followed by a chorus of laughter.

"O'Donovan must have arrived . . . the young one . . . " said Granville after a pause. "The men are teasing him. He's to be married."

"Ah," said Osbert, squinting at his watercolour of the shell, "and a good thing, too. He's a wild one."

"They're all wild at that age, and the girls, too."

"But charming."

"Yes . . . quite. What about O'Malley's wife who was away. Have you seen her about? Will she ever speak about it, do you think?"

"They say never . . . and she won't do cures."

"It's a shame, I mean that we can't record her experiences. As for this disease, it won't come here."

"No . . . why not?"

The shouts in the garden had stopped and the surroundings were quiet except for the sound of a rake, quite close, near the window.

"Because this is Antrim. Our peasantry are fine. Look at the cabins Father provided. Listen to them sing. And *we're* here. The landlords in the West are all absentees. We look after our people and they have the 'Tenant Right.'"

"A good thing, too," said Osbert, watching as his brother dipped his pen into thick blue ink. "A good thing since they eat nothing but potatoes, as well."

"And some oatmeal, and milk. Did I tell you, by the way, that at last we're to get a National School." Granville would talk all morning rather than revert to the listing of Latin terms. "And about time, too. They're everywhere else, all over the country."

"A National School? Then what's to become of O'Malley's establishment *en plein air?*"

"Perhaps he could teach in the National. Better than worrying all the time that the inspector would come and shut him down. And a reliable salary. He's a good man. Perhaps they'll hire him to teach there."

"Unlikely . . . he's Catholic . . . and a great companion to the island priest."

"Oh yes . . . Catholic . . . I'd forgotten. It'll be the farm for him then, all the time. And his father the hedge schoolmaster

68

before him. What a shame . . . still, I suppose it's all for the best. Except we'll probably get someone from God knows where with small Latin and less Greek."

"No doubt."

Wʜᴇɴ pressing the few linen napkins that had been owned by Brian's mother, Mary always watched the patterns and pictures emerge from the wrinkles as the fabric smoothed and stiffened under the iron. Three connected castles, a shamrock, a Celtic cross, a hand.

She loved doing this. Brian had said that he had no real knowledge of how his mother had acquired these objects, which suggested privilege, table manners, and banquets, but that they were used only on special days – those few occasions when there was red meat to be had, or whenever there was a wake.

Mary had only fragments of the legends attached to the pictures, her own associations being stronger than the fragile narratives she had heard as a child.

"Look," she said to her own child, who crawled on the flags near where she worked. "Look, Liam," she crooned, holding a bright white square like a holy cloth in front of her torso, "there are the three castles: Dunluce, Dunseverick, and Kinbane. And there," she nodded with her chin towards a spiral in the corner of the napkin, "there is *Slough-na-More*, the swallow of the sea near the island where I was born, and it's your grandmother who lives there still."

The child regarded the cloth with large, clear eyes then turned to reach for a wooden spool with which he had been playing.

The hand meant something else, Mary knew, a robber or a king. In her own mind was a hand that wavered under water but she pushed her inner pictures of this aside. The linen itself came from the factories in Belfast. Brian had described factories to her; huge rooms full of people making the same things at the same time, machines the size of cabins and with more noise than the sea. She would like some day to look at these factories, though Brian said it would be death itself to work in them even for a day.

It's much better, he had told her, to work at planting things in the earth and in the mind, and then there's the quiet and the patience to wait for them to bloom.

In the geography book she read aloud to Brian in the evenings there were lists of crops from lands she'd never seen; long columns of national products which her husband said were loaded onto boats and transported from country to country. There were engravings of exotic fruits – coconuts, pineapples, bananas, oranges – and certain plants that changed the taste of soup boiling in the pot. Cinnamon, Brian said, once tasted was never forgotten, was longed for ever after. He showed her the tear-shaped island where it grew and she thought about longing for something so far away.

Brian came in now, earlier than usual because of the wetness of the summer day. He sat on the rush chair which creaked under his weight and he picked up his son, running his large right hand through the child's red curls. He looked tired.

"Were there many today?" she asked him.

"No," he answered, "no. The same, only five."

Three eggs rested on the table where Mary had placed them earlier in the day, and one potato, old and crumpled, from last year's harvest. "Will they not come back?" she walked towards him. "For your teaching. There's all the girls who were so fond of you."

"I was too easy with them. They were fond of me for that . . . not for the Latin."

Mary helped the child down from his father's lap where he was beginning to squirm. "Well, whoever he is at the National School, he'll not be like you. He won't have the gift of it, the teaching."

Brian reached across the table and picked up one egg. It fit perfectly in the palm of his hand. "Next year at this time there will be no more hedge schools anywhere," he said. "Their days are gone. There will be no one left willing to listen to me or any of the other schoolmasters talking about the Greeks. The people are poor enough and the children will be educated by the government."

Mary was silent. She looked at the eggs she had pulled that morning from their own roof. It would need to be fixed soon. "They're nesting in the thatch again," she said to her husband.

He walked across the width of the cottage and peered through the glass panes of the window. Mary knew there was nothing to be seen out there in the rain. Returning to the chair, he sat down with a sigh and folded his thick arms across his chest. The child began to cry for his feeding. As she unbuttoned her blouse for the baby to nurse, Mary turned to her husband again. "What are you going to do, then, if the school is finished?"

Brian sighed and leaned back in the chair. "I don't know," he said. "I'm not much of a labourer. Perhaps if I improved the farm –"

"I could spin," Mary interjected, "there's something to be had from that. There's your own mother's wheel sitting untouched in the corner. And then there's the seaweed. I know how to gather it like the women on Rathlin."

"Yes," he said quietly, "there's that."

The child's hand reached towards Mary's face. "Brian," she said softly, "will you regret the school so thoroughly?"

"Yes . . . I will regret it. A child learning to read . . ." he began, but left the statement unfinished. "And it's the end of us," he said, "with them teaching our children. There will be none of us left, you understand, in the way that we know ourselves now."

Mary looked down at her child. "You'll teach Liam," she said, "and myself?"

"Yes."

"And the farm will prosper and the children will be taught. They will have learning."

"The poetry will be gone from our people," he said bitterly. "There will be none of it left at all. And no more scholars on the road. The way we know it . . . it will all be finished."

"You'll continue with your own poems, Brian. You don't need to gather the children to continue with your own poems."

"Ah Mary," he said sadly, "what I write is hardly poetry. It was the one scholar with the gift that I was waiting for, who never came, to my very great sorrow. My father taught his whole life and only had two with the gift, and they scattered off then to the roads with the correct amount of passion in their hearts and the old language and the weather on their tongues . . . that and all the old tales. One came by here once. He came by here after my father was dead and he himself was old, and he sat where you are sitting now. He was a man who could twist a sentence into a song. His whole life on the roads doing that. He remembered my father, so he came by here to see the spot again where my father had given him learning. His kind will not be seen again. There's not one that I gave the learning to who could twist a sentence into a song, and, now, with the school declining, I'll never have the opportunity."

He rose and flung another lump of turf onto the fire. "And my own son," he said angrily, "my own son will be taught at this National School."

"No," said Mary, "no. We won't allow it."

"We won't be able to stop it." He crouched over the fire, attacked it with the bellows until it shone, angry and hot. "The old language will disappear forever, and all the magic and the legends. It's what they want, what they've always wanted, to be rid of us one way or another. I'd thought the old beliefs were bad for the people. I'd thought that when they were in no danger of disappearing. Now that I know they'll be gone it saddens me deeply, Mary." He turned his back towards her. "That and the language," he said. "To think I had the mule stupidity to be teaching the children English and Latin and Greek when it was their own language I should have insisted upon." He leaned the bellows against a stool that stood near the fire. "It's enough to break a man's heart at his own stupidity," he said.

"Don't take on so, Brian." Mary reached across the nursing child towards him. "The children still have the language, and beliefs are what they are. There are great truths in the old beliefs . . . they'll not disappear as fast as all that."

Brian slammed his fist into the open palm of his other hand. "They can be beaten and starved out, and they can be silenced, Mary. They can be educated out. And don't I know the truth of this. I have none of them myself, though my own father, an educated man, and Quinn over on the island were always talking about things inexplicable."

The couple were silent. Mary placed the baby, who had fallen asleep in her arms, into his cradle and crossed over to the hearth to prepare the evening meal. Brian moved towards the door. "I'll be outside for a bit," he said, "to look at the field."

"It's raining, Brian."

"There's a bit of a break, now, and I won't go far."

Alone, Mary knew there was something hidden inside her, a lost thing she could find again when she had need of it, for she

74

had fragments of the old beliefs. They were gone from her husband but they had not been completely stolen from her . . . had become dormant, instead, in a kind of winter sleep. Any kind of return would be accepted by her, unquestioningly. A stone, a song, a green eye, the interrupted gesture. Something in her wanted finishing.

There was a story about a woman who had danced across a moor and over the cliffs at Rathlin to her death, and a belief that when her body washed up at Fair Head this was how the place received its name; from the look of her beautiful blonde hair moving in the water near the rocks where her skull had broken. Mary couldn't recall who had been the girl's partner in the dance but she could imagine the paleness of him, his torn shirt and liquid eye. She could imagine the blood of the young woman aflame in his embrace, every colour of rock, turf, and sea swirling, and the belief in him strong in the bones of her slender ankles – one wrist clasped by his beckoning hand. It was in herself, in her own beliefs, to dance like that, though she kept the idea hidden. And it was in her also to twist a sentence into a song if she chose to sing at all.

Brian ate his supper in silence, dipping the potato in the milk and looking past his wife to the fire. He peeled away the shells and pushed the eggs whole into his mouth savagely. When he spoke, at last, it was to no one but himself, as if he wanted to deliver his thoughts out into the room in order to rid his mind of them.

"To think that the little schools were started in the time of the Penal Laws, in response to oppression, when they wanted none of us educated. It's as if our people have always been hungry," he said, "for knowledge. And when they had nothing at all they still produced the few miserable pennies it cost to keep a schoolmaster alive. They've always had this hunger, you see, for the day that words can be spun into meaning. Nothing could keep them from it. Two hundred years of hiding the hunger, and then hiding the nourishment of the learning in the small makeshift schools." He placed his hands flat on the table in front of him. Their largeness was manifested in their length rather than in their width. They were the hands of neither labourer nor farmer. "There's a rare beauty," he said, looking at his hands, "in something hidden and secret, and it's a rare kind of education to be got in hidden places."

He was not speaking to her but Mary answered him anyway. "Yes," she said, "there's a rare beauty in something that is hidden."

As they ate their supper of bacon, eggs, potatoes, and milk, the clouds parted and the low sun broke through, sending a beam in the window and lighting the tops of the folds on Brian's sleeve, enriching the various soft browns of the scattered eggshells. It came to rest on a pile of books that occupied a three-legged table in the corner. Moving through this harsh light to the child or to the fire, Mary seemed to appear and reappear to her husband, who remained with all but his sleeve in shadow.

Outside, the moist earth steamed in the sudden blaze and, in a valley two miles from the uplands on which O'Malley's cottage stood, a mild breeze awakened, stirring marsh grasses and making thorn bushes lurch in odd ways. One by one the leaves of the planted fields there turned over. Had anyone been watching they would have seen the beginnings of a black stain speckling otherwise healthy foliage. As it was, one small boy, playing with stones and sticks and a puddle of rainwater, lifted his head and sniffed the air, unable to identify the new perfume, a portent carried on the wind.

These are the beginnings of despair. The clouds part and the

76

last rays of sun blanket a landscape of unspeakable beauty. The blue sea is covered with a carpet of stars, cormorants sail near cliffs where their young flourish, and smoke drifts from cottages where meals have been taken in peace. The sweet, dark smell of the change is confused with that of hidden roses. Not one bird pauses in song, anticipates the hunger.

The breeze crept under the cottage door. Brian, reading Latin near the window, lit his pipe at the exact moment that he might have inhaled the terrible sweetness. Mary, however, recognized something in the air that made her think, for a moment, of cool white skin stretched over the muscle on an arm. The air smelled of loss – of a beautiful absence. It caught in her throat and she brought her hand briefly to her lips as if to silence herself.

Then the wind changed direction, the sun set. Soon it was time for sleep.

THAT winter Osbert and Granville tramped around the countryside with campstools as usual – weather permitting. At Murlough Bay, Osbert sketched the view of Rathlin Island and Granville composed a lament for the hundreds of women and children who had been slaughtered there in 1576 by the Earl of Essex in his attempt to tame "Wild Ulster." Although he could not, from this distance, see *Crooknascreidhlin* (the hill of the screaming) or *Langraviste* (the hollow of the great defeat), where he assumed the massacre had taken place, just looking at the cliffs of the unfortunate island moved Granville to poetry. In fact, he had confused his disasters: both locations were the sites of equally brutal attacks on the part of Scottish soldiers a hundred years later.

The brothers also visited the now-abandoned hedge school. Osbert made several drawings, inside and out, so that it would be recorded for posterity, and Granville wrote two long narrative poems, one entitled "A Lament for an Abandoned Hedge School" and the other, a dramatic monologue, called "The Hedge Schoolmaster's Lament." They had seen this gentleman once or twice during excursions to the cliffs at Fair Head. As was the case with all the tenant farmers and cottiers in Antrim, the schoolmaster's potato crop had failed. But he was managing the winter well, he said, had eggs from the chickens and milk from the cow and a bit of money set aside so that he could last until next year's harvest.

"And your wife, sir?" they asked, anxious for a glimpse.

"Quite well," he had replied. "Thinking of spinning now that the child is weaned."

"And your friend, Quinn? Is he still developing his intellect . . . with your help, of course, and that of the Supplement to the fifth, sixth, and seventh editions?"

"He visits once a month or so," Brian was unconsciously stabbing the ground with the pitchfork he carried in one hand, "and we talk some about the Supplement, for which we're very grateful," he added, touching his hat nervously.

"His people are well?"

"They have lost their potatoes." The schoolmaster examined the sky. "They have some corn but there is hardship among them."

Osbert said that this year's harvest would set things to rights, and Granville maintained that crop failures never occurred two years in a row. Neither mentioned the new National School or the empty hedge school where the unattended wattle had begun to sag, and the thatch was full of mice and birds. They complimented the schoolmaster on his improvements to the farm and continued on their way. By the time they reached Lough Crannog the light was absolutely perfect.

Mary was beginning to leave the house behind. It had sheltered and protected her early in her marriage, throughout her pregnancy and childbirth, and while she was nursing the baby. It had kept its stone arms around her while she learned to read and while the first awkward nouns were scratched by her on the slate. The new world of books was kept dry and safe by it. Its fire had bloomed daily as a result of the plentiful supply of thatch provided by her husband. She had come to love its two lamps and four napkins, its stone flags and simple table. The sheets, the pillows, the small panes of glass in its few windows. The six rush-seated chairs and the one flat stone at its threshold. She loved the iron pots she used for cooking and even the troublesome hens that ruined the thatch by nesting in it. She loved the corners and the broom with which she removed the dust that collected where the walls met the floor. The drowsy sameness of each day. The comfort of binding oneself to the maintenance of life.

But as the first winter following the crop failure progressed, the change began to nudge her towards other activities, the way small animals nose their young in the direction of the wider world. Brian was a torn man. His crops had failed, his school had weakened and eventually died. He spent his days guiltily building and tearing apart his few drystone walls – improving the farm – or sometimes he worked on into the night angrily cutting turf, though his modest barn was filled to capacity. Mary saw him in the distance, hunched over his own father's turf spade, obsessed, as if this one tool from the past, alive in his hands, could make the present disappear. He did not speak to her about his discontent.

Liam thumped the door with his small fists and clambered up onto the stool to slap his palms against the window glass when his father left for the field until, at last, his mother dressed him warmly and allowed him out into the physical world where he watched, mesmerized, Brian's love-dance with labour. Eventually the child, himself, began to dig in the earth, caking the undersides of his delicate new nails with mud. He is no longer all mine now, thought Mary. The field has claimed him as it claims all the men . . . those who are not chosen by the sea. She looked at the curve of his miniature back as he crouched over a pile of dirt and said to herself, "This is the way his life will be, bent, under a darkening sky."

When it came time for the spring sowing Mary rose in darkness with her husband and followed the light of his lantern to the field. Lights from neighbours' lanterns speckled the hills, and the coming dawn was a red ribbon where the land rose up to meet the cliffs. As they silently shovelled the earth into small hills, or placed the seed-potatoes into the ground, an apprehension began to grow in her that some sudden calamity would take hold of them in the midst of this cold, dark calm. The gradually increasing red light that struggled across the soil, the broken earth at her feet did not dispel the fear and she continually looked over her shoulder to the cabin as if she expected the thatch to be ignited by the expanding crimson. Reflected in the panes of the window, the sun looked like fire and Mary clutched Brian's sleeve instinctively, then moved her hand away again when she realized what it was. The face he turned to hers in that moment was dispassionate. He appeared to be anxious to return his attention to the soil as if his soul were being stitched, with each planting, into the earth.

Mary sensed that the soil was inert; asleep in a way that it never had been before. Pebbles were coated in an oily moisture that did not clear in the morning light and that caused the coldness of buried things to cling to them. On the island, Mary remembered, there had been places so barren that fields had to be created, over time, out of living materials: dung and seaweed and the spines of recently eaten fish. It was the grass that grew in the sea that made the best soil, and as Mary stooped to make another planting, in her mind she saw the island men and women moving up from the strand with their dark, glistening burdens on their backs.

Liam, with his small face blurred by sleep, called her from the cabin door and she went to him to give him a cup of milk. Later, as she dressed him, fitting the trousers over his warm, sturdy body, she began to want to think of ways to put some life back into her husband's field.

It wanted a touch of the sea in it, Mary thought; a touch of the sea's long hair.

She rose in the dark and moved across the room, searching for her shawl. The child whimpered and Brian unfolded into the warm spot she had left in the bed. Through the window glass she saw the moon hugging the horizon. The latch fell behind her like a penny dropping into a jar and she stood still in the wake of this sound with her hand extended as if to stop it.

As she walked to the sea with the wicker creel on her back, light began to touch the growth beside the path, and the lakes below her – one with its circular island – rose up silver and alive.

She felt that she had never walked here before.

There was only the field in her mind and the sea plants she must gather to feed it. It was a mile from the cabin to the cliffs.

Though she didn't know this, the knife that she carried had lived indoors for two centuries after serving as a weapon in Cromwellian times. The creel was one woven in sorrow by Brian's grandmother when she was mad with grief over the death of her first-born son.

All of that quieted now, by time. The passion and even the memory of the passion, forgotten.

The knife scrabbled against the floor of the basket as she descended the cliffs through the cut in the rocks named Grey Man's Path, the long view opening before her. This coarse beauty – the ragged island offshore and the dark tumble of difficult coastal landscape – was implanted in her bones, making her sure-footed on its surfaces. The tide was out, as she knew instinctively it would be, and large boulders clothed in ribbons of weeds stood awkwardly exposed.

The pale sky shone on the knife. She worked steadily, listening in the stillness to sea birds and the grating sound of metal on rock, her back to the waves whose skirts spread across the sand, her own skirt drenched by the dew through which she'd passed. Her discarded shawl lay like a corpse at her feet.

There was an air of sorrow about this work which involved a series of gestures that caused her to resemble a woman pleading for mercy then letting her arms drop in resignation and helplessness. But the basket filled quickly and soon she paused to press its contents towards the earth with her palms so that water drained through the weave and disappeared into the sand.

When she was finished she bent down to pick up her shawl. Then she straightened her spine, placed her hands on her lower back, and lifted her face to the sky. There had been a roof over her for so long, the complexity of the clouds startled her in ways the landscape hadn't. She turned, then, tentatively towards the sea, squinting as if she expected it to strike her. But as it showed her nothing but water, and none of its sounds spoke to her, she squatted to fit the creel's leather straps over her shoulders. Then, using the muscles in her back and legs, she slowly lifted her burden and, with her body bent at the waist, she began the long climb upwards. Twenty minutes later, by the small lake with the island – the water closest to her cottage – she saw him standing in the reeds near the shore.

As she moved through the grass, bent under her load that smelled of the sea, the word "Moira" moved with her, its two syllables becoming clearer as she lifted her face to the lake. She saw that he who called her swayed like the reeds and shimmered in the early-morning sun, and she slid the straps from her shoulders and walked towards him with her spine straight and her throat open to the air. In her arms he was as cool and as smooth as beach stones, and behind him the water trembled and shone.

When he entered her she was filled with aching sorrow. His cool flesh passed through her body and became the skin she would wear inside her skin. She heard the rocks of lakes and oceans rattle in the cavity of his skull and then in the cavity of her own skull. A battalion of young men, their bright jackets burst open by battle, their perfect ribs shattered, their hearts broken apart, marched in his mind and then in her mind, and so she came to know all the sorrows of young men as she lay on the earth; their angry grief, their bright weapons, their spilled blood. Then across his forehead and hers sailed a pageant of all the ships, proud and humble, rough and fine, in which young men departed for the violence of the sea.

There were any number of ways for young men to die. Some had been flung by vicious currents against granite, some had watched the ocean's ceiling close over them while the fish they had caught swam free of the nets, some had died violently outside taverns after singing songs of love. Some took up arms against injustice and had been killed publicly on scaffolds or privately in ditches at the hands of oppressors, the poetry of politics still hot on their lips.

Dancers, poets, swimmers. Their distant blood ran in Mary's veins until he who lay in her mind slipped back into the water.

As she walked towards the cottage she looked back once. The lake was a shield of beaten brass flung down in the valley under a full sun. She lifted her basket and moved across the field.

And yet, like the landscape, there was nothing smooth in her.

SOME weeks later, Osbert, tired of views and vistas, and stirred by the mania for natural history that was sweeping like an epidemic through England, began to collect the strange, delicate life-forms that existed in the coastal tidepools. He would place these fragile treasures in a bucket of sea water, and then carry them home to his new aquarium where they would survive for almost a week while he drew and painted them leisurely, in the relative comfort of the musty Puffin Court library. After eight days or so, however, these enigmatic creatures would rise to a scummy surface and begin to smell in such an unpleasant manner that he would be forced to pitch the whole putrid soup into the rose garden and head for the shore to search for fresher specimens. Granville had responded to his brother's new interest by writing a poem entitled "Lament for a Sea Mollusc Trapped in Osbert's Aquarium."

When he was engaged in this activity Osbert paid little heed to the gorgeous small world he was disturbing. His specimens would gain significance and reality only when he got them home, put them under the microscope, and accurately reproduced them on paper. But by then, of course, they would be dead.

Today, as always, he worked carefully, scooping the creatures out of the pool with a glass jar. He lost some, those of such fragility that they came apart when subjected to anything other than the ebb and flow of the sea water that replenished their habitat. He cursed, then, quietly under his breath, and reached for a larger, stronger example of the same species. The day was not warm and his hands were becoming numb from exposure to water. He thought, with great affection, of the fire he had left burning at Puffin Court, and then, intermittently, of the carriage he had left at the top of the cliffs.

He heard the woman before he saw her. He might have missed her altogether, the hiss of the sea covering most other noise, but the knife rasping on rock was an unfamiliar-enough sound to catch his attention and he turned just at the moment when her shawl, which might have disguised her, was blown back from her copper-coloured head.

Although she was thirty or forty yards in the distance, he knew immediately that she was the woman who had been away, and she for her part, sensing his scrutiny, held still, her knife in one hand and a dark mass of hanging weed clasped in the other. Across the sand, he could tell, she was looking steadily at him.

Osbert was greatly excited. Granville, he knew, would have been even more so. Whatever it was she was doing did not interest him at all, but he sensed that it might be a key to communication. Were this communication to take place he would desperately want to take notes, but had, alas, neither pencil nor paper with which to make a record of what she would say, if she would speak at all. In his agitation he dropped the jar he was holding in his hand and several sea anemones were left to perish on the sand. Without pausing to retrieve it, he walked across the beach towards the woman.

When he was close to the rock she stood near, Osbert smiled brightly. "Madam," he said, "may I perhaps be of some assistance?"

"Assistance?" she asked.

Osbert was caught off guard by the fact that she had

answered his question with another question. He cleared his throat. "Yes," he said, "I thought I might help." He looked at the seaweed in her hand. "You are, I believe, removing specimens of this particular kind of seaweed."

"Sir?"

"You have so large a quantity here, I thought . . ." Osbert looked down at the basket, then back towards the woman, "I thought . . . why *do* you have such a large quantity?" he blurted despite himself.

Replicas of Mary had gathered seaweed along the coast for hundreds of years, singly, and at certain seasons, in groups. She knew suddenly that this man had been blind to them, her people. "It's for the field, sir, the patch . . . to make the plants grow properly." She lowered her eyes and, remembering her shawl, brought it back up to cover her hair.

Osbert was greatly surprised by this piece of information but felt it prudent, under the circumstances, not to show his reaction. Instead, he assumed a sympathetic expression. "They haven't been growing properly, have they?"

"No, sir," she answered quietly.

This was not the direction that he had hoped the conversation would take, and he had virtually no idea how to move into the area where he would be able to glean some useful information for his folklore collection. He clasped his hands behind his back and began to rock from his heels to his toes. "Ah well," he said, "things can only get better." And then, when she said nothing in reply to this platitude, he abruptly asked, "Do you know who I am?"

"Yes, sir," she answered quickly, "you are one of the gentry from up at the Big House."

"Yes, yes . . . that's it. And you, I believe, are O'Malley's wife. Am I correct?"

87

"Yes, sir."

A terrible silence followed this, during which Osbert felt it necessary to cough several times. Sea birds called overhead and, for no reason that he could fathom, they reminded him of the Hill of the Screaming on the silent, calm island that dominated the sea beyond this strand. Osbert had rarely felt so uncomfortable in the presence of another. He stared at the sea with great concentration as the woman stood patiently in front of him.

"Well then –" he began.

But, to his astonishment, she interrupted him. "Please, sir," she said, "what was it that you were doing?"

"Doing?" he repeated. Curiosity was not a state of mind that he associated with these people. Imagination, superstition . . . but certainly not curiosity. For a moment he wondered if her question might not be impertinent, but before he could clearly define her behaviour, he found himself answering in much the same way that he might have had she been someone of his own class.

"Doing? Why, I was collecting specimens of sea anemones to observe and study . . . and to draw . . . when I take them home. Little creatures, you know, that live in tidepools." There, he thought, there's an end to it. Perhaps he could just come out and ask her directly, Do you have a daemon lover? But, to his increasing amazement, she persisted.

"Excuse me sir," she ventured, "but why do you do that?"

"Why do I do that? Why do I do that?" He rocked again nervously on his heels. "I do that," he answered finally and emphatically, "because I like to do that."

"Oh," she said.

"It passes the time," he added, feeling foolish and then slightly piqued that he needed to justify himself to her. Not one of his tenants had ever questioned him like this. "Well, then," he said, again, most anxious now to be gone, "I suppose –"

She interrupted him again. "Sir," she said, "I'd like to see them, the creatures you are talking about."

He was almost annoyed. "Whatever for?" he demanded.

"To see why you search for them and look at them there in the water."

Osbert had a brief, inexplicable memory of himself as a child, standing in a large, cold room with a smoking fire at one end, holding up a single sheet of paper towards his mother who was giving it but cursory attention. "What has Granville been doing?" she had asked. The drawing had been of a tenant's cabin with a corpulent chicken dominating the roof. His mother, he now realized, was interested in neither the subject matter nor her child's rendering of it. "Why," she had asked, "have you not been drawing your Cave Walk?" There was something in the open, questioning face of the woman before him that brought to mind the child that he had been then.

"There are many different kinds," he said, "and they can be very difficult, sometimes, to see."

"Yes," she said, as if in agreement.

They squatted together on the sand within a rocky enclosure, whispering and pointing to things that were almost invisible, this strong communication between a peasant woman and a gentleman being so nearly impossible that neither thought consciously about it until later. Osbert told the woman, whose name he discovered was Mary, the Latin names for the many species that he knew, and she listened attentively, then asked, to his great private delight, if the Romans themselves collected and drew tiny sea creatures. He wondered how she, a poor woman, knew about the Romans at all, but he answered that there was one, the first great natural historian, who would have been interested.

"It's lovely," she said, "a garden like this. Colours I'd never thought about. See how calm and clear . . . like a mirror with our faces in it, except that behind our faces there's a whole world of things alive and being beautiful."

Osbert decided that he would remember that line about the mirror and the worlds for Granville. Then, uncharacteristically, a desire came over him to keep the knowledge of the line to himself.

The silences between them as they looked into the pool were comfortable now. The woman, it seemed, was enchanted by the fragility and gracefulness of what she saw so that words came to her slowly. "See how that one moves," she said, once, "as if it were unfolding some great secret there in the water."

Osbert looked, and it was true, the anemone was unfurling itself, tentacle by tentacle, its movements a slow dance, as if it were revealing each mysterious aspect of itself ceremonially, and for the first time. The landlord was on his hands and knees now beside the pool where he could see, not only his face and that of the woman reflected, but also the shadow of her hand passing back and forth along the floor of the tiny pond. "It's remarkable," he agreed.

"Small weeds," she said, moving her hand, here and there, tentatively across the top of the water now, "in the same current. They know each other, I think, these weeds and these creatures."

Osbert smiled at this suggestion. The rough weave of a shawl such as the woman wore had never been in such close contact with Harris tweed, but Osbert did not think of this. Everything about him had been manufactured somewhere else, in another country; everything, including his bones and the cellular construction of his flesh. She, however, had been built out of the materials of this country. She's like a child, he thought, the way she looks at things.

"I would like," she said, "to be able to walk in a field like this. These colours. These dances."

"I will capture some specimens for you," announced Osbert, generosity rising in him like a tide, "and you may take them home with you and watch them there . . . for a while."

The woman did not answer but rose, instead, to her feet. Then she shook her head. "Why would I take this world apart so that it could never be again?" she asked, looking down at Osbert, at the tidepool. "If I could go into this world I would go and come away again and leave it all undisturbed – the small caves, the beautiful creatures. I would take none of that away with me."

Osbert, who had been left by her in a ridiculous posture on all fours, rose with as much dignity as he could muster and began to brush sand and other detritus from the knees of his trousers. "Well, then . . ." he said, embarrassed.

But she laid her hand on his arm. "Please," she said, "I shouldn't have said that. It's a curse I used to have that I thought was gone . . . these speeches. It's just when I saw the little pool . . . I'm sorry." She looked at him with such earnestness and genuine concern that his heart, much to his surprise, warmed to her again. "And," she added, "I've never looked like this, at a tidepool, and you took the time to show me. I'm grateful." And then she added, "Sir."

She bent to lift the creel and walked away. When Osbert looked at the strength of her back and shoulders, admiration passed through him for the pride in her. It did not occur to him to be in love with her but a totally unfamiliar emotion stirred in him so that he wanted to call her back, to put his hand on her shoulder, to acknowledge the brief flash of understanding she had granted him. But it was useless, he knew – their worlds divided the second that she had stepped away from him. Half-heartedly he knelt again to remove a few more specimens from the pool, but her words stayed on his mind; not what she said, exactly, but the way she had spoken of visiting the closed world of the pool, its dances, the landscape of it. When he looked up again both she and her basket were gone.

On the way home in the carriage, with the pail of sea water sloshing at his feet, he remembered the look in her eyes when she spoke the word "undisturbed" and he let the horse stop and stand completely still for ten minutes, though his driver was not with him and he sat outside the vehicle in the icy wind with the sky threatening rain. Then he flicked his whip and tugged on the left-hand rein so that the animal would retrace its steps. When he arrived at the pool for the second time he angrily tossed the contents of the pail back into the water and strode quickly away, guilty and miserable. He saw his footsteps and the woman's and he could tell by the shape of hers that the soles of both her boots had holes. He was becoming confused, irritated, and sad. He would tell his brother, he decided, absolutely nothing about the events of the afternoon.

The next morning at breakfast, however, he made an announcement. He would no longer collect sea anemones. Instead, he intended to paint the tidepools in their entirety.

When Granville looked surprised, Osbert explained that everything in the tidepools was connected, and that to remove life from them would be like tearing gold out of the earth.

Later that afternoon Granville began to compose a poem entitled "Lament for an Empty Aquarium."

Back by her hearthside she told her husband of the meeting with the landlord from the Big House. Liam sat on Brian's lap, saying over and over all the new words he had learned. "Table," he said, or "stone." "Are we not to be speaking some Irish?" she had asked as the list continued. But Brian answered, simply, that it was no use to be talking a language fit only for a God-forsaken place such as this.

"But you said –"

"What does it matter, now, what I said?"

"It matters to me."

"It won't soon."

She told him about the tidepool – its colours and creatures, but he interrupted her. "Them and their tidepools," he said with contempt. "We're to be starving and they're to be collecting refuse from tidepools. Christ, is there no end to blindness and stupidity?!"

The child slid down from his father's lap and ran across the room to fetch the rag doll his mother had made for him. When he had it, he edged over to his mother's knees where he stood silently fingering its button eyes.

"But," she said quietly, "it's lovely they are when you look at them closely. There's colours there you'd only dream of and things that are alive – creatures – though its flowers that they –"

"Mary," Brian interrupted, "Mary, come back from wherever it is that you spend your time and let me tell you the news from Skibereen. Quinn says they are dying there like flies. That the ditches and hedges and gutters and streets are full of them – the corpses. And the workhouses packed with disease and thousands of people dying on the country roads that lead to them. There's nothing to be had and shiploads of grain leaving the ports every day for England. Great God!" he shouted towards the sky framed by the window. "What will they do to us next?!

They'll do nothing is what they'll do, for there will be none of us left. Even Quinn admits there's no amount of prayers will save a single one of us. And he, himself, showing his haggard face in this room with his clothes hanging on him like grave clothes on a skeleton, the hardship being so severe out there on your own island."

"But the fishing."

"It's all gone terribly wrong. Quinn says the English and all the other Protestants have stolen the souls of the men so they haven't the strength or the heart to fish. Young lads, he said, sit daily down by the water, staring at the sea as if it were a stranger, and the children, he says, impossible to coax from the cabins into the sun. All of the people coming together list-lessly, even for wakes, and recently, he said, not coming together at all."

"And Mother always said –"

"Your own mother, Mary, weakening on her bed and me without passage money for the ferry. You'll not see her again, that's one thing certain."

"No," she said fiercely, "it's not as bad as that! There's been scarcity before. We've all had the winters, and many's the time there's been fevers . . ."

Brian clutched the curls on his head with his hand. "Not like this," he said quietly, and the tone of his voice frightened Mary more than it would have had he been shouting. "This is the end of us. Even though we're better off here than in the rest of the country, it's the end of us, too." He kicked over the basket that she had brought with her so that the dulse lay scattered between them. "Surely you don't expect your child to live on that forever," he said.

"Not forever, just until –"

"Until what, Mary? There'll never be a healthy crop again.

94

It's the very ground we were raised on gone bad . . . turned to poison. We're finished." He raised his other arm towards his head and ran the heels of his hands across his forehead, cupping his skull finally in the curve of his fingers. "Finished," he said again to the floor or to his knees on which his elbows rested.

The child began to cry and Mary drew his head to her lap and stroked his hair and his soft cheek. When he was comforted she stood up and bent down to retrieve the dulse from the floor, over and over again until she had made a dark hill of it on the table. Then she took the pail from beside the fire and headed towards the door. We still have water, she thought, water to wash and to cook. But the memory of the black slippery mass on the plates made her throat dry and her ears ring. Outdoors, the stone wall of the well pressing into her hipbones, she looked down into the circular depth. Her own thin face gazed back at her, practically unrecognizable, and farther away, it seemed, than it ever had been before.

Returning to the cabin with the water spilling in silver beads over the edges of the pail, she suddenly dropped her burden on the flat stone in front of the door and snatched the last scrawny hen from the thatch by its rough yellow ankles. With the bird flapping and screaming at the end of her right arm, she turned and walked towards the small stone barn to find the axe, which she used, not as a blade, but as a club until her skirt was covered with feathers and blood. Then she folded to a kneeling position on the dirt floor and wept into the remaining down of the creature's still warm, pliant breast.

Her husband looked at her when she entered the cabin, her face streaked with blood and tears, dark stains and feathers on her clothing, but he said nothing – just dipped the pen he was holding into his last bottle of ink. Mary pulled the feathers

95

from the bird's meagre body, letting them fall, like snow, to the floor while the child picked them up in handfuls and hurled them into the air.

After a long while Brian spoke. "There'll be no eggs now," he said. But by then the calming smell of roasting meat was draining the anger out of the air.

Mary washed her face and hands in the remaining water from the pail and asked her husband what he was writing.

Just a diary of the weather, he told her, there being nothing else to report. A summary of the conditions of the month of November, 1846. Then, tilting the notebook up from the table, he read it aloud to her.

"Great quantity of fine, thin-clouded days," he had written, "with only three storms. West wind nine days, south wind eleven days, north wind eight days, east wind two days. Seventeen days of soft, cold rain, one day of ice and several of hoarfrost. Moonlight three nights, the others entirely dark."

MARY was alone by Lough Crannog on a grey day, her basket filled with limpets and the smaller edible seaweeds she had picked from the rocks near the ocean, the wind in all her worn and ragged clothes. Everything about her was torn, flapping, as if she had been transformed into a bundle of ancient banners blackened by time. It had been a day of stone, she thought; stone being the only property to hold still in the face of the icy wind. And it was the property that she knew best, these cold days; each detail of the wet rocks from which she picked nourishment for her child, her husband, and herself being what she saw when she was seeing with her outer eyes.

She, standing in the wind, looked at her two thin hands, the nails cracked where she had scratched them over basalt, the knuckles raw. Then she lifted her skirt and looked at her bruised shins and the skin of her legs which had turned red and purple with cold, and she wondered how love could still beat its insistent wings in the heart of a body so altered and twisted by the labour of moving two miles back and forth to the sea, each day, in search of sustenance.

It was this fierce desire of the heart in her that she was beginning to confuse in her mind with the bodily hunger that was creeping, by inches, each week, a little further into their cabin.

The skin of the lake was wrinkled by wind, making it appear impenetrable, and she wanted to gaze into its depths, believing that a world like that of the tidepool waited there – its colours and unique geography. But even on calm days this lake would reveal its beloved secret only when it chose, and showed her now a shield made of light and a plenitude of reflections from the world of the actual.

He came, sometimes, when she had given up hope altogether that he would touch her, and often, it was true, he did not approach her at all. How strange the stir in the air that was not wind and the slant of the light that was neither moon nor sun, and both these things signalling his arrival. Something already broken in her opened further, and he came in and showed her sights she had never known about and spoke an understood language that she had never heard.

Today, with everything in the world thrashing around her and the brutal noise of the sea still in her head, it was the sudden absence of cold that heralded him, and she opened her arms as if to embrace a warm morning. Today he was bright water with the flash of sun in it and the tumbling shadows of leaves. Now he taught her a history that she saw behind her eyes.

Coming from the island and living, as she now did, on the high, open land that led from her door to the cliffs, she had never seen a forest but, as he touched her, one grew over her head. He showed her the sapling that would grow to be a great tree. And then the great tree being cut down for the timber that would build the ship that killed him. He showed her the forest in which the sapling had flourished. She was surrounded by shivering green, by light glancing from leaves and nuzzling bark. Small butterflies burst from dark places, their wings illuminated and extinguished, and moved by the way the breeze tossed light. He was the touch of this light. Then he was the evaporating drops of moisture that shone like stars on the forest floor before entering air. All was fragmentation – notes of birdsong scattering through the atmosphere, the way the foliage dispersed rays of sun until the voices of the birds were the voices of a million moving shadows. "Life," she heard herself say, and "green."

"I lived here, once," he told her with the voice he had put in her brain and in her heart, "but I did not know the roots of the sapling, and the sapling, itself, did not anticipate the axe." Shimmering light was thrown from all surfaces and rested nowhere.

The woods suggested, in their uncertainties of space, transparencies of light – their rumours of entities glimpsed, then lost – that some magnificent event was always on the edge of taking place, and Mary knew her own presence in the forest, or the forest's presence in her, was such an event. He, the illusive light, the drop of water, even now disappearing from the blade of grass, the fallen leaf.

There was another voice that belonged only to her and she used it beside the lake to make a song for him. "*Oh soft, sweet voiced one,*" she sang, "*thin clouded as a moonlit dusk, you put pictures beside me in the grass and there is the long stretch of you at my side. Washing over me, you are cities, forests, bright bursts of birdsong. You bring as gifts to me all that murdered you. Gentle drowned one, heart's darling of the storm, I remember you when the pot is empty and hunger kicks its boots against the door.*"

Some of the winged specimens in the Puffin Court collection were so old they fell to pieces in Osbert's fingers as he removed them from their hinged boxes, causing the floor around him to be covered with colourful, if faded, detritus. All morning he had been studying the wings of butterflies under the microscope, watching a fragment of their patterns come into startling focus – slashes of orange or lavender, edged in black. He imagined, as he gazed, his father as a small boy, chasing these baroque beauties when they were alive, netting them, killing them, mounting them. A child's faded printing identified each specimen. It had been three or four months since his encounter with the woman at the tidepool. Osbert had captured nothing since that time.

Granville, greatly pleased by his own cleverness, was writing a lament for Ireland in which he compared the country to a butterfly who, having hatched gorgeously from the cocoon, was captured, killed, and confined in an Englishman's cabinet where, "She glowed like other beautiful things, but stirred no more her ancient wings."

Streaks of moisture were drying on the windows, leaving faint grey paths, and outside in the courtyard scores of puddles were beginning to shrink in diameter. The brothers could hear the maid clanking about in the scullery and the hounds yapping in the kennel. The wind shook the sashes in the frames. Under his eye Osbert saw a thundercloud of dust on an insect's wing and several filaments on a black leg. He wondered where the creature had flown fifty years before.

"Isn't it marvellous," said Granville, finishing his poem with a flourish, "that as brothers we are so like-minded?"

"Hmmm," replied Osbert as yet another ancient wing came apart in his hands. A few aborted attempts at sketching huge wing fragments rested by his right elbow.

Outside, a flowerpot was pushed by the wind from the edge of a stone bench.

"What was that?" both brothers asked nervously and in unison.

Engaged in their usual employments, they had, nevertheless, been listening all morning for sounds outside the walls. It was rent day. In previous years the cottiers had arrived promptly at 10:00 a.m., caps in hand, money in fist, and had humbly paid their dues. The smell of the coffee and buns that were generously given in return ever since Puffin Court was born, permeated the air. It was now 11:06 a.m., and though neither brother had commented upon the phenomenon, not a single tenant had appeared.

Granville, no longer distracted by his composition, began to pace, noisily, around the wooden perimeter of the room beyond the edges of the carpet. He cleared his throat a number of times, and now, flourishing a silk handkerchief, he blew his nose. He looked forward to rent day enormously, as it gave him a chance to scout for more folklore and to enquire into the quaint and amusing events that made up his tenants' simple lives. At that moment he was beginning to feel like a child whose friends had failed to materialize for a long-anticipated birthday celebration.

"Would it be too much to ask," said Osbert testily, "for you to sit down and stop fidgeting?"

Granville collapsed into a chair of red damask much worn by previous generations of Sedgewicks. "That microscope," he commented, "what does it really tell you about life . . . I mean beyond those sad, barely discernible, wriggling animals you showed me in that drop of water?"

Osbert neither answered nor looked up. He had discovered that the eyes were missing from one of his father's butterflies. He wished he had been able to witness the various stages of their decay. When was the moment when they disappeared completely, and did they depart simultaneously?

"Can you see, for instance," Granville continued, "how they survive and what exactly it is that they eat?" He rose to his feet once again and, forgetting his brother's admonition, walked towards the window with his hands clasped behind his back. "And when that drop evaporates, that drop of water they inhabit, do they then also become vapour? Perhaps they are mysteriously catapulted towards another drop. Vapour returns to the clouds, doesn't it? So perhaps the little wriggling creatures move up there, reassemble their families, and return to the earth as rain."

Osbert was now sketching vacant eye-sockets.

"What a life!" Granville exclaimed after a long silence. "You must say, what a life! Floating up to the clouds," he waved his right hand heavenward, "only to be flung back down to earth. And no control, of course. The animals would have no control over any of it." He narrowed his eyes and peered through the window, down the drive. "What on earth," he finally whined, "can possibly be keeping them?"

Osbert pushed his microscope away from him and turned the sheet of drawing paper face down on the table. "I don't know," he said, folding his arms and leaning back in the chair. "Has this ever happened before?"

"You know it hasn't, not ever."

"Have you spoken with any of them recently?"

"Not for some weeks – I've been reading galley proofs. Have you?"

"I haven't been out and about . . . the weather, you know. Are they going about their labours as usual?"

"Yes . . . I suppose . . . I haven't really noticed." Granville returned to the damask chair. "Surely they wouldn't rise up, would they, against us? Not when we appreciate their history and all those songs and stories and the like. They haven't gone and joined secret societies or anything like that, have they? Not the Molly Maguires or the Hearts of Steele or those other ones, those Whiteboys. Have you seen words like BEWARE CAPTAIN MOONLIGHT or any other such nonsense scribbled on walls? Has anyone said anything?"

"Not to me, they haven't. But then they wouldn't, would they?"

Granville was becoming agitated. "There's no need for societies like that here. We *live* here. There's no middleman and we've always been fair. Furthermore, I, for one, understand the sorrows of Ireland. I, in fact, have given a *voice* to the sorrows of Ireland."

Osbert recalled the woman on the beach. "There has been hardship –" he ventured.

"But, as you said," Granville interrupted, "not here . . . not in Ulster. Or, at least, not great hardship."

"There is never great hardship in Ulster."

"Never!"

"Could we have the day wrong?"

"No."

"Well then . . ." The brothers, embarrassed by this aberration, did not meet each other's eyes.

"Do I remember correctly," Granville asked suddenly, "that O'Donovan's to be married tomorrow?"

"Yes . . . I believe so."

"So they'll be having a sort of ball – fiddle music and the like, dancing and drinking, of course – in O'Donovan Senior's barn."

"Most likely."

"I believe that we should attend." Granville had begun, again, his nervous pacing. "Doesn't that seem to you like an excellent suggestion?"

~

Like the schoolmaster, the groom's father, Jim O'Donovan, was a smallholder; a man who, in the past, had managed tolerably well on his few acres, feeding his family on eggs, milk, potatoes, and oatmeal, and having his income supplemented by his wife's spinning and occasional weaving. His lease was renewed annually when he paid rent from the supplemental income, and, in his heart he felt, if not entirely free, at least somewhat independent with two cows, a donkey and cart, and one small plough.

Only one of his sons would inherit the holding, subdivision being something he could not agree to, due to the meagreness of his land. The remaining boys had moved, or would likely move, to Belfast or Derry to take their places behind the power looms that would eventually put their mother out of business altogether. His two daughters would, with luck, marry the inheriting sons of other smallholders such as himself. The bridegroom in question was to inherit the farm, though in the past he had earned his keep as a labourer on the vast Sedgewick estates.

O'Donovan Senior was not pleased with the match his son had made; the girl being the daughter of a cottier, or one who had been allowed to rent a cabin and potato plot in return for permanent labour in the Sedgewick corn and grain fields, and hence part of a social order lower than his own. But he was a romantic and rather than have his son mooning around pubs singing songs of love and death – as he, himself, had done at a similar age – he gave his consent to the marriage and agreed to allow the wedding feast to take place in his modest barn, the girl's father having no barn at all.

Except that, times being what they were, there would not be much of a feast, the O'Donovan family having been forced to drop to two meals a day of milk and potatoes, and were it not that his own parish priest was a friend to Father Quinn on the island there would have been no whiskey at all. But Quinn had agreed to contribute a small amount of his hoard as his own people, he said, hadn't the heart or the strength to drink it.

O'Donovan Senior, moving now with the wedding party, down the rocky, ill-repaired road from the church at Ballyvoy to his barn, had little strength of heart left in himself. He looked at the couple who walked in front of him, his son Hugh dressed in trousers far too short and the bride dressed in a gown that her mother had made for her from a bedsheet that had seen better days and the mother's own tattered veil which mice had obviously nested in. During the Mass, he had prayed, heretically, that the ragged bride who walked before him would be barren, knowing her to be another mouth to feed at his own table. His wife had wept through all the Latin prayers and the couple's vows. There was no joy in her tears.

They had invited few of their neighbours to their barn. The schoolmaster was asked because he had once said to O'Donovan that Hugh was quick at his studies and had filled the father's heart with great hope. And his quiet wife who had been away, Father O'Brien from the church at Ballyvoy, of course, and Father Quinn as a result of the generous donation of drink, and an old bachelor, by the name of Kavanaugh, friend of the family and well-known fiddler. O'Donovan, even in these grim times, had insisted that there should be some music and some dancing, were the company's spirits to rise as a result of the whiskey. At first the old man said he would not come, until O'Donovan, in desperation, had shaken his feeble shoulders and shouted "We're not dead yet!"

The small party made its way past silent cabins where no one sprang to the doorways to watch, past plots filled with the black leaves of ruined potato plants, past meadows decked with the ironically healthy wildflowers that decorated the bride's head, into O'Donovan's barn where a scant supper of oatcakes, cheese, and stringy hens' meat lay waiting. For many this would be the last time they would taste wholesome food. It was fallen upon almost immediately and without conversation and washed down, by old and young alike, with whiskey.

The old fiddler was the first to look up and then rise from the table. Repeating the line that had brought him to O'Donovan's barn, he announced in Irish and in a voice disproportionately strong in comparison to his wasted frame, "We're not dead yet." Then, with a surprisingly graceful gesture, he picked up his fiddle and bow.

Anyone standing a mile away on the slopes that led up to Knocklayd Mountain would have been astonished by what was about to take place in the still landscape before them. The day was sultry, overcast, and almost entirely silent – not a breeze to turn a leaf on a tree. Coolanlough, Ballyvoy, Craigfad, and Doon, and all of the Sedgewick estate seemed frozen and abandoned, it being evening and the field labourers having crept dispiritedly home to their cottages. Then, gently, a ribbon of pure sound emerged from the door of one whitewashed barn and wound over the blackened plots, around the ancient raths, under the hawthorn hedgerows. Two hawks, gliding over the valley, seemed to pick up this ribbon in their beaks and carry it on their wings until the whole region was filled with the terrible, beautiful tune borne of an old man's heart and hands.

It took only a few moments for people all over the area within hearing distance to emerge from the doors of their cabins, for they were hungry, not only for food, but for the music they thought had left them forever. Out of the dark interiors the ribbon of music drew them, old women leaning on sticks and babes who had barely learned to walk, pale young girls and young men, too, whose strong arms had grown thin. Some of the elderly had not staggered into the light for weeks and now stood blinking at the white sky before lurching forward in search of the song. Soon there appeared several streams of moving flesh which joined to become a river travelling slowly towards O'Donovan's barn. Without exception, each person was weeping.

In a short time a dark lake surrounded one whitewashed building and held still for some minutes. Then, like a biblical sea, it parted so that the old man could enter it and stand, still playing, at its centre. When he had finished he lowered the bow and the fiddle. The hawks circled overhead. At the door of the barn the small wedding party looked silently at the crowd of equally silent neighbours, until, from the midst of the crowd, one woman's voice was heard singing alone.

> O bonny Portmore, you shine where you stand,
> And the more I think on you, the more I think long.
> If I had you now, as I had once before,
> All the Lords in old England would not purchase Portmore.

It was not of her own landscape – the earth beneath her feet – that the lone woman sang, but of a lost world that encompassed all losses. By the second verse five or six other women had joined in and the fiddler had begun to pick out the tune with his bow. Mary, knowing this to be a song about the vanished woods of Ireland, remembered the forest that the other one had shown her, and the song pushed its way out of her mouth before she was aware that she had joined the chorus.

O bonny Portmore, I am sorry to see
Such a woeful destruction of your ornament tree.
For it stood on your shore for full many a long day,
Till the long boats from Antrim came to float it away.

There was great sorrow in the song and great joy, also, that the privilege of sorrow had not yet been cast from the people who sang it. The land they stood on had heard songs such as this before and it would hear them again, for it was the music that could not be starved out of it. The women knew that their bones would sing in the earth after their flesh had gone, and the men, who now joined them, knew that the song would make its way through the coming generations.

The birds of the forest do bitterly weep,
Saying where shall be shelter, where shall we sleep.
For the oak and the ash are all cutten down,
And the walls of bonny Portmore are all down to the ground.

This was the anthem that greeted Osbert and Granville as they rode in the carriage towards O'Donovan's barn. Their driver, an old man himself, stopped so that the music would be undisturbed by the sound of horses' hooves and squeaking axles. Inside, the brothers looked at each other for some minutes, then regarded the floor, embarrassed by the tears that, for reasons they did not understand, were beginning to fill their eyes and by a confused longing that they felt must be evident in their faces.

"I believe," said Osbert, when the song had finished, "that they are unable to pay. I believe that's why they didn't come."

"Yes," agreed Granville, wiping perspiration from his forehead, "yes . . . that must be it. Should we turn back?"

Osbert wanted to turn back; back to the cases of kept things, to the Cave Walk, the long rooms of Puffin Court. But he was suddenly ashamed of his desire to avoid the misery. "I think we should go," he said quietly. "I think we should give them this." He jostled a small leather bag full of coins.

But, as they came nearer to the people, the bag in his hands seemed to shrink until its insignificance was painful to look at, to hold, or to offer. "No," he blurted, just before they were to turn down the lane that led to the barn. "No . . . you're right." And, tapping on the glass, he motioned for the driver to turn around.

"These are very bad times," said Granville.

Osbert did not answer. He was trying to remove from his mind the disturbing idea that his brother looked ridiculous in his velvet breechcoat, the lace cuffs of which danced in the jolting carriage; that and the even more disturbing idea that he was his brother's mirror image. He removed his handkerchief and held it to his mouth and nose as they passed a particularly putrid potato plot.

"What are we going to do?" he asked as he pocketed the piece of cloth. "We must do something. I didn't tell you this because I didn't believe it, but the talk is that they've been fainting in the fields . . . from hunger."

"There's too many," Granville thumped his knee with his fist, "I tell you, there's always far too many of them! There ought not to be weddings like today – it ought not to be allowed. How are we to manage?"

∽

When Mary had seen Father Quinn rolling a barrel of the island's whiskey towards the barn, the morning on the beach three years before came into her mind with such clarity she believed she could recall each wave that had brought the darling one to shore, though she knew this was impossible – nothing being more complicated or unique than the breaking of the surf. Still, the inner picture had caused her to join, emotionally, with the other women in the singing of the sorrowful song. She, like them, believed that they would all soon die and she believed that death would sever her, not only from the world that included the straw under her feet and this pathetic whisper of a wedding, but also from the other world that it had been her privilege to visit, and so she doubly mourned.

The crowd had begun to organize itself into the various activities that accompanied such occasions, though at this time their celebrations were subdued; the dances quieter, more courtly and resigned. Couples circled each other warily and left a space between them for the third dancer that they knew was among them. Hands touched tentatively or did not touch at all. The girls, especially, danced as if in the grips of some great physical pain, bending over their own arms at the waist or twisting at odd angles away from the young men dancing near them. Faces were almost always averted.

With Brian beside her, Mary walked away from the agony of the dancing, across the barnyard, towards a group of young men who were quietly arranging themselves into a pattern she did not recognize. Concentrating fiercely, they were seated on the ground with their backs straight and their legs extended in front of them. In two long lines that gradually converged at each end they faced each other, while, in the centre of the shape they made, which was almost that of a diamond, a tall man and a boy loitered, slouching, their hands in their pockets, a much-mended bedsheet on the ground between them. Two older men surveyed the group then turned at intervals to search the sky.

"What is it that they're doing?" Mary asked.

"Waiting for the wind . . ." said Brian, "I think they're waiting for the wind."

"But why . . . why should they be waiting for the wind?"

"I've only seen this at wakes," said Brian as if he were talking to no one but himself, "and indoors. But now I see that it's different . . . and that will be what the sheet is for."

"And what –"

"Wait and you'll see." Brian shook his head. "It's a sad pass," he lamented, "when the games for wakes come to be acted out at weddings."

The fiddler had begun to play again, this time a livelier tune, and the old men were coming forward to take their turns dancing with the bride – a wraith composed of bones and bedclothes. One gentleman, diminished and ancient and totally dependent upon his stick, seemed to waltz with that object rather than with the girl. The wind, absent all day, appeared and unfurled her bridal veil which, in its fragmented state, looked like a collection of torn clouds.

Then the shout raised by the young men thundered across the crowd and echoed from the four principal parts of the landscape: the town of Ballycastle in the distance, Knocklayd Mountain, the Sedgewick demesne, and the moors that rose up to the cliffs. The fiddler lowered his bow, the bride stopped dancing, the whole company froze, then turned.

Having leapt onto the shoulders of the tall man, the boy stood there balanced perfectly. With one hand over his head and the other by his side he clutched the sheet which had opened itself to the wind. The men who formed the diamond shape had locked arms, and their bodies sloped back from their hips. Mary stared, confused. Her husband cursed – then laughed. Just as she was about to ask him again she understood: the men had used their slim bodies to construct the hull of a ship, their legs for the thwarts, their torsos for the sides, their arms for the gunwales, the young boy and tall man for the mast. Only the bedsheet – the inanimate – moved; a sail twitching in the wind. After the initial shout, the men held motionless; even their faces were entirely still.

An answering cheer came from the assembled neighbours. And then, to Mary's amazement, the word she thought was hers alone was flung across the landscape.

"Away, boys, away, " the people were shouting, their fists punching the new, brisk wind.

That evening was one of the few that the Sedgewick brothers had ever spent apart. Osbert, his expression sullen and private, disappeared into the library with a decanter of claret and Granville retired to his bedroom with cold compresses for his sick headache. There he lay, fully clothed in boots and breech-coat, with damp, white cloths covering his eyes and the mournful song running and running through his mind during the moments when he wasn't mentally cursing his father and his father's father for leaving such sensitive souls in the posses-sion of this unholy mess.

About midnight, when he was trying to summon the strength to put on his white nightgown and cap, he heard the sound of pounding footsteps in the hall and assumed, fatalisti-cally, that the Whiteboys, the Hearts of Steele, and the Hearts of Oak had all come at once to get him. But it was only his brother who burst through the door, wildly excited, his forefin-ger marking a spot in one of the volumes of the new edition of the *Encyclopaedia Britannica*.

"I know what's to be done!" shouted Osbert, breathlessly.

"All we have to do is sell one or two Gainsboroughs and it's *fait accompli!*"

"What's to be done?" sighed Granville, who was in fact experiencing a great deal of relief not to mention surprise that his brother would agree to part with any work of art for any reason.

"Here . . . look at this." With a triumphant flourish, Osbert slapped the book down on his brother's featherbed. It was open at the pages that described the British colony of Canada.

By January of 1848, the rumour that the landlords were to send a number of cottiers and their families to British North America began to circulate, in various forms, from cabin to cabin. Some said that every Catholic in County Antrim was to be evacuated, along with their donkeys, chickens, and tools. Others announced that since the county was a sinking ship from which decency demanded they be removed, only the women and children would be going. Another rumour, one closest to the truth, suggested that families would be hand-picked for the adventure by the landlords, the rest left to work the fields until they dropped of starvation, harvesting food destined for the surfaces of British tables.

As the talk increased, the word "Canada" was spoken hundreds of times a day – on the roads, in the fields, near the doors of dismal cabins, at firesides – and pictures of the country, itself, began to be assembled by those who claimed to know something of the terrain or those who had once spoken to someone who had received a letter from across the sea. The optimists maintained that all who went there became rich, that golden nuggets tumbled in the streams, that vegetable crops were acclimatized to grow in snow, that fruit trees bore blossoms and fruit all year round – the latter being preserved, always fresh, by a thin coating of ice. The inhabitants, they said, lived in beautiful houses made of unmeltable ice in which they moved on skates from room to room on ice floors. When questioned, these sages said that the cold was another kind of cold altogether, a cold unlike anything ever experienced in Ireland. More like a dryness of the air, this cold, which froze everything around it, produced comfort. The settlers, they said, were so comfortable that they skated about with bare arms protruding from light cotton shifts, plucking the fruit (which was a different kind of fruit altogether – transparent and jewel-like) from the unstoppable orchards. Snowshoes were described, to an assembly struck dumb with amazement, as boots with baskets on the bottom or shoes with frozen nets encircling them. These, they claimed, were issued to every settler on arrival; arrival itself being determined by the moment when the ocean stopped and the comfortable ice began. One was then expected to tramp away from the ship in search of the perfect home of ice (of which there were thousands – empty and waiting), the thatch on their roofs in perfect frozen repair.

The pessimists, as is often the case, spouted theories that bore more, though not much more, resemblance to reality. They scoffed at the tales of the optimists, saying that, although the cold was extreme, there was little, if any, ice at all. This was because the country was too new and, as a result, like all new things, in a state of great agitation. Nothing, they said, ever held still long enough to freeze. The water in all the lakes and rivers (of which there were many) tumbled and cascaded and climbed mountains and flung itself over cliffs and hungrily gobbled boats with more appetite than the waters of the Moyle. Everything was growing, they asserted, all the time, and a man who stood still for too long was likely to be pinned to the ground by rambunctious vines eagerly seeking light. Because of this growth, the pessimists continued, everything became, or had already become, too large. The mountains were unclimbable, the rivers unfordable, the forests impenetrable, and the trees in them unchoppable. The potatoes, if planted at all, were, in the end, unharvestable, in that, because of their remarkable growth, they were too heavy to be removed from the ground. And if by some miracle they were harvested, they were inedible because they continued to grow in the digestive tract after they were swallowed, causing certain death.

The optimists agreed that everything *was* larger there, but speed, they argued, more than made up for the problems caused by size and distance. Wagons, they said, swept through the countryside on long knives pulled by huge, strong horses and in the odd moment when there was no ice to be had, one could avail oneself of boats of paper (another kind of paper altogether) that were so light and so swift that even the natives who designed and built them were astonished by the progress that they made on a sunny afternoon. Furthermore, the natives were on such good terms with the "others," – the faeries – that they could count on the crops growing and the farm animals multiplying and they would generously use their influence in order to improve the lot of any starving Irish peasants in their midst.

But the pessimists maintained that the landscape swallowed almost everyone who approached it. Gigantic insects were described that tore the livers out of the sides of men, women, and children, and packs of wolves moved through crowds like threshing machines. Storms, they said, snatched infants out of the arms of their mothers – even indoors – and rivers overflowed aggressively, demolishing everything in their path. Moreover, it was futile to attempt to make roads through forests because trees reappeared as soon as they were cut down. Thousands of Irish men, who were always enlisted to break trails and make highways, had been sealed forever into forests and never seen again.

For a few weeks the arguments between the two factions distracted the people from that fact that their children's faces were becoming old and pinched, that their own bodies were practically unrecognizable from lack of food, and that the winter that they were attempting to survive was the darkest and coldest of the decade. When, at last, the selected families were announced, those going rejoiced in the theories of the optimists and those remaining behind were consoled by those who maintained a negative view.

Then, into the cabins of all came a perplexing pamphlet, kindly donated by the landlords and entitled "Colonel Tarbutt's Guide for Settlers in Upper Canada." Both optimists and pessimists were snubbed, at this point, in favour of those, of either persuasion, who could read. Generally, the guide confirmed the opinions of the optimists and brought great joy to those about to depart. The perplexity was brought about by the appendix, which the Colonel had called "Suggested Accoutrements for a Gentleman's Pleasant Pilgrimage," and in which he had listed, in alphabetical order, various items that he, a veteran of the trek, felt should be taken along on a journey to the northern portion of the new world. These included ancestral armour, andirons, artillery, barometers, bath chairs, blazers for boating, bugles, caddies for tea, candelabra, castor oil, Christmas decorations, cricket bats, eau-de-Cologne, engraved prints of Windsor Castle, Buckingham Palace, and the Queen, Epsom salts, field-glasses, folio for pressed wildflowers, golf clubs, two good hounds for hunting, ledgers, maps, microscopes, pianos, port, quinine, rose bushes, scotch whisky, tennis racquets, umbrellas, and Wellingtons. A final entry at the bottom of the list suggested that several pots of marmalade be packed and that a type of British plant known as "haws" be brought along so that pleasant hedgerows might replace those infernal rail fences.

A great silence filled the field where those who were illiterate had gathered to hear the reading of the list, and the child – a boy of twelve – who had read it to them, hung his head afterwards as though he, himself, were responsible for the cruelty of its contents and the wretchedness of the group to whom he gave the information. One woman, who had recognized only eight or ten of the words recited, asked, hopefully, if perhaps the words were French – the only language other than Irish or English of which she had ever heard. The boy said nothing but walked away with the other quiet members of his family.

For days after the reading of the list, each man, woman, and child who had heard it was away in contemplation of possessions that had been loved and lost. One remembered a chair with a carved pattern on its back, another a brooch given to her by the butcher's son who had later jilted her. A few china pitchers painted with flowers came to mind or silver-plated spoons. One recalled the head of a china doll she had found on the side of the road and had kept carefully in a secret spot until her brothers had discovered and smashed it. The men thought mostly of livestock, a beautifully marked calf or a particularly healthy lamb or piglet. One old man, with tears in his eyes, thought about his cherished, bad-tempered rooster, whom he had called Cromwell and whom he had been forced to eat only two weeks before. Fiddles, flutes, and pocket-watches sang and ticked in the minds of the people and well-made harnesses and trusted turf spades squeaked and crunched. A middle-aged man thought, with great longing, of a wheelbarrow, picturing clearly the way the boards had aged and weathered and the two smooth spots that his grasp had worn on the handles.

So concentrated had the people been in the past few months on the effort required to balance the idea of leaving Ireland against the cold and their hunger that they had forgotten the previous stages of hardship when the potatoes rotted in the fields, meat disappeared from the tables and then eggs and then milk, until finally the table itself was gone and the familiar stools that stood near it. But now when they dwelt upon their vanished possessions they did so with a terrible sense of loss. Many had only the clothes on their backs and some only one rough blanket, and, knowing this, they gathered their thin families together and crept into the dark of their empty cabins where Colonel Tarbutt's Guide was torn in anger and tossed hurriedly onto what remained of their turf fires.

During the course of the next few days, however, when storms painted the hills white or covered the rocks in glittering ice, another kind of possession began to build itself in the cottiers' minds, and one by one men rose weakly from their attitudes of despair and began to describe to their wives and children what they had seen in their waking dreams.

She is the colour of mahogany, they said, and taller and larger than the hall the landlords inhabit. Forty-five wings unfurl from her and her body is studded with nails of gleaming brass and she is clothed in ropes made from silken threads. The planks on her decks are polished and golden and reflect the fire of the sun and below them are rooms filled with emerald light caused by the fine green glass of her windows. Swifter than the gulls she is and as smooth.

Slowly, the ship was built, timber by timber, in the crumbling cabins, until the emigrants-to-be held her in their hearts as the greatest possession of all. Then the little withered children staggered out into the rain where they built her themselves with sticks and bark and leaves, and sailed her on mud-puddle oceans, towards the other shore.

Osbert and Granville expended several boxes of vellum paper making lists and tallying accounts. They had already demolished reams of writing material sending enquiries and requests off to passenger-brokers, most of whom, it turned out, were either completely corrupt or utterly stupid. One had offered the suggestion that all Irish peasants should sleep on the deck – for their own good – because people of this class were unused to beds and bedding and were therefore uncomfortable when provided with such amenities. Another had attempted to charge them three times the going rate for each man, woman, and child. By the time the landlords had selected fifty of the most destitute families for the passage, things were more or less settled. Some of their tenants had expressed the wish to proceed to the United States on arrival where they had family or friends who appeared to be already established. Others claimed they would look for employment in the cities of Toronto or Montreal. Only a few stated that they wanted Canadian land; those who were strong, or those whose characters had instinctively wedded them to the soil and who could imagine no other way of life.

Osbert was amazed to discover that he could acquire uncleared land for these emigrants – for little or no money – on the northern edges of townships with strange, unpronounceable Indian names. One particularly cynical land agent in Derry suggested that he should defer payment until the people arrived, since it was likely only half would survive the journey.

"But the ships are clean and well maintained," Osbert had replied, "and the food on them is of the highest quality, yes?"

"Oh, absolutely," said the land agent, turning away with a smile.

Granville, rereading the list of those who were to emigrate, was surprised to find the schoolmaster's name pencilled in at the bottom.

"What's this?" he asked his brother. "Is he so bad off then?"

"Bad enough," Osbert replied.

"But he's a smallholder . . . surely we shouldn't have to bear –"

"He pays his rent to us."

"Still, with five acres he should be able to grow enough –"

"Enough what . . . potatoes?" Osbert demanded sarcastically.

"Well, we certainly can't start shipping away all the smallholders as well as the cottiers. Did he approach you?"

"No."

"Well, then, surely *you* didn't suggest this?"

"Not yet," Osbert was busily tidying papers. "I'm just about to. This afternoon, in fact."

"But why him? Why not O'Donovan or Flanaghan? What's this all about?" Granville was becoming annoyed. "Why not the whole country? Why *him* in particular? Besides, he's a good tenant, we should keep him."

"It's not him." Osbert longed to be out somewhere on the Cave Walk with his pen and drawing ink. He wished he was looking at a tiny life-form through his microscope; one that was incapable of conversation.

"Why *him*?" Granville demanded again.

"It's not him," Osbert sighed impatiently, "it's her. The wife . . . the woman who was away." Osbert glared suddenly at his brother from beneath fierce bushy eyebrows. "I won't have her starve," he announced, "I won't have it."

"She petitioned you, came begging."

"She certainly did not. She would never, never do that."

"Perhaps they don't wish to go." He looked again at the paper in his hand. "Perhaps they don't want this land you've obviously already arranged for them."

"Perhaps." Osbert twitched in his chair and began to pull on his left ear, a habit since childhood. "Perhaps . . . but I'll have to persuade them. They must go," he was thinking aloud now. "They must go because of the light."

His brother regarded him in stunned silence.

Osbert looked towards the window. "There's this light in her, you see," he said, "and it must not be put out. I can't explain it, but I know that it must not go out, must be kept, somehow, though I'm not certain at all that it will shine as well across the ocean as it does here. Nevertheless," he added assertively, "I will not stand by and see it fade."

"You've gone mad! How do you know this woman?"

"I don't."

"Then, what's all this nonsense about the light? Surely you haven't begun to believe their wild tales. Charming, I admit, but utter flights of fancy."

"It has nothing to do with that," said Osbert. "It's just this subtle light. I saw it that day by the tidepool." He was putting on his greatcoat and reaching for his walking-stick.

"What day? What tidepool?" demanded Granville.

Osbert did not answer. He was heading down the long hall past the glazed eyes of twenty stuffed puffins, towards the door.

From where she sat on the stone at the cabin's threshold, Mary was able to watch the landlord approach for a long, long time. At first he was only a dark shape, small, moving down the path that, from this distance, was no wider than your finger on the green hill. He caught her attention because, for the past few weeks, no one at all was to be seen moving confidently through the landscape. A few of the labourers in the morning and now and then the priest hurrying to administer last rites, but mostly the people's energies were drained by the labour required simply to continue breathing.

Mary, herself, had remained in this spot – her head against the frame and her back to the door – since she had dragged herself from sleep in the morning. Several bouts of cold rain had drenched her, but she hadn't the will to stir. Inside, her husband and child remained as motionless as she – the former staring at the same page in the Supplement to the Encyclopaedia hour after hour, the latter rolling his little wooden spool from hand to hand across the floor on which he squatted. Mary could not bear to see Brian wince when he looked at her. She knew all her beauty was gone.

They had stopped talking two weeks ago and now silence was a fourth among them. It had crept under the door and set up house in the kitchen the day that hope lifted like smoke up a chimney. Everything had been laid down to rust. Not just Brian's spade, which Mary could see lying diagonally between her and the barn, but the child's lists of new words and the man's long rants concerning the unfairness of his lot.

During the last of these outbursts Brian had smashed his fist through a pane of glass in the lower part of the cabin's south window and the shards were still scattered in the grass. Mary had spent at least one hour today picking up one fragment and then another, looking through each of them towards the sky, noting how cracks picked up reflections of stones at her feet or how bubbles in the glass distorted clouds. If you tilted the broken edge, Mary discovered, it would mirror this or that facet of their holdings, randomly. She had been doing this for a while, when she saw her own gaunt face reflected, and in shame and disgust she kicked the shattered glass away from her. She had forgotten all about her slate which lay near the hearth inside, a curved crack like a ghastly smile running from one side of it to the other, a few Irish words chalked on its surface. Sometimes she spoke to the darling, absent one in poems or in snatches of songs.

By the time the shadow of the landlord fell across the door-way where she sat, Mary had stepped into the day of the black stones and was reconstructing her discovery of the beloved other. "Lay your head there," she was singing or saying, "where the warm breeze can blow the sea from your hair."

Osbert touched her arm and pulled her back from the sea and the stones. Then he followed her into the cabin where she squinted at him, or at the places around him where the light came from the window.

"You must go away," he was saying, "emigrate to Canada. I've booked your passage. The ship sails from Larne in a few weeks – for Quebec. You will go with the others. There will be land there waiting for you – acres and acres – more than you can imagine. The ship leaves in a few weeks – at the end of May – from Larne. Her name is the New World."

Mary looked at the objects discarded on the cabin floor. A pot, a ladle. She had almost forgotten how they were used now they were no longer in their proper place. Her mind tidied nothing. Not until she looked at the lantern standing on the table. She would not want to lose the lantern, illuminator of journeys. She would protect it, put it in a cupboard until she needed it.

No one inside the cabin spoke to Osbert and he tried not to look at their altered faces. He stood for some moments near the window with his tweed cap in his hand, turning it and turning it so that his fingers touched the peak and then the back of the sweatband, over and over. Then he coughed nervously and departed.

No one inside the cabin had spoken, but as Osbert walked away he knew that even the child had agreed to go.

SHE placed the geography book on a large boulder and herself beside it.

In the early morning light the incised continents stood out in exaggerated relief and it seemed to Mary as if her own approaching journey had given them more weight and substance. The cracks on the spine, where she had repeatedly bent the book open, were even more visible; etched reminders of her paths through the words of the book. She would show the dark, darling one this Canada, this place where she was going. She would show him the long river that thrust into its body and the lakes shaped like boulders which Brian said were also inland seas with no salt in the water. There was some hope in her mind that the beloved other would follow her there, and there was fear that he would not. That the land that had grown him, the sea that had drowned him, and the lake that had housed him would keep him here, far from her, forever.

Now the water of Lough Crannog licked the rushes near the shore. Mary waited as she had learned now to wait, calmly, her hands palm upwards on her lap as if she expected them to fill with pools of rain. Bright glimmers of life darted near the water on blurred wings and occasionally a trout leapt, then plummeted, a flailing blade, into the lake.

He breathed and the air shivered with constellations of bright kindreds. "Now it's you," he whispered, "this is what you take with you and what you leave behind." She saw obsessed kings and warriors, torn by grief and guilt, monks curved over hinged books in scriptoriums, gypsies with roads flung like banners in front and behind them, women, terrible in the beauty of their first youth, and hags in tatters, the knowledge of years hanging like rosary beads from their crooked hands. A line of pale young men appeared, their shirts open to white throats, their sole employment to sing the great sorrows and then to die for love. The great scholars, distant, preoccupied, came to her carrying pictures of medieval poets; men and women from the bardic schools, lying prone in windowless rooms with large stones resting on their stomachs and ten thousand metered lines preserved in their heads. Saints held still, their raised arms thrust up to heaven for so many years that birds had come to nest in the cups of their hands. "These are not being shed," the dark other said to her, "they are accumulated." Then came the gifted teachers, and with them the moment when knowledge is passed from one mind to another.

He showed her the teachers poised on the edge of the moment – a brown-robed brother guiding the hand of an acolyte through the deliberate strokes of calligraphy, a gypsy woman demonstrating the exact turn of a bare ankle to a young girl eager to begin dancing, a sailor showing a cabin boy how to twist a length of rope into the patterns of various knots, a woman setting threads on a loom while her daughter's fair head was illuminated by the window that lit the task. And everywhere around was the quiet that accompanies the act of passing skill from one mind and hand to another. Last he showed her Brian gently breaking open the marks of the alphabet to reveal meaning and the light of understanding on her own face.

The phrases of lessons he placed before her. "No, like this," he said, and "Let me show you," and "Now you try."

"This is what you carry with you," he repeated, "this is your ship's cargo. And when you go, this is what you become part of."

Then she saw the world's great leavetakings, invasions and migrations, landscapes torn from beneath the feet of tribes, the Danae pushed out by the Celts, the Celts eventually smothered by the English, warriors in the night depopulating villages, boatloads of groaning African slaves. Lost forests. The children of the mountain on the plain, the children of the plain adrift on the sea. And all the mourning for abandoned geographies.

"And you," she asked, "will I take you with me?"

"Yes and no," he said. She saw that he was clothed in the feathered coat of a poet, that clots of birds' nests rested in his hands, and that small fires guttered near his feet.

As he moved into the lake he said to her. "It will be, at times, as if it were less hardship to be sleeping in the graveyard of your native land, to be asleep underneath the stones that cover your island in the sea."

Father Quinn came to see the emigrants depart – their sacks filled with pots, their heads filled with the beautiful ship they had mentally constructed, hunger clawing at their bellies. He approached Brian tearfully and thrust his beloved copy of Cicero into his hands. "You'll think of me," he said, "in some Canadian forest when you read this, I believe, and the walks we had looking out to Rathlin, talking about it all in better times. And as to her," he said, looking at the ground and reddening in the face, "she has been a gift to you, I think." He walked away, then, to join the priest from Ballyvoy in prayers and blessings for his people.

A year later Quinn and many of his parishioners were dead, their silver teapots left to tarnish in the far corners of their sad, dismantled cabins.

Granville strode back and forth from family to family ensuring that each had their tickets and their papers, assuring them that the ship's rations were plentiful, and speaking of the benevolent government in the new country. As the people bounced away in the carts their landlord was not aware that each man, woman, and child was composing a poem of farewell to a landscape they had believed would hold them forever. The groan that rose from the ones left behind would be part of a long eulogy that those who survived would never tire of passing down to their children and their children's children.

Osbert was not there. He was bent, instead, over his microscope, studying a drop of water. But the prolonged keening slipped under his window frame and filled the halls of Puffin Court, causing him to look up and around. He thought of the tidepool and the beautiful creatures he had wrenched from it and the light in the woman's face, and fear and loss came to sit beside him at his table until he covered his ears to free himself from the wailing that seemed to be pouring out of all the familiar objects in his room.

Brian turned towards his wife who was pale, closed off from him and the others in the departing wagon, her eyes lowered as if she were watching the edge of the road. Her lips were dry and cracked but they were moving and a thin sound emerged. Singing, she was singing. He leaned against her, wanting to share whatever prayer she had been moved to utter. The child's head rolled back and forth across her thin chest as the wagon jolted forward.

Brian caught the words of his wife's song. It was not a prayer she was singing:

If I were a blackbird,
I'd whistle and sing,
I'd follow the ship that my true love sails in.

And in the top rigging,
I'd there make my nest,
And I'd cradle my head
On my true-love's breast.

When Osbert slumped again over the microscope and peered down its miniature tunnel, he did so just in time to see that which he was looking at vanish. Although he had witnessed the moment of evaporation, magnified, many times before; this time it shocked and moved him to such an extent that he pushed the instrument away from him and drew the old red curtains all around the room.

II

A Bird on a Branch

Esther knows exactly what she is doing as she lies awake in the night. She is recomposing, reaffirming a lengthy, told story, recalling it; calling it back. She also knows that by giving her this story all those years ago her grandmother Eileen had caused one circle of experience to edge into the territory of another. The child that Esther had been had drawn circles like this with her compass when she was in school, had shaded with her pencil the place where the two circles intersected; a small dense area with white empty pools on either side – a partial, a fractional eclipse. The grey shaded shape, she remembers, had been like a single willow leaf lying on the page.

It is very dark now. Were it not for the cement company's pier, which sheds its light faintly over Loughbreeze Beach, the room at this hour would be utterly black. Sometimes it had been so dark in the forest, Old Eileen had told her, that night became more than air and absence of light, became something you drowned in or swam through until morning.

Esther lying still in her sleigh-bed feels like an Irish poet from a medieval, bardic school. She is aware that those men and women lay in their windowless cells for days, composing and then memorizing thousands of lines, their heads wrapped in tartan cloths, stones resting on their stomachs. Esther has neither rocks nor plaids with her in this bed but shares with the old ones a focused desire. Nothing should escape. Line after line must be circulated by memory among the folds of the brain. Not a single calf, for instance, should be permitted to

133

stray from *The Cattle Raid of Cooley*; the scent of the herds must be kept, always, within the range of the nostrils.

Soon cows will begin to saunter, casually, into Esther's story, their black markings like continents adrift on polar seas.

The cows are gone, now, from Loughbreeze Beach Farm, they have drifted into the cedars beyond the ruined pastures. There is no song, no call that will make them turn and begin the sedate evening journey homewards. They graze only in fields raked by the light of memory. Esther sees herself as a child recognizing the strength of memory, putting aside ephemeral, destroyable books as old Eileen's voice built a story within the closed rectangle of a room.

At the quarry the men of the evening shift are growing restless. They began to work in the midst of heat and light and are now labouring in chill and darkness of the hour before midnight. They are open-pit men, earth-movers, makers of dust and noise. They have never seen glistening rock walls lit by lanterns or experienced underground rain. All moisture is the enemy, they fear the Great Lake that is their neighbour. Hydraulic pumps work night and day removing groundwater from the quarry floor.

Some of these men have handled fuses, have prepared the blasting caps of dynamite under the late-afternoon sun. Some of them have pulled the rope that activates the alarm – the five short and two long moans that remind Esther of extinct telephone exchanges. All of the men have watched showers of rock spring up from the earth and fall again like grey fountains. No matter how long they have worked at the quarry they are always moved by this display of danger and power.

They are separated from the men on the lakeboat by an instinctive fear of water, a pier, and a conveyor belt, and therefore know none of the sailors by name. They are separated from the men at the refinery by forty miles of Great Lake. They never think about either of these separations.

Not a single herd of cattle grazes in their dreams though many of their fathers and grandfathers were farmers. Sometimes they have nightmares in which they are buried by an unforeseen fountain of rock or drowned by the Great Lake pushing angrily through the south wall of the quarry.

But mostly their sleep is untroubled, undisturbed or even comforted by the distant rumble of machinery activated by the men of the midnight shift who have come to take their place.

Esther is thinking about houses: the one in which she lies, the one buried by sand, the one struck by lightning. When she spoke of the curse of the mines, could Old Eileen have foreseen the annihilation of the geography of Loughbreeze Beach? Hers had been a life during which houses were being constructed, kept, embellished, a life during which forests were torn apart in an attempt to reproduce the pastoral landscape of the British Isles. This was one of the essential differences between them: in Eileen's world abandoned structures decomposed, sinking back into the landscape from which they had sprung. In Esther's lifetime she has seen architecture die violently. It has been demolished, burned, ripped apart, or buried. Nothing reclaims it. Just as the earth at the quarry is wounded beyond all recognition and no one remembers the fields that flourished there.

In truth, the white house nearly blinded the six-year-old boy. Although he had been in the new country for almost three months, it was, nevertheless, the first particle of the huge strangeness that he had allowed his gaze to rest upon. It shone in the Great Lake harbour like a lamp, brighter than the sun that lit it. As the lakeboat in which they rode moved through the waves towards shore, the house appeared to breathe heavily and draw itself up like something alive. The boy was afraid of it and enchanted by it and convinced that light was pouring out of, not into, its windows. In its rooms, he imagined there would be music like Mass being sung, but louder. Then he remembered Father Quinn's visits to his parents' cabin, and their own parish priest in the cold church, and suddenly he was not certain where he was.

The white house had broken in, through the boy's eyes, to everything that had closed in him, and now the stimuli of the place where it stood assaulted his senses. There were shouts from the men on the jetty as the boat drew alongside and the boy's ears rang with the sound. The heat of the sun on his hair and the warmth of his mother's hands on his stomach were suddenly heavy and oppressive, that and the moist air that did not smell of salt, though the water behind him rolled towards a naked horizon.

Not far from the boy, lying motionless on the deck, was a girl not much larger than himself who had died on this journey from Quebec. Her mother and father crouched beside her and

136

stared out over the lake while her brown curls twitched in the breeze and one fly crawled listlessly from eyelid to eyelid. The boy did not look at her, took the full brunt of the white house into his sight, instead, until his eyes watered.

What the child had forgotten and would not remember until years later were the crowded docks of Larne and the journey there, the suffering, starvation, the desperate throngs on the wharf. He had forgotten the dark belly of the ship where no air stirred and, as the weeks passed, the groans of his neighbours, the unbearable, unspeakable odours, his own father calling for water, and the limp bodies of children he had come to know being hoisted through the hatch on ropes, over and over, until the boy believed this to be the method by which one ascended to heaven. He had forgotten his own sickness which drew a dark curtain over the wet, foul timbers of the ship's wall and the long sleep that had removed him from the ravings of the other passengers until he wakened believing that the shrieked requests for air and light and liquid was the voice of the abominable beast, the ship that was devouring a third of the flesh that had poured into its hold. And after ten weeks crouched on the end of his parents' berth on the *New World*, and six weeks confined to a bed with five other children at the quarantine station at Grosse Isle (some lying dead beside him for half a day), he had forgotten how to recall images, engage in conversation, and how to walk.

Now the white house burst out at him from the collection of darker buildings in the new harbour; glass and carved verandahs and whitewashed clapboard. The reflections in the large windows of the white house held his attention because he thought he was seeing the house's own memories painted there. When he closed his eyes he could see a picture of the white house as clear and detailed as that which lay before him. Then, with his eyes open, he saw the Great Lake, some shoreline trees, and the masts of the boat jerking on the surface of the building's windows.

His mother placed one hand on top of his head, then moved it down to rest flat against his back while the other hand remained firm across his stomach. He looked beyond the house and the small harbour town, for a moment, to a line of hills and heard his father say, "That darkness there . . . that darkness would be the forest."

His mother did not answer but shifted, instead, the boy's weight on her lap. He was six years old and he had forgotten how to walk. She had come looking for him after they had been separated at the quarantine station at Grosse Isle in the middle of the St. Lawrence River. She had lifted him out of the bed. He had scarcely been out of her arms since.

A free land grant awaited them in Hastings County in Upper Canada and they should have disembarked at Belleville. His father had been standing at the railing when this town was pointed out – a bouquet of spires in the distance – and, realizing that they had taken the wrong boat, he had run back and forth on the deck pleading with various lake sailors to make the vessel stop. But they had told him that the boat went to Port Hope, that he must hire a wagon there to take him north, then back east. Brian spent the remainder of the journey pulling the few pounds he had been granted out of his pocket and putting them back in again, knowing all would be gone once he had paid the fare for the vehicle and purchased a few supplies.

The boy heard the mother of the dead child ask again and again, "Is there no priest, is there no priest to bury her?" until his own mother said "Oh God," and wept and rocked him and called him by his name, "Liam, Liam," while the white house he was looking at moved from side to side with her motions.

They had set foot on the new land twice before – at the quarantine island and the docks of Quebec – but Liam did not remember either time, so this crowded harbour and the gleaming white house with memories of the Great Lake painted on its windows was to be his kept point of entry, the beginning for him of the long story – a remembered birth. The child was being flung into a world it would take him years to know and understand. Even as he sat in his mother's arms, and twisted his neck to keep the white house in view, the great forests had been felled twenty miles back from the lake and, further north, trees at this precise moment were groaning and crashing through their neighbours' arms to the forest floor. In a few years' time, Liam would know corduroy roads and rail fences and stumping machines, horses and cutters and banks of snow taller than a man, and the webbed shoes shaped like teardrops that one must wear to cross fields in winter. He would know the smell of wood in newly constructed buildings and the view through glass to graveyards only half filled with alert white stones. He would come to be familiar with cumbersome tools invented to cut through the flesh of trees or to tear at earth and rock.

During the next few days as the wagon on which the family rode rocked and swayed over the mire of the roadbed, through forests that sunlight barely penetrated, Liam held fiercely to the image of the white house, believing that at the end of this journey its brightness would greet him. It would be a huge, calm lantern in these frantic woods, its clapboard smooth and clean, the Great Lake shining and alive on each of its many windows.

But when the wagon deposited them under the outstretched arms of massive fir trees and disappeared into the further realms of the forest they were filled with dread, knowing themselves to be in a region where nothing at all was constructed and everything was engaged in haphazard growth. What with illness, quarantine, and then waiting out the winter freeze in Quebec, it had taken the family a year to reach this spot. Now they were terrified of the paradise they had imagined. To the boy in particular, the flowers and grass had become huge and terrifying, he and his parents had been reduced in size, and the sky had been blocked, forever, from the world.

Mary and Brian left Liam at the base of one of the trees and began to use what they remembered from the old place to drive away their own fears. While the forest shrieked, whistled, and moaned, his father tied branches together, constructing a shelter reminiscent of the abandoned hedge school at Ballyvoy. His mother had gone further afield and was standing, partly concealed by trees, looking towards the ground.

She was far from Liam, gone from him. Now and then the wind moved low branches and bushes, revealing a portion of her grey skirt or the back of her head and gleaming red hair. She appeared so small beneath the trees Liam feared that she might fade altogether into the forest. There was nothing about her, from this distance, that faced her family. She was fragmented by the confusion of the trees, their shadows making her appear and disappear, and she flickered like a flame about to go out. Panic moved its cold hand down the child's spine. He drew back from a shadow that propelled itself towards him, and then again from a magnificent sunbeam that followed in its wake. He called his mother but the surf sound of the leaves and a flock of screaming crows masked his voice. He had scarcely been out of her arms since she had lifted him from the bed at Grosse Isle.

Liam rose shakily, and for the first time, to his feet and began to move unsteadily towards her. A tremendous amount of noise from fallen and breaking twigs, from branches pushed aside and snapping back into place, made him think that she *must* turn to him and witness the miracle of his steps.

But she was calling instead and looking away from him towards Brian. "Brian!" she shouted. "If there's a stream like this, should it not lead to somewhere . . . to a lake or the sea? Should it not lead us to somewhere else?"

THE first night the family huddled under a roof of cedar limbs on a mattress made from the boughs of the same tree. They lit the lantern, which had miraculously survived the ocean journey, the lake voyage, and the jolting of the wagon on the road to this spot.

Soon their shelter was invaded by moths the size of the eagles they remembered from Ireland, and these frightened Liam to such an extent that Mary and Brian decided to abandon themselves, and him, to the impossible darkness. They lay, stiffly, side by side, eyes open against the inky black, certain that if they succumbed to sleep they would be torn to pieces by wild animals. Mary wept quietly and the boy pressed himself against her to absorb the comfort that her body gave. Brian measured his weakened frame against the forest outside and prayed for the strength to swing an axe. In their secret hearts Mary and Brian believed that having survived famine, disease, an unbearable ocean voyage, and separation at the quarantine station at Grosse Isle, it was their destiny to die in these moaning woods where heaven was blocked from their view by leaf and wood. The month was August, the air sultry. There was neither moon nor stars. The man, woman, and child were exhausted. Eventually they slept.

The next morning they cooked some of the salt pork and cut some of the bread they had got in Queensborough, a rough village they had passed through shortly before the wagon stopped to let them out. In their confusion they had no idea how to return to this pocket of civilization, not being able to determine the direction from which they had come. Still, the road, hardly more than a track, and the indentations the wagon wheels had left in the soft mud, gave them some comfort. They ate squatting by the roadside, not speaking, and wiping their mouths with the backs of their hands.

The boy heard the noises first and lifted his head from his food like a small animal that has smelled danger. Brian and Mary froze, became alert, stiffened their spines, as from every direction the noise of sticks breaking and twigs snapping moved towards them. Men with wild hair and unkempt beards began to emerge from between the trees, followed, in some cases, by women of indeterminate ages. The men carried huge tools, saws the length of curraghs and axes with blades the size of a horse's head.

Liam began to whimper as his parents rose cautiously to their feet. Then he heard the largest of the men speak to his father in a voice whose lilt was familiar and Irish, and out of the baskets they carried he saw that the women were pouring a river of food. More and more people arrived, from all directions, until Liam believed that some of the forest's trees had been magically transformed into human beings.

While the men chopped trees, their wild hair flying, their bare backs glistening, the women sang the song of the axe; a metallic series of sounds, a brutal cry. When the men faced each other in pairs, swaying backwards and forwards in unison – sharp teeth of the saw cutting the wood between them – the women sang the song of the saw, the notes of the melody, long and thin and piercing. Soon the staccato song of the hammer filled the new raw field of light that had been installed, squarely, in the midst of the forest. When the roofbeam of the cabin was raised, the song became an announcement of victory, a celebratory shout in which the men joined. Later, even the children sang the mellow-toned song of warmth and comfort that accompanied the building of the stone chimney and hearth.

Liam watched the crude cabin rise and remembered the white house which he now believed had abandoned him. He saw his mother move among the other women, shy and slight, in the midst of the enthusiasm of their songs. He recalled the shapes of the previous night's menacing insects and imagined himself smothered by their wings inside the log house. Then he saw his father walking easily among the other men; his back straightened and arms strengthened by shared work and companionship and he straightened his own back and practised his new steps on the unfamiliar ground.

Late in the afternoon the boy walked over to the stream that his mother's attention had fixed upon the previous day. He looked through the clear water to a sand bed, where small fish swam, and downstream to a collection of bright pebbles. No boulder, no log stopped or changed the direction of the stream. His mother had said "somewhere else" and "elsewhere." Eventually, Liam knew, this water would carry him to the bright home whose memories of water he had seen in its windows.

W̲HEN summer was finished the family was visited by a series of overstated seasons. In September, they awakened after night frosts to a woods awash with floating gold leaves and a sky frantic with migrating birds – sometimes so great in number that they covered completely with their shadows the acre of light and air that Brian had managed to create. Sumac burst, in the course of one cold night, into clusters of red flame and the dark pines swayed in a strange wind. The autumn change was so profound, so convincing that both Mary and Brian felt that it was an aberration that might be permanent, and this, because it frightened them, they did not speak of. Only Liam sensed in the stir of the air a preparation for something else, and he responded to this by standing in the midst of the swirling leaves shrieking with nervous, wild laughter. He gathered the chestnuts that pummelled the ground and looked into the tiny demonic eyes of hysterical squirrels. When he visited the creek he often saw his mother standing quietly further downstream, passive, inert. He, fascinated by a swerving current, the twitch of a fish, the way gold leaves were swept towards the somewhere else that she had spoken of, wanted to know what it was that held her there, so silent, unmoving, entranced by water.

Although Liam had almost forgotten the open breadth of the abandoned country, his mother's songs could bring back to him the interior of the old cabin; the cot he had slept in and the black pot hanging over the fire. The flat stone near the threshold had appeared, once or twice, inexplicably in his dreams, dissolving just before he woke. Occasionally a Gaelic phrase would wander through his mind and he would say it aloud to a forest that had never heard its like before.

Liam began moving less tentatively each morning into a world of unchartable visual richness – the shimmering planet of the forest. Leaf and leaf and shadow, shadow and sunlight scattered there, and over there, by the wind. In this vibrant September he remembered the terror of late summer storms that had darkened noon and thundered at the door while lightning tore at the tops of thrashing pines, and because most of his previous life had been erased he played with these memories and even the fear connected to them as if they were bright new toys.

His father, having sown his first crop of winter wheat, would leave the acre of light, for a few days, to open up the west end of the road with the other men, for government money, and on other days ride in a neighbour's wagon into Queensborough for supplies. The yellow paper covering the cabin's two small windows was replaced by bubbled glass and Liam learned the word "mullion" which sounded in his mouth like the liquefied view of trees he saw when he woke in the morning. When the wheat struggled towards the light, late in September, it looked stunted, embarrassed by its own uniformity near ragged stumps and untamed wilderness. Later in the season, his father would harvest it by hand and take bags of it in a neighbour's wagon to O'Hara's Mill, returning at night with five bags of flour and a weak calf in exchange.

Sometimes Liam spoke to the calf, who looked at him with mild, brown eyes. The boy believed that they were both children, that the calf, also, had turned six years old.

By the end of October, Liam spent his days running along the edge of the forest, his high laugh piercing through a golden and red shower of leaves. The woods appeared to be breaking apart, like a coloured-glass window, to let in light and air. His father brought back from the company of men a hundred words for trees and bushes and made the boy say them to his mother in the evenings. At night Brian told stories in Latin – a language that Liam didn't understand but loved nonetheless for its soft sounds, the *Ulli, arum, alla, orae*, which tumbled near the fire.

No one in the small family had ever seen fires such as these, their experience being limited to smouldering turf, and at first they spent full evenings staring, transfixed by the sight of the rabid flame that gobbled dry wood and became ash in the space of an hour. Mary, exasperated by the fire's greed – its need for constant feeding – told her child about turf fires on the island where she was born that had lived, without the aid of a match, for two hundred years. You buried a piece of turf, she said, in the evening ashes and fanned the flame out of it the following morning. It was in those hearths, she maintained, to keep a fire at their centre. But she did not tell him of the cold ash of their last days in Ireland or how, in desperation, she had thrust the grey powder into his mouth and her own.

Winter arrived suddenly and with fierce determination in November before they had learned how to make the fire last the night. Liam woke to a thin covering of ice crystals on his blanket and, not knowing that they had been formed by the moisture in his own breath, he thought that the coverlet itself had begun to freeze and wondered how it kept him warm. Three days later the first of the winter storms plunged down from the north while the boy and his parents huddled, stunned, against the cabin's southmost wall and prayed that the pessimists back in Ireland would not be proved correct in their predictions. When they had survived the second and then the third of these catastrophic occurrences, their terror abated somewhat, though not enough that they went willingly, or often, into a world either darkened by white storm or painfully bright as a result of sharp sun on snow. Winter became a season of waiting, almost of hibernation, the odd neighbour breaking into the trance of the cabin, the calf growing miraculously, near the hearth, to adulthood, its dung burned daily on the hungry fire.

Spring eliminated the visits of the neighbours altogether as the road became a river of mud, caused, first, by an unthinkable quantity of melting snow and then by unceasing rain. When the white flower they called "trillium" blossomed into an unbroken whiteness on the forest floor, Liam thought that winter had returned. He was able to walk about outside, then, and help his father, a little, with the building of a small log barn for the cow, or with the sowing of grain and potatoes until Brian departed for the government work on the roads and Liam was left alone with his mother.

Mary had begun, as before, to stand beside the stream, late in the afternoon, with her arms hanging loosely at her sides, as if she were resting after the completion of a significant gesture, and when the wind came Liam could see the sun burn in the hair bundled at the back of her neck. He loved her fiercely, then, though he knew she was gone from him and that whatever she sought did not concern him. She had spoken of the stream only once in the winter, asking his father if it had been killed outright and whether or not it would be likely to return. He had assured her that it would, that it was alive, even then, several feet under the snow, though the boy noticed that the certainty in his father's voice when telling the names of trees was no longer there.

When the stream did return, it was not at all what the father, the mother, or the child had expected. Swollen to five times its usual size, it hurtled past the acre of light, taking some recently ploughed earth with it. It was dangerous and untouchable and revealed nothing of what lay beneath its surface. It made a sound similar to the waters of the Moyle but unlike anything the family had heard in the new land.

Liam was forbidden to approach the water at this time for fear he would be snatched by the monstrous stream and carried off to somewhere else altogether.

Returning from the roads, Brian shone, brilliant, in the cabin doorway, then moved heavily into the interior across the basswood floor. Over the winter he had made five or six pieces of furniture: three chairs, a table and, as the thaw began, a hooded pine cradle. He touched this lightly in passing, ran his hands over Liam's hair, then approached his wife, who stood beside one of the windows.

"I need a wheel," Mary said, "and some wool. I need some moulds and some wax for candles."

"How are you, Mary," the man asked. "Does it move?"

She stretched and placed her palms against the small of her back. "Yes," she said, "I think I felt it kick."

The boy watched his father look at his mother's belly. Outside, the air erupted into urgent cries as a flock of geese travelled over the trees towards the north.

"Was the work bad?" the mother asked. "Did you go far?"

"The men spoke of starting a school," said Brian. "Three miles to the east on the other side of Queensborough. They are looking for a master."

"What good will Greek or Latin be to the children here?"

"What good were they to the children in Ireland?" Brian was

excited by the possibility of education. "The Greeks," he continued after a moment, "could never provide anything but intellectual food."

Liam thought suddenly of the visit of the man they called the itinerant preacher some weeks back. "I've come to provide some spiritual food!" he had announced at the door. "What?" he had said later, "You are Papists? Well, never mind, it's the same God, the same Christ." There was something, however, that made the boy believe that there were many Gods, and many Christs, and that theirs and the preacher's were not the same at all.

Liam watched the shadows of twigs, just beginning to leaf, move in a startling rectangle of sunlight that lay on the floor between his parents.

"We didn't go far," said Brian. He began to scrape dried mud from one boot with the toe of the other. Clods of it littered the floor at his feet. "Not far at all. Only to the small lake below Madoc. We worked, mostly, on the bridge."

"What lake is that?" Mary asked.

"It was the one we crossed on our way here."

She remembered the bridge from before, when they had first come to the forest, the sound of the wagon wheels on the planks and how she had looked over the edge towards the water, dark beneath a silvered surface. She remembered looking to the left and to the right where the lake blossomed, a mirror image of itself, beyond the pinched narrows that the bridge spanned. "Used to be," the driver had told Brian, "that we'd raft settlers across, and all their belongings and horses and wagons too – before the bridge."

Brian sat down, stretched forward to unlace his boots, then leaned back in his chair, sighing. Even in the interior gloom Liam could see that his father's face had been tanned by the outdoor labour. "Not far," Brian said again, adding that he had seen men in narrow boats on the lake dressed in the skins of animals, their hair long like a woman's. He turned to address his son. "They passed right under the bridge but did not speak to us. And what manner of men, Liam, do you suppose they might be?"

The boy leapt to his feet and ran to his father's side. "Indians!" he shouted, and then asked more quietly, "Were you afraid?"

Brian laughed. "They were as mild as pups . . . but fine-looking. Talking they were, and singing, among themselves."

"Were there women with them," asked Mary. "Or children?"

"No women . . . no babies. The pathmaster said they were a company of hunters from a village of them somewhere at the western end of the lake. They are called Algonquins, or sometimes Ojibway."

"Algonquins," repeated Liam, slowly. "Ojibway."

That night Liam heard his parents talking in bed, his father lamenting the lack of oxen of his own and worrying over the logistics of clearing more acreage. The men, he said, claimed there was a shield of rock six inches under some of the earth here, that a man could do better by burning the trees on his land for potash. Liam wondered if the ash was the same as that which collected under the cooking pots his mother used. Then he heard his mother say hesitantly, "Our stream, does it run to that lake, then?" and his father telling her that it ran to a river called "Black" and that it, in turn, ran to the lake below Madoc.

"The lake," his mother asked, "does it have a name?"

The cabin was dark and outside the night was very still.

Somewhere in the forest an owl asked a persistent question; a familiar sound, now, to the child who knew that no one – nothing – answered.

"Brian," Mary asked again, her words thickening with the suggestion of sleep, "what is the lake called?"

"Moira," he said. "It's Moira Lake."

After this, the silence in the cabin was so prolonged that Liam assumed his parents had gone to sleep, and he closed his eyes and turned on his side towards the wall.

THAT summer, during the final months of her pregnancy, Mary experienced an attack of energy so intense, a surge of such pleasurable strength, that she began to savour industry. Various new tools made their way to their cabin and became intimate companions – extensions of her new, vibrant body. She loved her largeness, her presence filling every space she occupied. Even the forest seemed to be comfortable with her confidence as she strode among its trees or searched the bark of maples for the lungwort that she used instead of yeast to make her bread rise.

The need in her was great to create objects where there were none before; to cause cloth, candle, butter, bread to come into being under her hands. Demanding nails and planks and a hammer from her husband, she passionately banged together shelves and a rough cupboard for her pantry and, beginning with one hen and a rooster, she raised a brood of chickens for whom she constructed a tidy henhouse, making her husband laugh with surprise. She named the fowl after remembered things – Rathlin, Antrim, Moyle, Crannog – and in doing so, destroyed, for a time, the awful power of memory itself. There was no desire in her to make and sing poems, and no wish to stand quietly in the late afternoon searching the stream.

With money from the roads, Brian had been able to pur-chase crocks and sealer jars, cutlery, tools, dishes, farm imple-ments, and finally, for his wife, a wheel and loom. Starting, as they had, with nothing, the two adults were like gods creating a universe. The arrival of a pewter jug or a soup ladle could be an occasion for celebration. Household goods were fondled or stroked like pets, and under such care developed an animate life, a soul.

Once a week, in the late afternoon, while Brian worked outside and the child ran free, Mary heated water over the fire. She poured the liquid into the large wooden tub and removed her clothes in order to bathe. As there were no mirrors in the cabin she had lost the sense of her reflected face, had learned instead, during these afternoons, the skin and bone and muscle of her limbs, the tight drum of her belly. She was delighted by the soft skin of her thighs and the firm curve of her calves. She was powerful and resplendent, the child turning in her womb, the warm fingers of water seeking the hidden corners of her flesh.

Afterwards, she'd take a stool to the front of the cabin and comb out her long, damp hair in the sun. To the child Liam, hidden in the trees, the unbound hair seemed like a river of secret thoughts flowing from his mother's skull. He wanted to touch and become part of it, but he would never approach her at these moments, sensing that his presence would be an intrusion. He held still, kept himself concealed, and gazed from a distance.

As an adult this was how he would remember her; her head unleashing a torrent of fire, her throat exposed to air, her pale hands sailing down the red banner, pulling it apart so that sun and wind could enter it, the wall of forest shimmering with heat and light.

And himself excluded from all the drama that emanated from her.

He would not remember how he had sat on a stump outside the cabin two months later while a forest the colour of his mother's hair was shattered by autumn winds and the sound of her cries filled the air, how he had covered his ears and squeezed his eyes shut, painting a picture of the white house in his mind, its windows and porches, its simplicity, so unlike the exterior of the small, dark cabin.

When the neighbour woman showed him the baby and told him that her name was Eileen, Liam turned away in disgust and demanded his mother so vehemently that he was allowed to enter the cabin where she lay on a rope bed with all her wonderful hair plaited in a thick braid. But when she opened her arms the baby was placed in them and Liam stood apart at the end of the room.

In the weeks that followed, Liam spent the days squatting between the house and the barn, sulking and drawing lines in the dry mud with a stick while inside his mother bent over the baby, the fire, and wept. Her loom was silent, her spinning wheel still, until, one morning, Liam entered the kitchen and saw that there was colour in her face and a brightness in her eyes. She was packing a bread-and-butter basket for his father, who would leave that afternoon with the pathmaster.

Liam wondered whether or not his father might be taking the baby with him on his journey and pictured quiet days spent alone with his mother. But his father laughed and said he had not the equipment with which to feed it and his mother laughed too and embraced him.

That night Liam's mother taught him lullabies, singing them in both Irish and English. "*Dusk is drawn and the green man's thorn is wringed in wreaths of fog,*" they sang together, and "*Slumber from the dark wood comes to hold the world in thrall.*" Then she showed him how to change the soiled cloth that was wrapped between his sister's legs. Shyly Liam told her about the great white house and asked her if she remembered it.

When she said she did not, he announced that one day it would be his and he would bring her with him to live in it.

"And what of your baby sister?" his mother asked. "Will she be invited as well? Will you look after her?"

Liam was silent. He looked at the small fists curled like snails inside the cradle.

"Surely it is in you to look after small Eileen," his mother said softly.

"Yes," he said, wanting to please, "it's in me to look after her." He was basking in his mother's warmth, the feel of her hand on the back of his neck. She rocked the cradle with her left foot but her hand was on the back of his neck and her eyes were on his face.

The next morning, when Liam's dreams were pierced by the infant's voice, he rolled over and looked across the room. His mother's bed was vacant, the coverlet pulled across it smoothly as if she had not slept there the night before or as if no one had ever been there at all.

The day was bright and clear, though the low November sun threw the shadow of the forest wall a great distance until, in the middle of the afternoon, it covered both the barn and the cabin. The boy spent most of the day in the sun, just beyond the house. In these spaces he believed he was still connected with his home – could place his hand on the edge of the shadow of the roof – but was also separate enough to ignore the baby's crying. By the time the sun was blocked entirely by the forest, silence had fallen inside the cabin.

It was in this partial dusk that Liam began to learn his parents as beings detached from him. The small field of winter wheat, the rich, as-yet-unharvested green, which he had helped his father sow, bent in the breeze as if preparing for the scythe. Various implements his father's hands had held were propped against the barn wall, and looking at them the boy remembered how the muscles in the man's back changed when he worked. He tried to imagine the span of time until his father would return, mud from the roads caked on his boots. But because such things as time and work and journeys had always been defined by his mother and father, he was unable to conceive of the length of a week, a month, or even a night.

At first he had not allowed the idea of his mother to enter his mind at all, but, as the day darkened, and the increasing wind set her solitary white apron flapping on a string tied between two saplings, he called her name once and, without waiting for a reply, ran towards the forest and peered into the gloom. Standing entirely still he saw birds dart and chipmunks leap, and when he had remained frozen at attention for some time a female deer sauntered with her fawn across his line of vision not ten yards away. It was not his mother. "I am seven," he whispered, thinking for the first time about his age.

At twilight he turned his back to the eastern trees and walked towards the log structures feeling terribly the chill of the approaching evening. Inside, night had already arrived and Liam had no skills with which to combat it and none to combat the hunger that had, quite suddenly, attacked his belly. Eventually he found a bucket of water near the door and a crust of bread on the table. He ate and drank, warily, uncertain as to whether he might be punished. Then he groped his way through the cabin's objects until he recognized the soft skin of candles, and he held them, one in each hand, for at least an hour, willing them to produce light. The baby had begun to cry again so the boy crawled back and forth across his father's basswood floor until his hand brushed the pointed end of one of the cradle's rockers, and he pumped it fiercely up and down attempting to achieve silence. He heard the thud of the small body hitting the sides of the interior as the wailing increased in intensity. Digging his fists into his ears, he shouted what he could remember of the lullabies his mother taught him, until, magically, a slim bar of light appeared on the table before the window. He staggered across the width of the cabin to the door and out into a world of icy wind and moonlight.

It was then that he saw his mother – or what he would later, in his dreams, call his mother – slipping in and out among the pines on the opposite side of the stream as she had sometimes done in playful moments during their happy summer, making a game of it. Her form appeared and disappeared, multiplied, and then reduced itself. The moon was a huge ball thrown by her into the sky and the boy stretched his arms up towards it glee-fully for a couple of moments before he ran towards her, laughter bubbling out of his lungs and over the dark field of winter wheat. As he approached she withdrew behind the cedars and spruce where thick black erased her. Liam crept away across scrub chalky with moonlight and frost. Humiliated. Then he half-turned and saw the multiple versions of her, straight and thin and white. His blood thundered in his ears at the sight of the many hers – one for him, one for his father, one to silence the baby – and he was running again towards the stream. Dark boughs moved up and down like huge wings across the bodies of these women. Liam stopped short. His vision changed. He ran his hands, in agitation, back and forth across his homespun sleeves. "White birches," he said aloud, using the name his father had taught him, and repeating it, his voice a high song no one heard, "white birches, white birches."

He spent the night underneath the cow. He took one blanket from the cabin, after flinging another hastily over the wailing cradle, covering it completely. Then, frightened of the barely discernible shape it made in the dark, he slammed the door behind him. In the barn the animal's heat drew him to her side. He placed his face against the tough, warm wool until, becoming drowsy, he scrambled down to the straw where he was strangely comforted by the slight shift of a hoof or the involuntary shudder of flank muscles.

During the early, still-dark hours of the morning Liam dreamed the baby had grown to huge proportions, had burst through the cabin walls, its arms and legs flailing in forest and fields, its cry a deafening roar. He opened his eyes and clawed through the dark to the barn doors, swinging them open to a weak, grey dawn, then realized the monstrous sound came from behind him where the cow bellowed in pain in her stall. Relieved, he stumbled back and burrowed into the straw near her front hooves. As she groaned, the faint light from the opened doors revealed a cloud of fog issuing from her mouth and nostrils into the cold air. The child, remembering his mother's cries, the baby's wails, and now hearing this hollering cow, turned in the straw away from the source of the sound and saw the udder stretched tighter than his mother's swollen belly and bluish milk drooling from the end of the teats.

At first, while the cow howled with impatience, Liam held the cylinders of flesh in his two small hands, willing the milk to stream forth as he had seen it do under the attentions of his mother and father. When nothing happened he wrapped his arms around the engorged udder and embraced it until the cow roared in agony and the boy was hurled back onto the straw under the assault of the sound. The animal moaned and then became, for a moment, silent, and Liam was able to hear the faint cry of the baby in the cabin before the cow began again her desperate noise. Lying helplessly in the straw, Liam recalled the frail replica of the cow that his father had sold in town two months before and thought of his own mother's frail replica now singing its hysterical song in the cabin, and he wept into his rumpled sleeve, adding his own voice to the chorus. He was linked by need to this sorrowful orbit of flesh and he shrieked in anger at the unfairness of his own appetite. In fury he searched the barn for an oak bucket which he subsequently flung under the grotesque skin bag. Then, grasping the teats with all the violence of his desertion and desire he crushed the warm flesh in his hands and the liquid gushed into the wooden receptacle.

He was awkwardly moving into what he remembered of adult rhythms, while the cow moaned softly and was comforted.

Liam pushed open the cabin door and stood listening in the half-light, the bucket steaming under his hand. When he heard nothing he dropped it heavily to the floor, spilling some of the liquid and causing the noise to issue again from the cradle. He seized a tin cup from the table, dipped it into the pail, and drank with his back to the howling wooden box. The milk calmed him and eventually he walked to the cradle and threw aside the blanket.

His sister stopped crying and regarded him with clear, green eyes while he recoiled from the stench which rose from the cradle and filled the room. Then, as he withdrew, she began again a sound that reminded Liam of the call of a sheep. The boy collapsed on a stool, put his head in his hands, and shouted the words of a lullaby towards the floor. "Sidhe sail their boats till dawn upon the starry bog!" he yelled.

When her wailing grew louder he dragged the bucket towards the cradle, snatched a spoon from a shelf and, almost gagging because of the smell of urine and faeces, he began, quite gently, to pour milk into the small mouth. Most of the liquid travelled down either side of the baby's face and into the folds at the side of her neck. That which passed her lips caught in her throat and caused her to cough so violently that her face turned red, then purple while her limbs pumped urgently beneath soiled cradle cloths. When the seizure passed, the boy carefully lifted another spoonful from the pail, holding it level, and the baby's tiny lips moved towards it. Liam spent more than an hour bending first towards the pail, then towards the baby, concentrating so fiercely that the world became the circle of the oaken bucket on his left, the rectangle of the pine cradle on his right, and the white oval of the milk-filled spoon floating from one to the other. Then, scrutinizing the small face, he saw that she was asleep.

The cloths of her bed were soggy with spilled milk and urine. The surrounding air was filled with the reek of her. But Liam had achieved silence. He opened the door and listened to the absence of noise from the barn, noticing a cold rain had begun to fall. With distaste but determination he undressed his sleeping sister and threw her putrid garments into a puddle beside the front stoop. He washed her with water from the bucket near the door and set her shrieking once again from the shock of the frigid cloth. He stuffed her arms into a flannel garment he had dug out of a wooden box along with strips of white material, which he tied around her legs and buttocks. She quietened once again.

While he was performing these tasks, his teeth chattering with cold, he remembered a tin box, no larger than an adult's hand, and the thin wooden twigs with coloured heads that filled it, and with this memory came the knowledge of how his mother had produced the heat, the light, the fire.

Three days and nights passed in the company of the cow, the fire, the baby – the waxing and waning of heat and sound and light. Once or twice Liam heard the sound of a wagon rumbling on the rough concession road but, locked within the pattern of his tasks, he did not attempt to intercept it. Once, while he was carrying a bucket of water from the creek, someone he knew galloped by. The man waved and Liam barely returned the greeting, as if fearing that one gesture disconnected from the sphere of labour he had built would break the spell and cause his world to fragment.

On the evening of the third day the baby smiled when he approached her cradle, and he stopped, then, and picked her up, holding her warmth against his chest for a long, long time. She had become his, they would always be connected.

Brian, returning, heard his son's high, thin, singing voice. As he approached the cabin he saw his wife's apron shuddering, like a ghost, a memory, on the string between the trees. He was composing words of praise for the boy but his body was chilled and hollow because he knew, without enquiries, that there was an emptiness about the place. Something had claimed his wife as she had been claimed once before; some other history or geography had taken her away. But this time nothing at all would be left in her place, except two children, one of them unweaned.

Tomorrow Brian would scythe the winter wheat, cutting

down the summer green with the despair of a man who has known hunger and desertion.

Now he would enter the warmth his son had made, and take the young boy's body in his arms.

SOMETIMES when Brian looked around the interior of his cabin he thought he could actually see his wife's absence. The air seemed odourless, empty, and so clear that all the objects she had touched and then abandoned were well-drawn, unbearably distinct, their colours deeper, their edges sharper, so that it was painful for him to look at them. Her goods and her gear, he thought, remembering a song. Then the song itself ran over and over in his mind:

The people they say that no two are well wed,
But one has a sorrow that never was said.
And she smiled as she passed with her goods and her gear,
And that was the last that I saw of my dear.

There were times when, humming this tune – looking at a churn or an apron – he thought he might go mad.

Liam spent some of his time beside white birches, stroking the pale paper skin with his fingers or staring at clusters of the slender trees from a distance, until the snow came to stay and in the white world they were no longer startling enough to hold his attention. His mother's disappearance tied him closer to his father. They shared the loss and a silent agreement that they would never speak about the loss.

With the coming of winter a sad calm fell over the little family, interrupted only once when a well-meaning matron from Madoc arrived in a rattling sleigh with the intention of adopting the baby girl. Liam, sensing the purpose of her visit, crouched by the cradle, growling, and when the woman drew near he lunged and bit her ankle. She departed, then, in great wrath and declared to her friends at church meetings that, like most Irish and all Papists, the boy was mad and dangerous and his father dim-witted and unable to speak. As the sound of the sleigh bells grew fainter and fainter, Liam had sobbed in his father's arms, the baby pressed between their bodies. "She's mine," he whimpered. "She's mine, she's mine!"

~

Four years passed and the world around them opened. The forest parted its dark curtains and allowed the entrance of a few more ragged settlers, who did their best to till the rocky land, and a couple of wild-looking Scandinavian prospectors whose finds led to a scattering of iron and tin mines.

Brian was introduced by one of these men to two thin boards, curved at one end, which could be strapped to a man's boots. On these one could glide over the surface of the snow at great speeds, using a long pole for balance. His first attempts at this method of transportation were disastrous, leaving him trapped face-down in awkward positions in the snow while the prospector bent over with laughter near the barn. When the Finn departed for the foothills of California he left his strange equipment with Brian. "Learn to use them," he said, "and you'll go down in history as the first bog Irishman on skis."

Liam – now eleven – and Brian worked together, taking their grain to O'Hara's Mill at Bridgewater, growing potatoes, corn, barley, oats, and breeding a modest menagerie of animals. A family of Holstein cattle was mothered and grandmothered by the cow Liam had called Moon in memory of the night he had spent with her, the ball he had seen in the sky, and the white circle of redemptive milk which had filled the oaken bucket.

His father named the first-born bull McGee, after the editor of a newspaper called the *American Celt* that he was sometimes able to get his hands on at the mill when O'Hara had finished reading it. This man McGee is a poet, Brian would tell his son on winter evenings, and a great believer in the music and literature of Ireland. He is a wonderful champion of our people here on the other side, and younger than I can ever remember being. He gave a lecture tour throughout Upper Canada. He's a man, Brian asserted, that any Irish man, woman, or child should want to listen to. He understands the injustice, he said, the terrible black heart of it.

Liam paid him no mind. He was more interested in seed catalogues. He wanted to make everything he could grow out of the ground. He was only a boy but rumours had already reached him of farms with vast, lush acreages. Some day he would grow sugar cane and pineapples. All he remembered of Ireland was a flat stone beyond the threshold of a door, the rest of the past had fallen away.

The first time Brian had applied to the Board of Examiners at Madoc, offering his services as a teacher, he was refused. Claiming that they objected to his lack of formal training, and the distance he would have to walk from his farm to the nearest schoolhouse, this group of Methodist men, many of whom were in the process of founding Orange lodges in their various villages, were in fact suspicious of Brian's Irish background in general and his loose association with the "Popish church" in particular, and not a little put off by the large store of knowledge he insisted on displaying during the interview. After a few years, however, when the tiny log school on Concession Road

Five remained untenanted, they overlooked their secret Orange Oath to stamp out all those of Papist inclination, and offered Brian twenty pounds a year to instruct between fifteen and twenty students, many of whom were of Irish parentage themselves. Liam did not attend the school. He was left at home to take care of small Eileen and the animals while each day his father walked or travelled on skis the four miles there and four miles back.

Brian had been especially moved by the schoolhouse the first time he inspected it. Everything in it and around it – from the log frame to the benches for students and the master's desk and chair – had been hand hewn by the earliest settlers twenty years before. It was neither made of wattle nor concealed by hedges, but it was kin to the forest that surrounded it. And its existence and survival seemed so unlikely and against the odds that, in spirit, it reminded Brian of the little, desperate academy that he had kept in Ireland. He decided he would teach some of the Irish language to his students, until the school inspector insisted that he stop. Liam was taught at home and he, in turn, instructed Eileen. This system operated so well that Liam was advanced in the classics at eleven and she, whom they called the baby, could read and write by the age of four.

Brian's loneliness for his wife was most acute in the evenings, though assuaged somewhat by the presence of the children. But, now and then, when he saw Eileen's cloud of red hair glowing in the firelight or noticed a distant look in her green eyes, he experienced a chill of recognition and wondered if it were wise to tell the stories of the old sorrows deep in this forest so far from home. But because of his belief in the influence of landscape, he hoped that the tales were as divested of power, far from their native soil, as the German and French and Danish fairy tales that the children at his school were beginning to learn in their Upper Canadian Readers.

The road that passed in front of the acre of light – which had, itself, become several acres of light – was becoming the site of a capricious and irregular parade, sometimes consisting of one or two appearances a day, sometimes allowing a week to pass before another spectacle revealed itself. Tinkers, peddlars, cobblers, mail coaches, circuit riders, and travelling medicine shows, all moved along its surface. Once, a small disoriented circus appeared, seeking its next engagement at Tweed. The ringmaster was horrified to discover that he was heading northeast instead of southwest and cursed so loudly and so eloquently that Liam decided the man must be a poet and an orator like the man McGee whom his father went on and on about. The resident parrot of this company, which the boy was told had originally belonged to a pirate, chanted "bones and blood, bones and blood," as the troupe and its vehicles drew itself together, turned, and lurched away. When he had expressed his amazement, Eileen had simply looked at her brother and said, "Birds can talk the same as you and me."

In winter, after the ground solidified, visions sped past so quickly that Liam hardly had time to register the sound of bells and run to the window before the excitement had disappeared on steel runners. Sometimes he saw only an icy fog, composed of the breath of humans and animals and cast over the dark glimpsed shape of something he was never quick enough to interpret. And sometimes, when he was certain that he had heard bells, absolutely nothing at all could be seen beyond the white wall of snow created by the wind between the cabin and the road.

On an icy morning in February, before light, Liam's seven-year-old sister woke him to tell him of a dream. While their father banged the stove lid and nudged the fire back towards flame, she spoke of a dark bird and waves frozen near a long stretch of beach.

"But you've never seen a beach," said Liam sleepily. "You've never seen a wave."

"And the bird talked," she said, ignoring his interruption, "and wore a top hat and smoked a pipe."

"There's a story like that in the reader."

"No there isn't. The bird flew to my shoulder and said things . . . but I don't remember."

"Get yourself dressed. You'll catch cold." Liam himself had been dreaming of a woman, and being fourteen, he wanted to go back to sleep to find out what was under the blouse she had begun to unbutton.

"No, I do remember," announced his sister. "No, I guess I don't. But he's coming here."

"Who is coming here?"

Eileen looked at him with impatience. "The bird, the black bird," she said.

"McGee says here," said Brian, reading a year-old newspaper called the *New Era* and dropping it page by page into the flames, "that Orangeism is a threat to *all* Canadians."

The frost on both the old window and the newer, larger one was turning faintly red. "It's going to be a fine, clear day," said Brian, straightening after his attentions to the stove and stretching his arms out so that they were level with his shoulders.

"He's coming here," said Eileen, "and he's bringing something with him for me."

"You should spend some time with Moon today," said Brian to his son, "and read some Latin to her. She always enjoys Latin when she is pregnant. Some Ovid, I should think, would be best."

"She'll calf soon now." Liam sat upright and shivered. "Jesus, it's cold."

"No swearing," said his father. And then, "It will be at least a month yet."

Eileen ran barefoot in her white nightgown to her father's side. "He said that it's for you, too, and for Liam."

"What is?" Brian asked.

"Whatever he brings when he comes."

"Who? Eileen, dress yourself this instant."

The small girl walked across the cabin to the window and breathed an oval landscape onto the glass. "It's shining," she said. "All of the ground is shining. I'll never catch cold because I was born here and I love the snow."

Brian selected three or four books from the shelf and bound them together with a leather strap. Among them was the geography book that had so delighted his wife. For the first time in several years her face came into his mind as he handled the faded brown volume, just as if he had seen her an hour before. He unbuckled the strap and removed the book, placing it on the right-hand corner of the table. "Teach Eileen some geography today," he said to Liam. "Something warm . . . Asia."

"Asia," repeated Eileen, liking the sound of the word. "Asia, Asia. When I have a little girl I will call her Asia." She turned away from the glass, and the steam from the cast-iron kettle boiling on the stove immediately obliterated the miniature window she had made there.

"He hasn't come, yet," she said, rummaging through the pine blanket box, looking for her woollen stockings. "There are no birds out there at all."

As his father predicted, the day was bright and clear and windless, and this caused the pageant on the road to thicken and become more colourful. Sleighs full of everything imaginable passed at intervals by the cabin, this being the ideal weather for transportation. In the space of two morning hours Liam had watched sail past his door cupboards, cookstoves, pigs, grandfather clocks, a collection of yapping hounds, an outhouse, stacked cages full of white geese, and a team of fine horses pulling a sledge while their owner sat, perched on a round stool, playing beautiful music on an upright piano. Then a group of French and Finnish loggers skied by, singing loudly, and heading in the direction of Madoc. None of this could lure Eileen from the new window where she could see the forest and the place where the stream lay hidden under the snow. No amount of coaxing or threatening could lead her from this window and into the realms of geography. Finally, Liam, exasperated, wrapped himself up in several layers of wool and left the cabin for the barn in order to read to the cow.

He and Moon were lost in the enjoyment of the *Metamorphoses* when Eileen, covered only by a thin shawl, flew through the barn door and announced, "He's coming now, so you'd better come with me."

"*Who's* coming?"

"The black bird! He'll be out of the forest soon."

Liam sighed, marked his place in the book with a piece of straw, ran his hand affectionately across Moon's swollen side, rose, and took his sister's outstretched hand.

She led him to the cabin's back stoop and they both looked

between the two young maple trees that had once been saplings holding a rope and an apron, out towards the darkness of the forest, squinting in the intense light. Liam shifted his boots in the snow. "Eileen," he said softly, after a few moments. "Eileen, there are no birds here."

"Just *wait*."

"I'll wait until one hundred. I'll start counting now."

At forty-one, Liam saw a group of men emerge from the woods at the place where the hidden stream bent towards the field. Six men were carrying what appeared to be cedar boughs on their shoulders. Another, who walked in front of the others, was wearing a top hat and smoking a pipe.

He was no longer a young man, and because of this his face was lined and in some spots furrowed. He was tall and straight, however, and the two braids that hung from his top hat were coal black and shining. The cut of his coat was exactly like that of an English gentleman, but made of buckskin, and beautifully, though not extensively, decorated with beads. The same material covered his legs and feet. His hands, even in these frigid temperatures, were bare.

As he approached the cabin with his entourage he removed a gold pocket-watch from his waistcoat, looked at it for a moment, then snapped the case shut. "We have arrived," he shouted at the amazed children, "exactly at noon, and that is good."

As he got nearer, Liam could see the crow feathers that stood like smoke-blackened toy soldiers all around his hat band.

"That is good," repeated the man's followers.

He walked up to the children and solemnly and formally shook their hands in turn, but he kept his gaze focused on Eileen. "Another one," he whispered. Then, without turning around, he addressed the six men. "Put her down," he said, "so the children can see."

The burden of boughs was lowered to the ground and there lay the beautiful, pale, frozen woman. Like the tall man she was dressed entirely in buckskin, though her jacket was lacking the ornamental beadwork and her hair was loose, framing her white face with a cloud of fire. Frost had collected on the edges of this cloud, in the wisps of curls that adorned her forehead, and on her eyebrows and eyelashes, and this had the effect of making her appear to be almost translucent beside the dark branches of the cedar boughs that had supported her. The skin on her face and neck and her bare hands was so perfect, so unblemished, it might have been created more recently than Eileen's. Her lips were frozen into the shape of a faint smile.

After he had looked down at the woman for a few moments the tall man with the crow feathers in his hat sat abruptly down on the back stoop, and his companions walked back to the forest and disappeared from sight. The children had not uttered a word, had not made a sound.

The odd trio that was left behind stood now with their heads bent, looking towards the frozen woman. Their motionlessness was so complete that, were it not for the steam that unfurled from their mouths and nostrils, they might have appeared to have been frozen themselves. Nothing around them moved – no bough on tree nor cloud in wind nor rabbit pumping over snow. The road was empty. A long silver tooth hung from the waterspout over the rainbarrel. Moon was quiet in her stall, as were all of her relations in theirs. Roosting hens fell asleep, their feathers unruffled. It was the dead of winter. Nothing in the deep earth had begun to pulse towards light, no sap ran and hibernating animals, curled in their burrows, drew breath at infrequent intervals. So fixed was the whole atmosphere, not a red-gold hair on the head of the beautiful frozen woman or the slender child quivered. The boy's hands, which were normally never still, hung wooden and static at the ends of his sleeves. The man's briar pipe no longer smoked.

It was into this tableaux that Brian, having set his pupils free to enjoy the fine winter day, glided on his skis, singing.

"Look Papa," said Eileen as he swept towards her. "Look, it's a big doll."

With Brian's arrival the world unlocked. A frigid breeze blew a veil of powdery snow across the face of the dead woman. Brian sat down on the back stoop. He looked towards the forest and then began to weep. Eileen, terrified by her father's outburst, kept repeating, "It's a doll. It's a doll." Liam stuffed his hands in his trouser pockets and walked off angrily to join Moon in the barn, where he read the *Metamorphoses* aloud in a passionate voice for the remainder of the afternoon.

Brian tried several times to persuade his son to come into the house but his words were drowned in a slew of Latin phrases. Even Eileen was unable to move him. At sunset the barn door creaked open and Liam, without looking up, recognized the smell of pipe tobacco and saw, on the straw beside him, the shadow of the feathered top hat.

Liam continued with the Latin but the shadow did not move. Finally he closed the book and turned to face the visitor.

"My name is Exodus Crow," the man announced in a strong, clear voice. "The crow was my father's spirit-guide and, in time, became mine. He is a wise bird who survives hardships and who loves that which shines. He is a bird with a strong voice who insists on being heard. Because he sits high on the top branch of the tallest tree in the forest, and flies even higher than that, he can see many things at once and so is a good guide. Because he flies fast and calls loudly he is a good messenger.

"I am called Exodus because my mother, who was taught to read by a churchman, lost interest in the Bible halfway through the Book of Exodus. She loved the name Exodus and was doubly disappointed therefore in this book. Genesis, she said, was full of many stories: the man with the boat full of animals, the woman whom Snake made bite the apple, and many dreams and vision quests. There is a great deal of manitou in this book called Genesis. This book called Exodus, she said, was not worthy of its name because it was filled with battles for land and the making of laws. And the Great Spirit changes after this first book from making animals and trees and rocks and flowers and dreams and visions to making battles for land and sending down laws. My mother did not like this but she liked the sound of the word Exodus and wanted to give the name a better home. She called me Exodus."

Silence filled the barn after this series of sentences. Liam pretended to study the cover of the closed book on his lap but Moon twisted her great neck and looked with her liquid eyes at the figure in the doorway.

This seemed to encourage the tall man to enter a little further into the barn and to resume his speech.

"My mother, who is dead, believed in the manitou that is a part of everything," he said. "Your mother was filled with this manitou. Now she is dead as well. But before she died she told me to go to her children and tell them her story, for they were small, she said, when she was forced to leave them. Her story will move through me as easily as a wind through the pines of the forest. Like Crow I will be heard. Your sister wants to hear the story, your father wants to hear the story. But you, who will move forward and make the change, *must* hear the story. And yet, by your silence you are telling me that you do not wish to hear it."

Liam still said nothing.

"I will tell the story to the whole family. If you were one of my sons you would go into the forest now for a long, long time to find out who your spirit-guide is. And when you knew that, and when you had lived with this silence of yours in the woods for a long, long time, you would be a man. But you are not one of my sons and you are not of my people. If you hear your mother's story it will be the same as seven long days and nights in the forest alone, you will be cold and afraid, but when you have heard her story it will be as if you had reached out and touched your own adulthood."

Moon dipped her large head and began to chew thoughtfully on some straw. Liam saw the calf shudder inside her body.

"I am thinking," said Exodus, "that this cow has much manitou. That is the spirit that is everywhere and that we, the Nishnawbe, believe in."

Exodus closed the bottom half of the door quietly behind him and left Liam bisected by its shadow. The boy resumed his Latin-reading to the cow, but he was having more and more trouble turning the pages. His hands were blue with cold, and, besides, he couldn't shake the feeling that Moon was no longer listening.

Their shared grief on the back stoop had created an immediate bond of trust between Brian and Exodus Crow, and when they had finished weeping the Irishman had opened the door of his cabin with genuine welcome. He knew that Exodus held the mysterious narrative of the past seven years in his mind, and that the tall, dignified man had brought the frozen woman home, not just to return her remains, but also to tell her story.

But, so far, the Ojibway had revealed only three things: that he, his friends, and their burden had left Moira Lake one and a half days before, that they had walked on the ice of first the Black River, then one of its tributaries, and that he was sorrowful because the woman had been a friend to him.

When the boy entered the cabin both men were devouring pea soup and large chunks of bread. His father motioned for him to join them but he shook his head and walked to the far corner of the room, behind them, where they could not see his face. The sound of the liquid entering the men's mouths sickened him. They had betrayed his mother with their hunger. She was abandoned, lying in the snow, while they built fires, enjoyed food and warmth, and erased the sight of her by staying behind a dark log wall. He wanted his father's grief to dramatize itself, there, in the room, wanted the words of his own anger to pass his father's lips.

"I will build a box for her," Liam said, at last, his words a challenge.

His father did not reply but Exodus turned fully around in his chair to address the boy. "It's good that you said that," he murmured. "It's good that you spoke because now I can tell you about your mother."

Exodus, returning after an autumn hunt with a sledge piled high with deer and rabbit, had first seen the woman in the woods on the northwest shore of Chuncall Lake, which was now called Moira. It was not a lake in which people fished because a great number of Iroquois had been slaughtered nearby and their bodies thrown into the lake, producing, it was rumoured, flesh-eating fish so fierce that they ripped out the throats of those who attempted to capture them.

"This is not really so," said Exodus, "as I, myself, have passed many times over this lake in a canoe and have seen the peaceful fish gliding below the surface. Nevertheless, it is the custom to fish elsewhere."

He had seen her because of the sun on her copper hair and had almost taken her to be a deer or some other animal, so odd had been this colour. But then he saw her brown skirt move in the woods and her white face; these things and also her green eyes which looked at him through the trees. What was a white woman doing in the forest with the first coat of snow on the ground? Was she, he wondered, a ghost? Then he remembered that white ghosts stayed in the houses they had built and never in the woods which, it was said, they feared.

She came towards him and with gestures of her hands made it clear that she was hungry and wanted food. By this time Exodus had seen that she had made a small hut of sticks and pine boughs, outside of which there were the remains of a fire and some fish bones and fish heads. It was as though she had been on a vision quest and had just, the previous day, broken her fast. Evidently she did not fear the fish of the lake and had somehow managed to catch them.

Exodus indicated to her that he could speak English. "How are you?" he had asked.

"I am fine," she had replied, "but hungry."

"Where do you live?" Exodus wanted to know.

"I live here," she said, and with such certainty that Exodus had to remind himself that this could not be true.

He built a fire then and cut some meat from a carcass on the sledge and began to cook some food for her. She did not speak while he was performing these tasks but watched him so closely that Exodus knew that every move he made was being memorized. He was studying her boots, which he concluded would never get her through the winter. At one moment, while he knelt over sticks and flame, the wind blew her skirt to one side exposing one alabaster leg, so soft and smooth that Exodus knew that she had not been in the woods for very long.

They ate in silence, the woman squatting by the fire and Exodus sitting across from her. When she was finished she sighed and folded her legs under her body, sitting back on her heels with her hands clasped together on her lap.

Then Exodus asked, gesturing towards the fish bones, "If you were able to catch fish and you were hungry, why did you not catch more?"

"Because, yesterday morning when I went to the lake it was covered by an icy shield."

Exodus laughed, as much because of the strange lilt in her voice as because of what she was saying. "But you must make a hole in this shield," he said. "Then the fish will come."

"Then they are not killed by this ice?"

"No, even later, when it is very thick, they are not killed."

Exodus was uncertain how to discover where it was she had come from and uncertain also of how to persuade her to return. Finally, he determined to ask her directly if she had always lived in the forest.

She told him then about her troubled country and how she had lived on a small island across the waters of the Moyle two miles off its shore. She told him about the Children of Lir who had lived for three hundred years on the waters of the Moyle, and how they had lived there as swans. She told him about Grey Man's Path down to the water, about the beautiful woman who had danced over the cliffs and whose long hair floating near the rocks that killed her had given the name Fair Head to the point of land near where she fell. She told him about Finn Mac Cumhail and the Fianna, about Finn's great dog Bran, and about the poet Oisín who had disappeared into Tír na nÓg, the land of the young, and who had returned centuries later to argue for the old ways and the old beliefs with he whom Oisín called Patrick of the Crooked Crozier. She told him of "the others," those who lived under the ground and those who lived under the water, and how they were around always and in everything and how they made the most beautiful music – a music so sweet and so sad that once it was heard it was never forgotten. She said that on her island there was no man and no woman who was not somehow haunted by it.

When she stopped she had been talking for a long, long time and she looked at Exodus almost as if she were surprised to see him there and asked "Do you believe me?"

Exodus *did* believe because, he said, it was as if his own mother were telling the stories of the spirits.

He believed her so completely that for the first time he felt there might be some wisdom in the white people beyond what they preached from the Book of Exodus, and he knew, as he had said to Liam, that this woman was blessed with manitou, and because of what she had told him he felt a great kinship with her.

So he told her about the manitou – the spirit that is in everything and that is moved by earth and air and water and light. And he said that her hair contained the light of the rising and the setting sun and by that she was blessed. He said that there were sky worlds and cloud worlds and water worlds, and spirits that live in them that were friends to men and women and upon whom men and women must rely for the food that grows out of the ground and for success in the hunt. And then he, Exodus, looked at the woman and asked if she believed him and she said that, yes, she believed him.

Exodus said that he knew then that belief was everywhere in the forest around them and in the lake whose covering of ice shone through the trees and in the clouds and in the wind that brushed the boughs of the pines. So he told the woman of the first missionary who had visited his grandfather, and how this missionary had spoken of Moses and God and Jesus. His grandfather had listened and had believed what the missionary said. But when his grandfather told the missionary about the spirits that surrounded and protected his tribe the white man had scoffed at him.

"I believe you," the grandfather of Exodus had said. "Why don't you believe me?"

Exodus knew that the woman understood him and that he understood the woman, but he wondered about her survival in the woods.

"How long have you lived here?" he had asked.

"Three days."

"And you will return now to your house?"

"No, I cannot return."

"But the winter will worsen."

"I cannot return."

But the woman read the questions in his mind, drew a long breath, and answered.

"I am loved by the spirit of this lake," she said, "this lake that shares my name – Moira. This spirit first found me when he lived under the waters of the Moyle, which I told you about. Then when I lived on the large island he came to me in a dark lake near my home. In this land I thought he had forgotten me until I heard of the lake called Moira. Then I knew where he was. I will stay near him now until I die. I am loved by him and he is loved by me."

Exodus Crow had kept silent. He felt that the ears of the forest were opening wider, listening. The sun had moved behind a cloud and the lake was a grey blanket on the other side of the trees.

"Do you believe me?" the woman had asked him. And when

he remained silent she said, "I believed you – why don't you believe me?"

"Her eyes," Exodus said, now, to Brian, "glittered a little with amusement when she asked this."

Brian's own eyes were shining with tears but he nodded, remembering his wife's sudden, delicate displays of humour.

"I finally answered her," said Exodus Crow. "I said that I believed her, because I did."

Brian began to move around the cabin lighting lamp after lamp, pulling lanterns and candles out of cupboards and down from shelves and lighting them too. He wanted a sudden brilliance to fill the room, to clarify what the tall man was telling him. "But I am her husband," he said, a taper burning in his hand.

Exodus agreed that this was the case and that the two children, who had pulled their chairs close to the table, were her children. "And they still are," he said. "In this world. She was from an island in the other world. And I was her friend. The one from the water was not *of* this world. He was her spirit-guide."

"I taught her to read." Brian looked instinctively towards a pile of books at the other end of the table.

"I know, and you taught her about distant lands. She told me. And she told me that you knew that she had been, as they say on the island you came from, 'away.' But because you did not believe this, you could not see when she went away again."

"To live in the lake," said Eileen.

"To live beside the lake," corrected Exodus. "Perhaps now she lives in the lake."

Brian lit the last coal-oil lamp. "Had she chosen to come

182

back . . . I loved her." He paused. "But she didn't come back," he said.

"There is this fierce love in all of us for that which we cannot fully own," said Exodus.

The interior of the cabin was so bright now that Eileen's eyelashes shone and several miniature candles were visible, reflected in her eyes. Beyond the walls, the light from the cabin windows moved across the snow, onto the face of the frozen woman. Then, as the night grew more agitated, and as snow lifted from the ground like large skeins of silk, her face darkened, and shone, like a beacon on a distant shore.

"The whole world is an island," said Exodus, "and all who live in it are island dwellers – walkers on surfaces, floaters on water, standers on mountains. No one is ever *in* anything until they have been touched by what she was touched by."

"I wanted to be a poet," said Brian, "but there was nothing in it, my poetry."

"She had songs that she had made for the water-spirit from the otherworld island and they were pleasing," Exodus addressed Liam, now, respectfully, as if he were a man of the same age. "She sang them with a good voice."

"I haven't heard my wife's voice for seven years. Why didn't you make her come back?"

Exodus turned to Brian. "After I had seen her the first time I dreamt I saw a golden fish who sang in words I did not recognize and I knew what I should do. I should help this woman to stay near her spirit and to live there in the forest. And when I told the others they agreed that that was what I should do. But to live near the spirit I knew the woman would have to learn concealment, accuracy, and endurance. I would build strong shelters so that she would be able to withstand the winters, and bring firewood for her comfort. I would bring her deer meat and teach her how to boil the sap in April for the sugar that can be got from it. I showed her how to make tea from the young shoots of the hemlock, and she liked this. And I showed her how to sew together the skins I brought so that she might have clothing to cover her."

Brian said nothing. Liam had partially relaxed and was now slumped in an arrow-back chair, fingering a crust of bread that lay before him on the table.

Exodus Crow had more to say. Clearing his throat he began again. "When she had been in the woods for more than one winter she told me of the woman called Deirdre who had lived happily in the forest with three warrior brothers, one of whom she loved, until a bad king had killed them, and how she had died of sorrow."

And later she had told Exodus that she knew, now, why Deirdre had loved the forest for living in it, as she, herself, had, and learning it well, the branch of one tree could gladden her heart. After she had been in the forest for several winters she told him dark things; about the time of the stolen lands of her island, and of the disease, and of the lost language and the empty villages and how the people who once sang were now silent, how the people who once danced were now still.

"It is true," said Brian bitterly. "Those who haven't died are scattered, and their voice is broken, their words are gone."

"She told me a frightening thing," said Exodus after several moments of quietness. "She told me that on the big island there were once forests as thick as those here in this land but that the old kings and lords of England had cut down each tree until only bare hills were left behind."

"That is true also," said Brian.

Exodus leaned across the table and looked steadily at the Irishman. "And so I told her," he said, "that some white men had seized my people's land and killed many animals for sport and abused our women."

The hands of the two men lay flat upon the table but their eyes never left the other's face. "What did she say then?" asked Brian.

When Exodus replied there was a break in his voice. "She embraced me and said that the same trouble stayed in the hearts of both our peoples."

When the next day the men and the boy prepared Mary's grave, they found that she had been blanketed during the night by snow.

"We should find a hollow log and some more cedar boughs," said Exodus.

Liam was watching his sister who lay thrashing on the ground making snow angels. "I want to make a box," he said.

"We will not be able to enter the ground far enough for one of your boxes."

"I will make a thin box," said Liam with such intensity and anger that the men decided to let him proceed, and moved to their own tasks.

Liam worked in the carpentry shed that he and his father had built on the side of the barn, the smell of the cows seeping through the wall. While he hammered nails into pine he visualized his mother's walk down the creek to the river that ran to Moira Lake, running the narrative against his own struggles with Moon and the baby. He took what he knew of the banks of the small stream and added the farms of the settlers he was acquainted with and those he had heard about – one or two villages such as Bridgewater and Hazard's Corners – and with his mind caused both the stream and his mother to wander through them. He placed tracts of impenetrable wilderness between these pockets of civilization so that her journey away from him would be difficult; in places, barely manageable. He invented huge fallen trees that blocked the way and boggy areas that slowed her footsteps. Sometimes he stood still with a nail in his teeth and the hammer hanging, forgotten, from his fist, while his mind travelled the creek and then the river; the stones and boulders, the frills of the rapids, the hard rock bed of it.

Occasionally, in his mind, he made his mother fall awkwardly to the ground and push herself slowly to her feet, twisting her neck and looking back to the place where she had left her children. She was staggering along the dark ribbon of water that threaded itself through forests and swamps. At any point she might have paused – when adjusting one of her boots, for instance, or when she looked at her own face when drinking from the inky river. She might have changed her mind and made this walk a return to him rather than a desertion, for until she reached the lake she would have still been his mother. He was certain of this. But try as he might to force his mind to lope downstream, to watch her approach rather than withdraw, he could see her only in profile, or with her back turned against him. He laid down the hammer and pounded his fist against the wall of the shed until slivers entered the soft flesh of his hand.

By the time he had thumped the last nail into the shallow, slim box, his mother was a silhouette standing on the shore of a shining expanse of water; one of several trees rooted in an alien landscape. Sap was running through her veins, the blood that she shared with Liam forgotten in favour of a view of a lake.

It pleased him to know she would be buried inland.

As the men bent forward to lift the woman into the box that Liam had made, Eileen came swiftly from behind them and thrust her child's body between her father and Exodus. Then, sinking to her knees, she moved her small hands through the folds of her mother's soft buckskin clothing until, from a pocket on the left of the breast, she removed a braided circle of red and black hair.

"This is mine," she announced with satisfaction. Then, running away towards the house, she called over her shoulder "It's for me!"

The men exchanged puzzled looks but did not speak of the incident.

They dug a plot beside the creek the woman had followed, attacking the ground with pickaxes, Liam working with more passion and energy than the two adults. They covered the spot with logs and boulders so that animals would not disturb the grave, Exodus chanting words in his native tongue, Brian saying the rosary in Latin.

Liam stood apart from them, staring upstream away from the direction his mother had taken. He could see neither the water, which was buried under snow, nor the ice which he knew covered the water, but the stream-bed to the north made a slender road through the forest; a neutral road, in that he knew his mother had not walked that way.

The pickaxe he had flung to the ground when the work was

finished, half of which was buried in a drift, became an exaggerated question mark in the snow. Everyone's footsteps were visible everywhere, as if there had been a great crowd assembled for the woman's funeral. Instinctively, however, no one had trod upon Eileen's snow angels which looked, now, to her brother, like the remnants of sad, inexplicable skirmishes that had taken place in the yard between the house and the barn.

Brian was describing the construction of the long, pine table to Exodus. How he, himself, had seen the single board it was made from out at the sawmill at Queensborough. The huge tree trunk, he said, sliced like bread. And now there was this essential piece of furniture. Manufacturing, he announced, was flourishing in both Elzivir and Madoc townships. He chanted a list of new enterprises. "Sam Rawlin's Tannery, Pringle's Brickyard," he said aloud and with some pride.

His guest listened politely, and, after Brian was finished, he said, "I wore this hat and brought this pocket-watch to have a connection with the people that she came from. It is not the custom of my people."

"No, no of course not," said Brian, suddenly embarrassed, his mind full of bricks and boards and machines.

"Do they put boards on the ground in Ireland?" he asked. "Do they have floors?"

"Sometimes . . . but often it's only earth for the floor and straw for the roof."

"So I thought," said Exodus. "She did not seem disturbed by the earth for a floor."

Liam entered the cabin, glanced at the men, and threw a load of firewood noisily to the left of the door. Then, aware that he had the men's attention, he walked away from them to the farthest corner of the room.

"We're low on kindling," said Brian. "The lamps need filling. And what's the news of Moon?"

Liam did not answer.

"She's a wonderful cow," said Brian to Exodus. "She's been with us almost from the beginning. Liam, here, is her favourite. I think they talk to each other. Does she talk to you, son?"

Liam rose up impatiently and approached his father. "When is he leaving?" he demanded. "He's been here for days now, when's he going?"

Eileen, who had been playing with three cornhusk dolls near the fire, said, "He's not going yet."

Turning abruptly in his chair, which made a shrieking noise on the basswood planks, Brian shot an angry look at his son. "That's about enough," he said. "I'll not have you –"

"Wait," Exodus interjected. "The small girl is right. I'm not leaving yet." The room around him held still as the tall man rose to his feet. He crossed the floor to the corner where the boy had retreated and where he now sat with his long legs bent over a squat barrel. "I'm not leaving yet," he said. "Because of you."

The boy flung a lock of hair angrily from his forehead and then glared down towards his shoes. A thin film of perspiration had collected on the sparse, fine hairs on his upper lip. His Adam's apple moved awkwardly up and down his throat. "Don't stay on my account," he hissed. "There's no need to stay on my account."

"Look, Papa," piped Eileen, "the sun this early in the morning."

"There is a need," said Exodus to the boy.

"And what's that, then?" Liam's skull lurched on his neck

189

as he, once again, flung the hair from his eyes. The gesture was that of someone involved in physical combat with the invisible.

"I haven't given you your mother back," said Exodus, "and I can't leave until I do."

"She's dead," blurted Liam bitterly. "She's out there under the ground."

"That's not what I mean."

"What *do* you mean?"

Exodus was quiet. Then he said, "I will go out of this house now and when I come back I will know. I will tell you then what I mean."

"He's a kind man," said Brian, after the cabin door closed.

Liam said nothing.

"It's not necessary for you to be rude to him."

"How long are you going to let him stay?"

"As long as he wishes. He was your mother's friend."

Liam laughed. "If he was her friend why didn't he bring her back years ago? Why did he let her freeze to death? Why did he let her live out there like a savage?"

"She wouldn't have come."

"How do you know?"

"I know."

"She was your wife. She belonged to you."

"She was my wife, but she did not belong to me."

"Who did she belong to then? Do you believe in this spirit?" Liam had risen to his feet to ask this question. "Do you?" he demanded. "Do you believe in this fairy tale?"

"I didn't used to."

"So, do you believe in it now? Have you gone mad?"

But Brian did not answer, just shouldered his skis and set out, as he had done most every day for the last several years, to teach the children at the small log school.

Liam returned to his seat on the barrel and Eileen brought two of her cornhusk dolls to the place where he was sitting and put one on each knee of his old grey trousers. "Yes, he believes it," she made one of the dolls say to the other. The toys appeared to leap and twist when she made them speak. "He believes it," the second doll said, "because it is true." Liam watched the dry corn leaves, the skirts of the dolls quiver just above his knee.

Later in the afternoon, as Liam crossed the space between the house and the barn, he saw Exodus sitting in the groin of the willow tree that grew on the other side of the creek. His back was turned and Liam was glad of this as he did not wish to be observed by anyone as he walked across the snow which still had Eileen's angels and the men's footprints pressed into it; these things and the oblong shape of the litter that had held his mother's body.

It was now that time, which comes on certain winter days, when a cloud-covered sky looks no different from the frozen earth beneath it, when branches of trees could be roots thrusting into an opaque earth. There would be no moon, no stars tonight. His father, Liam knew, would glide into sight on the edge of a darkness that would follow him down the road between the trees, waiting to settle over the house until the moment he closed the door and laid his books upon the table.

The boy found Moon agitated, banging her hips against the boards of her stall, collapsing onto the straw, then rising again, awkward and groaning, to her feet. When she saw him she arched her back and lifted her tail as if she wanted to urinate, then she rotated her large head on her great neck and cried out in a voice so human Liam had to force himself not to turn away.

His father, he thought. Where was his father? Moon had always calved at night in the company of Brian, her bellowing touching the children's dreams, causing them to stir and whimper but never waking them. Suddenly a picture of his father came into Liam's mind, wrestling by lamplight with this beast who resembled so little the serene animal at whose side the boy had grown. "Jesus," the boy said under his breath as the cow sank to her knees then rose again, pounding the left side of her ribs against rough pine planks.

The cow crashed onto the straw, where she lay on her side, her body swollen, the steam of her breath causing a veil of mist to obscure her contorted features.

Black and white, thought Liam mindlessly. This cow is so black and white. Nothing should be this black and white.

Just as he finished the thought, a river of clear liquid surged out from under the cow's tail and onto the straw, freezing there on contact. A shadow interrupted the light from the door – Eileen's white face. Moon's eyes rolled back into her head. When Liam turned again, the child was gone.

By now he could see the white membrane of the birth sac emerging between the calf's back legs, and two grey blocks floating inside it. Hoofs, he thought. A contraction moved through the animal's abdomen and she groaned and panted. "Please hurry . . . please," Liam whispered, fighting back the nausea that was rising to his throat. "Please, Moon, make the baby." But the sac slid no further from the body of the cow, who now breathed as if she were speaking. "Awl, awl, awl," she seemed to say.

Liam began to concentrate, helplessly, on the head of a nail that projected from the barn wall. Why was it there, what normally hung from it? Who had taken the hammer in one hand and this ridiculous, insignificant piece of iron in the other? He would ask his father why this particular nail was here? It irritated and confused him and he flicked at it with his fingernail. Then, as Exodus exploded through the doorway and pushed him out of the way, the sleeve of Liam's jacket tore on this nail.

"No," shouted Liam when he saw the knife gleaming in the tall man's hand.

Moon roared as another contraction ricocheted through her belly. Exodus had the steaming forelegs in his hands now. The whole stall was boiling with a fog composed of hot breath and the mist that rose from the blood and water. Liam focused on the three-cornered rip in his jacket – how to mend it, what needle, what thread? – until he could force himself to look at the calf that lay convulsing on the floor.

"It's not breathing," he said to Exodus. "You killed it with the knife."

Exodus did not look at the boy. He lay the trunk of his body over the twitching calf and turned its face towards his own, one hand removing mucous from the tongue and nostrils. Then he placed his mouth over one of the cow's nostrils and exhaled slowly. The calf shuddered and was still. Liam watched Exodus open the calf's mouth and again press his face into the small animal's snout. Moon struggled to her feet and, as she did so, the afterbirth slipped from her body. She was looking behind her for her calf. Liam watched Exodus remove himself gently from the small black-and-white body, then watched the calf rise, the thin legs trembling like young birches in the spring.

Exodus guided the baby animal by the neck, smoothly, towards its mother's teat. "I know what to do now," he said, passing Liam on his way out the barn door.

The boy followed him but stopped three paces from the barn, distracted by the sight of a figure coasting down the road, pulling night behind him like a cloak. Brian waved. Liam tried to return the greeting but found himself instead bent over his stomach, retching into the snow.

No matter how often she was called, or how persuasively she was coaxed, Eileen would not come down from the tree, claiming that she had not finished thinking.

When she entered the house several hours after dark, she stamped the snow from her feet for longer than was necessary. Brian was putting fresh hay in the stall but Liam was in the cabin, huddled over a glinting needle, his jacket, and a long black thread. Soup bubbled on the stove and there was bread in the oven. The boy's brows were drawn together over his nose as he squinted at the sleeve. Eileen unwound a long, woollen scarf from her neck, ceremoniously, waiting for her brother to look up.

"Have you seen the baby cow?" he asked, finally, when she neither moved from the door nor spoke to him.

She smiled then, and with an air of great confidence said, "Exodus says he knows what to do. He's gone away now for a little while, but he'll be back, that's one thing certain." She crossed the room to look into the pot on the stove. "I'm hungrier than ever," she announced. "And the baby cow," she added, replacing the pot lid, "he said the baby cow must be called Genesis."

"He's gone?" The needle was a miniature sword, bright, between Liam's thumb and forefinger. "But I wanted . . . Did he walk back along the river?"

"No," said Eileen, settling herself at the table to wait for her father to return from the barn. "First he turned into a bird, then he flew away, high up, very high over the trees."

Liam was not satisfied with the look of the stitches but they held the fabric together. The needle moved in and out, smoothly, through the cloth. Eileen stood near his shoulder. "Papa says he'll get me coloured thread in Queensborough to make pictures on the pillowcases. I could make a picture on your sleeve."

Each spring from then on, Liam would set out in search of Exodus, nosing his canoe through the tributaries of the Black and the Moira rivers that crossed the two townships that made up his immediate geography. He would often portage, searching for hidden water, stubbornly moving away from the creek that crossed his own property, believing that to follow the route his mother had taken would never lead him to the man he was looking for. Moreover, he was often needed at the farm, and the journey to the lake that his mother had claimed as hers had assumed such hugeness in his mind he could not imagine a return from it except as an old man. Ulysses staggering home under the weight of the adventure, sailing back to an abandoned and completely altered family. He knew he could never leave Eileen for that long, could not leave her at all, he believed, for more than a few days.

Years later he would say that this was the time when he learned the woods. Until then, the edge of the forest seemed a wall, protecting darkness from the acre of light; a territory lacking the colourful, linear sequences that made up the road and its pageant. The picture it had presented to him had been flat, without dimensions, coloured by trees whose names he had learned only at his father's insistence. Now, when he walked among these trees, their low boughs touched his face and hands while around him hidden life rustled and fled. He glimpsed fur bursting from the earth and heard the outraged screams of winged creatures hidden from him by a canopy of leaves. Everything around him moved or was moved.

He never fell in love with the forest but came to admire and respect it. It had captured his interest, and as it broke apart in his mind into the millions of facts of its existence, he grappled with it, detail by detail, overcoming his vague fear. And his anger. No longer a beast who had swallowed his mother whole, the forest became, if not a lover, almost a friend. Once or twice, when the canoe was balanced on his shoulders, he met bears, large good-natured gentlemen who drew back and stepped aside to let him pass. He was never lost; no two parts of the forest were the same. With practice he had no trouble recognizing the singular construction of each of a thousand similar pines.

As the years went by, the late-spring forest quest became a ritual. The sombre river and creek waters, their surfaces like heavily varnished Renaissance paintings he would never see, turned into inviting highways. He would not find Exodus and eventually, by his nineteenth or twentieth year, he forgot that this had been his original intention. He would find, instead, rock and bark and swamp and cedar and strange, narrow liquid highways the colour of mahogany, and, for the time being, that was enough. And he would learn particular things about soil, decay, seeding, and growth. Light and air. Tender green. He knew he wanted to make things grow, wanted, above all, to nurture, to be a farmer.

His father grew older, and with each successive winter, weaker, his journeys to and from the schoolhouse taking him a little longer each year until finally it was necessary for him to set out and return in darkness. His robust, kind face had collapsed into creases and folds, and there was something sorrowful about the sagging skin at his neck. On winter evenings he told grimmer and grimmer stories: black potatoes, cabins filled with skeletal families, children devoured by rats, the coffin ships, mass graves on Grosse Isle, Cromwell, and the long history of the persecution of the Irish race. He was troubled by the presence of flourishing Orange Halls in his own county, knowing that many of his Protestant neighbours had taken the pledge to eliminate Catholicism wherever they might find it. One of the men on the roads, a drifter who had joined then abandoned the Lodge, had recited the secret Orange Oath to Brian, laughing at its arrogance, but the words had burned themselves into the schoolmaster's memory and after a few drinks at night he would sometimes repeat it to his children. "'I swear that I am not nor ever will be a Roman Catholic or Papist,'" he would announce. "'Nor am I married to nor will I ever marry a Roman Catholic or Papist, nor educate my children nor suffer them to be educated in the Roman Catholic faith, if in my power to prevent it.'" Afterwards he would strike his forehead in anger and disbelief. "They brought the hate with them across all that ocean . . . across all that water," he would say, staring out the window at swirling snow. "It hardly seems possible."

He told his children of an incident he had read about a few years before in a newspaper at O'Hara's Mill. Aggressive crowds of Orangemen had attacked the St. Patrick's Day Parade in Toronto, causing a riot to occur during which a young Irish Catholic father had been stabbed in the back with a pitchfork. The murder had gone unpunished. He had never until now mentioned the incident to his children, but his knowledge of it had broken something inside him.

His eyesight was becoming weak and he had no patience with spectacles so the pleasure he had taken in long bouts of reading could no longer distract him from the consideration of the old troubles. Brian now sensed old threats being reiterated, old wounds being reopened.

He knew his hero, D'Arcy McGee, had left the United States for Montreal, had entered Canadian politics, and was now Minister of Agriculture and Immigration. This gave Brian some comfort; this and the Irish revolutionary songs he loved to sing to his children – songs with such heartbreakingly beautiful tunes that his daughter, Eileen, had committed them all to memory by the age of thirteen. On winter afternoons she cheerfully sang about the hanging of brave young men, wild colonial boys, the curse of Cromwell, cruel landlords, the impossibility of requited love, and the robbery of landscape while she built snow castles under the brilliant slanting sun of several Januarys.

The year that Eileen turned fifteen and Liam twenty-two, Brian learned that his hero and hope for the future, McGee, had been sent by the government to the International Exposition in Dublin. It was 1865. While in Ireland, McGee returned to his native town of Wexford for a short visit. There he spoke about the problems of Irish immigrants in North America and the follies of political activism. Brian was well aware that as newly appointed Minister of Immigration McGee was an expert in the former topic, and as a participant in the disastrous Young Ireland uprising of 1848 he was an expert in the latter. McGee had railed against the demagogues he felt were promoting Fenian political activity in North America and had discussed the flaws in the Irish Catholic character that left that group open to manipulation by such creatures. He had announced that he and his fellow Young Irelanders had been, politically speaking, "a pack of fools." The speech devastated many of his Irish Catholic supporters on both sides of the Atlantic, many of whom believed that McGee had been somehow bought off, bribed, or blackmailed.

On an evening in June, when his eyes were particularly tired, Brian asked Eileen to read the text of the speech to him from a newspaper.

She stood in profile beside the window where the light was good, her hands whiter than usual against the tan paper and the print on it, and read in a voice stripped clean of emotion D'Arcy McGee's catalogue of the frailties of his own people. She had not yet the experience to respond to the words she was saying – growing up in the forest, she was innocent of identification with any group. No collective voice had made itself heard in her mind, and so she articulated words such as "squalor" or "illiteracy" or "idleness" in exactly the same tone of voice as she might have used when reading aloud a poem or a fairy story. Outside, birches were heaving in a brisk breeze. When she finished she put the paper down on a stool beside the stove and turned to ask her father a question concerning his supper. It was only then that she saw that he had been weeping.

"Such betrayal," he was whispering. "And he an Irish Catholic himself. Such betrayal."

After that he never mentioned McGee's name again.

At the school Brian began to teach the children an entirely different history of the British Empire than the one outlined by Egerton Ryerson in his prospectus for Upper Canadian schools. Speaking in the confidential tones of a man imparting wisdom by a fireside, he told of the land seizures which preceded the plantation of English and Scottish Protestants in Ulster. Turning slowly from the slate board as if his body were an old hinge, he would glare out from under bushy brows at what was to him now a blurred sea of small faces and demand that some young scholar recite the rights that were denied Catholics in Ireland during the eighteenth century at the time of the Penal Laws.

He scratched the words "They could not . . ." on the board, and the children, delighted with the game, would shout out the answers, enthusiastically and in unison.

"Purchase or lease land," they cried. "Become educated, practise a profession, vote, run for public office, practise their religion, own a horse worth more than five pounds, keep the profits from their rented land, or speak Gaelic."

"And what is Gaelic?" he would say.

"Gaelic is the language of scholars and poets."

He was warned several times about this approach to history, but because the men of the community trusted him – despite his Catholicism – and the children loved him, they were hesitant to let him go. Later, however, in June of 1866, when a small band of Fenians stumbled over the border from the United States, determined to fight for Ireland on the closest plot of British ground, their sad, ineffectual skirmishes caused such a widespread outbreak of anti-Irish sentiment that the Board of Trustees for Madoc Township voted unanimously that Brian should be retired from active duty.

Liam had just finished giving fresh feed to Genesis, Leviticus, Acts, and Ruth (Moon had died the year before of old age and had been buried tearfully by the small family near the spot where the mother lay) when he heard his father's voice in the distance. "For freedom comes from God's right hand and needs a godly train," he sang as he strode into view. "And righteous men must make our land a nation once again."

As she had the year before, and in the same month, Eileen stood by the window with a newspaper in her hands. This time she was reading the words of the Fenian Proclamation that General Sweeney had brought with him when he had attempted to invade Canada. Her father sat with his arms stretched out in front of him on the table and his head moving up and down. Liam, watching him from the other side of the room, could not decide whether his father was nodding in agreement or whether his head was becoming too heavy to hold upright because of weakness.

"'We come among you.'" Eileen read, "'as foes of British rule in Ireland.

"'We have taken up the sword to deliver Ireland from the tyrant.

"'We do not propose to divest you of a single right you now enjoy. We are here as the friends of liberty against despotism, of democracy against aristocracy.

"'To Irishmen across the province we appeal in the name of seven centuries of British iniquity and Irish misery.

"'We offer the honest grasp of friendship. Take it Irishmen, Frenchmen, Americans. Take it and trust it.

"'We wish to meet with friends. We are prepared to meet with enemies.

"'We shall endeavour to merit the confidence of the former. The latter can expect from us but the leniency of a determined but generous foe, and the restraints and relations imposed by civilized warfare.'"

"For this they took away my children," Brian said. Then he walked into the back room and flung himself down on his bed.

Eileen turned to her brother. "I thought the words were beautiful," she said. "I thought they sounded like poetry."

A week later, after dictating a long letter concerning Ireland's lost voice and stolen poetry, a letter that his daughter dutifully transcribed, Brian turned his face to the wall and died. He was fifty years old and his body was that of an ancient man: exhausted and withered.

Unable to bear the scene of his father's death, Liam was sitting on the stoop outside the door when his sister laid a small hand on his shoulder. She placed the paper into his hand. "He said he wants one copy of this to go to Exodus Crow," Eileen told her brother, "and another to some priest in Ireland called Quinn."

Liam didn't answer. He was thinking about how his father had died so quietly in the late afternoon, at the time of day when, in previous years, he had skied into view on the road, his coat a dark sail, night hurrying behind him as if trying to catch him up.

THE farm did not prosper despite the presence of Genesis, Leviticus, Acts, and Ruth; warming the barn in the winter with their large bodies and startling the calm green of the pasture in the summer with their precise black and whiteness. His few crops were meager and stunted. Shortly after his father died, Liam began to consider opening up two or three more acres so that he could grow feed corn for the cattle. Taking a carving knife in his hand he walked all over the land he now owned, plunging the blade into the earth every twenty yards. He found solid rock six inches under the soil in some locations and three inches under the soil in others. The rest of the property consisted of steaming muskeg, humming with mosquitoes in summer and projecting the ash-grey remains of dead cedars through a smooth, indifferent cover of snow in winter. Liam came to understand that his father's salary, insignificant though it had seemed, had nevertheless provided much-needed cash. There were now times at night when the young man, awakened by a furious north wind late in winter, experienced the acid taste at the edge of panic and the high, shrill buzz of panic in his mind. The scattered neighbours whom he had come to know along the road, cabin Irish like himself, had either died out, leaving decaying log homesteads behind them, or were living a life of squalid poverty – sweetened now and then by the availability of homemade whiskey.

He wanted to think about the things his father had taught him: the various names for trees, a few Irish revolutionary songs, the love of animals. He thought instead about his mother's hair in the sunlight. It was she who had told him how a field could be created, over a period of years, by the patient application of seaweed on dry rock. The weed, she had said, must be carried on the back in a basket strapped over the shoulders. She also said that the walk from any sea was always uphill. His child's mind had envisioned an ocean growing the wildflowers he was familiar with – Queen Anne's lace, black-eyed Susans – as she spoke. But it didn't matter now. Here he had neither the sea nor, it seemed, the time, never mind the patience. These things were as irrelevant to the ground on which he now stood as was his father's *Greek Lexicon* or *Oxford Anthology of British Verse*. Neither the English poets nor the Greeks had anything at all to say about farming the Canadian backwoods.

One warm sunny day in late March of the following year, Liam remembered the small library of reference books at the back of the log school, and he removed the skis from the place where they had rested against the wall since his father's death, strapped them on his own boots, and set out over the old route. He sailed by a pine forest that was a slash of green on either side of him, past squatters' shanties and abandoned farmsteads. Sometimes, he glided through a section or two of hardwood trees among which the sun ricocheted causing shadows on the snow that mirrored oddly the corduroy construction of the road bed. His father lay underneath the snow now. A mild man, enraged, then made silent. His grave had not yielded to the shape of the earth as Liam's mother's had, almost immediately, and as Moon's had in the space of a few months. *Rian fir ar mhnaoi*, he had said to Eileen just before he died, the Irish already sounding unfamiliar, untranslatable in their ears.

When he called for Mary they had not known whether he wanted the Blessed Virgin or his own wife, whose bones lay whitening a hundred yards from where he raved. Liam remembered sitting on the back stoop, avoiding the moment of his father's death. It was then he had recalled that *Rian fir ar mhnaoi* meant the trace of a man on a woman. He had whispered the phrase to himself, over and over, until he felt the pressure of Eileen's hand near his neck.

The school of which Liam's father had been so proud sat boarded and nailed, a late-winter drift on the west side almost reaching its eaves, the glass in each of its four windows, if not broken, was covered with a coating of dust from the previous dry summer. The bell for which Brian had fought long and hard was gone from the little wooden tower, and now a frayed grey rope swung in open air like a mutilated memory. Liam removed the skis and, with the sorrow and anger upon him, waded through the heavy spring snow to the front door which was easy enough to kick open, the force of this carrying him in one stride into the centre of the dim, remote room, where he saw before him the remains of his father's world in a new land.

On the slate board at the head of the room was chalked a map of Ireland, spotted with the Gaelic names of territories, towns and villages, bays and rivers. A series of arrows twisting in improbable directions, suggested fierce, unprincipled, alien invasions. Between the tiny shape that represented Rathlin Island and the large mass of Ireland itself, were three white dots, and Liam knew from the stories his father had told that these were the Children of Lir, biding their storm-tossed tenure as swans on the waters of the Moyle.

Next to the map was a list of Gaelic nouns written in his father's hand, and beside them their English equivalents written in the hand of a child: "famine," "sorrow," "homeland," "harp," "sea," "warrior," "poet," and the word "castle,"

interrupted after the first syllable – the chalk that wrote it resting on the ledge beneath the board.

Liam saw in his mind, then, the scene about which his father
would not speak. The child dutifully writing what she had
learned, the few other students squirming in their seats, their
teacher standing to one side with his arms folded, nodding as
this collection of words flowed down the board, a map filled
with violent arrows and forbidden words occupying the space
that separated him from the small scholar. And then the surprise entrance of the trustees, their anger and his father's arguments, the child in the midst of this abandoning the word
"castle," carefully placing the stub of chalk on the ledge, and
returning quietly to her seat.

What was it that lodged the homeland so permanently and
so painfully in the heart of his father? What terrible power had
that particular mix of rock and soil, sea, grass and sky that its
sorrows could claim him and cause him to draw its image on a
wall built in the centre of a forest thousands of miles away.
Concentrating, Liam suddenly recalled, quite vividly, his
father's turf spade, its worn handle and the spots of rust on its
blade; that and a steaming haystack. About the departure,
and the misery that preceded and followed it, he remembered
nothing at all. His first real souvenir was the act of arrival –
immigration – and a white house with water dancing on its
windows.

His father's stories, which had entertained him as a child
while wolverines yodelled beyond the cabin walls on sharp
winter nights, had left his centre untouched. But his sister, he
knew, had ingested the stories, their darkness – the twist in the
voice of the song, the sadness of the broken country – and had
therefore carried, in her body and her brain, some of that country's clay. She who was born into a raw, bright new world would
always look back towards lost landscapes and inward towards

inherited souvenirs, while he sought the forward momentum of change and growth, the axe in the flesh of the tree, the blade breaking open new soil. He feared, more than anything, the twist in his sister's song and the days she spent thinking in a willow which, all those years before, Exodus Crow had chosen for her. He could not imagine a future for the vast part of her that turned inward. She has spent, he thought, too much time in the woods alone.

Liam found the books he was looking for, standing on two rough shelves at the back of the room. They smelled of mould, were covered with dust. There, among the *Canadian Series of Reading Books*, among the *Elementary and Advanced Arithmetics*, between the *English Grammar* and one old stained volume of the Supplement to the fifth, sixth and seventh editions of the *Encyclopaedia Britannica*, he located the *Canadian Geological Survey*. His father, he remembered, had ordered this text for the school with great excitement, paying for it out of his own salary, claiming that it had important things to say about the composition of the new land. Liam wanted to know about this composition. He wanted to make things grow in it.

Opening the book to the first map of Upper Canada, he located the position of Belleville on the edge of Lake Ontario, then moving his finger due north past Moira Lake he found the approximate location of his farm, noting that the shading of the map had changed from a dot to a slanted line pattern. These slanted lines filled the enormous area that hung, like a lady's fancy lace collar, from the neck of Hudson Bay, one ribbon falling into his own county. According to the words at the bottom of the page, this vast territory was called The Canadian Shield. It covered hundreds of thousands of square miles. There were no pauses in its pervasiveness, no exceptions to its continuity. It had been put there by an ice age that would never happen again, it would be there for all time, and it was made of solid rock.

Liam looked up from the map and was confronted with the Irish word for famine; Brian's handwriting, stark and white, on a black slate board. He closed the book with a snap, thinking of men more enterprising than his father, men who had started iron mines, who had burned acres of forest for potash, who talked about machines while waiting for their grain to be ground at O'Hara's Mill. None of them was Irish. Some had stood at the door to this room when a child stopped halfway through the word "castle" and placed the chalk on the ledge.

His father had known about the shield of rock and had never told him. Had known about the barrier that would keep Liam from everything he wanted. The enterprising men, he suddenly believed, had been right to dismiss him.

Still holding the book, Liam snatched a cloth from the top of one of the desks and reduced the final remnants of his beloved father to a grey smear. Chalk dust filled the sunlit air like snow as Liam turned and, after kicking closed the door of the cold iron stove, left the place forever.

Skiing back towards the cabin and finding that he had, unwittingly, brought the *Canadian Geological Survey* with him, he tossed it among the trees that lined the road. It disappeared immediately from view, immersed in a bank of heavy, melting snow.

As the cabin and the few acres of light came into view, Liam felt as abandoned and helpless as he had the day, seventeen years before, when he awakened to find his mother gone. He heard Eileen calling to him from the willow tree on the other side of the stream.

"The creek is open further upstream," she cried. "It's open and running because of the sun today."

He glided over to the bank, then stopped, cautious about melting ice, and began to shout at her, "What are you doing up there? You're not a child anymore. How will you get across this ice now?"

"I did everything," she yelled back. "I baked four loaves of bread. Your shirts are clean. I'm thinking . . . and talking to the bird. Don't worry about the ice, the bird says it will hold me."

Liam ignored her answer. "We're going to church tomorrow," he called.

Eileen's laughter tumbled across the field near the creek. "Have you gone mad?" Eileen was standing now, hugging the large branch on her left. "Anyway, there is no church for us. Father said we'd have to travel too far to go to church. Too far there. Too far back."

"We're going to the Methodist church in Queensborough," Liam yelled. "And you're going to wear some nice clothes. You're seventeen years old and it's time you got married."

Eileen laughed again. "I'm not going," she said. "Not ever!"

Liam shook his ski pole in the air. "You're going," he shouted. "You're going to meet and marry a man who sells furniture, or who takes iron out of the ground, or one who owns a saw mill, a grist mill, a tannery!"

"Butcher, baker, candlestick maker," chanted Eileen.

"You cannot," he roared, "spend the rest of your life in a tree! This farm will never grow anything but boulders. We *live* on the Canadian Shield. Everywhere we walk we're kept out of. You will go to church."

"Boulders? What do you mean, the Canadian Shield?"

"A blanket of rock! So you're going to make something of yourself. You are going to marry a gentleman. No farmers, no teachers, and no, *no* poets!"

"*Are* there any poets here?"

"No."

"Then I'm not going to church. *You* get married. I'm never getting married. Last night," she announced, "I dreamed I was a fox in a burrow."

"A fox in a burrow," Liam muttered as he skied towards the cabin. "A fox in a goddam burrow."

"Don't worry," he heard Eileen shout from behind him, "everything's going to be all right. The crow told me."

"Jesus Christ," he said, throwing his poles down in the snow, "the crow told her! No one but a goddamed poet would marry her anyway."

The next morning, after walking six miles through ankle-deep slush, Liam and his sister entered the frame church and settled themselves in at the back. The whole congregation looked towards them, then each member turned to his neighbour and whispered the word "Papist."

As the hysterical preacher raved about sin and death, Liam noticed that the sun had changed its position in the room and was now making a furnace of Eileen's red hair. One by one the men in the church, as if drawn by its heat, turned their heads to glance at her, then quickly looked away, as if the fire of her hair might blind them.

"It is possible," the preacher barked, "that you have already sinned to the uttermost."

Liam felt a pressure on his shoulder and the warmth of his sister's body next to his. He saw her coat move up and down with the rhythm of her breathing.

"To the UTTERMOST!" the preacher repeated.

The men kept twisting in their seats to look at Eileen, then quickly averting their gaze. Some of them brought their hands up to the backs of their necks, nervously, or straightened their spines in a determined manner. His sister's head, the fire of her hair, lay heavy on Liam's shoulder. She had fallen fast asleep.

Until he saw the men twist in their seats, Liam had not known that his sister was beautiful. He had not known how dangerous beauty could be. The smell of fear was in the air. The broad backs of the men seemed ready to burst from their Sunday suits. His sister was asleep and her hair was on fire.

Liam wanted them both to become children; to spend day after day playing the games he had invented, when much younger, for Eileen's instruction. He wanted experience reduced to the simplicity of the problems in the arithmetic schoolbook of which he had come to be so fond. He thought, now, of those restrained, strict narratives and of the uncomplicated desires of the people featured in them, and he wished to be a child again, interested in how much it would cost a nameless man to buy thirteen bushels of apples at eleven pence a bushel.

He put aside, for the moment, the man he was becoming, the one who had considered giving his sister away to men who were both drawn to and afraid of her beauty – men who would never know her.

Eileen slept on, untroubled by the tension in the room. When the service was over Liam shook her sleeve and took her hand. She looked around the church and then at him, startled and confused, not understanding, at first, precisely where they were. During those few seconds it was as if she didn't recognize him at all.

Halfway through the month of May, after a wet spring had swollen the creek into an impressive brown river, Liam and Eileen saw a man walking on the water.

The small crops of wheat and oats, which had been sown in oozing mud, were beginning to change the colour of the earth. Leviticus, Genesis, and the bull who had been renamed Acts by their father after D'Arcy McGee's Wexford speech, were inching through the pasture, grazing. Ruth was nursing her new calf. Liam was pushing the hand-plough through the garden near the cabin door, Eileen following – with seeds for tomatoes, cucumbers, beans and carrots – and singing.

Liam was certain that he could hear the scrape of the shield beneath the blade of the plough. In his dreams it hung like an iron collar around his neck, banging heavy against his breastbone as he walked, creating such pressure on his lungs that he awoke gasping. Pushing the plough before him, now, he was thinking of the lush land that bordered the Great Lake Ontario, land owned by men whose names were Smith or Johnson – not a Murphy or a Callaghan among them. Port Hope, he recalled, had been the name of the harbour where, as a child, he had seen the white house. The rivers and creeks in his county, he knew, flowed away, towards this fertile territory, as if fleeing from rock. He had seen raindrops hitting the water that swept by his property and had imagined their journey southwards, away from the granite barrier, towards prosperity.

Behind him, Eileen abruptly stopped singing. Liam, lost in a terrifying daydream in which the shield had broken through the thin soil under his feet, turned towards her silence and saw her staring fixedly at the water, one hand still in the sack that held the seeds, her whole body tense, alert. He followed her line of vision, dropped the plough to the earth, and raised his arm to block the interfering glare of the sun, holding it there until he appeared to be locked in a gesture hovering somewhere between welcome and self-protection.

Genesis, Acts, Ruth, Leviticus, and young Numbers had all glided towards the creek end of the pasture and were now facing the opposite shore, their tails swinging in unison.

There was an old man walking on the water, towards the acres of light.

The figure, dressed in white trousers, jacket, and shirt, and outlined by the dark firs behind him, had long white hair, streaming out from under his pith helmet. He looked so much like the engraving of Moses Liam had seen at O'Hara's Mill that the young man wondered, for one split second, if he shouldn't have paid more attention to the preacher in the Methodist church. He abandoned that thought almost as quickly as it formed, however, in favour of the one that followed. This was no ordinary Old Testament prophet, he decided, this was a ghost.

"The crow said –" began Eileen, but before she could finish, the ghost began to shout gleefully. "You're here!" he cried, staggering on top of the water. "You're here . . . magically unchanged, and in the middle of a forest! I've so much to show you! You're here! I'm here! And see how much of *it* is here. Isn't it wonderful. The flora! The fauna!"

"Yes," Eileen called back, "it's wonderful." And then to her brother she whispered, "I wonder what he means? The crow said that –" She was interrupted, again, as the ghost, having successfully crossed the surface of the water, crashed into a heap at the feet of a group of vaguely curious cows who responded to this invasion by slowly lowering their heads to observe the visitor more closely. Liam and Eileen ran to where he had fallen on the bank.

"I've been eaten alive by the buzzing air," the man was saying to the cows, "and sick as a dog in the halfway houses." Remaining in a seated position he unfastened a large pack from his back and dropped it to the ground with a groan of relief. "But it's all been worth it," he continued. "I've made one thousand and one sketches of everything." He leaned forward to extract two long poles from the water. "These stilts," he said proudly, "are my own idea. I've heard of men who would walk twenty miles to cross a bridge when all they needed was a pair of stilts." He slid them under a rope that was tied around his pack. "They're a tad troublesome," he admitted, "in the bush when one encounters low limbs of trees and such, but well worth it when one encounters rivers. But this place," he enthused, throwing his arms skyward, "that forest" – he waved a hand in the direction of the opposite shore – "is one vast tidepool teeming with life! I've made one hundred drawings of fungi alone! But my dear," he rose to his feet and faced Eileen, "how perfectly splendid to find you – it took me longer than expected to find the spot." He peered into the young girl's face. "I *have* found you, haven't I?"

"I don't know," said Eileen to the stranger. "Have you?"

"And who are you?" he asked Liam. "Not the hedge schoolmaster, that's certain."

"My father is dead," said Liam.

"Dead?" The old man bent forward, opened his pack and removed a pair of spectacles. Only one lens remained. He closed his naked eye and looked at Eileen through glass with the other. "Of course, dead, you're just a child though strikingly similar. Your mother . . . where's your mother?"

"She disappeared," said Eileen, "then she died."

"Oh," said the old man quietly. "Then you wouldn't know about the tidepool."

"No," said both young people together.

"But I know about you," said Eileen. "Crow said you'd be coming."

"Crow?"

"Oh, it's nothing," said Liam, embarrassed. "It's just that sometimes she thinks she talks to birds."

"Good!" barked the old man. "Wonderful!" He shouldered his pack with remarkable agility. "My name is Osbert Sedgewick," he announced. "I'm from Ireland. My brother and I knew your parents. He's dead now, my brother. Everything has changed . . . quite completely. I'm very thirsty. Could I have, do you think, a cup of liquid refreshment? I was going to show her all the sketches. I left everything alone, you know, didn't alter anything. I did *so* want to show her the sketches."

"You can show me the sketches," said Eileen quietly. "I would like to see them."

Osbert Sedgewick stayed with Liam and Eileen for a month and a half, or rather, as it turned out, they stayed with him.

His presence filled the cabin with an air of pleasant formality, something like a precise contrapuntal tune. The young people were charmed by him. He allowed Eileen to use his tiny bricks of blue, yellow, red, and green to colour his drawings of flowers and leaves, and later presented her with four carefully sharpened pencils so that she could make the drawings herself. Liam showed him how to paddle the canoe so that the rivers and creeks might become an entry rather than a barrier to the forest. Brother and sister were both astonished by the old man's

216

table manners. He had travelled with a linen napkin in his pack, encircled by a silver ring with his name engraved on it in flowing script. At meals he unfurled this piece of fabric with a flourish as though he were magically conjuring the plate, which steamed in front of him. While Liam gobbled his dinner with a spoon, Osbert's long hands performed a graceful dance around his food. Eileen finally hunted up the four linen table napkins her mother had brought over on the boat and persuaded Liam to use one of them.

Though strong from a life-long addiction to walking, Osbert was utterly inept at farm chores, so he made himself useful in other ways: filling the oil lamps before nightfall, picking wild raspberries while out sketching, tramping six miles to Queensborough and six miles back with supplies in his pack and the news of the world under his arm. He was delighted by the progress of the new country; wanted to ride the Grand Trunk Railway that had been built between the cities of Toronto and Montreal, looked forward to the successful completion of the confederation of the provinces, admired the Irish-Canadian McGee whose speeches indicated that he was deeply involved in the logistics of this confederation.

"A wonderful orator," Osbert told the young people. "A good politician, but a terrible poet. This latest speech of his – 'The Mental Outfit of the New Dominion' – is a stunner!"

"Father was disappointed in him," said Eileen. "He believed that the Irish had been betrayed by him."

For many weeks Osbert had avoided all talk about Ireland, carrying on instead about the different species of fir trees in a particular patch of forest or listing the seven varieties of woodpecker he had spotted during the day. Then, gradually, gently he had begun to introduce the topic by asking Eileen to sing "Kerriswater" or "She Moved Through the Fair," turning to

Liam when she had finished and saying, "Those are fine songs," and asking, "Do you know any?" until, finally, the young man, himself, began to ask questions.

When Osbert told the young people about Puffin Court, its stuffed birds and landscaped walks, Liam believed the descriptions to be part of a mythology similar to the stories Exodus Crow had told about his mother and the spirit of the lake. But Eileen's face changed, grew flushed and troubled until, with all her father's anger and sorrow, she faced the visitor. "You were not my father's friend," she said, her voice low, flat. "You were his landlord."

Osbert did not answer right away, but looked at his long white hands which rested on the pine table. "I was his landlord," he eventually said, "but I was not as bad as some."

"And who are your tenants now? Or did they all die?"

"I have no more tenants."

"So they are all dead?"

"We sent most of them away – here – some died on the voyage."

"Will you get more?" asked Liam eagerly, thinking of vast acreages under the plough. "Is there a great deal of grain?"

The door slammed as Eileen left the cabin. An uncomfortable silence followed. Then Osbert answered. "There were tons and tons of grain. It was shipped to England. There was a terrible famine – worse in the south. Some of my tenants died. The rest we paid their Tenant Right and sent here. Your parents were among the first to go . . . and you." He dipped his head towards Liam as he spoke the word "you." "We sent so many away that there was no one left to work the estate and no money left either."

"So you came here?" said Liam.

"No . . . not right away. My brother never saw it clearly. Men would drop dead in the fields, and he couldn't see it. When there was no money left he couldn't see that either. He wrote terrible poetry – even worse than your McGee did – just went on writing terrible poetry. Then he died."

"And you?"

"I sold the demesne, all the stuffed wildlife, the cases, the library, the walks – everything – to the first person who wanted it."

Osbert got up and walked across the cabin to the corner where his pack rested. From it he pulled two tin cups and a bottle he had brought back with him from one of his trips to Queensborough. He poured the amber liquid into first one cup then the other, gave one to Liam and raised his own high into the air. "I sold it to a whiskey factory," he said. "A goddamed whiskey factory. Afterwards I visited my brother's grave and poured some of this stuff all over the grass. 'Write a poem about *that*,' I said." Osbert swallowed the contents of the cup, coughed, and grimaced. "I, myself, do not care for the stuff, but drink it now and then, nevertheless."

"My father wrote poetry, sometimes," Liam said. "He said it was bad poetry." Liam felt the alcohol burn through his chest, at the place where, in dreams, the shield was lodged.

"Your mother was the only one of them that had the real poetry . . . because she was 'away.' I never heard any of her poems but I knew she had them. She showed me a tidepool once and I never forgot. She changed something in me. I wasn't in love with her but she changed something in me. Granville, my brother, could never comprehend it – though he wanted her story, you understand. We collected folklore. He thought he loved the legends – but you can't love something you don't believe in and he never believed a word of it." Osbert poured himself another cup of whiskey. "A very bad poet," he repeated. He swallowed this time without the grimace. "*Rian fir ar mhnaoi*," he murmured.

"What's that?" said Liam, sitting up straight, his attention sharp.

"Something I found written on a slate in the cabin where you and your parents lived. After everyone was gone there was just this slate lying broken on the floor. I pieced it together. Someone had written *Rian fir ar mhnaoi*."

"That . . . that's what my father said just before he died." Liam raised the cup to his lips. He allowed the liquid to rest in his mouth for a few moments before swallowing it.

"I have no idea what it means," said Osbert apologetically.

"I know what it means." Liam was beginning to enjoy the whiskey now. "It means that my father may have been a bad poet, but I think he believed in poetry."

"Here's to bad poets everywhere," said Osbert, lifting his cup a few inches off the table.

Eileen spent the night in the tree, unwilling to enter the cabin where the man who had owned her parents sat drinking, believing that should she make the concession to return she might, somehow, declare herself to be his tenant.

It was a clear moonlit night. Everything was either dimly luminous or shadowed. The stars resembled the gifts that the crow had given her: sparkling metals from the creek-bed, graphite, pyrite, sometimes crystals of quartz. He was her bird; her secret. She had tried once or twice to share him with her brother but his lack of belief had eliminated the possibilities for the crow in any other life but hers. Once, the bird had swaggered up to her with a glass button in his mouth, and later with one made from mother-of-pearl. He had brought her a drawer full of brilliant things: belt buckles, a silver ring, coins, watch fobs.

The orange light of the cabin's window burned all night

long, disturbing Eileen's sleep, until she had to shift her position to place one of the tree's limbs between herself and this beacon. Even then she was awakened several times by voices, howling, laughter.

Although she didn't know this, the man and the boy finally fell asleep at the table, three-fourths of the whiskey demolished. Liam with his head on his arms and a puddle of vomit near his left foot, Osbert sprawled back over the chair, his nose pointed skyward, his mouth wide open as if yelling at God. Neither had thought about Eileen, sensed her overnight absence.

In the morning the crow awakened her by racketing around in the leaves and complaining in her ear. The willow tree in which she opened her eyes was a miracle; its feminine skirts and long hair passive in the breeze, exotic as a palm on the edge of a woods composed mostly of rigid jack pines and dense cedars. In winter, Eileen ran her hands over its supple bones, climbed high and watched the forest. In summer, she parted its curtains and stepped inside its mystery. She could hardly see out during the day. The long lip-shaped leaves moving in the wind and the shattered sunlight giving the surrounding air the look of green water. Her father had said the sea was green – the creek was the colour of polished wood. It had never occurred to Eileen that water could be blue.

Blue was the colour of the crow – his sheen – a glaze painted over black. Black as the name of a river the colour of polished wood.

Tilting his head, now, the crow fixed her with one bright eye and then the other. His beak glowed like the cabin window in the evening. Every morning for seven years Eileen had awakened to his laugh but this was the first time she had awakened into his world.

"Is this landlord *him*?" she asked petulantly, pushing the hair back from her face and allowing her legs to unfold over the large limb where she had slept. "Is this landlord the one you said would come?"

The crow rocked, laughing, on his branch. She heard him repeat the word "Landlord" and the word "Him." Then, after performing a sort of side-step along his perch and looking coyly the other way as if fearful of being overheard, he told her that there were no landlords, there were no lords of the land.

Eileen parted the willow fronds in front of her – just a few inches – so that she could see the cabin. The bird pecked fiercely under his wing, ignoring Eileen altogether, then dived through the soft green screen to the quick-running creek, splashed there and returned with what appeared to be a piece of the sun in his mouth. Eileen held out her hand but he scraped away across a twig, teasing.

"Aren't you going to give it to me?" she asked.

The crow appeared to be panting, his beak held open by solidified light. He edged sedately towards Eileen, one step at a time, his eyes fixed on something in the distance. Then he dropped his most recent gift into her palm.

Afterwards, he perched briefly on her shoulder, his talons clutching homespun cloth, before catapulting away, leaving Eileen immersed in flickering green. She was calm, decided, clutching a precious gift, and hungry for breakfast.

It took Liam two days to recover from the whiskey, but something had broken open in him during its tour of his body. He was still in awe of the man who had poured it for him, but they had become closer, like soldiers who had been wounded in the same battle. They compared injuries and anecdotes, laughed about Liam staggering outside to pee, howling at the moon, lecturing the cows in the barn. They recalled with astonishment that, at one point, Osbert had read aloud from a newspaper one of D'Arcy McGee's long diatribes against Fenianism, embellishing it with wild gestures and a thick Irish brogue.

Eileen noticed that the tone of her brother's voice had changed; that he attempted to move his blunt peasant's hands gracefully when he spoke, emulating Osbert – eager to please him – wanting some of his breeding to come to him through the shared light of the oil lamp. He did not seem to understand, as she did, that what Sedgewick was after was the children's absolution.

The old man walked as far as Madoc, returning the following day with an ox, a cart, two tombstones, and a stonecutter. Eileen presumed that one of the monuments was for her father, the other for her mother. But Osbert, having been greatly moved by Liam's maudlin account of his childhood with the cow, had wanted a memorial for Moon. Appropriate verses were composed and chiselled onto marble surfaces. The stonecutter was invited to spend the night. Another bottle of whiskey was consumed.

After two cupfuls, Liam began to rave about the shield. "It's all over," he said. "All over the country except on the front, down by the Great Lake. This land will never grow anything but scrub pine. There's a shield, you see, that keeps the growing from happening."

"There are some lovely birches, though," Osbert interjected.

Liam remembered that he had thought a birch tree was his mother in the moonlight. Now birches looked to him like bones rattling in a winter wind. He knew the forest too well. He was losing interest in it. "There's so much rock," he said. "How's a man supposed to farm when under everything there's all this rock?"

"Mines all over the place, though," said the stonecutter. "Lots of iron ore – Marmora, the Seymour mine – some quarries, marble, lithographic stone."

Eileen was at the other end of the table, colouring Osbert's drawings of daisies. She gently placed her brush beside the pad, rose to her feet, and ascended the ladder to the loft where she now slept. Within moments she returned to her place and began to watch the men carefully, her watercolouring abandoned.

"The only metal worth pursuing," announced Osbert, "is gold – the great stabilizer of the universe. A worthwhile quest . . . a wonderful healer. The moral question, of course, is whether it should be removed from a landscape fortunate enough to contain it. Personally, I would say not. Leave it alone, I would say. But human greed . . . well, there you have it."

"I'd get it out of the ground fast enough," said the stonecutter.

"My point exactly."

"I don't care about it one way or the other," said Liam. "I just want something to *grow* in the ground . . . don't want to take anything out of it that I didn't put in myself. Anyway, the only gold around here is what's in this bottle," he poured an inch of liquid into his cup. "There isn't any gold around here."

"Oh yes there is," said Eileen.

"Is that so?" the stonecutter grinned at her. "How can you be so sure?"

Eileen unfurled the fingers of her right hand. Her palm glittered.

"You see," she said to her brother, "the crow knew all along about the gold, he knows what to do." She was speaking to her brother but her eyes never once left the old man's face.

"Like particles of broken lightning," Osbert was saying, "just like particles of broken lightning."

Sedgewick paid for the property with a large bundle of pound notes which had been lying, all along, in the bottom of his pack. They were filthy, mouldy, and smelled of the block of cheese against which they had nestled during Osbert's trek through the bush, but, resting on the table, the notes stood half a foot high. Osbert removed an inch for himself and pushed the rest towards Liam. "Whiskey money!" he exclaimed. "Let us sing the praises of flowing streams: the one that bubbles through the demesne at Puffin Court and makes whiskey; the one that hurries towards the Black River and gives us nuggets of gold."

"How much is there? How much is this?" asked Liam.

"Never counted." Sedgewick folded his arms and leaned back in his chair. "But quite a lot, I should think. Don't spend it all at once." He laughed loudly at his own bad joke, then rapped his knuckles on the table as if bringing a class to attention. "A stable spot in the universe," he said, "is all I ever wanted – and this forest tidepool of quivering life." Then looking sharply at Liam, he reported, "Tidepools ruined all over England, you know. A man called Gosse wrote a book about nature near the sea and people of culture crowded the beaches seeking the tidepools, lifting the life out of them with nets." His expression was grim. "She would have hated that. Your mother would have hated that."

When she had entered the green world of the tree, later in the day, the crow confided to Eileen that the only problem was that from now on her family would be visited by the curse of the mines.

He dug his beak into the flesh of the tree several times as if to illustrate his point.

Eileen was watching the way the leaf shadows moved across the skin on her arms, that and the way the spots of sun caused the crow's sheen to roll back and forth across his feathered body like lamp oil on water. She would be leaving soon and hoped to take these things with her. She placed her index finger on the crow's neck but he wouldn't look at her and so she slipped between the green curtains, got into the canoe, and paddled to the opposite shore. As she was pulling the boat up onto the bank she heard the crow from inside the tree. But the foliage was too thick. She could no longer see him.

She took with her only textures, slim leaf shadows on her arm, and a knowledge of how dark can shine. The bird would be, in the future, something she almost remembered when she awakened at the most silent hour of the night with an unidentifiable feeling of great loss upon her and a flutter of dark wings near her heart.

Even before Liam and Eileen had decided how and when to leave the acres of light, the road parade, which had dwindled to a few miserable souls as settlers discovered the impossibility of farming solid rock, became more colourful and exotic than it had ever been in its short history. It had taken only a week or two for the news of gold, carried on the lips of the stonecutter back to Madoc, to fan out from there and into the wide world. Now the pageant that spilled out of the forest and by the cabin door was so intriguing that Genesis, Leviticus, Ruth, Acts, and young Numbers rarely left the road side of their pasture where they stood lined up like a military colour party, chewing thoughtfully, watching the action.

The usual collection of ragged, bush-crazed prospectors that are conjured by even the hint of a discovery of gold were joined by half-pay officers, members of parliament, enterprising American businessmen, a gaggle of scrapping orphans, cowboys on horseback, an escaped chain gang, sailors, coureurs de bois, and a quiet trio of sandalled and habited monks from Quebec. And then one day a chattering, laughing wagonful of whores from Montreal appeared, dressed in colours and fabrics the likes of which neither Liam nor Eileen had ever seen.

"Those, my dears," said Osbert as this spectacle rounded the corner and came into view, "are, if I am not mistaken, ladies of ill repute."

Their leader – and driver of the team that pulled the wagon – was a round goodnatured woman called Madame Beausejour who explained, first in French, then in English, that although she and her *petites filles* intended to set up housekeeping they had, more important, brought along their *équipement de prospection*. The girls, then, proudly brandished pickaxes and pans, the latter of which they banged in a tambourine-like manner as they went joyfully on their way singing French log-driving songs.

Hamlets of hastily constructed huts, shacks, and hovels sprang up in the area overnight and gave themselves names such as Eldorado, Enterprise, Nugget Niche, Beaucoup D'Argent, Eureka, and Coeur D'Or. In the space of three weeks the population of the town of Madoc tripled. Barber shops, beer parlours, and the offices of barristers were born, fortune tellers flourished. Hardware stores and hotels came into being and board sidewalks unfurled on the edges of muddy new streets named after Aztec warriors and Inca gods.

The staid festivities, which had been planned months before, and which celebrated the confederation of the provinces on July first, escalated into a pagan display of gold fever. When Madame Beausejour's *petites filles* walked into the town park, swathed in transparent blue silk and offering to represent *les lacs et les rivières du Québec* in the Methodist women's tableau entitled "The New Dominion," for instance, a riot nearly ensued. Spurned by the town matrons, the girls broke into the Orange Hall from which they removed several colourful banners. With these they marched through town demanding *liberté, égalité, fraternité*. The town band concert, which was to include some hymns and a few recently composed possible national anthems, was drowned out by talented prospector-fiddlers playing reels, strathspeys, waltzes, and hornpipes. Aged Canadian veterans of the War of 1812 began arguments with aged American veterans of the War of 1812, each claiming that they had won the day – and small, fierce re-enactments of various notorious battles ensued. A group of would-be Fenians, made bold by the liberal supply of whiskey, rescued the Orange Order banners from the girls and rode around the perimeter of the park on white horses, calling themselves Silly Billys and Worshipful Masters and hurling insulting replies in the direction of the hecklers in the crowd.

A second invasion of gold seekers followed close on the heels of the first. Two or three weeks after the last of the celebration's fireworks had faded from the night sky, the roads began to fill with German, Swedish, Polish, and Finnish immigrants diverted from their original destinations by the news which had now reached the docks at Quebec City. These were joined by the odd recently emancipated American slave and some thin, worn Civil War veterans who, despite their artificial limbs and obvious shell-shock had made the long journey from Virginia to Canada.

It was against all this that Liam and Eileen eventually made their way; the girl frightened, clutching her brother's sleeve, having never in her life seen such crowds of people, the young man purposeful, bursting with such forward momentum that at times he believed he could actually feel the shield melting, like ice in the sun, around his lungs and heart. Behind them, at one end of a five-foot rope, and pausing to graze more than Liam would have liked, walked Genesis, chosen to accompany them partly for her name, which Liam considered to be suitably symbolic, and partly because she was the one who most resembled her mother. With them they carried only that which they could fit into the packs on their backs. In Eileen's case this included watercolours, two small sketch pads, a geography book, some clothing, four linen napkins, a tiny braided wreath of red and black hair, a broken piece of blue china, and one black crow feather. Liam stuffed his pack with socks, an extra shirt, some overalls, and the thick bundle of pound notes. In his left hand he carried a lantern, which was fortunate because, finding the halfway houses full of gold seekers and the roads clogged with the same, he and his sister soon decided to travel at night. They slept during the day in cool morning rooms in which the smell of whiskey, tobacco, and sweat lingered after the departure of the previous night's collection of prospectors, and which, in the afternoon, responded to the summer sun on the roof by heating to impossible temperatures.

They were released from these periods of baked, drugged unconsciousness into the soft, windless twilights of one small town after another. Evening games were winding down, the hymns of choir practices poured out of open church doors. Liam and Eileen were aware that these worlds had nothing to do with them, but they were aware also that everything in these worlds paused and turned to watch two young people and a cow pass through the tidy residential streets and out into the night. When darkness fell they were often in a woods made silver by moonlight, surrounded by the ochre circle – four yards in diameter – provided by the lantern, and beating off the clouds of moths that flew into their faces or covered the glass that held the light. By daybreak they had usually walked through a couple of sleeping villages where dogs announced their arrival and departure and where cats were sometimes coupling noisily. There was always, they noted, one candle burning somewhere, and a toy – a doll, a hoop, a ball – left abandoned in a yard. Occasionally, a horse or cow, whose attention they had caught, would canter or saunter across a wet dawn pasture to meet them and strain against the fence rails while Genesis mooed softly.

They were heading for Liam's first harbour on the Great Lake, retracing the route their parents had taken over seventeen years before, but as the rhythms of their nights became established they believed they would walk like this forever, out of pattern with the life around them, discreetly moving from settlement to settlement. Deloro, Marmora, Blairton, Prevenau, Havelock, Asphodel, Indian River. Lantern light and swerving moths and a single candle behind glass their only points of reference.

As they travelled steadily westward the land opened up revealing, at dawn, lush farms with huge porched barns and beautiful, well-maintained red brick houses, tree-lined lanes and formal front gardens. Now and then a flamboyant scarlet mail coach hurtled importantly past in the first part of the morning, leaving them choking in the dust it had raised.

"I have never in my life," Liam remarked, "received a letter."

Then one morning, remembering, he hailed an oncoming coach by flapping two white envelopes in the air. He handed the driver his father's letters addressed to Father Quinn, Rathlin Island, County Antrim, Ireland; and to Exodus Crow, Moira Lake, Madoc Township, Upper Canada; these and a ten-pound note that happened to be resting on the top of the pile in his pack. The confused driver sat speechless, astonished, looking at the money in his hand, unable to continue on his route.

After a week of walking, the morning sun disclosed in the distance the town of Peterborough – its river a ribbon of silver, its steeples shining. Eileen and Liam stopped for the day at the inn at Downers Corners, unable, after a night of travelling, to face the density of this large centre's population. Liam explained to his sister that it would be necessary to pass through this place in order to reach the road that turned south and led to the Great Lake; a lake much larger than the long narrow one whose starlit company they had kept for the past two nights. An innkeeper told them the narrow lake was called Rice by the Indians because of the wild rice that grew near its shore, at its marshy edge.

"What about that Indian, Exodus Crow?" asked Liam, lying by his sister's side on the feather mattress while stunned summer flies buzzed at the margins of dusty glass. "And what did you mean about the gold and him knowing what to do?"

"I don't know," said Eileen truthfully, vaguely, falling gently into sleep. "I think I used to know, but I've forgotten."

For the brother and sister the loosening and letting go of their physical past was as simple as making a left-hand turn after the commotion of Peterborough. Now the road they took south drew them down into a space forsaken by a vanished glacier towards the remnant Great Lake it had left behind. Hill by hill they descended in the dark, their lantern burning oil purchased at the previous inn and echoed by the rows of lit windows in the big houses of the prosperous farms they passed. Even in the darkness these estates pressed themselves so firmly into Liam's visual memory that the old log houses and the small log barn began to lose shape, to melt away like the shield. Genesis veered to the right or to the left at the end of her rope, turning her head and enlarging her nostrils, inhaling the smell of healthy herds fed by fertile pastures. On either side of the road, maples grew so sturdily and stood at such precise distances from each other that Liam and Eileen put aside their memories of the thick, continuous pines and cedars that had lined the tracks of their childhood.

At first light on the third southward day, at the crest of yet another of the hills that lay in succession before them like a huge, soft staircase, the boy, the girl, and the cow stood utterly still in the centre of a road that was, half a mile later, to transform itself into the main street of a hamlet called Rossmount. They watched, almost without breathing, as a blood-red sun quivered on the eastern horizon of an expanse of water unlike anything Eileen had ever seen and recalled only vaguely by Liam. It was twenty miles away and a thousand feet beneath them, yet it dwarfed every feature of the surrounding landscape simply by its presence.

"Sweet Jesus," said Liam. "Holy Mother, Sweet Jesus, look at that lake!" His sister had turned her back to the view. "Eileen," he said, "look! We're going to live somewhere on the edge of *that*."

The lake had already changed colour, the sun hovering, full now, an inch above its edge. "Look at that, Eileen!" Her brother grabbed her shoulders but she twisted away, unwilling to turn so that he was forced to circle round to examine her face. "What's the matter with you? Look at that incredible lake."

"I can't look," she stammered, "I'm afraid. I think it's mine but I'm afraid." She leaned, exhausted, against Genesis. "It's mine and I know nothing about it. It doesn't have another side."

"Yes it does, yes it *does*." Her brother was impatient, eager to join the world. In the fields that were spread like draped tables in front of them he could see the patterns of the August harvest of barley and acres of rich, green corn. The sight moved him. He wanted to run wildly down the hills, then fling himself, gasping, into the arms of the magnificent lake.

"It has another side," he said to Eileen. "It's just that we can't see it. You remember. America is over there on the other side."

"No," said Eileen, turning slowly and resuming the journey, her eyes on the stones of the road. "I feel it in my heart. There's no end to it, no end to it at all."

III

The Trace of a Man on a Woman

WHEN Esther was a child she collected stone snails from the beach, placing them in jars and baskets all over the house until her practical mother, overwhelmed by the quantity, had demanded that they all be thrown back on the shore.

"And if you have any white stones," the old Eileen had added, speaking for the first time in a month, "throw them into the water."

"What do you mean?" Esther had asked. But the old woman had lapsed, once again, into silence.

The midnight shift at the cement company is made up of men quite different from those who work the daylight, twilight, and first darkness hours.

The midnight men begin their tasks, these summer nights, under a thick carpet of stars they rarely notice, their machines being so powerfully exposed by other forms of light that everything beyond the glare is a black wall. Because the spaces in which they move are enclosed by the night, the men might almost be redesigning the shapes of rooms. Unlike their colleagues on the day shift, not one of them has ever bent to the quarry floor to rescue a fossil released by dynamite. Neither have they taken fossils home as gifts for their children.

They are not dynamiters – the government does not allow explosions in darkness – and so they have never been present when the most recent wall of the quarry fragments, folds, and collapses, dust rising from it like curtains of rain. The noise they make is strong and relentless, and, because the wind and lake are often calm on summer nights, all pervasive. They are out of step with the rhythms of the rest of the world and, as a result, their family lives are sometimes troubled.

Everything they do, everything they have done for the last thirty years, has crept into Esther's dreams.

They represent the most dangerous kind of shape changers: those who cannot see, because of darkness, beyond the gesture of the moment.

A forest child, Eileen was disturbed by the immense fact of the lake. Her landscape had never included a phenomenon this imposing, this regular. But mostly she was disturbed by its familiarity; her sense that she was related to it in ways she couldn't understand. She knew immediately what it would sound like when she stood on its shore and how it would change tone and texture as the sky changed. This ocean of a lake was hers; a possession she had inherited at birth, but one she had never requested – an unruly relative that must, sooner or later, be reckoned with. It frightened her. It's mine, she had told her brother, not knowing at all what she meant by the assertion other than that it was true. She would have to live beside it, its voice forever in her ears.

Liam refused to rest after their last night's walk. "We'll reach the harbour by nightfall," he told his sister, "and sleep there in a real town hotel with a dining room and silver forks and spoons. We'll use the manners Osbert taught us. Tomorrow we'll buy some land and a house. We'll buy a horse and a carriage and you can have a parasol."

"What's a parasol?"

"Something that looks like a big flower that ladies hold over their heads."

Eileen's mind was filled with the left-over images from night journeys and the imposition of this lake upon her life; its invasion. "I don't want a parasol," she said.

Her brother ignored her comment. "We'll have a herd of a

hundred cows," he said, "and fourteen acres each of everything that grows. We'll hire workers."

Later he said, "I've counted forty-three ships on the lake – nine steamers and thirty-four sails."

The road bent in front of them, leading them towards a village. They bought bread and cheese from a general store and ate it in the trembling shade of a maple tree. As evening fell, the harbour of Port Hope caught gradual fire below them as they witnessed from the last slope its gas lamps ignite one by one, and all the ships reflecting artificial light in the waters of the lake. Then a din from the west startled them as a train – its windows ablaze – flung itself across a trestle bridge which, from this distance, looked too delicate to hold the weight implied by its clamour.

"That was a locomotive." Liam was impressed, wide-eyed. "Soon we must ride on a locomotive."

Eileen was more comfortable with the lake in the darkness, though the air was moist with its presence, and only when the train rattled over the trestle bridge was she able to stop listening for the conversation she knew the waves were having with the shore.

Liam and Eileen did not stay in either of Port Hope's brick hotels with dining rooms and shining cutlery, their rooms being fully occupied by promoters, speculators, and financiers attracted by the town's new prosperity. The proprietor of the British Hotel dismissed them curtly from his lobby, suspicious of their ragged appearance and more than a bit put off by the mention of the cow. His colleague at the American Hotel on the opposite side of the street was more garrulous. He told them the story of the railway and subsequent "boom" of the town, and directed them towards the harbour and an establishment sometimes known as the Seaman's Inn and sometimes as Canada House.

As instructed, they walked beside the steel lines of the railway which led to the docks. This harbour, Liam said, resembled nothing that he could remember. There had been no railway here, he told Eileen, when he and his parents had arrived, and none of these grand houses; he pointed to the few Gothic mansions, recently built or in various stages of construction, on the hill behind them. He said he thought there had been one white house with many windows near the shore but he supposed it would be gone by now with all the new wharfs – lost to the "boom." In the unnatural light Liam looked paler to Eileen, thinner than he had on all their night voyages, his hair in the gaslight an odd shade of pink. "It's a pity about that," he said, referring to the house.

They heard the inn before they saw it – music and men's voices, laughter and the odd curse. When it loomed into view, lit against the dark lake, it appeared, even from the rear, to be in a state of great agitation, the structure vibrating with the activity it contained. Eileen heard a fragment of an Irish reel she recognized, then the sound of breaking glass. Through the back windows she could see the large torsos of rugged men lunge in various directions, meeting and parting in what looked to her like serious combat. After she and Liam rounded the corner and began to climb the wooden stairs that faced the beach stones and the lake, Eileen realized that the boards beneath her feet were shaking. She watched as Liam tied the cow's rope to a porch railing, then allowed herself to be guided over the threshold and into a riot of male dancing.

A shoulder swung by, inches from her face, a grizzly beard heaved into sight and disappeared again. Eileen flattened herself against a wall as a line of broad backs veered in her direction then dived away from her towards the other side of the room. The pandemonium of a train crossing the nearby trestle bridge – the longest and highest in Canada, the clerk at the American Hotel had told them – was all but drowned out by the thumping of hobnail boots. Arm in arm, five leaping men thrashed against the bar, from which several gleaming mugs instantly jumped and shattered. Men in pairs clasped each other by the shoulders, kicking their legs wildly to the left or the right, entangling themselves with stationary chairs which were held aloft for a few moments before being hurled against the wall.

After a few more thunderous moments, all noise abruptly stopped. The men collapsed on tables, chairs, the floor, the bar, their great ribcages heaving from exertion. Then, as though ordered to do so by an invisible commander, they all turned in unison and calmly regarded the newcomers.

"I'm Captain O'Shaunessy," said a stout, grey-haired, bearded man behind the counter. "What can I do for you?"

They were given a large, sparsely furnished room overlooking the Great Lake, whose waves they would hear all night long when the sound of them was not overwhelmed by a passing locomotive or sporadic outbursts of dancing downstairs.

"They're mostly all seamen from the lake," Captain O'Shaunessy had told Liam as they climbed the stairs. "They're all drinkers and they're all dancers. They'll all live to be a hundred so long as they don't take the lake for granted or sail with anyone else who does. I'm about a hundred myself, though I've never counted. Never once took her for granted. There are five hundred and forty different kinds of weather out there, and I respect every one of them. White squalls, green fogs, black ice, and the dreaded yellow cyclone, just to mention a few. There are quite a few that cannot be mentioned at all, for if you do they'll come to seize you even on land – far inland. I'm retired now but I still don't take the lake for granted. If you want anything just ask for my brother. His name is Captain O'Shaunessy."

"But *your* name is Captain O'Shaunessy too."

"Of course it is. I'm his brother. Because of the lady I'll give you the room with the door that leads to the upper verandah. You can sometimes spot ten different kinds of weather from there. You should see the lake when winter's coming on," he added ominously, "or when she's working up to a purple riptide." He opened the door noisily with a large iron key. "Have a good sleep," he had said as he turned again towards the stairs. Both Eileen and Liam thanked him, but their voices were lost in the deafening racket of accordion music and pounding feet.

Mornings at the Seaman's Inn were relatively tranquil; the dancers either snoring in their rooms or sailing respectfully over the surface of the Great Lake. Eileen awoke to a shimmering ceiling, an empty room, and the sound of a passing train. Shortly afterwards, her brother slipped through the door. He had already been out walking and had bought bread and apples for their breakfast. While he ate he paced back and forth through a patch of sunlight on bare pine boards.

"It seems impossible," he said finally, "but it has to be. I went down to the water, turned around, looked at the Seaman's Inn, and there it was."

"There *what* was?"

"The house . . . I could see the reflection of the lake in its windows. I though that it was gone, but there it was. All those windows."

Eileen could see a lighthouse through the window. She focused on this rather than on the lake. The quivering light around her gave the impression that the room was full of rain.

"My first memory," her brother was saying, "looking back at me. I wonder if Father remembered it as well." He turned towards the window. "Why didn't I ask him?" The young man threw open the window and pitched an apple core out towards the lake. "Sometimes I have no idea where I am. If the light hadn't been just right, if the lake hadn't been in the windows, I would never have known where I was." He pushed the window closed. "I'm going to buy it, Eileen. I think it's supposed . . . that I'm supposed to buy it. A house . . . all those years in my memory. I'm going to buy it."

"All right," said Eileen, rapidly pulling on her skirt, "but where is it? All these wharfs and docks. Take me to see it."

"I don't have to take you to see it. I don't have to take you anywhere."

"Liam . . ."

"You are standing in it. The white house in my memory is the Seaman's Inn."

Negotiations proved difficult. The inn was owned by the two retired Captains O'Shaunessy, identical twins whose only differences lay in their Christian names – Sean and Seamus – and in their states of mind. Sometimes both stood behind the bar, sometimes only one. But which one? Sometimes it mattered which one, other times it didn't. Sean wanted to sell, but Seamus didn't. Then Seamus agreed to a fixed amount and

Sean became maudlin after several whiskeys and gave a long, tearful speech about the lake.

"I've never taken her for granted," he said to Liam, "but I've never left her behind neither. I've slept on her bosom and sprawled by her side. I wouldn't sell the Seaman's Inn for a pair of mermaid's tits. Where are these boys going to dance, I ask you, if I sell this inn?" He gestured magnanimously around a room filled with burly customers. "And what about her?" he jerked his thumb over his shoulder in the direction of the lake. "If I were to sell the Seaman's I might offend her and she'd send some of her weather to get me, no matter where I went." He leaned across the bar and looked fiercely at Liam. "She'd send the magenta maelstrom to get me. And," he added, darkly, "she'd send it to get you, too."

"Well," laughed Liam, "that *would* be a problem. My sister here says our family has the curse of the mines on it already and it would be a shame to add a purple maelstrom to that."

"And why would that be now . . . this curse of the mines?" Seamus strolled towards them from the other end of the bar. He directed his question to Eileen, who sat primly on a high wooden stool near her brother.

"Because of the mines that will be all around our old property. We sold it, and someone said there would be a curse . . . but I don't remember who."

"And what kind of mines might they be, Liam?" Seamus solicitously poured several inches of whiskey into his lodger's cup.

The young man sipped slowly, pausing for effect. He set the drink carefully back down on the bar. "Gold mines, Captain O'Shaunessy," he finally said. "There's a terrible quantity of gold on that property we sold. And we sold it," he added, "for a very good price." He placed a newly purchased felt hat on his head. "I'm off to take care of some business, now. You'll look after my sister, I assume." He eyed the men in the room suspiciously. "If one of them touches her," Liam said, "there'll be more than a purple maelstrom to deal with. I've lived in the bush for a long time. I know how to fight bears."

Liam's business took him into town every afternoon of the following week, leaving Eileen in a room full of Irish lake sailors, safe in the custody of one Captain O'Shaunessy or the other, often both. She remained near the bar with her back to the lake silently embroidering flowers on white cloth and listening to the captains argue about the sale of the inn. "You're a fool, Seamus . . . the lad's got gold money," or "The lake's in our blood, Sean . . . to sell the Seaman's would show a lack of respect," or vice versa, depending on the time of day or the mood of the speaker.

Both men specialized in a kind of monologue that could only be referred to as a rant, often breaking from private argument to preach to the entire room. "What do you think, boys?" one or the other would say. "Captain O'Shaunessy, here, says we should abandon you all, leave you to dance unsheltered by the walls and the roofbeams of the Seaman's Inn, leave you with no home to return to after you've been out there paying your respects to her, not taking her whims for granted, enduring her tantrums, patient with her doldrums. Like Cromwell himself he'd rob you of your rightful home and cast you off to the four corners of the world for the simple want of a place to drink and a place to dance. It breaks my heart, it does, to think of you all scattered and the lack of respect this scattering shows to her."

The sailors nodded sagely, listened quietly, knowing that a similar speech would likely be delivered the next day by the other Captain O'Shaunessy.

After one of these passionate declarations, late in the

afternoon towards the end of the week, when the room had resumed its discussions of dance steps and lake schooners, and the captains were polishing glasses and quarrelling quietly and more or less amiably, and Eileen had gathered enough courage to sit facing the front where she could glance, now and then, through the window to the lake, the door of the inn opened and within seconds the room's population was on its feet. Tables were pushed back against walls, chairs were stacked in teetering piles, fiddles were brought to chins, accordions were squeezed between arms, and the crowd, which had pressed itself around the door, parted into two cheering halves as into the room danced a tall, straight, curly-haired young man. The two captains O'Shaunessy embraced and wiped tears from their eyes. "It's him," they said in unison to Eileen. "The brightest and the best. God be praised, he's back. Aidan Lanighan."

"The antidote to the poison of Cromwell," said Seamus.

"The offspring of the sons of Usnach," said Sean.

"The treasure of the old world."

"The pleasure of the new."

Aidan Lanighan twirled meteorically around the room, grasping, in welcome, the hands of everyone near him, slapping the biceps of all he knew, ruffling the hair of his special friends, and finally running his fingers almost absently through Eileen's long red hair. In minutes everyone in the room had felt the ephemeral, lightning strike of his touch. He skidded to a momentary stop in the centre of the floor, then exploded into a jig that was at once an expression of vehement gaiety and furious lament. Head, arms, hips, legs, feet, fingers, and facial muscles engaged in a frenzy of precise motion, gathering energy from the lake, the light, the blood pumping through the arteries of all the other men around. It was as if Aidan Lanighan were at once creating and annihilating the room, taking it with him into his own space, his vitality causing the late afternoon sunlight to plunge recklessly through the west window, the lake to push its rhythmic song under the door, the old accordion to become orchestral, the hair and the eyes of the men to shine. He sprang out of the jig and into a combination of sudden leaps, step-dancing, and violent turns. In a miracle of tone, stress, time, pause, tempo, silence, and thrust, the histories of courtship, marriage, the funeral, famine, and harvest were present in the inn.

Eileen's embroidered flowers fell from her lap to the floor. Her throat was dry, her heart flailing. An Irish phrase *Rian fir ar mhnaoi* rattled in her head, the sound of it in the gestures of the man before her; her father's lost language, alive and leaping, miming its own story in a new world by a Great Lake. The Fianna, the Children of Tuireann, desperate departures, centuries of reunion, her mother's withdrawal, and every wicked manifestation of Great Lake weather was in this dance which was now airborne and drumming at the same time. In the midst of the last alacritous gesture, a dive through yielding waters, Aidan Lanighan moved one hand again through Eileen's hair and swept the other across the floor. He smoothed over her thighs the piece of cotton she had dropped, and disappeared into the crowd of joyful lake sailors.

Eileen stared for a full minute at the unfinished rose on the white cloth. It is scarlet, she thought. The thread from which her needle still hung looked like a line of blood descending to the spot on the floor where Aidan Lanighan had bent to retrieve it.

She stood up and walked across this place, up the stairs, and into her room.

"Hey," called one of the Captains O'Shaunessy, "I'm supposed to be keeping an eye on you. Your brother said . . ." But by the time he could tell Eileen what Liam had said she was leaning against the closed door, gazing directly across the room, through the window, out to the lake.

Liam returned in a new frock coat, gold watch, white shirt, bow tie, bowler hat, and spats, looking self-satisfied and prosperous. He was carrying a load of cotton dresses in his arms as he entered the inn.

"She's gone to her room," he was told by one Captain O'Shaunessy or the other.

"And she won't come out."

The captains exchanged meaningful glances and cleared their throats noisily, waiting for Liam to question them further. But knowing his sister was safe, Liam was swollen with his own news, bursting with it, eager to announce it. He tossed the bundle of dresses over the bar, where they reclined like a swooning woman, removed a map of the lakefront from his waistcoat pocket, smoothed it out with the palms of his hands, and prepared to address the proprietors of the inn.

"There's a terrible lot of lake on that map," said Seamus.

"She dominates it . . . she rules the map, she does," agreed Sean.

"See how small Port Hope is compared with the vastness of her."

"Insignificant."

"Trifling."

"Gentlemen," Liam interrupted, before the captains could gather the steam necessary for a full-scale sermon on lake currents and nautical disasters. "Gentlemen, I have purchased a hundred acres of land, a mile and a half of lake frontage, ten cleared acres, a hardwood forest, two springs, and a creek."

The captains were silent.

"Best farmland in Northumberland County, in Upper Canada, possibly in the world!" Liam thumped the bar with his fist. "Grows apples, potatoes, corn, barley, wheat, oats, alfalfa, and any kind of garden vegetable. Excellent pasturage for sheep, goats, horses, cows."

"And how is she getting along, your cow, in the stables?" asked one Captain O'Shaunessy, politely.

"Fine. Comes equipped with two barns, toolshed, a wharf, and a boathouse."

"A wharf?"

"A boathouse?" the captains raised their eyebrows.

"And a small log house, a well, and a chicken coop. It's right here," Liam pointed to a spot on the map, some twenty-five miles east of Port Hope. "Just below this village called Colborne."

"Colborne, is it," said Sean. "Now there's a place."

"A real hellhole," said Seamus.

"What kind of a fool would want to start a village two miles up from the lake?"

"Only an American of British descent."

"A United Empire Loyalist – Joseph Keeler – a cursed Orangeman."

"He's dead now, God be praised."

"But his son isn't, and he another cursed Orangeman."

Liam ignored these comments. "All this year's crops are up and flourishing, some harvested, barns bursting, livestock included in the price, and we take possession September first. Drinks all round!"

"What's today?" asked Seamus.

"August twentieth." Sean put his arm on his brother's shoulder. "It's a terrible pity, that, don't you agree Seamus, and we willing to sell the Seaman's Inn for a fair price."

"Knowing, of course, that you and your sister would take such fine care of it."

"And us planning to build another inn downshore a bit."

"With a solid floor. Hardwood." Seamus rubbed the toe of one boot back and forth across a worn pine board under the bar.

"What do you think of that, boys?" Sean addressed the room. "Captain O'Shaunessy and I planning a fine new inn for all of you and this youngster here breaking his part of the bargain . . . and he an Irishman." He shook his head sadly.

"But you said you'd never sell the Seaman's Inn," Liam reminded them.

"That's what we said."

"But that's not what we meant."

"We meant we'd never sell it to an Englishman."

"Or an Orangeman."

"Or a Frenchman."

"But you are an Irishman."

Liam was dumbfounded. "It was a whim," he said, lamely. "I remembered this building from when I was a child. I fell in love with it."

"And now you've fallen out of love with it? Now there's a fickle character."

"Inconstant."

"Listen, I can't farm railway trestles and wharves and warehouses." As if to prove Liam's point, the six-fourteen roared overhead, heading west, towards Colborne.

One of the Captains O'Shaunessy slowly poured the young man a whiskey. "Now would you be calling that a problem, Sean?" he asked. "This youngster, here, wanting the Seaman's for a house and wanting also to farm that land down by Colborne? Would you be calling that an insurmountable problem?"

"No, Seamus," the other man polished a glass, thoughtfully. "I'd be calling the British Empire a problem, or the famine, or the coffin boats, or the fact that our own Prime Minister has become an Orangeman. Things like that are problems, but certainly not living in this building and farming that land."

"Drinks all round!" cried both Captains O'Shaunessy in unison. "Drinks all round! On the house!"

WHEN in residence at the Seaman's Inn, Aidan Lanighan danced twice daily, at five in the afternoon and then again at eleven. He spent the rest of the day sitting pensively by the window, brightening when greeted by an incoming sailor, then sinking again into a reverie that appeared to have nothing to do with his whereabouts. This state of mind was exactly the opposite to the one in which he exploded into the dance. The other men in the room glanced at him with fondness – sometimes adoration – often touched him on the arm or the shoulder in passing, danced a little better, themselves, in his presence, but mostly left him alone to think his mysterious thoughts.

Eileen, who had now taken to spending most of the day sitting on the upstairs verandah staring out at the lake, crept downstairs each afternoon, ostensibly to find her brother, but really to watch Lanighan perform. She was always wearing one of her new cotton dresses – high at the throat and tight at the sleeves. Her childhood had glided away from her on dark wings. She had only recent memories in her mind: the lantern-lit night walks, the rattle of the trestle bridge, the traffic on the Great Lake, and this man's disturbing dance. His eyes, she realized, were greener than her own. She thought that he was beautiful.

She ate some but not much of the lake fish and potatoes presented to her in the tavern room. Slim already, she had begun, after her first glimpse of the dancing, to lose weight.

Liam was distracted, paid little attention to her, embroiled as he was in long, difficult negotiations with the O'Shaunessy brothers or visiting the land agent on Walton Street. At night he stayed downstairs until two or three a.m. Eileen lay on her metal cot, watching the reflecting harbour lights flicker on the ceiling until she heard the sound of Lanighan's dance begin at eleven o'clock. Fifteen minutes later, when it ended, she turned her face to one side and wept quietly until she fell asleep. She never remembered her dreams. Both she and her brother had forgotten her birthday, but she awoke on one of these mornings knowing she was seventeen years old.

On the fifth morning after Lanighan's arrival, the weather became sultry, the lake agitated, pitching six-foot breakers at the end of the pier for no apparent reason – there being no wind – and Eileen, innocent, until quite recently, of large bodies of water, watched from her verandah with a combination of fascination and horror; much the same way as she watched Lanighan's dancing. It seemed the waves had become somehow trapped in her head so that when she moved she was dizzy with them. Her premonitions, which as a child she had never doubted, had completely deserted her. She realized she had no idea what would happen to her – believed that she might be trapped in this world of pounding waves and leaping men and shrieking trains and shuddering trestles for eternity. She stepped back into her room, walked around it three times, and decided to go downstairs.

Lanighan was sitting quietly at his table. Behind his head, through the window glass, Eileen could see the spray from the pier leap and descend.

She walked up to the bar and faced whichever Captain O'Shaunessy stood behind it. "I need to know one thing," she heard herself whisper.

"And what's that?" The Captain O'Shaunessy leaned towards her.

"Why does he never speak?"

O'Shaunessy beckoned her closer still. "He never speaks," he hissed into her ear, "because he has had his heart torn out by the traitor McGee – who was *our* voice, mind you," the bearded man gestured to all the Irishmen in the room, "until he turned his voice against us, a few summers ago in the old country, and has been doing so ever since, at every opportunity. And he having to flee the homeland when he was younger than Lanighan, there, with a price on his head because of the Young Ireland uprising. And now, in the *Montreal Gazette*, he says he will list, with no proof, mind you, the names and addresses of his fellow countrymen he claims were part of the Fenian uprisings. It's a strange world, my dear, that allows a man to turn against the longings of his own native heart, and when he does there's a cloud hanging over the heads of all Lanighan's brothers."

"Do you think he talks to his brothers?"

"I'm speaking of those of the spirit, not of the flesh. They all turned silent when D'Arcy McGee turned traitor to the cause, joined forces with that Orangeman Macdonald. This was to be *our* nation, you see – that's at the heart of it. There's more of *us* in the bowels of the lakeboats or in the city factories, or on the roads, or building the canals. McGee talked great lakefuls of words, but, in the end, he turned traitor. They'll stay quiet until he turns back again, as, being Irish, he should, turn back again to the cause."

"Is that all, then?"

"Is that *all*? The entire hope of the Irish population trampled into the dust by the political greed and ambition of the one we looked to for our solace and salvation? Are we to be ignored, used as workhorses, as badly treated here as we were there? I'd be silent myself if it were in my nature . . . but it's not, nor in my brother's neither."

"Is he a Fenian, this Aidan Lanighan?"

"He is a patriot."

"But he *can* talk?"

"Talk, is it? Talk? Oh, he can talk. But most important, he can dance."

Eileen was drugged by the lake, but, with repeated exposure, she was developing tolerance.

This she accomplished by long vigils on the verandah, which were offset by pacing the dark hall of the second storey of the Seaman's Inn – all the doors closed at noon, the noise of the Great Lake cushioned.

We'll be leaving soon, Liam had said, to go to the land south of Colborne. Then, he told her, everything would be perfect, forever.

"Have you ever been in love, Liam?" she had asked him one evening.

"No, but I intend to be soon. I'll need sons for the farm, and a wife."

"Aidan Lanighan's had his heart torn out by that man Father talked about . . . that man called McGee, the member of parliament. They say he'll be silent as long as McGee is silent . . . about the Irish misery."

"What does this Irish misery matter, Eileen? We're in Canada now, we're Canadian, not Irish. I don't even remember Ireland and you were born *here*. Soon we'll be living on the new farm and I'll have a wife, some sons, a hundred cows."

"And what will I have, Liam?"

He smiled indulgently at his sister. "You'll have a large room of your own with a wonderful view of the lake."

One night she opened the door of the room and walked hesitantly along the dark hall to see the eleven o'clock dance. She stopped on the third step down and, quite uncharacteristically, crossed herself, before continuing the descent. Once she entered the room, she dodged the galloping dancers and approached the bar.

"So, you've come to see the last performance?" said one Captain O'Shaunessy.

"The lad is off on a grain boat tomorrow to plead with McGee," said the other.

"And how will he do that if he won't talk?"

Both Captains looked at her with surprise. "Haven't you been watching? He'll dance. It's what he's been practising here all week . . . his petition to McGee."

"He'll *dance* it?"

"Yes, and he'll break the man's heart in his breast if he isn't completely lost to us."

"But how will he know what Aidan is saying?"

"A true Irishman always knows what a dancer is saying."

Lanighan, when he began to dance that night, broke Eileen's heart in her own breast. His feet hammered the boards, his arms whipped like swords through the air. Eileen read the gestures as demanding space, territory, a promised land, hills, the sky. She heard the dance shout passionate declarations and make pleas for justice. She saw the young man's pulse beat in his neck and the veins throb at his temples, his dance keening, then yelling with joy. Lanighan pivoted, lashed out, the sweat from his hair raining on the room. The Great Lake thundered, the trestle bridge rattled, and all of Aidan Lanighan's beautiful, long muscles elongated further, making him larger than the tavern room that contained his prancing oratory.

Eileen watched all this from under partly lowered eyelids. Then she watched herself rise and join the dance. Walls loomed and receded. She danced herself behind Lanighan's eyes and knew, suddenly, the dark pitch of the bellies of lake-boats, intense political agendas, a sordid slum childhood, nights in crowded Montreal boarding houses. She knew Lanighan's voice, his abandoned song, his pain, his silence. His hand, as it had once before, swept through her hair, his mouth was open and his breath was in her lungs.

For a fraction of a moment a dark bird, unjustly forgotten, seemed to fly across her forehead, beating a tattoo of its own sorrows and betrayals. Then it was Aidan Lanighan's hair, so close she could see the slashes of reflected gaslight on all his black curls. He was radiant, blazing, and she his attached shadow. If he shone his light elsewhere she would disappear. Her brother's shocked face slid by, the grinning Captains O'Shaunessy, the huge sailors of the room on their feet cheering, clapping the rhythm of the dance; this protest, this proclamation, this celebration. Aidan Lanighan's open mouth was so close to her ear, she knew she was being inhaled by him – herself a series of complicated messages sent by a network of nerves through his brain and body. She would share his silence, provide him with a voice.

The room calmed, its blurred walls snapping back into focus. At the climax of the dance Aidan Lanighan had grasped Eileen's arm just above the wrist and had thrust it up over her head where her fingers curled reflexively into a fist. She looked at this – her pale arm, the etched creases where her knuckles bent, the skin tight over the fragile bones, the ordinary button on the cotton cuff of her white sleeve. His hand, the colour of the Great Lake's sand, clutching this. She broke from him, then, and ran to the wooden stairs.

In the dark hall she searched her empty pockets for the key which was, though she didn't know this, lying in the dust beneath the bar, having leapt from her clothing in the heat of the dance. She rattled the doorknob so furiously and loudly she missed Lanighan's footsteps on the stairs, was made aware of his presence by the warmth of his breath at the nape of her neck. She placed her damp forehead against the cold wood of the door. Then she turned.

While he caressed her she told herself the brief, brutal story of his life, composed partly of the things the captains had said to her and partly of the songs she had sung, innocently, as a child. Moonlight militias, love of comrades, humiliation, defeat. The blunders of revenge-crazed leaders. Brothers in arms left to grief-choked deaths near foreign woods. The trafficking of pathetic quantities of weapons back and forth across the Great Lakes, long nights creating vehement rants for political papers. It was Eileen's first history of the world, told to her, she believed, by this man's hands. She, who had spent most of her childhood behind the swaying curtains of a willow tree; she who had seen her own father strangle on his last, Irish words, knew suddenly that it was also her own story she was hearing inside her head while the young man's desperate hands ran back and forth over her heart. She understood that he knew how to use silence as a weapon, that he would not speak the history until McGee turned back to his people, as he would do, could not help doing, when he saw Lanighan's fervid dance.

She believed everything, the urgency of his body, the touch of his hands, the pressure of his mouth, the insistence of the narrative that ran and ran in her mind. In his arms she was assaulted, stolen, by a learned mythology.

She heard her brother's footsteps on the stairs. Her body

stiffened. "I know where you are going," Lanighan whispered to her. "I'll find you when I can."

He burst from her arms and over the sill of the open window at the end of the hall.

"Where did he go?" Liam hissed. "What did he do to you? I didn't even see him leave the room."

"There's no one here," said Eileen, her hand clasping the pistol Lanighan had hidden in her pocket. "I lost the key."

Each syllable was a blade cutting her throat, these first lies to her brother. She had given her real voice to Aidan Lanighan. He would bring it back to her, she knew, when he returned for her and the gun.

On Monday, September 2, 1867, the population of the town of Port Hope and most of the population of its neighbour and rival, Cobourg, turned out to witness the launching of the Seaman's Inn. Crowds filled the wharfs and lined the boardwalks in front of the warehouses. Children shinneyed up lampposts. Carriages full of the well-to-do moved sedately down the hill from the mansions on Dorset Street, leaving behind a few prim old ladies who found the whole fuss slightly vulgar but who, nevertheless, gazed at the lake through field-glasses from the widow's walks on top of their roofs. All the stores on Walton Street were closed and, even though it was Monday, not a piece of laundry flapped on lines in the back gardens of less prestigious neighbourhoods.

For the past few days while the Seaman's Inn was prepared for its journey, Liam and his silent sister had occupied a suite in the American Hotel, the Captains O'Shaunessy being housed in rooms on the upper storey of the same establishment. In the fancy dining room at night, after Eileen had wandered vaguely away from a scarcely touched supper, the three men discussed her condition.

"Captain O'Shaunessy and I believe she's been visited by 'the terrible calamity,'" Sean told Liam. "She's fallen in love with a patriot and there's no cure for it."

"There's nothing in it," said Liam, annoyed. "She'll be herself in a day or two."

My grief on the sea, how the waves of it roll.
For they heave between me, and the love of my soul,

quoted Seamus.

And my love came behind, he came from the south.
His breast to my bosom, his mouth to my mouth,

added Sean.

"There's nothing to this," said Liam, but without his former conviction. Even during the excitement of this time, as he stood on the edge of his future which appeared to tumble before him like a well-maintained road, Liam would pause now and then to study his sister. He was, as always, bewildered by her behaviour. Who was this girl to whom he was bound by emotion and blood, who had shared rooms and landscapes with him? She remained mysterious to him; the patterns in her mind as indecipherable as they had been on summer evenings in the cabin when, without speaking, she would step out the door, cross the creek, and enter the willow tree – sometimes not returning until after dark.

Now it was as if she hadn't returned at all, as if she were keeping apart from him, locked inside a shimmering green world to which he had no access. He wanted to pick her up and hold her against his chest as he had when she was small, to recall her to the real world of plans and schedules and accomplishments.

Now the plans for the departure of the Seaman's Inn were in full operation, the two Captains O'Shaunessy shouting orders, positioning their burly clientele in strategic positions, making use of the shiny new whistles they had bought on Saturday from Cooper's Hardware Store. At the end of a series of four high-pitched blasts, the building groaned and rose from its original crumbling foundation in the loving arms of eighty lake sailors. They turned the structure around and set it down on a collection of spruce logs which lay across the sloping beach leading towards the water. At this point the building began to roll at a dangerous pace in the direction of the waves so that the eighty strong men were obliged to run beside it, grabbing at window and door frames in an attempt to slow it down. Eventually, a barge was pushed as close to shore as possible by a little steam tug. Then the eighty seamen sloshed through the water, and the inn groaned again as they finally shoved her onboard.

Liam insisted that he, his sister, and Genesis make the journey to the shore near Colborne in their new home, the captains piloting the tug that pulled the barge. It took half an hour of complicated manoeuvring to place a gangplank successfully between the end of the pier and the verandah of the inn.

Led by Eileen who looked neither to the left nor the right, Genesis walked calmly up the swaying plank as if she had spent most of her life at sea. Liam spun around, tipped his bowler hat to the crowd, waved, and blew kisses. This was his second-to-last excessive act and, years later, after seasons and seasons of farming, he would talk about it to anyone who would listen. "I turned, I tipped my hat, I blew kisses to the crowd, and we floated her downshore, twenty-five miles to Loughbreeze Beach" – the name he would give to his farm, a part-Gaelic moniker in memory of his father.

The Captains O'Shaunessy had removed much of the old furniture from the building in order to use it in the new, but they had left a sleigh-bed and a dresser in the room which Eileen and Liam had occupied for the past few weeks. And, in sly deference to Eileen, they had not removed Lanighan's table from its place by the window.

Eileen sat at this table now and watched the town of Port Hope become small and distant as the tug pulled the barge out of the harbour, past the white lighthouse, and onto the lake. Soon the sand and stone beaches, poplars, soft bushes, willows, pastures, orchards, and forested areas of the Great Lake's shore-line coasted by, wrinkled and distorted by the window's irregular glass. Some of the trees, she noticed, were already tipped with red, and goldenrod was scattered like pollen in passing meadows. Once a seagull landed on the outside sill and looked at her quizzically before opening surprisingly large wings and wheeling away.

The inner ledge of the window was pitted and scarred, its paint flaking or gone altogether in some places. Sometimes this held Eileen's attention more than the beautiful, rocking shore-line, but mostly she examined the brown surface of the table on which Aidan Lanighan's arms had rested. After she had stared at the wood grain for a long, long time, she glanced out the window and saw smooth, green hills like Aidan Lanighan's shoulders and fields full of tall grass that moved in the wind like his hair.

"I know where to find you," he had said, as cold steel was slipped into her pocket. "Keep this for me."

"He's had his heart torn out," she whispered, now.

The village of Lakeport nudged its way into the right-hand corner of the window, dipped out of sight, then appeared again, its small population waving from the shore.

Genesis, looking bored and sleepy, stood placidly by the bar, stumbling slightly as the floor tilted. Liam was stretched out on the floor, his bowler hat on his face, seasick.

Eileen turned from the landscape and rose from the table to

pace the tavern room, searching the planks under her feet for the exact spot where Aidan Lanighan had lifted a fabric rose in his hand and then placed it carefully on her cotton skirt, a gesture that now seemed so intimate that, recalling it in this heaving, shimmering room, caused her to close her eyes in pain.

She had spent the few days after Lanighan's departure, before the Seaman's Inn was emptied of furniture and clientele, moving in a seemingly random manner from table to table of the tavern room that now swayed around her. She appeared to be lost, drifting, but was, in fact, swimming in the currents of conversation that flowed among the men, absorbing information about Lanighan, focusing on anecdotes and opinions with such intensity that the faces of the speakers and the words they spoke would remain permanently in her mind. She felt that years later, were she to spot one or another of these sailors in a crowd, she would be compelled to greet him as though he were a lost confidante, so vital were the histories their memories contained. Listening to them, she had been stepping carefully through the episodes, real and rumoured, of Lanighan's life; the way he, himself, was said to have journeyed among the garrison towns of the Great Lake and the long river as a regimental tailor. Now, she had learned, he stayed mostly in Montreal, doing private piecework, restlessly changing places of employment so that he would have time for the vague political activities that were described by the men in emotional rather than factual terms.

"He's had his heart torn out by McGee," she had heard one of the men say, and another, "It's how it is with all of us and how it always will be. We're shaken by it."

But Eileen cared little how shaken they all were, wanted from them only the one man's wound which she would claim as her own: the energy that caused him to dance frantically across a room and then to push her shoulders against a wall and bury his face in her neck. That and a view of the man McGee who had lured Lanighan into the role of a distanced petitioner, leaving her behind, dazed, entranced, utterly without power – a captive, now, of heaving architecture, afloat on a Great Lake.

The engine of the tug shuddered and then stopped. Eileen looked through the window and saw a long sickle-shaped beach composed of smooth grey stones which became pebbles near the shore. Behind this, tall poplars flickered in a light breeze and the fixed, dark shape of a large barn loomed at the edge of a cedar woods. Mentally, she allowed Lanighan to press, again, his mouth to her ear. "I know where to find you," he whispered, her own lips silently mouthing the words as she rose from his chair to disembark.

In Liam's last excessive gesture he tore off his coat and shirt and trousers and dived from the verandah of the inn into the lake. When he reached the shore he kissed the beach, one of the poplar trees, the barn, and the grass near the small, soon-to-be-demolished log house. "Then I dived from the verandah," he would, in the future, tell anyone who would listen.

While the O'Shaunessys, Liam, and a gathering of men from Colborne carefully manoeuvred the Seaman's Inn onto the new foundation that awaited it, Eileen walked the stony sickle-shaped beach from one end to the other. Through the clear water a few feet from shore she could see small limestone plateaus extending out into the deepness of the lake. They reminded her of the maps in the geography book, the continents lying like oddly shaped tables on the floor of the ocean, each shoreline implying the form of the land mass opposite so that the whole world seemed unfinished – frozen in a state of perpetual separation – longing for reunion. She no longer feared the lake, its size and power, knowing it could cause Aidan Lanighan to appear, magically, on its horizon. The air around her was moist, expectant, the stones under her feet filled with etched memories of previous life-forms.

She would speak little – become silent, a person who waits. She would hold Aidan Lanighan in her mind. And he would recover her.

As the white clapboard building settled on its new foundation its former identity leaked slowly from it, the views from all its front windows, where the Great Lake still danced, changed utterly. From the west, the idea of orchard and pasture slipped into its rooms, from the east barnyard, pigsty and chicken coop, and, in the north, the dark tumescent shape of the cedar bush pushed its shape, and, in the late afternoon, its shadow towards the wooden walls. The smell of smoke and whiskey that had filled what used to be the tavern room diminished by degrees and was replaced by other, earthier odours. No longer vibrating under the pounding of sailors' feet or the frenetic clatter of trains on the trestle bridge, the house assumed a state of sedateness that was almost refined. Then one night, about a week after their arrival at Loughbreeze Beach, both Liam and Eileen were awakened by a harsh noise followed by low guttural moans – the last ghosts taking their leave. The building would not be agitated by anything at all, now, for a hundred years, though its cells would hold onto a latent tendency towards this kind of experience. Liam would never again refer to the structure as "The Seaman's" or "the Inn" and it relaxed, with grace, into its new, more banal existence as farmhouse.

The tavern room, soon transformed into a large, comfortable parlour, would remain for Eileen powerfully lit by the energy of Aidan Lanighan's dancing in the same way that the upstairs hall, even with its doors open to bright rooms, clung to the velvet darkness of his furtive caresses. At night, when she undressed by lamplight in her large room with its view of the lake, she examined her shoulders, neck, and breasts, certain that at some time or another she would be able to detect permanent evidence that his hands had visited there. She kept his only tangible gift, the derringer pistol, buried beneath her two white nightgowns beside the braided red and black hair and the one glistening black feather, whose significance she was never able to recall.

During the day she watched her brother wed himself to the land. Often she saw him in the fields digging like a child with his hands buried in the rich soil. Sometimes he would run back to the house from the orchard with an oversized apple in each hand. "Look!" he would often shout as he displayed a packed corn crib, a fat ewe, or a basket of eggs from the chicken coop. Once he strode through the kitchen door and dragged Eileen across the yard to the barn where they stood silently in the dusty light, Liam with his hat clasped to his breast, his face rapt as if visiting a great cathedral.

Eileen assumed the household chores, quietly and steadily. As if in a trance she moved easily, vacantly from task to repetitive task. Her brother, anxious to preserve every perfect vegetable in the kitchen garden, had provided her with a pantry full of sealer jars and three huge copper kettles. When the equinoctial gales of autumn began to toss the lake and rattle the stones on the beach, Eileen was immersed in a room full of billowing vapour and the smell of cooked fruit, her hands holding glass the colour of lake water and the floating swaths of gauze she used for straining seeds and skins. She cooked meals for her brother and the three hired men, who had been originally delighted by her appearance but whose ardour had cooled when their jests and compliments were met with absent-minded indifference. "She must be promised," one had said to another.

In the mornings she crossed the wind-twisted yard to milk Genesis and the half a dozen new cows she had not taken the trouble to name. Then she would feed the chickens and return to the order she had created in the house. The kitchen windows displayed her laundry shuddering like angry pennants against the dark cedar woods. In the parlour windows the lake churned, and clouds of golden leaves swept from the poplars through the air. Eileen's fires, fed by equinoctial oxygen, burned with a sharp, orange brilliance, flames inside the Quebec heaters thrusting like blades out of the flesh of pine logs. While working, she kept one eye on the horizon for the sail she was certain she would be able to identify as his, and Aidan Lanighan's voice whispered in her ears.

Then one morning at the end of the first week in October she woke at dawn to a world from which turbulence had been removed. The autumn gales had finished. She walked out onto her upstairs verandah, searched the horizon for a specific sail, looked east towards the long arm of Presqu'ile Point and Bluff Island which formed its outstretched hand, then down to the subdued, clean lake water, licking the pebbles at the shore.

Liam and the men were already active downstairs, banging stove lids, starting crackling fires with dried cedar kindling, and shouting to each other about the glorious day. Aidan Lanighan's voice had gone from Eileen's head in this weather, though she was not empty of his presence. The physical world, however, in the sharp autumn light, was engaged in an act of blatant exposure which cut through her preoccupation and allowed her to see, quite distinctly, not only the sand bars of the distant peninsula, but also coloured pebbles on the floor of the lake twenty feet from the edge. Since her arrival, she suddenly realized, she hadn't moved further than three hundred yards from the house.

Surrounded by the dark green of cedars that afternoon, her back to the lake, she remembered her solitary childhood – snow angels, her father's voice, her mother's frozen face and red hair surrounded by white, something that could be a wing the colour of a moonless night sky with blue highlights, a swaying green curtain. She recalled her father's songs, cheerful tunes informed by grim narratives, or melodies suggesting the paralysis of great love. *It's you who have left my heart shaken, with a hopeless desolation, as before you I stand.* Eileen, singing quietly, bending back the boughs of cedars, moved forward while the lake's whispers faded. Sometimes she had only fragments of the songs, so she invented endings for half-remembered lines or created whole verses that resembled the original only in tone.

It was some time before she discovered that she had been following a well-trodden path which had led her out of the evergreens and into another part of the woods altogether where she was surrounded by the rough trunks of hardwood trees, a steady precipitation of coloured leaves, and the sound of a second voice joining hers at the end of a verse of "Renerdine." From between two sumac bushes there emerged a dark-skinned, blue-eyed girl, who looked directly into Eileen's face, threw her head back, and laughed out loud.

"Who are you?" the girls asked each other simultaneously.

"I live here," they both replied.

"You are the new people, then," said the girl, "with the big house that was a boat. I live *here*," she announced openly, grabbing Eileen's wrist and pulling her along the path between the twin fires of the sumac bushes. "I live with my father who has been here since '48. He got tired of the boat being so long from Quebec, and it was summer so he counted to twenty, jumped overboard, and swam to shore. He liked the look of the beach, you see, and there was no one on the land then. But he's never been one for living right on the water. So he walked eight thousand and nine hundred paces into the forest – one for every week of misery inflicted on the Irish by the English – and he built his house and went further north, on foot, every day, looking for some kind of work. The work was hard to find, but he found my mother in a matter of days – days, he says, just like a miracle. She was Ojibway," the girl announced, proudly. She stopped suddenly and searched Eileen's face. "You're not English, are you?" she asked suspiciously. "No . . . I thought not, you're Irish, like my dad, and I'm half that and half Ojibway because of my mother. She's dead now."

"So is mine . . . and my father, too." Eileen was surprised at the ease with which she responded to the talkative girl. "But I have a brother," she added.

"We're almost at the place now. My father has gone to work on a barn today. He said, 'They won't like it, Molly, that we're on this land, them in that fancy house. We'll just have to be quiet for a while and let our presence be known, gradual-like.' This is a wonderful day because you've come to find us."

"I didn't really come to find –"

"And you and I having so much in common we'll be like sisters, because of the Irish and our mothers being dead."

"I have a black feather," Eileen said to the girl for reasons she didn't quite understand. "And I think there was a bird."

"Dad has birds all over him when he works, and chipmunks that run up one of his arms and down the other."

They had come to a small clearing in the woods. In it there was a shanty with a tin stovepipe, a modest-sized workshed painted bright orange, and a yard filled with logs, planks, sheets of tin, and sawhorses. Above the workshop a sign proclaimed, THOMAS J. DOHERTY: SIGN PAINTER AND BARN

EMBELLISHER. But, most surprising, the surrounding area was scattered with a multi-coloured collection of wind machines that clattered and whirred in the breeze, and miniature mechanical figures churning butter, milking cows, running on the spot, riding horses, some solitary souls making ridiculous gestures with their arms or kicking wildly with their legs. Rags of various colours flapped frantically from wires supported by stakes at one end and attached by hooks to either the house or the shop at the other, causing both the surrounding forest and the clearing to look as if they had been torn to shreds. The walls of both buildings were covered with horseshoes, except those of the front and the side of the workshop, which were dressed with paintings of cows, rendered in profile and standing in a series of improbable landscapes.

"Those are what he does," said the girl, pointing to the painted cow. "Big on barns for money. He's doing one today."

"And these . . . ?" asked Eileen, looking towards the frenetic wooden figures.

"Those he does," said Molly Doherty, "for art."

Molly Doherty was her first friend, and Eileen would always love her. Never impatient with Eileen's quietness, her reticence, the dark-haired girl talked to her about anything that came into her mind – wild berries, the lake, her father, her mother's people, horses, travelling medicine shows, coveted hats – allowing Eileen the luxury of occasional companionship. She never demanded that Eileen reveal her darker side though she guessed that that side existed. She told her about O'Doherty Island which was situated off the northern coast of Ireland, how her father had said it was full of yellow meadows, white cows, and three times fifty of the world's most beautiful women. "Dad says he left the 'O' in his name with one of the beautiful women there, and he'll take me back, some day, to retrieve it."

"My mother came from a northern island," said Eileen. "One called Rathlin, where there were women who carried baskets of sea plants on their backs."

"O'Doherty Island is much different from that . . . you wouldn't be able to compare them at all, those two islands."

"Why not?"

"Because, to you it would be invisible. O'Doherty Island can only be seen by members of the O'Doherty family."

"An otherworld island."

"Yes, one of those."

"My mother's own island was closer to that than you think . . . but I can't remember why. There was something about the sea and a lake. There was a bird that belonged to me, or her, but I don't know which."

The girls talked everywhere: out on the jetty, sitting among the beach stones, walking through the woods or, if the weather was awful, as it often was, huddled inside the cluttered shanty. Only once did Molly search for information that Eileen did not willingly reveal.

"Do you have a sweetheart?" she enquired with uncharacteristic shyness.

It was early November by then and Eileen had been carrying the tension of waiting on her neck and shoulders like a taut bowstring. Still, she didn't want to loosen the string by confessing Aidan Lanighan to her friend; wanted to keep even the pain of him private, jealously hoarded, close to her blood. His continued absence was a strong thread strapped to her body, pulling her towards him.

"No . . ." she said, "not really."

"Me neither," Molly confided cheerfully. Then, seeing that

her friend's face had clouded, she changed the subject. "My father can do something else, you know."

"What's that?"

"He charms skunks."

Since the beginning of October the smell of skunks had increased in intensity at Loughbreeze Beach until now it permeated the air almost as far as the village of Colborne, and, when the breeze was from the east, well past the hamlet of Lakeport. Liam had never seen the culprits, though he kept his rifle handy for just such an occasion, but the smell of them was always with him. When there was no wind, the stench was overpowering, causing one of the hired men to quit in disgust and, once, disturbing Genesis and the other cows so much that their milk soured. Eileen did not mind the smell as much as the others did. To her it was a manifestation of the helplessness of her own state; Aidan Lanighan's after-image clinging to her like a lingering odour. Often, while washing dishes in the kitchen at night, she would gaze out the window to the dark yard and see white, fleeting exclamation marks on the grass. But, by the time her brother entered the kitchen, they would be gone – on night duty. The skunks, according to the hired hands who could live with the stench, would hibernate soon, emerging in June with litters of five or six kittens. By the smell, one of the men said, you could tell there were at least a hundred of them already.

This irritant was added to that which Liam called his "other problem in paradise": the squatter that he knew inhabited the north end of his woodlot.

A few weeks after Eileen had met and become friendly with Molly, Liam tramped out into the woods to investigate, and found Doherty, himself, working on a wind machine in the cluttered yard. "The name's Thomas J. Doherty," he had said, forcefully, knowing the purpose of Liam's visit and not looking away from the two pieces of coloured wood that he was attempting to join together.

Liam tried to ignore the torn banners that bounced in the air around him. "How long have you been living here?" he asked.

"That depends," said Doherty, pounding a pedestal for yet another carved milkmaid into the ground, "on what you mean by living." He stepped back and squinted at the post. "And, of course, what you mean by here."

"Here, on this spot, on this farm."

"A very short time indeed."

"But I thought –"

"A very short time in comparison to the long history of English injustice to the Irish. You're Irish, yourself," said Doherty, smiling beguilingly. "You've got some of the music on your tongue."

"Never mind that," said Liam. "This is my land. You can't just go on living here."

"Now, look at that little girl go!" Doherty had fixed his wind sculpture to the top of the pole. "Isn't she wonderful?"

"You must find a place of your own," said Liam weakly.

"The last one let me stay." Doherty settled himself down on top of a tree stump and slowly, casually, lit his pipe. "And he a Scotsman, name of McCormack. Sold out to you, did he? A shame that . . . the farm going so well: no pests, no problems, no bad smells. Said he wanted to write a book about some place called Patagonia. I don't know how to write myself, but I can talk and I can paint. And I can –"

"I'll give you two weeks," said Liam. "Take it or leave it."

"Well, I think I'll be taking it and leaving it," said Doherty. "Leaving it in that I'm not going anywhere, and taking it in that I'll have the two weeks and many more."

Liam saw the round face of Eileen's black-haired friend in the window. She raised her hand as if to greet him.

"Two weeks," repeated Liam in his new, landowner's voice.

"I can make your life a lot easier or a lot harder," Doherty called to Liam's retreating back. "The last one had no troubles. Your sister, now, there's a fine girl. She and my Molly have made friends."

As Liam walked back towards the barn and house, the skins of white birches flickered at the edges of his vision and sumac burned. He could tell that the wind was dropping, the smell of skunk becoming even more powerful than it had been on the previous few evenings. It was the smell of an anger, milder, more subtle than that which he experienced in adolescence. The sumac was the colour of something else altogether, something that anticipated more than the fierce winter he knew would come sweeping, in just a few weeks, up the lake from the east. He tore two or three branches off as he passed, and placed them, when he got home, in one of the sealer jars which he had bought for Eileen and which she had not yet filled.

A week later Eileen returned from visiting Molly to find the lake in a furious uproar under the sullen sky, but there was no wind around the farm buildings and the smell of skunk was heavy in the air.

Liam was tossing hay in the barn, randomly but doggedly as if he were trying to create a new topography inside a closed, controlled space.

"Mr. Doherty charms skunks," she said to him. "Molly told me."

"Oh, for God's sake, Eileen."

Eileen climbed two rungs of the ladder that led to the loft.

Holding on with one hand and one foot, she allowed her body to rotate slowly. "I believe her," she said.

Liam snorted with contempt. "Yes, and you used to talk to birds."

"I did?" Eileen swung around in the opposite direction, her hand a hinge on the wooden post. "Molly is half Ojibway," she said absently.

Liam stood up straight for a moment and leaned on the pitchfork. "Remember that Ojibway, Exodus Crow, bringing Mother back? Father was marvellously taken with him. It took me a while, but in the end I liked him too." A strong waft of skunk invaded the barn. "Jesus," said Liam, "I can't stand much more of this. Maybe this is why McCormack sold the farm, though Doherty claims he had no trouble at all with skunks."

"I don't remember the Ojibway," said Eileen.

"That's impossible," said Liam. "You liked him best of all." He resumed his work. Eileen stepped down from the ladder and walked along one beautiful board, which had been polished by grain. She could see her breath in the chill and her hands were numb with cold.

"So now you're a landlord," she said to her brother, her back turned to him.

"What do you mean by that?" he asked suspiciously.

"Well, you've got all this land and you've got people living on it and you're going to evict them."

"I bought it fair and square. I didn't seize it or anything. I paid cash."

"To whom?"

"To McCormack . . . you know that."

"And who did he get it from?"

"It was granted to him by the Crown for being in the British Army. What's this all about, Eileen?"

"And who did they – I mean the Crown – get it from?"

"They didn't get it from anyone, Eileen, it was just here, that's all."

The bottom of Eileen's skirt was covered with grain dust. She bent to brush it off. "I think they got it from someone." She reached into her pocket and pulled out a flat almost-rectangular stone, tapered at one end. Showing it to Liam, she said, "Molly says it's a skinning knife. I found it on the beach."

"Very interesting. Jesus, will this smell ever leave us?"

"I think that the English took the land from the Indians same as they took it from the Irish. Then they just starve everybody out, or . . ." she looked directly at Liam, "they evict them, or both."

Liam did not answer.

"So now you're going to evict some people from land you never would have had in the first place if the English hadn't stolen it . . . and if they hadn't stolen Ireland."

"Ireland doesn't have anything to do with it."

"Yes it *does* . . . you bought it with an Irish landlord's money."

"Now, he isn't a bad sort," said Liam defensively.

"That's because he isn't a landlord any more. It's *you* who are the landlord now."

Liam threw down the pitchfork, "When did you get so high and mighty and political? Why don't you run for Parliament if you know so much? And what is this anyway? Suddenly you're three times as talkative as you've been in months, except that what you say is crazy. I just want to farm the land . . . is that a crime? You live here too," he added.

Eileen walked towards the barn door. "If I were you," she said, "I'd give Mr. Doherty a chance with the skunks."

"Doherty has six days to get out."

"Give him a chance with the skunks, Liam," Eileen stepped over the barn's threshold. "You'll be sorry if you don't."

Liam did not speak to his sister for two days, but on the morning of the third day she saw him disappear into the cedar bush, then reappear an hour later with Doherty and Molly in tow.

As they passed the house Eileen saw the saints' medals jingling on Thomas J. Doherty's cap, and she heard him explain to Liam that the moss was growing on the west side of the maple trees and that this could only mean that the winter would be fiercely severe. They were heading for the beach. Eileen grabbed one of Liam's jackets and joined them there.

Molly had two large baskets in her hands. "Dad's making me collect the white stones," she explained to Eileen, "while he does the prayers. God, there's a powerful smell of skunk around here."

"Does this mean –"

"If the skunks go your brother says we can stay. And Dad's thrown a barn portrait of some cow called Genesis into the bargain."

Doherty was telling Liam that it was necessary to pray to saints that had connections with animals. "St. Jerome because of his lion, St. Francis because of the birds, and St. Patrick because of the banishing side of things. I come to you as a barn embellisher and a skunk banisher," he said proudly. "And as an Irishman and a devout Catholic.

"Now, it's a sad thing about skunks," he went on, "in that they have no patron saint of their own . . . they being native to North America and saints being native to the other side of the Atlantic Ocean. And the poor little devils could never stow away to get across, in that their whereabouts is so easily detected. So they have to be contented with the saints of other animals. It's a sad thing, that."

Liam nodded and looked over at Eileen, raising his eyebrows sceptically.

"Now, if St. Patrick could only have returned to do something about the English snakes," Doherty was saying. "But God must have had some larger plan."

Eileen bent down to pick up a white stone for Molly's basket, then she straightened and searched the horizon. At the edges of limestone shelves, seaweed moved in the water like long green hair. She felt comfortable, almost happy, occupied with searching, stooping, gathering. The Great Lake was speckled with pinpoints of brilliant light, as if some large power had flung down handfuls of stars. The white stones, when she found them, were cool and smooth and rested easily in the palm of her hand. Molly chatted noisily and taught Eileen how to skip flat shards of limestone over the ruffled water. "I like your brother," she said, "and he'll be better-natured after the skunks go."

Two days later the smell of skunk was stronger than ever. Doherty, when consulted by Liam, reminded him that the darkest hour was just before dawn and that patience was the virtue the Lord God cherished above all others. The farmyard was decorated with circles, arrows, and question marks, all made of white stones. And Molly, following her father's directions, had placed the words GO FORTH AND MULTIPLY ELSEWHERE on the grass where they shone in the sun in front of the long front porch.

Eileen feared for her friend. "What if they don't go . . . the skunks, I mean?" she asked her brother on the evening of the second day.

Liam put down the book he was reading, "I think they'll go . . . probably tomorrow. Besides, I don't notice the smell as much," he said vaguely, and then, as a great surprise to Eileen, he added, "Anyway, a portrait of Genesis would have been enough for me to let them stay."

The next morning at sunrise, while she was clearing the breakfast dishes, Eileen looked through the window and saw a crowd of skunks stroll casually into the woods and disappear. Thomas J. Doherty and Molly arrived an hour later to gather up the stones. "They have to be thrown into the Great Lake one by one, these white stones, otherwise the skunks will be back next year with their young," Doherty confided.

Liam emerged from the barn, shook Doherty's hand, and accompanied Molly and Eileen to the beach for the stone-throwing ceremony. Even though her eyes were mostly fixed on the horizon, where any moment a particular sail might reveal itself, Eileen couldn't help but notice that her brother was showing off, performing. With body twisted, his boots grinding into the beach pebbles, he attempted to fling his stones impossible distances out over the water.

It was a crisp day in late autumn. In Port Hope the last nails were being hammered into the latest version of the Seaman's Inn while the O'Shaunessy brothers stood on the shore, admiring the new building and arguing about the date of the official opening. Further north, in Elzivir Township, Hastings County, Osbert Sedgewick was pasting a variety of brilliant-coloured leaves into an album he'd made himself out of birch bark bound together with fence wire, and watching a man he'd hired from Madoc install a decorative wrought-iron fence around the gravestones.

And in Ottawa, the new nation's capital, the Irish-Canadian politician, D'Arcy McGee, excluded from the Dominion's first cabinet despite his efforts to bring about Confederation, limping badly because of an ulcerated leg that had flared up in the stress of the past few months, made his way slowly towards Parliament Hill. In this first parliamentary session of the new Dominion he would occupy a seat he'd barely won in the autumn election. His enemies were stalking him, his political friends abandoning him, and his electorate, the Irish poor of St. Anne's riding in Montreal, were confused by him, if not embittered. He was five foot three inches tall, uncommonly ugly, a sentimental and prolific poet, and his liver was half ruined by a lifelong fondness for the bottle. But when he opened his mouth to speak, the world around him stood at silent attention; his words a subtle net thrown over the chaos of any crowd. He had the gift and the curse of this; the ability to entrance, then to cause either permanent devotion or rage. When McGee opened his mouth to speak no one within hearing distance had the power to turn away.

In recent months he had opened his mouth to speak far too often.

Eileen took to reading the *Irish Canadian*, a Toronto hebdomadal she had discovered in Doherty's shanty and one which she remembered hanging from a wooden rod in the old Seaman's Inn. It contained an odd assortment of bad poetry, serialized romances, mildly stated manifestos, outraged letters to the editor, notices of eye and ear clinics, gossip, obituaries, birth announcements, reports of practical jokes, political satire, invitations to meetings of the Hibernian Benevolent Society and the St. Patrick's Literary Society, exaggerated editorial rants and a Believe It or Not column of freakish facts, and was considered so dangerous a Fenian menace by the authorities that its editor was regularly thrown in jail – sometimes for as long as six months – thereby making its circulation and distribution highly erratic. By the time the paper reached Eileen it was clipped, torn, scribbled-upon, and months old, having arrived, weeks late, at the home of one of Doherty's barn clients and moving from there into the barn embellisher's hands. Eileen read every line, marvelling at the miscellaneous details which included references to the twenty-three horse-flesh markets of Paris, France, and to the fact that the poet Tennyson spent long days, reading, meditating, and writing seven or eight stanzas. She absorbed the eloquent lines of McGee's latest outbursts against Irish nationalism and his denunciations of Fenian sentiment in Canada, which were reported with scornful comments attached. Her brother said the paper was nonsense and that he did not wish to see it lying around in his parlour. After that Eileen read it in secret, the door of her room locked. She was not going to give it up. She knew it was full of hidden messages from Aidan Lanighan. In its sentences she could feel the throb of his pulse.

Outside the windows, the Great Lake had begun to toss floating chunks of ice towards the shore. All sails had disappeared. This paper became her only connection to the heat, which she kept in dream and in memory, a thin silver chain linking two birds flying. It was December. Snow covered the stones. Sometimes Eileen heard the sounds of a train travelling on the track a mile north of her, its whistle an animal's cry. Her favourite poem from the paper was called "The Patriot's Bride," and it ended with the lines:

'Tis the deep unrest of her pure white breast
For the fate of this hapless land.
And the spirit that sighs for the wild uprise
Of some brave and patriot band.

On December afternoons she ironed, sometimes the same blouses and shirts, over and over again, while she whispered lines from the *Irish Canadian* aloud to herself as though committing scripture to memory. *"Darkness," said the young stranger after a silence of some minutes, "and light,"* or *Deeply regretted by all that knew him,* or *The fruit in the minds of the oppressed peasantry,* or *In Philadelphia one hundred able-bodied coloured men, all of whom served in the late war, offered their services to march to Canada's border to fight for Irish liberty and independence.*

Sometimes she merely chanted lists of new words, words she had never used in ordinary conversations: "munitions, indignation, assertion, benevolence, infamous, conspiracy, contemptuous, oblivion, detrimental." One headline caught her attention and stuck in her mind, the rest of the article having been torn out. D'ARCY MCGEE ON THE RAMPAGE! it announced, followed by one disjointed phrase from the text which began "After his calumnious Wexford speech . . ." She had looked up the word "calumnious" – "full of trickery" – in her father's old dictionary, which Liam had carried in his pack on their long night walk, then she had looked up the word "rampage." "Storm, rage, rush about," the dictionary told her. "To go about in an excited, furious, violent manner," it said. It was what she wanted, she knew, this rampage, and she resented its excesses being in the custody of the betrayer.

She was ironing in the afternoon, applying heat and pressure to cloth, inhaling the smell of clean linen, the word "rampage" thundering in her mind when she saw Aidan Lanighan at the end of the lane. At first she thought that Liam, who had taken the cutter into town, had gone into the ditch and was return-ing on foot. Then she saw the colour of the walker's hair against the snow. He was hunched into the wind, his hands pushed into his pockets. She couldn't move, could barely blink. He was smaller than she remembered, his posture bent. Eileen watched herself run down the lane, her hair a fire in winter, but found she was locked in the pose she had entered when she first glanced through the window; one hand reaching for a clean shirt waiting on a chair back, the other holding the iron upright, her mouth still forming the shape of the last whispered sound. Then her joints unlocked and she sprang to the door, knocking over the chair, the iron as she ran out into the winter air. "Christ," she thought, "Liam will see his foot-steps," having believed all this time that his path to her would be a traceless journey moved by wind over the lake. When she reached him she grabbed his sleeve and dragged him towards the barn. He laughing in her grasp, his hair filled with snow.

In the loft he thrust his hands into her clothing, seeking her skin, and she gasped at the chill of his fingers, her face at his neck and the breath from both their mouths visible everywhere.

"Are you alone?" he asked.

Her face was flushed, perspiration at her hairline in spite of the cold. "Liam's not here, if that's what you mean."

"I need to stay for a few days."

"But he'll be back and he won't let you in."

"I can stay up here . . . just for two nights, then I'll jump the train for Montreal."

"Where have you come from? Where have you been?"

"Toronto."

"It'll be cold out here . . . you'll freeze."

"There's straw . . . I'll manage. If you bring me food, I'll manage."

At the sound of sleigh bells Eileen scrambled down the ladder, shaking the straw from her skirts as she descended. "I'll come in the dark," she whispered.

The kitchen, when she entered it, was full of the smell of smoke, though the air was bright and clear. Eileen righted the overturned chair and stooped to pick up the iron where it had fallen. It had burned a black triangular shape into the floor, some singed varnish was still attached to its underside. The mark, itself, she thought fleetingly, looked like the charred hoofprint of a huge beast.

Subsequent generations of the family would be superstitious about removing the board with the mark on it, but they wouldn't know why. When they questioned her, Old Eileen would shrug and look the other way. But the young girl that she was now ran her fingers over its surface, feeling the heat still contained in the wood grain. To her it was evidence of her own emotion; the moment of contact with the dream, Aidan Lanighan's hand burning the flesh at her waist.

Late that night she removed from a hook on the woodshed wall the lantern that had lit the dark summer walk, and with several matches in her pocket, and pork, bread, and butter wrapped in cheesecloth under her elbow, Eileen walked across the new-fallen snow, willing a wind to spring up before dawn to erase her footsteps. Standing under the loft she lit the wick and began to climb the ladder, placing the lantern on the overhead beam, so that her arrival was preceded by golden light and leaping shadows. Aidan Lanighan was curled up, trembling on the straw. The night was clear and cold; stars penetrated the spaces between the boards on the other, darker side of the barn. While he tore at bread and meat, Eileen assaulted him with questions, demanded the details of his life. He would not tell her why he had been in Toronto, and offered, instead, a scant account of his childhood in the Irish slum of Griffintown in Montreal. Like Liam, he had arrived in Canada a famine child, his mother dying in the fever sheds, his father becoming a poorly paid labourer. He told her that he, himself, had been apprenticed as a tailor by a neighbour. It was easy work, he said, could be done anywhere. He was thinking of moving to Ottawa.

He'd been in jail after the Fenian invasion, and his father as well and "as many Irish-Catholic wretches as the bastards could lay their hands on." Many of his friends – even some priests. "None of us," he said, "had anything to do with it. Some of them had never even heard the word 'fenian' before. It was a disgrace."

"I know all about it," said Eileen. "Do you know the editor called Boyle?"

"Yes, I know Boyle."

"I've been reading his paper and understanding it. I've been understanding the injustice."

"Injustice, is it?" he was amused by her use of the word.

"And about the man McGee – his speeches."

"I've heard McGee, many times."

"And he a turncoat. St. Anne's is his riding is it not? Isn't that where Griffintown is? And now he's turned traitor."

"How would you know about that?"

"It says so in the paper. You know Patrick Boyle and hasn't he a way of saying things in his paper?"

"I don't know about that."

"But he has, you must see –"

"I don't know," Aidan Lanighan interrupted, "because I never learned how to read."

Because of the cold, they gained, on that first night, a fractional, disjointed knowledge of each other's bodies, Aidan allowing four or five inches of cloth to separate around a breast, Eileen unbuttoning six inches of shirt to place her cheek against the fur near his heart. The pain of his entry into her body caused her to cry out and he covered her mouth with the cool curve of his palm until she whimpered and quieted and began to feel the pain being replaced by a kind of sorrow which she would only later recognize as pleasure. Afterwards he wept, briefly, before collapsing into an agitated sleep during which his limbs twitched as if they remembered dancing. Eileen was aware of hot liquid on her inner thighs and the slight touch of his tears running down her neck. She covered him with the thick paisley shawl her brother had bought for her in Port Hope, and gazed at his smooth face for an hour in the lamplight, his breath clouding the air between them, her own breath coming in convulsive jerks, and her hands, as she tried to straighten her hair and button her clothing, shaking.

When she stood to leave, Aidan awakened and clutched at her skirt, pulling her down beside him. "Listen," he whispered, "it was in the cell that I taught myself to dance, at night when the others grew tired and lonely and pulled into themselves. I could whistle, so I did that for a while, till the guard shouted at me to stop. But I wouldn't stop. I whistled more and I began to dance and dance until the men came cheering to the bars of their cells. I was beaten once for dancing, but I wouldn't stop."

"Did you dance for McGee?"

"I tried."

"But he never understood it?"

"No, he never understood it."

During the following two days she would sometimes slip out of the house with warm milk from the cow or a bowl of porridge, but mostly she kept close to the kitchen, not wanting to arouse her brother's suspicions. The second night she undressed Lanighan and ran her hands all over the unfamiliarity of his body while he lay shivering and laughing in the cold. Then she flung her own clothes onto the straw and lay beside him, seeing her long soft leg beside his harder, darker one. His skin tasted of salt and dust, his mouth on her nipple the only warm spot in a frozen world. When they could no longer bear the chill they burrowed into the straw, the discarded clothing, and attacked each other's heat, gasping with exertion. Eileen was devastated, torn apart by the new pleasurable sorrow. Lanighan wrapped her hair around his neck like a scarf and they both slept, bound together.

Once, waking suddenly, Eileen shook his shoulder. "I remember you," she said, her hand clutching his hair. "There's something in me that remembers you from somewhere."

"The Seaman's Inn."

"No . . . somewhere else. How could I know you this well?" She pulled on her woollen skirt, her boots. "We'll never leave each other, even if we have to be apart."

Eileen reached for the knife she had brought with the bread and meat. Bending forward in the light she cut a length of her hair and handed it to him.

"Keep this always," she said. Wind shook the barn and pushed its way through several cracks. Aidan groaned and covered his legs with straw. "You take all the warmth with you when you leave," he said.

The next morning he was gone.

Snow hurtled past the windows of the farmhouse at Loughbreeze Beach. Aidan had departed in the middle of the early-morning storm, leaving no footprints in the yard. Eileen stared hard at the straw, now, wanting it to hold some formal imprint of his body, a memory of his presence. But there was nothing of him there, no souvenir. Nothing except the long piece of her hair, looking discarded and dead in the weak winter light. He hadn't taken this one gift she had given him and, she suddenly realized, he hadn't even asked about the pistol.

Walking through the house, Eileen felt helpless, grief-stricken, and enraged. For days, after cursorily performing chores, she toured the locations that had been touched by Aidan's existence. The parlour that in another life had been shaken by his dance, the upstairs hall where he had first pushed his mouth against hers, the dark triangular mark on the kitchen floor caused by his appearance in the lane. Angrily scrubbing floors, she avoided the spots where he had stood or leapt, fearing that the brush and suds might erase any trace, any scent of him from the architecture that held her – from her life.

At night she lay awake while storms howled and the house creaked in the wind, inventing a community for him – a brave and patriot band – composed of the few scraps of information he had given her, the Celtic sagas of "old sorrows" her father had told to her, and the bizarre combinations of fact and fiction she read in the *Irish Canadian*. In her dreams, McGee loomed, a crouching beast, an awkwardly shaped iceberg, she on a far shore and Aidan beckoning from its summit.

Her father had often sung the Irish song about Castle O'Neill to her in the evenings while she sat on his lap near the fire. Once, she asked him to translate, and her child's mind, drawn to the picture the words painted, had retained one verse. She had sung the words one winter day when the empty threads of the willow were covered with frost. She had been surrounded by glitter; the shadow of the tree's branches a network of blue veins on the snow. Now she whispered the words as she toured the house, "No dowry I hope for of sheep or cattle or lands, but my two hands supporting your head like a clustering branch," and never thought about the branches that had often supported her.

Three days before Christmas, Thomas J. Doherty dragged a fir tree down the path that emerged from the cedar bush and into the parlour, then returned the following day with an assortment of birds he had carved and painted for its branches. Eileen cooked a goose for her brother, the Dohertys, and the hired men. She made plum pudding with hard sauce and cut star-shaped cookies from damp flat oatmeal batter. But the house seemed to her to lean in odd directions as if in memory of its lake cruise, and the jagged chunks of ice which filled the little bay looked sharp and threatening. Liam and Molly sang Christmas carols together and one of the hired men had an accordion. Eileen fought the desire to dig her elbows into her side and bend over in pain. The bright ice on the lake was impossible to look at. Neither the winter orchard nor the dusky cedars surrounded by snow soothed her. There was no neutral view.

She created Aidan over and over, gave him lines he had never uttered. "I love you," he said in her imagination. "You are my heart's darling." Then, looking into the hell of the cookstove fire, she would think, He forgot my hair; he didn't even remember that he gave me the gun.

The bands of wild rovers, desperate warriors for justice, and heartbroken Irish nationalists that she had concocted as a family for Aidan Lanighan were never still in her mind. They galloped over hills with the wind in their hair or leapt back and forth on the trunks of enormous, floating trees as she had seen men do in logging season in Elzivir Township. They ran by night with the moon on their shoulders, and when they sat at the table and talked – using the new phrases she had learned from Boyle's paper – they were tense, straight spined, poised for flight. They had in their bodies the energy of the young horses she remembered pounding recklessly through the dawn fields she and her brother had passed that summer. They were brothers-in-arms, fiercely loyal, and their arena was the new dominion. Though they were all men, she believed that she was one of them, that Aidan Lanighan's touch had guaranteed her a role in the theatre, the performances, that made up their lives.

Soon after the January thaw, and the arrival of the arctic air that always followed it, the bay beyond the stony beach froze smooth and deep in frigid, windless air and the population of the village of Colborne came by cutter to the Great Lake, bringing skates and iceboats with them. Molly and Liam joined them, as did Thomas J. Doherty, his own iceboat sporting colourful sails and tiny decorative windmills. Eileen stood at the window where Aidan Lanighan had brooded, where she, herself, had watched the shoreline of the Great Lake glide by; and noted that the bay had become a public gathering place. Where once there had been only shining, limitless water, and the expectation of a particular sail, there was now a collection of bundled parsons and grocers, elder sons and youngest daughters, farmers and millers, wives, and spinsters. Something else was steering Eileen from the ordinary, she knew; separating her, making it possible for her to join her patriot band and lie in the arms of her lover. Even those she loved, her brother and the Dohertys, were able to skate happily among the throng, shouting greetings, in exuberant goodwill, while she had affiliated herself with Aidan Lanighan's unseen companions and all the old sorrows she believed they cherished. She put on her blue cloak and bonnet and drove the sleigh, as she did often now, to see the two-fifteen rattle by, heading noisily east, towards Montreal. She had, she realized, nothing of her own except her separation from the facile skaters, a memory of a young man's body, the dream of a corps linked by passion, and her fixed state of single-minded desire. And in an upstairs drawer her underclothes and outer garments, and three or four significant objects, one of them a pistol.

After the train had passed, and all traces of its pandemonium had disappeared from the atmosphere, Eileen waited, as always, for twenty minutes, believing that Aidan Lanighan had stepped down from one of its coaches at the station in Colborne and was making his way towards her sleigh having completed some clouded mission in Toronto. Then, when he did not come, she pulled angrily on the reins, turned the cumbersome sleigh around, and sped back to the lake and the bright, forgotten room where Aidan Lanighan had danced; a room from which, she was beginning to believe, he would be forever absent.

By the time her brother and Molly stumbled awkwardly on their skate blades into the house, she had already removed a fifty-pound note from the much-diminished pile which Liam kept in a cookie tin underneath his bed, and added it to her collection of special items in the drawer.

That night, while Liam walked Molly back to the shanty in the cedar woods, Eileen stared for a long time at the three-quarter moon over the frozen lake. The ice looked like tin, cheap and plentiful; the moon, itself, as though it could be easily flicked, like a coin, from the sky. No magic existed beyond the plans she created for Aidan Lanighan, and herself at his side. Since the arrival of the frigid air no new snow had fallen, and the ground beyond the porch was unyielding in the moonlight. She would search for her lover, leave this place.

In her large room with its view of the lake Eileen turned her back to the moon and wrote a verse into the long, undeliverable letter she spent her evenings composing.

I would know your shadow even outside in bright sunshine.
Bright hero and love for whom I have suffered censure,
It is your thick curling hair that has filled me with
   melancholy,
And it's parting with you that has left forever this pain in
   my side.

She stopped writing and looked for a while into the flame of the oil lamp. If he didn't appear at the end of the lane in two months she would have to go to find him. The paralyzed lake beyond her windows led to a wide river, and the wide river to

Montreal. She imagined skating there while the ordinary throng lay sleeping in their beds. Then she remembered the silver rails she visited each day. She would wait until spring, and if he didn't come she would go to find him.

Eileen drew a thick line through the word "forever" in the last part of the verse. She would not wait, not suffer forever.

Further north, in Elzivir Township, there had been a snowfall, and Osbert Sedgewick, extinguishing the last oil lamp in the cabin, looked out through the window. He was amazed at the delicate blue glitter of the acres of light and moved by the pattern that the decorative iron fence around the three graves drew on the drifts near the marble stones. He thought of Liam and Eileen, of their new prosperity in a fledgling land, how their children's children would walk free, serve no master, worship where they choose, answer to no one. He did not know that there was an inner theatre where a girl could build a prison. He did not see Eileen translating from myth to life the songs her father had taught her.

AFTER the fine day and the sudden bout of celebratory skating, winter attacked Loughbreeze Beach with exuberance, blizzard after blizzard shrieking inland from the centre of the lake. In odd, calm moments drifts crawled up the verandah steps towards the front door, frost blossomed on glass, the arms of fir trees bent under thick white capes.

Liam snowshoed daily to the Dohertys' home, often bringing Molly back with him in hopes that she would cheer up his sister, whose brooding had finally caught his attention. With Molly, conversation and companionship and laughter entered the parlour. She sometimes carried copies of the *Irish Canadian*. "Eileen likes to read it," she insisted in the face of Liam's objections, "for the poems." His sister's sadness confused and troubled him. If she wanted poems she could have them. It never occurred to him that politics and desire had seized her imagination, that during this short, severe winter they were creating a private blizzard in her skull, though the part of him that was like his father wondered why, if she wanted poetry, she did not turn to Latin or to the Greeks. But his own state of mind was joyous and electric. He had asked Molly Doherty to marry him – the sooner the better. He was anxious for sons, for more acreage under the plough, and, most of all, though he would not admit it, for a woman to warm his bed. Thomas J. Doherty was delighted with the arrangement, though he said, himself, that love was the greatest of the seven sorrows, so powerful that it had made him forget the other six.

For his birthday, which fell in January, Molly made Liam a cloth envelope in which to keep his two bow ties, and on its surface she had coyly embroidered the phrase "Not the Only Tie that Binds." Their happiness hurt Eileen.

In an old issue of the *Irish Canadian* she read about Thomas D'Arcy McGee, how he had threatened to expose the Fenians of Montreal and how he had made good on that threat in an early December edition of the *Ottawa Citizen*. Eileen scrutinized the list of names with a pounding heart, in the same manner that she had, months earlier, scrutinized the horizon for a particular sail. When she did not find the words "Aidan Lanighan" she was not sure whether it was relief or disappointment that she felt. In early February she read that McGee had been expelled from the St. Patrick's Society as a result of his "blasphemous charges." Eileen imagined Thomas D'Arcy McGee, a small man, a failed Fenian, no longer young, filled with envy, and self-serving to the end. She imagined Aidan, straight and shining, locked in debate with McGee; the beauty and virility of his dance. He was like Oisín in the land of the forever young; righteousness in his anger, the memory of a wronged brotherhood still hot in his brain.

"My people," she whispered, thinking of how her father had explained Oisín, Finn, and the Fianna to her. "Our people."

She wanted to be like Deirdre, running wild in the woods in the intimate company of doomed brothers. "All stories," her father had told her, "are born of sorrows." She sensed her own story unfolding without her as she cooked or slept or built fires, trapped by winter in a house from which all action had fled. Powerless, she had not even the ownership of her sorrows, they being attached inexorably to that which was absent. She wanted the power, the collusion, the potential for tragedy. During the day she gazed through Aidan Lanighan's abandoned tavern window, at storms out over the lake – storms of which she was not a part.

At night she dreamed that her soul was caught in the teeth of these storms, had joined their forces, was hammering the house, her prison. Then she dreamed that her soul stayed wedded to the energy of blizzards as they headed east, along the lakeshore towards the river St. Lawrence, towards Montreal.

By the end of March the ferocity of the winter of 1868 began to lose momentum. Temperatures soared, soggy drifts were replaced by tufts of grey grass and by barnyard mud, except in the half-acre hardwood lot where a large handkerchief of snow still lay undisturbed and shining. Liam spent his days oiling and polishing his new collection of ploughs and his nights midwifing a menagerie of healthy baby animals. He seemed never to sleep, his hours filled either with courting or birthing or preparing for the opening up of the earth. All the same there was a crisp alertness about him, usually associated with the well rested, a tidiness about his activities. Eileen found it difficult to define the change in her brother. She had lost the ability to recognize contentment.

On a Tuesday morning in the midst of this spring thaw, Eileen awoke resolved. She packed a case with blouses, clean underclothes, a hairbrush, a bottle of rosewater, and a pair of beautiful new white boots. To this collection of objects she added the braided hair, the black feather, the pistol, then closed the bag and hid it behind the cloth curtain that covered her closet. Humming an Irish revolutionary song, the fifty-pound note tucked in her camisole, she walked downstairs with an air of innocence and started the morning fires.

Liam was anxious to get to the livestock, so bolted his breakfast. As he passed Eileen on his way out the door he pinched her waist and asked, "How's the brooder this morning?" Teasing, not waiting for a reply. The other men, having been mystified by her for months, did not look at her or speak to her at all.

When the house was empty and silent, she visited all its sacred spots: windows, marks, certain floorboards. Superstitiously, she felt compelled to look one last time at the loft where she and Aidan had made love, where the exquisite sorrow of pleasure had first made itself known to her. But when she had put on her old brown boots and walked halfway across the yard she remembered that her brother was attending to the calves and cows and turned back towards the house. She couldn't bear to look at Liam's innocent face on this morning, was frightened of her love for him, of her blood connection to him, and almost certain that she would never see him again. Walking away she heard him speaking the Latin words of Ovid to the cows and she hesitated, recalling a light in a forest window, three modest graves, a field of winter wheat.

As she placed her hand on the door to the house, she could hear the sound of the past, her father's skis approaching, the lessons Liam had taught her. The frond of a willow branch waved in her memory, her mind briefly greened. Aidan Lanighan danced, his feet drumming a tattoo, a command. She must travel the muddy, wrecked roads, twelve miles to the station at Brighton where nobody knew her, must compose herself so that she would look like an ordinary girl on an ordinary journey.

She walked through the house and up the stairs to fetch her case, then came back down again. She left a track of muddy footprints going both ways; a confusing, remnant map of her intentions, suggesting a frantic uncertainty about the direction of her flight.

She ran across the yard and into the lane. Recently, as she had stared out the kitchen window, this avenue had transformed itself in her mind into a processional aisle leading to the arms of Aidan Lanighan, a way of access to an enriched life. She remembered him hunched at the end of it, emerging from falling snow.

Passing the cedar bush she thought briefly of Molly, her friend, her supporter. She remembered how Molly had looked in the grain field in August, her dark hair and skin, her white teeth and dress. How she would make a band with some grain stalks, tie a sheaf, toss it up in the air, make another band and tie another sheath before the first one hit the ground. To Eileen she had looked like a joyful, industrious juggler. Molly would be sitting now in the shanty mending linen for the wives in town, a stew she had prepared for her father's evening meal bubbling on the stove. She was a woman who loved the actual, who never doubted her own uncomplicated perceptions of the world, while everything solid around Eileen wavered and withdrew.

Liam would not be able to remove Eileen's footsteps from the stairs, suffering from the loss of her and anxious to keep some evidence of her. But Molly, strong and practical, in firm belief that Eileen would return, scrubbed the floors clean, and the stairs, step by step, ten days later when Liam brought her home as his new bride and mistress of the house.

In the future it would be Molly who made the farm pulse with energy so that barns would seem more substantial, the fields richer, the crops thicker; she who carried the cells of both the old world and the new in the construction of her bones and blood. As an old man, Liam would recall and then list all her accomplishments. She could carry a two-hundred-pound bag of salt on her back. She could stand at one end of the kitchen and skid fourteen plates down the long pine table and have each arrive at the correct spot. She could load sixty cedar logs onto the horse sleigh, drive off to Hayne's Mill, and return at dusk with enough shingles for a new roof.

"All I had to do," Liam would say, "was hang my pants at the foot of the bed and she'd be pregnant."

In the end Molly would successfully raise five children, four of whom were her own.

Eileen stepped from the train into ankle-deep water and into confusion. Disoriented and stunned by the overnight journey in the swaying railway coach, she stood entirely still for several minutes with her case hanging from her left hand and her skirts lifted and clutched into a lump near her right knee, watching the clods of mud that had collected on her boots during the walk to Brighton disengage, disintegrate, and float away from her – the last traces of her previous life. She wondered if the Great Lake she had abandoned had followed her here, unwilling to let go of its influence on her future. She recalled that she had always anticipated a sail, an arrival by water. Then she sloshed forward into the watery streets.

A boy in hip waders sidled up to her and, when she asked, he said, "C'est le fleuve dans les rues – the river in the streets – at each spring she is coming like this into the streets." Then, laughing and splashing, he jumped away. "You will be wanting a boat," he called over his shoulder.

She approached a policeman in rubber boots, assuming, because of his uniform, that he was a soldier. "Griffintown," she said, "where is Griffintown?" Her feet were already aching with cold.

He pointed to the south. "Down there," he said, "up to its arse in the river. As for me," he added, "I always felt that the whole neighbourhood would be much improved if they held it completely under water for twenty minutes or so. It appears God agrees with me."

Eileen stepped awkwardly forward in the direction he had indicated. When walking, she felt the water touch first her shins, then her knees, and she thought that the river was rising, but gradually she realized that the street, itself, was descending under her feet. Two small children bobbed by, singing, in a rainbarrel. Men approached her in punts, leering, and offering her transportation for free. She staggered away from them, frightened, pushing against the current, her lips blue with cold. I will die, she thought. I will die before I find him. Eventually a large woman, surrounded by baskets of clean linen, poled towards her on a section of wooden sidewalk. "Come on board, *chérie*," she said, "or you'll have no feet left to travel with. *Va t'en!*" she shrieked at a bearded man who was circling Eileen in a skiff. "*Cochon*," she muttered under her breath, and then to Eileen. "Where are you going?"

"Griffintown." Eileen's teeth were chattering as she crawled onto the makeshift raft, then, remembering a hotel mentioned in the *Irish Canadian*, she said, "I'm looking for the Old Countryman's Inn."

"*Oh, la*," said the woman, "*en bas*. Down on the quays. It will be murderous there . . . *vous avez besoin d'un bateau*. But I will take you part way."

The whole population of the city had moved, depending on its location and elevation, one or two or several feet skywards. Business was being conducted from second-storey windows. Wooden sidewalks, chained to front doorsteps, were being used as landing docks, or, in some cases, as parlours where people in rocking chairs sat smoking and chatting in the sun. Small boats were rowed in and out of large ground-floor windows. A cabinet full of broken china swept majestically towards an intersection Eileen and the woman were approaching, and had to be poled out of the way. Heading in the opposite direction, his long ears floating on the surface of the brown water, a dog paddled calmly past. Someone whistled from a rooftop and the animal turned left, swam through an open balcony door, and disappeared.

The raft was brought to a halt in front of a diminutive structure called Le Grand Hotel. "I stop here," the woman said to Eileen, then shouted, "*Un bateau, un bateau pour la jeune fille! Maurice, es-tu là?*" A grey head appeared from a third-floor window. "*Un instant,*" a man croaked testily.

"He is my husband, *mon mari,*" the woman told Eileen. "He has a boat tied up inside which he will not allow anyone to row but him . . . so I have to push the sidewalk to bring home *le nettoyage. Il est très stupide,* but he will not bother you because he is afraid of me. Maurice," she called again as an old rowboat nosed its way through the front door. The woman looked sternly at her husband, "She is looking for the Old Countryman's Inn," she said to him. "She is from some other place."

As Eileen sat at the bow of the rowboat, heading south, the waterline crawled up the faces of the buildings she passed. She could see islands, now, in the wide expanse of river, and the amazing span of Victoria Bridge, arching like a rainbow inundated at both ends.

"She will start to go down tomorrow," said the boatman shyly. "The ice is broken now, but you will need the third floor of the Old Countryman's because it is down by the quays and because of the water level."

Eileen was having trouble distinguishing between that which was afloat and that which was grounded. They had entered a poorer section of the city, now, where ragged families were huddled on thatched or tin rooftops, surrounded by tables, chairs, and a few miserable chickens. The odd stone building emerged at infrequent intervals looking like a ship moored in a harbour otherwise filled with wrecked vessels. Clumps of sod from submerged huts joined dancing chunks of ice on the water's surface. "Their huts," the boatman explained, nodding in the direction of one particularly wretched collection of individuals, and then pointing to a small floating island of mud and wattle and straw, "their huts melt each spring. The *Irlandais*, the Irish."

Then he asked, "Someone waits for you at the Old Countryman's?"

"No . . . but perhaps I will find news of him there."

"Then I will wait in case you wish to go somewhere else, Mademoiselle."

The proprietors of the Old Countryman's Inn were discovered in a third-floor room sitting atop the several wooden cases that contained the hotel's entire stock of whiskey.

"Except for one or two bottles that floated away," explained a round, balding man with a florid face.

"Mademoiselle is looking for someone," the boatman said.

"And who might that be?"

"Mister Aidan Lanighan," ventured Eileen, hesitantly, her face flushing.

The bald man beamed. "Lanighan, is it? Would you not be content with myself?"

"He said he lived in Griffintown," she added, looking towards the boards at the bottom of the boat.

"Well, he does, but then so do I." The man laughed aloud at her silent embarrassment. "Oh, go find him, then. Forty-three Rue Coleraine. Lucky for him he has the garret."

Eileen recognized the name. "Is it the same Coleraine as in Ireland?" She remembered her father speaking of the market there.

"Of course it is. Would there be any other Coleraine?" As he walked away from the window the bald man unfurled the paper that was tucked under his left elbow. Eileen was delighted to see that he was reading the *Irish Canadian*.

Eileen watched the partly submerged hotel withdraw, its waist encircled by water. A flock of large Canada geese dived, honking, from the sky, skidding across the surface on either side of the boat, raising a tremendous wake and filling the air with an argumentative babble. They swam towards a nearby bakery where loaves of bread had sailed into the street and now bumped gently against the shop's exterior wall.

The garret of 43 Rue Coleraine turned out to be the upper storey of a wooden house, ancient by new world standards, its foundations washed away by years of spring flooding, its clapboards askew. Built on such uncertain ground, the structure managed to lean exaggeratedly to the right and to sag simultaneously in the middle. Above the water level only the cedar-shingled roof, one dormer window, and two or three feet of lopsided clapboard were visible. All around the building were a variety of other roofs in varying stages of dilapidation – some thatch, some tin, some holding the unfortunate inhabitants, others empty, the residents having fled to higher ground. One old man sat smoking a pipe, his back against a crumbling chimney. It was he who pointed out the open window which belonged to number 43. He stabbed the air with his pipe stem and winked at Eileen. "He got home last night," he said, "late. Actually, he got home this morning."

Maurice brought the boat up to the window ledge. "Look inside," he said. "Is he there?"

Eileen saw a form, sprawled on a mattress. "Yes, he's there."

"*Eh bien, au revoir.*"

"I'll pay you. How much?"

"No charge . . . this has been a few hours of quiet on a pleasant day. *Faites attention*, be careful, you can climb in the window. You are in no danger. The river, she goes down tomor-row."

Eileen stood just on the other side of the window, listening to the water lap against the outside wall and looking at one perfect hand which lay in the path of the late-afternoon sun, the shadows of the lightly curled fingers raking across the palm.

That hand has touched me, she thought.

As her eyes adjusted, the rest of Lanighan's body came into focus, the chest moving under the even rhythm of deep-sleep breathing, one leg crossed over the other below the knee as if arrested in mid dance step, the arm that did not extend towards the sun flung across his forehead. The face was composed, washed clean of expression, the exact eyebrows mirrored by two dark circles under the closed eyes, the jaw shadowed by a three-day beard.

His beauty terrified her.

The wallpaper in the room was stained, missing altogether in some sections. Loosened by damp, in places it hung in large curls from the walls, rising and falling in the breeze which passed through the window. Above the mattress hung a picture of the Sacred Heart of Jesus, and Eileen was moved by this, imagining Lanighan finding the hammer and nail to hang it there. His mouth was open, like a child's. Occasionally his arm twitched. When she looked at his boots, which lay discarded, far from each other, at opposite ends of the room, Eileen's eyes filled with tears. She dropped her case lightly to the floor. The sound caused him to stir, then roll over towards the wall, but not to awaken. She didn't know what to do. There was nothing in this room but a mattress and a sleeping boy with a bleeding heart above his head, and nothing beyond the room but a river that had tried to imitate a Great Lake.

Years later, Eileen would tell her granddaughter, "This is

309

what love is like, one is asleep and the other is awake but you never know which one is dreaming."

She leaned against the ledge of the open window. The sun had already moved a half a foot across the mattress and was creeping through Lanighan's curls towards his eyelid. When it brushed his cheekbone he awakened, leaping immediately to his feet, looking wildly around the room.

Eileen crossed the floor, her arm held out to steady him. "It's me," she said, her hand on his shoulder. "I've come to help the cause."

"The cause," he repeated, still stunned by sleep.

"I've come to help you ruin the traitor McGee."

"You've come for *that*?" He shook his head to throw off drowsiness.

"I waited. I waited all the time," she said, "for you to come. But while I waited I learned more about the truth of things."

"The truth . . . ?"

"Our people . . . the oppression . . . the injustice," she declared passionately. "My father said they took away our language and our voice."

Lanighan walked slowly back and forth across the dark end of the room. "Your father," he said, "knew all about this, did he? How was it that your father stayed alive?"

"He's dead."

"But while he was alive."

"He was a schoolmaster . . . and a farmer, though Liam says the land was impossible."

"He was privileged."

"Privileged!" Eileen's face flushed. "Privileged? He almost starved to death during the famine."

"All of our mothers and fathers almost starved to death in the famine – many *did* starve! But your father . . . he had land, land and learning: two privileges. And now, Liam . . . land

and learning . . . the first bought with a landlord's money, the second acquired in leisure time. What about *my* people? What about the rest of us who had neither the land nor the leisure? What about the rest of us who have to live in this soggy rotten mess they call Griffintown?"

Eileen did not answer but backed towards the window. She could hear the water slosh against the clapboard, and for the first time she realized that below her there were rooms underwater. Outside, men were whistling and calling to one another in boats.

Lanighan ran his hand through his hair. "I'm only half awake," he said. "Never listen to me when I'm only half awake."

"Do you want me to go, then?" Eileen's voice trembled. "Do you not want me to be here at all?"

"I want you," he said. A statement, a fact. "I'm awake now. For a while I must have thought you were a dream."

That night the river water receded, unnoticed by the young man and the girl whose nightgown spilled like milk around them both in the dark. Eileen did not see that the mattress on which they lay was old and torn or that the blankets which eventually covered them were worn and faded, nor had she seen the crack in the glass that cut across the Sacred Heart poised above the bed.

She re-enacted in her mind the journey in lurching coaches and swaying boats, except that now the passing landscape was so altered by pleasure that her own transformation was deep and cellular. When she closed her eyes under the pressure of Aidan's body, a succession of images appeared in her mind – the bow of a boat bisecting flood water, the mud and stones of the road to Brighton, the footprints left behind on stairs, the wake made by a floating sidewalk, weeds trembling in a wind produced by hurtling machinery. The subtle consequences of flight.

She was annexing his power, felt it travel her bloodstream as they moved together, and for the first time she said his name over and over, the sound of it finally comfortable on her tongue, the beginning of a new language, the long and the short vowel sounds and the fierce consonant which joined and divided them. They were of the same tribe and she was strong in his arms, ready to seize the new territory.

"Aidan," she said, running her hand over the smooth curve of his shoulder. "Aidan, it's a wonderful name you have."

"It's a saint's name, hardly the one for me."

"But the sound of it . . ." she paused. "Is my own name, do you think, right for me?"

He did not answer. He had fallen, again, into the tunnel of sleep.

LATE the next morning Aidan and Eileen awoke to the smell of mildew and dissolved wallpaper paste; odours they had ignored the night before. They dressed and descended the damp stairs to assess the damage to the rest of the house. A film of pale brown mud covered all the furniture that had not been taken to higher ground and stained the cracked walls and warped floorboards. Detritus was everywhere: handbills, twigs, newspapers, hair ribbons, one glove, a toy boat and, in a first-floor room, a trout, imprisoned, drowned by air, flopping feebly in the half inch of water that remained. Aidan kicked open the doors of a woodstove and muddy water spilled onto his boots.

"They'll be back soon," he said, "to clean this up."

"They?"

"The ones that live here." He took Eileen's hand and led her to a small room at the north end of the central hall. "This is where my father died," he said darkly, "though there's nothing of him left here at all . . . nothing at all."

"When did he die?"

"Last year." Aidan rubbed dirt from the surface of one window pane, revealing a view of a narrow plot of mud surrounded by a broken board fence. "He was forty-eight. Died in his sleep. Heart failure."

"Do you have brothers and sisters?"

"Not any more. Only my father and I survived the emigration. My sister died on the boat and then my mother and

313

brothers were taken to the fever sheds. We never saw them again."

"I don't remember my mother," said Eileen, "alive."

The reek of rotten wood and mould was all around them, the air heavy, filled with moisture. A rusted stovepipe, from which the stove had been removed, projected from one wall, an ominous downspout which spat a trickle of brown water. Liquid ran like rats inside the walls.

"My father worked on the bridge out there," Aidan said, waving his arm towards the south, "and once when they were sinking a piling they came to some bones, and then more bones, and more bones. They'd found the mass grave, you see, where thousands of us were thrown. Everyone working on the bridge was Irish, so it was their own brothers and children and wives they were uncovering. They wouldn't go on with it" – he coughed – "they *couldn't* go on with it . . . no matter what the bosses said. There were fights. Some of the men sat down and wept. No one would turn another inch of soil."

He cleared his throat and looked away from Eileen. "They moved the location of the bridge, then, Misters Brassey and Betts."

"Out of respect?"

"There was *no* respect, Eileen, there is never any respect. You've come to the wrong place if you're looking for that. They did it because the men wouldn't work and there's no labour cheaper than Irish labour."

She noticed that his right hand was clenched.

"They pulled a huge rock out of the river the next week and the men decided it should be a memorial. So there it stands – one great Jesus rock and six thousand Irish under it. That's where my family is."

Eileen touched his sleeve. "We'll change everything," she said. "It's in us to change it all."

314

The house was leaking, ticking like a discrete collection of clocks.

"You think so, do you? McGee was our only hope. He had all our love and he never understood it."

"Yes," said Eileen, "he never understood it."

Eileen followed him that day through the dirty, sodden streets of Griffintown. Lanighan's world – a world awkwardly reassembling itself. People called to the young man from doorways and rooftoops. Some flung him the opening line of a song which he answered in a rich voice, finishing the verse before proceeding down the street. Others shook his hand and told him their troubles. He stopped often, to help women and old men return cumbersome furniture to drenched rooms, or to drag feather mattresses out into the sun to dry. He and Eileen ate on a street corner – a sausage, a chunk of bread – and drank from bottles passed to them through windows. Ragged girls leaning in groups against wet walls whispered and giggled as they passed, and Eileen felt her cheeks grow hot when Lanighan threw his head back and laughed, or, if he was greeted by name, burst into a brief bout of dancing.

He was a performer, continually on stage before the audience of his world, the most trivial of his gestures scrutinized and adored. Every street he entered changed around him, ripples of response were activated by his presence. Children clutched at his sleeve, gifts were spontaneously offered by adults. No matter the intensity of the small domestic dramas he and Eileen came upon, they were interrupted to allow the larger drama of Lanighan's presence to shine through. Eileen was bathed in his light, proud to be walking by his side, her skirt brushing the cuff of his trouser leg.

That night he went to a meeting at the Old Countryman's

Inn and would not allow her to be there with him. "Never have had a woman," he said, "in our midst. It would spoil the talk."

"But I'm one of you," she said. And when that did not produce the desired effect, "I'll wear trousers and hide my hair."

"Never," he said, holding it in his hands, "Never, never hide your hair."

When he was gone, Eileen wrote a letter to Liam – a letter she would never mail – filling it with sentences concerning love and injustice. "Soon," she scribbled, "we will go to Ottawa to sit in the House of Commons and listen to the traitor, McGee, who has turned against the cause of freedom for Ireland. It is not only for love that I stay here," she wrote, "but for our mother and father and all their hardships, and for your children, Liam, and my own. It is with Aidan Lanighan and his brothers that I can help to make the change. If you saw this place, these people, you would want to join us . . . but, remember, no matter what, I am your loving sister."

She folded the paper four times and placed it in a brown envelope. After writing the address she hid it in her case, her hand brushing the cold metal of the pistol she had almost forgotten was there.

The noise of poverty and despair rose through thin floors from the lower storeys of the house – snatches of angry conversation, a baby's wail, the sound of breaking glass – while the odour of damp and mould surrounded Eileen and settled on her skin and hair. She did not know how or where to bathe, was filled with dread when forced to visit the reeking privy whose contents had been liberally distributed by the flood throughout the yard. The heavy air was rife with the peculiar smell of smoke from wet cookstoves and unsuccessful fires, a smell not unlike that of decay. Mixed with this was the odour of decomposition from the corpses of several rats who had been trapped in the inner walls of the house when the water had risen.

Years later smells such as these would remind Eileen of love, these and the strange odourlessness of absence.

By midnight Aidan had not returned. Eileen had spent the previous hour following the rhythms of argument between a man and woman in the room directly below her. At moments of fierce intensity or soft, tentative approaches to reconciliation she was least able to decipher the subject of the quarrel, as though the intimacy of these contacts allowed no witnesses. In between, however, she recognized threats, warnings, accusations, denials rising to the indistinguishable pitch of chaos, causing sweat to stand in beads on Eileen's forehead. Finally, at the height of a crescendo of shouted language there was a pause, a silence that was then fragmented by sobbing and the sound of creaking bedsprings.

Eileen turned her face towards the damp wall and wrapped her thin arms around her body, imagining a clean, dry house for Aidan and herself, a territory free of conflict.

First they would enter the delirium of the argument so that justice could be achieved.

Overnight the remaining dampness crystallized in the cold. At ten in the morning Lanighan danced into a room whose walls were covered with a furry coat of frost. Eileen, watching his performance, laughed with relief, his return dispelling her fears, the cold, the wretchedness of the dark night. He pulled her down two flights of stairs to the kitchen of a woman called Mrs. O'Brien who had managed to coax her cookstove to burn comfortingly. A plump matron, she embraced Lanighan and examined Eileen with a mixture of curiosity, empathy, and suspicion.

"She's too thin," she announced, ladling out two bowls of soup, "and you too. Eat something."

Lanighan, still hungry after the soup, abruptly left the house to visit a French bakery where he was so beloved by the boulanger he was regularly given gifts of day-old bread and the odd patisserie.

While he was gone Mrs. O'Brien heated a copper boiler full of water so that Eileen could bathe, and bolted her kitchen door, "So that the rest of the starving tomcats in this place won't slip in through the cracks."

"He's a fine one," she said, "out all night and you upstairs waiting for him."

"He was at a political meeting," said Eileen defensively. "With his brothers in the cause."

"Oh yes . . . it's always the way." The older woman folded Eileen's discarded clothes over the back of a chair. "Them and their brothers and their causes, and us always cleaning up after them. Even the likes of him . . . them and their politics. It's in every man to waste his time on politics and leave us here to starve."

"But it's to stop the starving that they meet," said Eileen. "And I will meet with them."

Mrs. O'Brien poured more warm water into the tub where Eileen crouched. She turned her back and put the pot back on the shelf. "If you do meet with them it will be the first time they've paid any attention to a woman . . . at least in *that* regard. The only thing that's not themselves they pay attention to is the bottle. It's a terrible marriage, politics and the bottle. Look at old T. D. McGee himself. You'll have to stand by the stove to dry. There's nothing here not covered with mould. It'll be eleven Sundays before anything's dry enough to put more water in it."

Eileen stepped from the tub and walked, naked, towards the stove, leaving glistening footprints on the floor behind her.

The other woman eyed her dispassionately. "The likes of you could cause riots to break out amongst themselves, all politics and drinking aside."

"I've read that McGee takes a drop," said Eileen.

"It's more like an ocean he takes, though they say now he's given it up. That'll be the first man I've heard of to do so, if, in fact, he has."

"We're going to Ottawa to hear him speak," said Eileen.

"You and Aidan?"

"Yes."

"He'll be taking you with him, will he?"

Lanighan pounded on the door.

"I'll be with him now always." Eileen buttoned her skirt and began to tie the ribbons on her camisole. "And I'll go with him everywhere."

Mrs. O'Brien raised her eyebrows but said nothing. She crossed the room and unbolted the door. Lanighan presented her with a chocolate éclair which she gobbled hungrily. Afterwards she leaned forward to kiss him and left a bit of whipped cream on his cheek. "Eileen says you'll be going to Ottawa," she said slyly.

"Yes, some of us are going down to hear the old man talk."

"And you'll have to watch out for those friends of yours, that they don't get their hands on your girl, here."

"Oh, the lads," he said. "They're all right."

Mrs. O'Brien snorted contemptuously. "They're not all right Mr. Aidan Lanighan, and you know it. It's every one of them that's up to no good, yourself included. What would your poor father be saying, him having worked all his life to keep you alive, and you, now, up till all hours with whiskey and politics and never putting in a full day's work yourself. And preying on girls the likes of this one."

"I sew a piece here, a piece there," he said, ignoring the reference to Eileen. "I'm fast, I'm good at it. The others is tailors as well, and they work when they can."

Mrs. O'Brien snorted again. "Tinker, tailor, soldier, sailor . . . what difference does it make when you'll all end up in jail or hung."

Aidan began practising complicated dance steps near the stove.

"I hope to God," said the woman, eyeing him with anger and with love, "that I don't live long enough to see the day when you'll be dancing like that on the end of a rope."

"That," said Lanighan, "is never going to happen." He put his arm around the woman's wide shoulders. "So don't you worry yourself about it."

Mrs. O'Brien softened under his touch, and eventually patted his cheek.

"Be careful," she said quietly. "And look out for the girl, too. She's too thin."

"Who is she?" asked Eileen as they climbed the stairs to Aidan's room.

"She's my father's wife," said Aidan, "Or, at least, his woman. I suppose you could call her my mother. I think she likes you."

"She loves you," said Eileen. "That's one thing certain."

Their first argument broke into Eileen the way she'd seen a panicked moose crash into the forest in Elzivir Township, totally unmindful of bushes and trees in its path, damaging everything around it. She had become like the woman she had heard through the floorboards; had learned, even in this short time, the symphonic structure of lovers' quarrels. The theme

320

was the trip to Ottawa, the second movement the pistol which Eileen had believed Lanighan had forgotten. First he had told her that she could not come with him to hear McGee speak, which had caused her to weep and storm for hours while he remained on the other side of the room, blank, impassive, his arms folded. When she had calmed, and they had made love once again, he delicately asked if she had brought the pistol with her to Montreal.

"I could be searched," he said, "at any time. I left it with you because of that, but I'll be needing to take it with me to Ottawa."

Eileen sat upright in the bed, agitated by this new piece of information. Three of the men, besides himself, were going, Aidan had told her, and they would meet another two there. All of them had had their weapons seized when they were imprisoned at the time of the Fenian raids, and they dared not get more for fear of raising suspicions.

"You *are* Fenians, then?" said Eileen.

"No . . . no. Just interested bystanders."

"Then why do you need the pistol?"

"It's only for protection, Eileen, against bad possibilities. We're just going to Ottawa to hear what McGee has to say in the House, to get the information first-hand."

Eileen scrambled out of bed, dragging a blanket with her. She wrapped it around her body and sat firmly down on her case, refusing to move. "You'll not get any pistol from me," she said, "unless I go with you. *I* want information first-hand too. Besides, if I wasn't here there wouldn't be any pistol."

"I would have come to Colborne to get it from you. And you *are* here, Eileen."

"You were going to Ottawa before I came here. You were going without the pistol."

"I told you, I would have come to Colborne to get it, and anyway things have become more serious since then. You can't come with us, Eileen."

"I walked a hundred miles at night."

"With Liam."

"I'll be with *you* . . . and you're in a wagon." She would not get up from the case, leaned back against the wall, her eyes filling with tears. "Don't shut me out, Aidan," she whispered. "I love you too much to be shut out of what you do. We are together now, isn't it true, forever. I'll do anything you want . . . but let me be with you."

Lanighan looked at her crouched by the dirty wall. He walked around and performed a few half-hearted dance steps. "Eileen," he said softly, "you cannot even begin to understand." He paused, ran his hand through his hair, cleared his throat, and turned towards the window as if making an explanation to the whole world he inhabited. "You cannot even begin to understand what it is that I do. You couldn't be a part of it even if I wanted you to." He raised his hand, palm towards her, as if to halt an advance of carriages on the street below. "Which I don't," he added.

"You don't want me."

"I didn't say that."

"You don't want me with you."

"Not for this kind of thing. Not this time."

Eileen sat with her back curved, her hands resting on her lap. Rejected, excluded, the mythical journeys she had imagined with Lanighan snatched from her. She wanted his dramas, their urgency, as much as she wanted his body in her arms. She wanted to creep inside him, to be a vital part of his life, his politics. "Don't shut me out," she whispered again.

He sighed, placed his forehead against the wall, his hands in his pockets. "You can't come with me, Eileen. Give me the pistol."

A terrible silence filled the room. The sun, entering through the window, reflected angrily back from the cracked heart of Jesus. Then abruptly Eileen jumped to her feet and ran to where Lanighan stood. "Aidan," she said, her voice sharp and clear. "Aidan . . . isn't it still possible that you could be searched?"

"Yes . . . it's possible."

"Then why not let me come with you."

"Eileen –"

"No, listen . . . I could carry the gun. They're not likely to search a girl."

Lanighan looked hard into her face. "Jesus Christ . . ." he eventually said, "you're right, Eileen. I'll take you with me."

She had pleased Lanighan and now would gain entrance to the vibrant centre of his life, be sister to his brothers-in-arms. There would be drama and power, and change would sweep from their love like a cave giving birth to an important river.

"How beautiful this all will be," she said.

"Don't expect too much, Eileen, we're only going to hear McGee speak. And the pistol," he said, "it's just a precaution."

"It will be beautiful," she said, "to be with you among your companions and all of us thinking about the cause."

"The cause. . . ." He began, but did not finish, the sentence.

In June, dawn comes early to Loughbreeze Beach, lifting light with little difficulty over the flat eastern horizon of the Great Lake, just beyond the peninsula of sand that swallowed Esther's father's doomed hotel.

At this moment the midnight shift at the quarry stops for coffee: the machines rattle, purr, and are silent. It is an enchanted time. Men in dusty work clothes, whose passions, during other parts of the day, are focused on all-terrain vehicles and fast food, stroll up to the edge of the man-made crater, their styrofoam cups warming their hands, and look out over the calm water. They think about young women who are sleeping. They push their hardhats back and let the new sun touch their foreheads.

A crow outside the south bedroom awakens in a tree where he has always lived and begins to explain the dawn, the coming day, the previous night, the currents of the lake, the nature of the wind, which – though absent now – will soon stop dreaming and start moving everything it can. Esther has never slept through the bird's strident announcements. But on this, the last morning, she has not slept at all.

She rolls over in the old sleigh-bed. Her hips ache and one hand feels numb, as if it has been taken from her, or as if a gift she held in it has been permanently removed.

In her mind there hovers the face of an old lady – a replica of her own face which floats now on the square, white pool of the pillow. In this family all young girls are the same young girl and all old ladies are the same old lady.

There were evenings, Esther remembers, usually in summer, when her mother and her Grandmother Molly, her aunts and great-aunts would drink sherry and review the family deaths. The aunts would have spent the long, hot afternoon under the poplars, having left behind stifling farm kitchens further inland to inhale the air above the lake and gaze at the colour blue. Sons and husbands would have stayed on the inland farms, active in bright fields, the skin on their faces having been furrowed over the years by sun. Esther's father would sit at a desk in a far corner of the parlour, pretending to busy himself with a complicated tangle of family accounts, dreaming of his ruined houses.

The decanter, which Esther's mother would pick up absently while crossing the floor in search of something else – a photo album, a letter from a deceased son or nephew – would glow in her grasp. The aunts would glide, then, like ships towards the cabinet that held the crystal glasses, returning with prisms caused by late-afternoon sun in their nervous hands. Then would begin the litany of loss and memorable funerals. Portentous dreams would be recalled and deciphered. Esther's father would sigh and leave the room to make a sandwich in the kitchen. There would be no dinner on an evening like this until much later, and the meal, if and when it appeared, would be one made up of "leftovers and tears," as her mother would say.

"Leftovers and tears," whispers Esther now, as she hears the rock crusher being activated once again by men who have forgotten the beauty that held them only minutes before.

Old Eileen would sit silently through the descriptions of coffins and hearses, the references to the locations of graves, and the recitations of verses from various headstones. "Don't talk to me of death," she would say when the women were exhausted by memory and sorrow. "No, don't talk to me of death. I murdered love."

Then she would slowly climb the stairs, walk down the hall, and lock herself into the large bedroom with its wonderful view of the lake.

"Leftovers and tears" whispers Esther again as she drifts into the morning, into the last stages of the story.

Eileen was always afraid that she would lose Aidan somewhere in the city, that he would dive into a crowd of strangers and disappear. She had only a vague exterior map of Montreal's St. Anne's riding – of Griffintown – in her mind, and no knowledge of what lay in the interiors behind its walls. She knew nothing of the rooms and hallways beyond one damp house, but could imagine intimate gatherings, intimate corners, and Aidan in them. He was often gone at night and would reveal nothing of his whereabouts, as if he were deliberately withholding information. Then she would find herself wondering about and sometimes inventing the subjects of conversations, the faces of the speakers.

When she wasn't imagining the activities that occupied him when he was absent, Eileen thought about how often he had fallen asleep in her presence. She became unsure, then, of her place in his life and wondered whether her nearness bored, calmed, or exhausted him. All penned animals at the farm, she remembered, slept through most of the daylight hours, and then again at night as though wakefulness during confinement were an unnatural state.

Sometimes, however, he would practise dance steps in the room and Eileen would watch astonished by his skill, his grace. Often he called out the names of certain dances before he began. "O'Reilly's Lament," he would shout, or "Rolling Over the Waves." He looked straight ahead at the wall or out the window, announcing his performance to no one in particular, perhaps to himself, never to Eileen.

She would sit on the bed and watch him, imagining the increase in his heartbeat or trying to guess the tune that played in his mind as he moved, until one day she realized that he was not dancing alone; that his hand was outstretched to grasp that of another – or a chain of others – that his arm was bent so that another's could lock with his at the elbow.

She was devastated then, angered; she believed he had tricked her. Something she couldn't understand was hurling him back and forth across the room. He was being embraced by a family of invisible partners. She lunged forward and caught his sleeve. "Who are you dancing with?" she demanded.

He stopped moving, startled, looked at her in confusion, sweat sliding over his temples.

"Who are you dancing with?" she repeated.

"No one." He stood like a beckoning statue frozen in mid-gesture, one hand outstretched, muscles tense. Then he broke the pose. "Oh," he said, understanding, "none of these dances is for only one person. They are for two or four, sometimes as many as eight."

Eileen relaxed somewhat. "Then why do you dance alone?" she asked.

"Because," he said, one foot stamping rhythmically, keeping time with an inner tempo, "because there's no one else to dance with."

"There's me," she said, looking up at him from where she crouched on the bed, "I danced with you once."

"Yes," he admitted, whirling away, "but you didn't know the steps."

Now, even though the day was sharp and full of sun, because of the numbers of wagons and buggies passing in the opposite direction and the dust on the road, Eileen had the impression they were travelling through fog or that they were taking a soft brown cloud, like a parcel, with them to Ottawa. The fine powder collected in the folds of her skirt and on the sleeves of Aidan's jacket. When she put her hand over the fist in which he held the leather reins and took it away again, an imprint of her palm remained. Once or twice she leaned forward and brushed the dust from his eyebrows and eyelashes, and he looked at her in a puzzled way because he did not know what she was doing.

Aidan's companions, whom Eileen had imagined as bright warriors, were in fact taciturn, balding men, responding only when spoken to, obviously uncomfortable with the presence of a woman in their midst. They sat on a bench behind the couple, facing in the opposite direction, solemnly drinking from a bottle of whiskey which they passed back and forth between them, turning at intervals to offer some to Aidan who always refused. He had instructed Eileen to be silent about the pistol. It was resting between her breasts, its steel the same temperature as her body.

This dry open plain was so unlike the mouldering walls that had held Eileen and her lover for the preceding days that she was almost grateful for the clouds of dust that obscured the distances. The intimacy of her encounters with Aidan and the intensity of her responses, the minutiae of political details, the long, precise catalogues of unfairnesses and cruelties she had gleaned during the previous months of reading and waiting did not include the possibilities of long views and far horizons. She wanted no impression of that which was being passed by, just forward motion, the firmness of the young man's body, a conviction encircling them, and a long, hard look at the enemy.

"Aidan, what will McGee speak about, do you think?"

He stared straight ahead. The road led directly to Ottawa. "The country," he eventually answered.

"*Which* country, though?"

He flicked the whip in the air, trying to encourage the tired horses. "This country," he said, a note of irritation in his voice. "*This* country," he said again. "We're in Canada now."

Eileen put one of her hands in his jacket pocket, and when he did not respond or look at her she felt a flicker of panic. In Aidan she felt an anger, an emotion that excluded her, might even be against her. "I'd forgotten," she said, thinking of something she had read and trying to join Lanighan wherever his subtle anger had taken him. "He cares now only for furthering his own political career at our expense . . . he doesn't care any more about the Irish." The idea of the oneness of the tribe, the imagined collective voice, calmed her. There were no uncertainties.

Lanighan twitched and shifted his position on the hard seat. A buggy driven by a well-dressed man hurtled past, replenishing the cloud of dust. "He cares," Aidan said cryptically, "more than you know."

It was as if he were not speaking to Eileen, not speaking to anyone at all.

The dust from the vanished buggy settled on his hair and eyebrows. Eileen did not brush it away this time but, looking at his profile, at his hair whitened by the fall of dust, she thought, This is what he will look like to me when he is growing old.

She leaned forward to brush the fine brown powder from her new white boots. It was late in the afternoon and the shadow of the wagon and its occupants stretched out far behind them on the road. The gun pressed painfully into her breastbone and she returned to her previous upright position. They had been travelling for almost ten hours when the river, the forested hills of the Gatineaus, and the spires of Parliament came into sight. The surrounding air was now clear of dust, splotches of snow and puddles lay in the fields. Even from this distance the stone walls and slate roofs of Parliament – absurd in the middle of the wilderness – were visible. "It's beautiful," Eileen said, surprise evident in her voice.

"From this distance," said Lanighan. When they got closer, he told Eileen, there would be mud and broken wooden sidewalks and the shanties of the Irish lining a canal they had dug with their own hands. "But from this distance," he agreed, "it's the most beautiful thing in the world."

They met the other two men in the tavern at the Victoria Hotel on Wellington Street. Lanighan embraced the sandyhaired, better-dressed man, whose name was Patrick. He was younger than the rest of the company – except for Aidan. Eileen knew he was looking at her, his gaze a provocative, sweeping inquiry.

"My girl," said Aidan, explaining her presence.

Eileen moved her hand to her breast where the pistol was hidden. One of the men ordered whiskeys all round and the group settled in at an oak table.

No one spoke. Outside, Wellington Street was empty of traffic, growing dark. A lamplighter walked by like a ghost creating his own aura.

"It will be a long night," the sandy-haired man eventually said. "He doesn't speak until late."

Aidan straightened out his legs under the table, his chair pushing back slightly and scraping the floor.

A line from an emigration song her father had taught her kept running through Eileen's mind. "Come fiddler, now, and play for me. Goodbye to barn and stack and tree." She thought she knew what each of these features of an intimate landscape looked like, even though they were far away in a country she had never seen.

"I can wait until the hour," said one of the men who had come with them on the wagon.

Eileen touched Lanighan's knee and searched his face. He was far from her and she knew it. The lamplighter passed by the window again, awash in a sickly pink light of his own making. Aidan's arms were folded across his chest as though he were protecting his heart, denying Eileen access to it. She felt that she had displeased him, would do anything to regain his favour. She leaned forward, towards the table. "We are all fighters for freedom," she said, uncertainly.

Lanighan shot her a brief, silencing look.

The sandy-haired man called Patrick threw his head back and laughed. "Was there any particular kind of freedom you had in mind?" he asked, suggestively.

Eileen's face turned red and she lowered her eyes.

"She's a beauty, this one," the man said to Aidan, "and a rebel into the bargain. Here's to her . . ." He lifted his glass. The men chuckled but avoided eye contact with one another.

"There'll be a full moon tonight," the smallest, roundest, and oldest of the wagon men commented, "after the street-lamps are out. And they'll not leave the lamps on long after the moon is up."

The men rose to leave the tavern, and Eileen bent down to tighten one of the laces of her white boots, her hand involuntarily clutching at the gun beneath her clothing. She was drawn sharply back to an upright position by Aidan's hand on her arm, her shoulder-blade coming up hard against the back of the chair. Then, quite suddenly, Aidan was on his knees before her completing the task.

"Ah, yes," said the man known as Patrick, grinning, but

looking at Eileen with intensity. He winked and sang quietly behind Lanighan's back.

> And what's to tell any man whether or no,
> Whether I'm easy or whether I'm true.
> As I lifted her petticoat easy and slow,
> And I tied up my sleeve
> For to buckle her shoe.

Ignoring him, Eileen placed one hand on Aidan's dark head and for just a moment he rested his left cheek against her knee.

It was, though they did not know this, their last embrace.

BECAUSE of their largeness, the Houses of Parliament appeared to Eileen to be an overwhelming natural phenomenon, permanent, indestructible, their faces the façades of cliffs. To enter them would be like stepping into the mouths of great caves, to penetrate the earth and look upon all that had been covered, disguised by trees and gravel. The huge windows glowed with a molten light which spilled out over the grass and changed the colour of the stones at Eileen's feet. Behind the massive structures, on the other side of the river, the Gatineau Hills were covered by a dull sheen, grey under a full moon. Despite the crunching footsteps of her companions, Eileen could hear a continuous hiss of noise in the distance which made her feel as though her head was full of wind. "Chaudière Falls," one of the men told her. "Half a mile up the river." Aidan walked ahead of her, hurriedly, the intimacy of their moment in the tavern forgotten.

In the gallery of the House of Commons, Eileen looked first at the huge wheel-shaped gasoliers which threw a relentless glare into the carved corners above her, then down to the orderly collection of heads below. Someone was talking about Nova Scotia. Aidan, who did not sit next to her, nervously fingered the ticket the porter had given him. Eileen worried for a few seconds that she had lost hers. The gallery was warm. She could smell sweat and whiskey emanating from the bodies of the men. She clutched at the insides of her skirt pockets until she heard the crackle of the paper stub. Feeling light-headed, distant from the life pressing in around her, she was unable to follow the thread of civilized debate taking place below. Her attention had been trained towards the anticipation of drama, could not focus on the mannered theatrics of men in a Gothic hall.

Eileen looked at Aidan's profile, his dark lashes. He was blinking rapidly. Then she looked, again, down at the crowd of men below her. Were it not for the sideburns on one, the whiskers on another – the colour, the abundance, or the lack of hair – they would all have looked the same in their black top-coats and white shirts. This uniform, she suddenly understood, was a mark of power. She had never known men who dressed in clothes such as these. How was it possible that, attired in what Eileen imagined one might wear to a ball, these parliamentarians were engaged in arguments that were lengthy and dull. Hours empty of passion were crawling through the room.

"McGee will speak soon," the man called Patrick eventually hissed into Eileen's ear.

She was surprised, whenever she looked towards Aidan, at his alertness. His eyes were bright, his body poised, vibrant as if he intended to burst, shouting, into the centre of the room. After a few moments she saw him rise to his feet, bend, whisper something to one of the three men from the wagon, then to the man called Patrick, and leave the gallery.

"Where did he go?" she asked, the panic moving from her throat, down the insides of her arms. "What did he say?"

"Just a call of nature, darlin'."

Despite his fancy clothes, the man's sandy hair was greasy, unwashed. "He'll be back in a jiffy," he answered. "But," Patrick tugged on his left ear, as if shaking a message out, "he said you had a little something for me down that lovely front of yours. You must be cold. Why don't you wrap your shawl around you," he carefully draped the paisley fabric over Eileen's shoulders, "and pass the little something to me from under it so the others won't see. It's what Aidan wants you to do."

Eileen's blood beat in her brain. "He wants you to have it?" she asked.

"It's part of the plan," the man whispered, "part of the grand scheme. We're all fighters for freedom and Aidan says he's proud of you for being in sympathy with that."

Gratitude, a warm rush of it, melted the tension in her arms. Eileen wrapped the shawl around her throat and moved her hands under it.

The pistol was warm and damp, covered with her sweat.

When Lanighan returned to the gallery, he squeezed into a spot beside Eileen. The crowd had thickened in response to the rumour, telegraphed, even at this late hour, through the streets and alleys and saloons of Ottawa, that McGee would be speaking soon, and the seats behind them were filled to capacity with stonecutters, streetsweepers, waiters, cab drivers, ladies of the night, even a few ragged children.

"Are you watching?" Lanighan whispered. "Watch him and listen."

Eileen saw a small man rise to his feet and incline his head towards a collection of tattered papers on the desk in front of him, his hands nervously leafing, sorting, stacking. He would be responding to a motion on the part of the Nova Scotia Assembly that Confederation be repealed.

"They want to take it apart again?" asked Eileen.

"Yes," said Aidan. He was leaning forward, his elbows on his knees.

McGee was a long time organizing his papers, fussing.

The silence in the House turned into an almost audible apprehension. Eileen was certain that the light thrown by the gasoliers had changed, was more exaggerated, and that, as a result, there were more shadows in the room.

At length, McGee straightened, limped sideways to change his position behind the desk. Then he began to speak.

Aidan leaned against Eileen slightly. She could feel the heat of his upper arm move through the cloth of their sleeves and his thigh pressing against hers. She could feel his heat but she knew he was gone from her, lost in the quiet words being spoken by the man below, and she resented the fact that this person, of such insignificant physical stature, this turncoat, could lasso her lover's attention, hold it hostage. Even the enemy, she thought, envy burning through her bowels, even the enemy should not have the power to come between us. Then, as the speech escalated in tenor and pitch, she was caught by some of the lines.

"It's not only the lime and the sand and the hair in the mortar, but the time which has been taken to temper it."

Eileen thought of the long seasons that her mother had been away and how all that time was preserved, exposed, placid and frozen on her face.

"Time," McGee announced, "will come to the aid of impartial justice."

In the words "impartial justice" she heard the song of her father's tongue . . . the suggestion of poetry. She bent forward to scrutinize the speaker. The enemy, she thought, is a small, corrupt man. Where does his voice come from?

She looked questioningly at Aidan, her face registering the confusion that she felt. The country described by the speaker was one in which there would be no factions, no revenge for old sorrows, old grievances. Everything about it was to be new, clear; a landscape distanced by an ocean from the zones of terror. A sweeping territory, free of wounds, belonging to all, owned by no one.

The man called Patrick was sprawled in his chair, apparently asleep, but Eileen sensed Aidan's concentration – so fervent it enveloped his whole body.

McGee had come to a pause in his long address. Eileen was being shaken by sudden recollection; the privacy within the curtains of a willow, a dialogue with a blue-black bird. This, and a kind of music breaking into meaning. The words in the room had become like that, a significant message carried on cadence. She remembered now, for the first time, that as a child she had listened to a wise man.

"There was a man," she whispered to Aidan urgently, "a man called Exodus Crow. He knew things. He told me once – a long time ago – he told me there were no lords of the land."

Aidan pressed the air with his left palm, silencing her.

McGee was concluding; his performance now as mesmerizing as one of Aidan's dances. He was speaking to the whole room, his notes forgotten in the hand that rested on the desk in front of him. He was addressing them, he said, not as the representative of any race, any province, but as the forerunner of a generation that would inherit wholeness, a generation released from fragmentation.

The House exploded into sound. Thumping of desks, cheering, applause.

Eileen, released by the monstrous single-voiced roar from the trance induced by the little man's voice, allowed the phrase "not as the representative of any race" to strike her in the heart. This is the voice, she thought, this is the power that should be harnessed. Her father had talked about Irish eloquence. Without the race of his blood this little man would not have had the voice. He has betrayed, she decided, the voice, the suffering voice.

The bird in her mind flew away again, breaking through green.

Aidan was rocking backwards and forwards at her side as if in pain. "Jesus Christ," he was saying, "Jesus Christ, Jesus Christ." Lost landscapes through which she had never walked were unfolding, hill by hill, in Eileen's thoughts. To her, McGee was the worst kind of enemy, the truly guilty; the one who knows the beauty and betrays it.

Patrick was on his feet with the rest, clapping and cheering, his head thrown back.

Faking, thought Eileen.

Afterwards, Prime Minister Macdonald and the leader of the Opposition entered into a testy debate which Eileen was too distracted to follow. "Do we go . . . ?" she asked Aidan. "When do we go."

"Not until it's over."

"Then?"

"Then we go."

"All right," he said when the House was finally adjourned shortly afterwards, "let's get out of here."

Outside, standing confused in the shadow of the colossal building, the men were anxious and jumpy. "We should get moving," one of them kept saying. "We should be moving now."

The spectators were beginning to drift homewards in various directions across the moonlit lawn.

"We'll catch you up," said Lanighan. "I want to see him up close. We'll see you at Mrs. McKenna's Saloon. She's the only one still open."

"You'll recognize him," one of the men said, "by his white top hat and gloves. He wears the hat to make himself look taller."

"Where's Pat?" another of the men asked.

"Gone on ahead, I guess."

To Eileen's great joy Aidan had begun to play, absently, with her hair.

"That voice of his," she said as the men walked away through moonlight and chill, "that voice of his is something beautiful. It's our voice, but he's betrayed it."

Without answering, Lanighan seized her wrist and pulled her behind him, running to the right, towards the building called the West Block. They moved swiftly behind it, along its sandstone wall and out its gate, across Wellington and into O'Connor Street. At the corner of Sparks and O'Connor, Lanighan pushed through a break in a six-foot wooden fence and, dragging Eileen after him, entered an empty lot. Releasing her, he moved to the south side of the lot and flung himself down near a spot where two boards were broken at the bottom, leaving enough space for a man to look through or crawl through. Eileen followed and stood panting behind him. "Lie down," he gasped.

She scrambled to the ground. "What's going on?" she asked. "What about the others? What are you doing?" Eileen saw the shadows of sad, unhealthy weeds move in the moonlight on the boards to the left of her. To her right there was a makeshift door and a small shed with a sign in its single window. IRISH NEED NOT APPLY, it read. "Tell me," she said now, pulling on Aidan's sleeve. "Tell me what's happening."

"Don't say *anything*," he replied curtly.

They lay in silence for twenty minutes, Aidan quiet and private, Eileen suffering more from his withdrawal than from a sense of danger. No part of him was touching her.

The side of Sparks Street they could see underneath the fence was remote, bathed in dull moonlight. No wind, no sound of any kind entered this road except as an echo – footsteps or horses hooves – from another part of the city, followed by stretches of absolute silence during which Eileen noticed that Aidan was breathing in the way he sometimes did just before they began to make love, just before the frantic part when she didn't know whether it was his breath or her own that she was hearing. Now, in the space of a few seconds, she became aware of another sound, a peculiar combination of scraping and clicking, something like that made by the second hand on the large clock in the parlour at Loughbreeze Beach Farm. She thought of her brother and felt, for the first time, the dull ache of missing him.

Then the white top hat and one gloved hand of D'Arcy McGee came into view, then the glint of the silver handle of his cane; these glowing because of the moonlight, the rest of the man almost invisible beside the night walls that no lamps illuminated.

"Give me the gun," hissed Lanighan.

"What are you going to do?" Eileen was appalled by the anticipated act shaping itself in her mind. She looked out into the street where a shadow moved. A cloud, she thought, frantically, a cloud across the moon.

"I'm going out there," he was saying. "Give me the gun."

"No."

Aidan ripped at her blouse. "Give it to me, Eileen . . . I have to have it," he spat.

"I can't," she cried. "It's Patrick that has it. He said you wanted him to have it."

"Jesus." Aidan's face contorted before Eileen's eyes. "Jesus . . . He saw your hand go to the gun when you bent over in the bar."

341

"He said that you told him –" she began. Then her words were cancelled by the sound of a single shot and the sight of a white top hat rolling away, cartwheeling down a wooden sidewalk.

"What is it?" asked Eileen in terror. "What's happened? Aidan . . ." She looked again under the fence to the opposite side of the street. A dark stain was gathering around the figure which lay, like a bad drawing of a sprinter, askew on the sidewalk. Lights were beginning to appear in windows. The sound of calling voices, running footsteps, a crowd gathering. "Did you plan this? Did you plan to kill him?"

"*Plan* this?" Aidan was curled on the ground. "I *loved* him," he began to sob. "Jesus God, I *loved* him. I was here to protect him and now I've killed him . . . *you've* killed him. I was with him" – his voice became strangled – "not against him. My God, he was our only hope."

"But you said . . ." Eileen grabbed his arm but he shook her hand away. It was his least graceful gesture.

"Who knows what I said? What does it matter what I said? Don't you understand, I am what people like you call a goulagh – a spy – I was working *for* him against the fanatics – against people like you."

"People like me . . ." repeated Eileen slowly.

Carriages, policemen, were arriving beyond the fence. A woman screamed, someone called for the coroner. Eileen heard the word "dead" pronounced in a solid male voice.

"Oh my God," Aidan moaned, "it's my own death out there."

"I didn't know . . ." Eileen's voice was quiet, calm, but her heart was attempting to leap through her ribcage out into the street, the commotion, the murder.

The anger that Aidan felt was most visible in his mouth; the same mouth that had whispered endearments, that had

342

caressed every part of her body. "It was all play for you, wasn't it," this new mouth said. "All some kind of dream . . . some kind of goddamed otherworld island. You think this will make things better for our people?"

"I never wanted . . ."

Aidan staggered to his feet. He wiped his face with his sleeve, then thrust his fist towards her face. "Don't come near me," he hissed. "Don't touch me." He brought his fist back towards his own forehead. "It's all gone now, whatever there was to work for."

The leering face of the man called Patrick appeared briefly in Eileen's mind. "*I* didn't kill him," she called into the night, her voice shrill.

"You killed him." Aidan attacked a board with his fist. He did not look at Eileen. "Did you hear a single thing McGee said? Did you listen to what he wanted?"

Without waiting for her to answer he stumbled across the empty, pathetic lot, across broken glass and garbage, leaving Eileen standing alone, her hair filled with wonderful moonlight, her shadow in this moonlight bent at the waist on a rough wooden fence.

A picture of Aidan dancing in the attic room flashed through her mind, the way he curved his arm or extended his hand to accommodate an unseen partner. The captains at the inn, the lake sailors had all been wrong. His dance was not a petition to McGee; it was an expression – an affirmation – of partnership. Whenever Aidan danced, the voice of D'Arcy McGee had been present, dancing with him in the room.

"You never talked to me," she whispered to the emptiness. "You kept me out. You would not let me see the truth."

SHE spent the remainder of the night on the north side of the Houses of Parliament, seated on her shawl, her back against the curved wall of the unfinished Parliamentary Library, the grass around her silvered with moonlight and frost.

Coming here from the empty lot she had, for a moment, joined the growing crowd and confusion surrounding the body of McGee. Looking above the heads of the spectators she saw the whole city light up, like a fragmented nation coming alive, coming to its senses. Of the body she saw only one gloveless hand, its palm full of moonlight, and a narrow stream of dark liquid running in the gutter near where it lay. Then a policeman pushed her roughly aside. Apart from this one dismissive gesture no one paid any attention to her. She turned her back to the horror, walked down Sparks Street, veered to the left at Metcalfe, and made her way up to Parliament Hill.

She could hear the clock on the front of the mountainous building scrape and click, moving from minute to minute, reminding her of the sound of McGee's cane advancing down the sidewalk on Sparks Street. From the distance the sound of the Chaudière Falls reached her. When the clock struck four she became aware of the vibrations of the iron bells travelling through the stones at her back, and then the river speaking to her in a voice that she knew she would carry with her for the remainder of her life. A voice at home inside her brain because it had lain there for years – dormant – waiting for the correct combination of stimuli to activate it: the sound of rushing water, a love torn apart, sudden terrible knowledge, the release from the mortal dream.

As the sky behind the Eddy Match Factory across the river filled with light, the steady timbre of the water and rapids became sentences spoken in a soft female voice and Eileen accepted, without surprise, the presence of her mother's lost words.

So this is what it is to be away, her mother's voice told her. You are never present where you stand. You see the polished dishes in your kitchen cupboard throwing back the hearth light, but they know neither you nor the meals you have taken from their surfaces. Your flagstones are a series of dark lakes that you scour, and the light that touches and alters them sends you unspeakable messages. Waves arch like mantles over everything that burns. Each corner is a secret and your history is a lie.

Eileen turned her head to look at the solid wall against which she had rested for hours. It was not made of dark granite as she had believed, but rather a rose-coloured sandstone, benign, glowing with warmth. She reached her left arm across her breast and touched the stone beside her shoulder, trying to read the texture of its surface. It was solid, gentle, distant from her.

She gathered her shawl around her shoulders, stood, turned her back to the Gatineau Hills, and began the long journey home.

~

Liam was using the hand plough to turn the earth at the east of the house, making a kitchen garden for Molly, when he saw Eileen at the end of the lane, limping badly in her new white boots, her clothing torn and soiled, her hair tangled.

That morning he had awakened earlier than the others in the house and had hunted up the pack he had brought with him from Elzivir Township. There, in a small side pocket, he located the object he was looking for, something Eileen had found under her father's pillow after he died – a bone hairpin with a single thread of red-gold hair wrapped around and around it. The object spoke of frailty and loss and the scant, dissolving memory that is kept of one who has gone away. He would carry this object always in his trouser pocket, he decided, in memory of his mother, in memory of Eileen.

"Sweet Jesus," he said, now, under his breath. She had been gone for three weeks. He dropped the plough and ran up the lane. "Where have you been?" he yelled. "What's this all about?"

Eileen walked past him, staring at the house, while he staggered backwards in front of her, gesturing wildly.

"What does this mean, Eileen? You disappear . . . Christ, I thought you'd be gone for seven years. Where did you go? What have you been doing?"

The lake was choppy, a steel blue. A host of troublesome black birds were making a racket in the poplars near the shore. I must make a scarecrow for the garden, Liam thought, suddenly. Then he stared hard at his sister's face as they reached the door. He knew nothing about this woman.

"Eileen," he said parentally. "Tell me where you went."

She sighed and kissed his cheek. "I've given up on outer words," she said. "I live on an otherworld island. I'm going to lie down in my large room where I can see the lake."

"What the hell do you mean, outer words, other worlds?" Liam followed her into the house, past the triangular burn on the floor of the kitchen, through the parlour.

"I mean . . . explanations." And then, as if she were talking

346

to herself, "Yes, that's what I mean, explanations, interpretations."

Liam grabbed her shoulders and shook her almost roughly. "Tell me what's happened," he commanded now. "Eileen, tell me what's happened to you."

But Molly came between them and put her arm gently round Eileen's waist. "Leave her alone," she said to Liam.

As he watched the two women slowly climb the stairs, Liam heard his wife comforting his sister.

"You've come home now," she was saying. "I'll look after you. Everything will be all right. You've come home now to stay."

An old woman called Eileen saw something of herself in the puzzled eyes of a twelve-year-old girl. She had been watching the child for some time, waiting for the light, the wind, the position of the clouds to suggest when she should speak, when she should tell the story.

"I see you out there on the beach," Old Eileen said. "I see you, Esther, from my large room with its wonderful view of the lake. I am reminded of her."

The child Esther's face was dusted with gold freckles. She wore a white dress. It was September and she had just returned from school. There were multiplication tables in her mind and the correct spelling of the word "tenacity," but she wanted the pebbles at the edge of the shore and a boat to step into, which might carry her off. She turned in the room towards the corner where the old woman was standing, darkly dressed, looking like a shadow.

"Who do you mean?" Esther asked.

"Her," Old Eileen replied. "My mother with skin as perfect as ice. She is nothing like your mother, Deirdre. Perhaps it skipped a generation."

The old woman went to sit straight-spined in an upright chair, and Esther remembered that when her father had once brought a rocking chair into the upstairs room Old Eileen dismissed it angrily. "The world is already askew," she remembered her saying to him. "I hold still in my otherworld and let your world rock and tilt and veer. You of all people should know this," she had said to Esther's father, whose hand still rested on the wooden arm of the gift. "One of your houses was struck by lightning, the other buried by sand."

"When I die," she told the twelve-year-old Esther now, "the room with the view of the lake will be yours. You have lived with calm parents in cataclysmic houses. I think those houses were trying to push you out – to push you out towards the lake."

"But we could always see the lake."

"That's not good enough for the likes of you. The likes of you has to be *on* the beach, *on* the lake." Old Eileen leaned forward in her chair, thrusting her face closer to the child who had been gradually approaching her, "Where is the centre of the world?" she abruptly demanded.

Esther stood silently in front of her, holding onto a book she had forgotten to put on a table. She did not know the answer to the riddle.

"The place where you stand," Old Eileen said. "The place where you stand is the centre of the world."

"Imagine," the old woman said, pointing one talon-like finger towards the peninsula that unfurled itself out into the lake. "Imagine, everything over there is buried in sand, your father's hotel included."

"I know about that." Esther began to pass the book from one hand to the other.

"But do you know about the slowness of sand. Do you know about that? One morning you wake up, walk into your lush garden, and in one corner there's a small drift of sand sloping up the boards of the fence. The next week you are shaking sand out of the clothes you pull from your wardrobe. Soon there is sand mixed with the grounds of your coffee. No matter how hard or how often you sweep there is a thin layer of sand on your kitchen floor. Your garden disappears. Your neighbours have already disappeared. Where the orchard used to be there are curving dunes of sand. There is grit in every spoonful of food."

"I remember," said Esther though she was not certain that she did.

"Nothing but an ocean of sand." Old Eileen pointed again to the peninsula which shone in the late-afternoon sun, its dunes alive with light. Then she looked into Esther's eyes. "Politics," she said, "are exactly like that – when they are not like being struck by lightning."

Her face softened and she leaned partially away from Esther. "And love too," she added. "I only got the lightning not the sand in the garden, so I suppose I should be grateful to D'Arcy McGee for something."

"Why D'Arcy McGee?" Esther asked.

"He put me in my place," said the old woman, evasive now, wanting to step back into the territory of the child's life.

"Do you remember your father's house on the hill?"

Esther thought about how she and her mother always revisited their disappearing houses. At the site of the house on the hill, she remembered, they had discovered charred beams and irregularly shaped chunks of glass which had melted in the fire and resolidified into transparent boulders. She had found one of her doll's saucers, so delicate you could see your fingers through the china, intact, undamaged, resting on the rubble. She knew it must have fallen fifty feet from the nursery on the third floor, and sensed that, underneath the wreckage, there would be more dolls' dishes and other small unharmed objects.

"This house is waterproof," Old Eileen said. "We sailed it here, you know."

"Grandpa Liam told me." Esther placed her schoolbook with the others on a table in the corner.

"If I were you," Old Eileen smiled vaguely, "I would stay in this house all my life. If I were you, I would never go away."

"Have *you* ever been anywhere?"

"Only once." Old Eileen stared out the window towards the east. Esther believed the old woman could probably see as far as the Atlantic Ocean. "Of course, in the end you will be visited by the curse of the mines, but that can't be helped."

"What do you mean?"

"It has to do with the landlord, this curse," Old Eileen said, "and some furious digging in the ground."

"Grandpa Liam said there was a landlord who –"

"On the other hand," Old Eileen interrupted, "I've been away all my life." She rose and crossed the room – straight, prim, but slow, old. "I can't, you see, get the face of a certain young man out of my mind." She began to rummage in the upper drawer of the rolltop desk, then she turned and moved back to the stationary child. "Here," she said, handing Esther a braided skein of red and black hair, "and here." She produced a black feather, a shard of turquoise china. "It will take a long time," Old Eileen said, resuming her position in an upright chair. "It will take a long time to tell you the whole story. There are so many ways, you understand, of giving yourself away. I had a baby, you know, when I was very young; I gave her to Molly and Liam to raise. Call her Deirdre, I said to them, because of the sorrows."

AT 7:45 on a summer morning the night shift is ending. The men climb down from tin towers above conveyor belts and scramble over the sides of elephantine vehicles to the quarry floor. One pulls a lever and the rock crusher falls silent. A lake-boat called the *Sir John A. Macdonald* moans twice and, full of Canadian limestone – landscape and fossils – turns west, heading for another shore. The huge hole in the land beside the lake is fractionally larger.

Esther O'Malley Robertson is sitting against the pillows of her old sleigh-bed. She has never, since she took over the management of the farm, been upstairs as late as 8:00 a.m. But this is the last morning.

The crow completed his dawn monologue hours ago, is off in the cedar woods swallowing mosquitoes, murdering worms. In the distance Esther hears the shifting gears of several pickup trucks travelling the gravel roads too fast, driven by the men from the quarry who are eager to join their breakfasting families.

Esther is at the end of the story. She knows, without consulting mirrors, that, after this night, her face is even more like her grandmother's – is the face of an old woman. Just as, years before, while she sat listening to the narrative for the first time, her face had become more and more like that of a child called Eileen who had spent long summer afternoons behind the curtain of a willow tree.

Two mourning doves somewhere near the decaying barn

now resume their lifelong task of attempting to perfect the sound of loss. Soon their lament will be obliterated by the noise of the day shift at the quarry – the dynamiters, the drillers, the crushers – that and the roar of limestone hitting the steel bottom of yet another lakeboat, this one called the *Daughter of Confederation*.

Suddenly Esther remembers the collection of schoolbooks she had brought with her into the parlour the day her grandmother finished the story, the leather bookstrap which held them together, the brown bookbag. *The Dominion Workbook*, *The Canadian Speller*, the beavers and maple leaves embossed on their covers. All that, she thinks, is lost now; dynamited, gone.

When Liam died, a short while after his wife, Molly, his considerable savings were divided among his five children, one of whom was Esther's mother. The farm was given to Eileen, who outlived him by only a few years. After Eileen's death, Esther's mother and father moved to a small house in the village and Esther was left alone to run the farm as Eileen's will had determined she should. Esther had watched her parents depart, had turned and walked into the fields, dug her hands into the earth, examined the leaves of each crop. Later she ran her fingers over the bark of the orchard trees, strolled through the flickering woods. She was less staking out her territory than she was being claimed by something that was destined to be hers; the centre of the world, the ground on which she stood. She was, by then, thirty years old, tall and angular; with a banner of red-gold hair which she kept out of her way, bundled at the back of her neck.

He was drawn to her shore by the threat of a storm only eight months later. He anchored his boat in the relative calm of her bay with a gale coming up and waves slamming against the jetty to which he swam. Esther, lighting the first evening lamp, was made aware of his presence as the sound of his footsteps grinding through beach stones gradually overcame the sound of the surf. When she opened her door she was unsurprised by his dark curls, his pale hand and his bright green eye.

She was never to ask him about the rest of his life, though she knew he must have come from a fishing hamlet near the peninsula of dunes fifteen miles down the lake. But these details barely interested her. It was his swimming to her land, the storm, his journey over beach stones that mattered. The unpredictability of his arrivals and the certainty of his departures. Between his visits, when she found herself waiting, she knew it was for a kind of completion – his absence from, not his presence in her life.

Winter came, freezing him into the distance. In spring, while men from the village worked her fields, Esther stood in the mornings in her large room with the view of the lake and searched the horizon. But by then, as she came to realize, he was fishing other waters. The jetty, that fixed point of arrivals and departures, fell into disuse and then into disrepair as, storm by storm, it was dismantled by the lake until it became a rough collection of boulders.

The lake would become no longer fishable, and the only sails it carried would belong to the yacht clubs of the industrial towns and cities that had grown along its shores. Esther stayed alone on the land, the farm becoming a miracle of prosperity under her hands.

"Your mother – my daughter Deirdre – was brought up as Liam and Molly's oldest child," Eileen had told Esther.

"Why didn't she tell me? Why didn't Mother tell me?"

"There was no need – there was never any need – for Deirdre – for your mother to know. There is a calmness in her; she does not lean towards extremes. I had thought as I watched her grow up in this house, distant from me, believing that I was her aunt, that the past was finished, settled. I watched her grow up, marry your father, give birth to you. Her life is clean, I thought, clear of it all." Esther's grandmother looked into the distance. "And I was glad," she added. "Then her houses were destroyed and she came home, with your father, back to Loughbreeze Beach, back to the lake. And, even then, nothing of the young woman I was was present in her, and nothing of Aidan either." She paused then and looked hard into Esther's eyes, "You, on the other hand, are both him and me."

Old Eileen took the adolescent child to see the burn mark on the kitchen floor, the place in the parlour tavern where Aidan Lanighan's hand had brushed the boards, rescuing embroidery. Standing near these spots, traces of the sorrowful young woman she had been entered her attitude, her posture.

"He was always there, where he stood," she said. "He danced into rooms and utterly inhabited them. He was the energy of the real moment while I was always turning the moment into something else altogether. Inventing it. Interpreting it. You have this gift in you, the ability to be where you are, but I am in you as well and there will be times when you want to drift away. No more of this drifting," she said, looking out towards the lake. She sighed, "I'm tired now. I'll go back to my view of the lake. I always knew it was the only thing that would ever be mine."

Then, suddenly, at the bottom of the stairs, Esther's grandmother twirled around twice, her skirts swirling like those of a young girl at a dance, her face lit by memory. "Imagine this room," she said, "alive with leaping men and politics!" She paused then and the light in her face disappeared. "If I were you I would be where I stand," she said.

THERE is light in the sky as late as ten o'clock on a June evening such as this one.

A mile down the shore the cement company's pier looks almost festive bathed in the reflected remnants of a pink sunset and covered in red and green lights. *The New Dominion* appeared on the horizon an hour ago and is now slipping into place beside the rusted steel casings at the end of the conveyor belt. It is lit as if its crew anticipates champagne, dancing, not the avalanche of rock that will soon begin to fill its hold.

Night comes to the quarry somewhat earlier than it does to the water or the beach, its shadow moving from east to west across the raw, grey ground. Unthinkably bright floodlights are switched on causing the lines in the men's dusty faces to look exaggerated and exposing the torn rock, the scars, the fractures.

Now the land itself fragments, moves away from piers in boats named after brief histories towards other waters, other shores. No lamps at all are lit tonight in the empty house on Loughbreeze Beach. The men at the quarry, angered by something they don't quite understand, set their jaws and shift the gears of their equipment with grim forcefulness. Under the glare of artificial light the fossilized narratives of ancient migrations are crushed into powder. The scream of the machinery intensifies.

ACKNOWLEDGEMENTS

This book is a work of fiction; all characters, events, situations, relationships, and in some cases geographical locations are either a product of the imagination or have been worked on and transformed by the imagination. As a result, the physical and social make-up of nineteenth-century County Antrim in Ireland, or Elzivir Township and Northumberland County in Canada have occasionally been altered to meet the needs of the story.

Nonetheless, many scholarly works inspired and informed parts of the narrative. Of these the most important to me were: *The Great Hunger* by Cecil Woodham-Smith; *Visions and Beliefs in the West of Ireland* by Lady Gregory; *The Great Migration* by Edwin C. Guillet; and *M'Cahan's Local Histories* published by the Glens of Antrim Historical Society. Two books by T. P. Slattery, *The Assassination of D'Arcy McGee* and *They Got to Find Me Guilty Yet*, were enormously helpful to my understanding of the political forces surrounding the assassination of McGee. To this day uncertainty regarding the identity of the assassin remains. This book does not pretend to solve the mystery.

I first heard the traditional folksong "Bonny Portmore" on Loreena McKennitt's recording entitled *The Visit* (manufactured and distributed by Warner Music Canada). "If I Were a Blackbird" is traditional as well. I have also used two lines from "The Emigrant" by Belfast poet Joseph Campbelle. The epigraph at the beginning of the book is a traditional Irish triad taken from *Dánta Ban: Poems of Irish Women Early and Modern*, selected and translated by P. L. Henry (Dublin: The Mercier Press, 1991). All other songs and poems are inventions of the author, influenced, in some instances, by the reading of anonymous Irish poetry in translation.

Of the many people who either read and commented upon the manuscript or who aided with my research I would like especially to thank Stuart MacKinnon, David Staines, Dr. Palmer Patterson, Victoria Glendinning, Nelson Ball, Greg Murphy, Clifford Quinn, Mary Dalton, Tony Urquhart, Janet Turnbull Irving, Dr. Arnulf Conradi, Ellen Levine, and Alex Schultz.

Thanks also to Pamela Fawcett for her excellent typing skills.

I owe a great debt to the University of Waterloo Library and to Memorial University of Newfoundland Library where much of my research took place, and to the Canada Council and the Ontario Arts Council for financial assistance during the tenure of this project. I would also like to thank the English Department of Memorial University of Newfoundland and the English Department of the University of Ottawa for enjoyable and productive writer-in-residencies.

And, once again, a special thank you to Ellen Seligman.

Elsa Trillat

Jane Urquhart was born in Little Long Lac, Ontario, and grew up in Toronto. She is the author of seven acclaimed novels: *The Whirlpool*, which received Le prix du meilleur livre étranger (Best Foreign Book Award) in France; *Changing Heaven; Away*, winner of the Trillium Book Award and a finalist for the prestigious International IMPAC Dublin Literary Award; *The Underpainter*, winner of the Governor General's Award and a finalist for the Rogers Communications Writers' Trust Fiction Prize; *The Stone Carvers*, which was a finalist for The Giller Prize and the Governor General's Award, and longlisted for the Booker Prize; *A Map of Glass*, a finalist for a regional Commonwealth Writers' Prize for Best Book; and, most recently, *Sanctuary Line*. She is also the author of a collection of short fiction, *Storm Glass*; four books of poetry; a biography of L.M. Montgomery for the Extraordinary Canadians series; and the editor of *The Penguin Book of Canadian Short Stories*. Her work has been translated into numerous foreign languages.

Urquhart has received the Marian Engel Award and the Harbourfront Festival Prize, and is a Chevalier dans l'Ordre des Arts et des Lettres in France and an Officer of the Order of Canada. She has received numerous honorary doctorates from Canadian universities and has been writer-in-residence at the University of Ottawa and at Memorial University of Newfoundland, and held the Presidential Writer-in-Residence Fellowship at the University of Toronto.

Jane Urquhart lives in Northumberland County, Ontario, and occasionally in Ireland.